The Letters of Nicodemus

The Letters of Nicodemus is a fictional
account of the impact of the life and ministry
of Jesus Christ upon one of the lesser New
Testament characters. Against a vivid back-
ground of Jewish and Roman politics and
known Biblical events Nicodemus's letters to
his former tutor, Justus, reveal the bitter and
bewildering struggles between his frank incredulity in a Messiah who could never con-
form to the expectations of the Jewish
priesthood, and his deep need to know and to
accept the mysteries of Christ's words and
deeds.

JAN DOBRACZYNSKI

The Letters of Nicodemus

TRANSLATED AND
ABRIDGED FROM THE POLISH
BY H. C. STEVENS

HEINEMANN

LONDON MELBOURNE TORONTO

William Heinemann Ltd

LONDON MELBOURNE TORONTO

CAPE TOWN AUCKLAND

THE HAGUE

Published in Poland in 1952,
in Germany and France in 1956.
Published in this edition 1958.

© 1958 by JAN DOBRACZYNSKI

Printed in Great Britain

To Elzunia

Nihil Obstat
Daniel Duivesteijn, S.T.D.
Censor deputatus

Imprimatur
E. Morrogh Bernard
Vic. Gen.

Westmonasterii
die 11a December 1957

The Letters of Nicodemus

The Letters of Machiavelli

. . . This illness, Justus, has completely worn me down. I have always had strength and to spare, and have always been pleasant and understanding in my relations with my fellows. I have never suffered before from this endless irritability, impatience, and intolerable need to complain. But now I am developing all the unpleasant characteristics of a hunted creature, like a wild vine ready to twine over any hedge. In the past I was always able to deny myself. But today I find it difficult to observe even the prescribed fasts. And I am more and more at loggerheads with the other members of the Pharisaic Grand Council. Their everlasting disputations over purification and discussion of new homilies bore me to death. A man can observe all the prescriptions of the law scrupulously every day of his life, and still gain nothing by it. Why is it my daughter who has been attacked by this disease? All the law is summed up in the words of the psalm: 'Do, O man, as the All Highest commands, and He will never forsake thee.' Never . . . There are not many who have gone so far in fasting, observing the laws of cleanliness, who have offered up sacrifices, meditated on Talmudic homilies and expositions of the law, as I have. There is something wrong somewhere. Surely I have not committed so many sins that the Most High finds it necessary to punish me with this terrible misfortune? True, we have to remember the case of Job. But, to begin with, the Edomite was not a believer; and besides, he did not know how to serve the Almighty Lord: he flatly refused to recognize that every man sins if he doesn't incessantly watch over the purity of his thoughts and deeds. And finally, it was he himself whom the All Highest smote, not someone as dear to him as Ruth is to me. To look on helplessly while disease consumes the body of the one you love most: that's something to which one can never be reconciled.

9

I have to talk about it to everybody I meet. Before long people will flee from me, for I infect them with sorrow just as others infect with leprosy. Only one thing still saves me: my work. When I am composing homilies, and when in my homilies I speak of the greatness of the Unnamable One, I am intoxicated as though with wine. I know there is growing appreciation of my homilies. Though there are some who criticize them. And that is especially painful to me. People don't seem to realize that living, as I am, always in the presence of Ruth's illness I can only use hard words, which will not take polish. At times I feel like a tortoise, which draws in its head and legs, and would rather not put them out again than expose itself to painful suffering. Though how could anyone suffer more than I do? Surely a man who, in his fear of further suffering, has grown incapable of denying anything, has drunk in full measure from the cup of human suffering?

I am depressed, too, by the circumstance that I have met with this affliction at the very moment when the world is plunged into such grievous confusion. You are not the only one who has realized this. Here, too, a fever has worked its way into the people's blood. There have never been such passionate disputes in the Grand Council and the Sanhedrin. The quarrels have found their way out to the temple courtyards, and at times they develop into fights, in which, sad to say, even wise and respected doctors take part. Usually the Zealots are brought in to settle the fiercest conflicts: it is horrible to think that those Zealots hire themselves out to murder for money. Older and more experienced men say similar disturbances were prevalent some twenty years ago, when bands of robbers descended into Judaea from Galilee again and again. The Romans restored order, and I have to admit that they are more easily to be borne than the tyranny of Herod and his sons. But now there is something in the air, like the disturbing breath of a storm still hidden beyond the hills, yet already at hand. Every man is against every man. It is an open secret that the Roman Legate in Syria hates the Roman Procurator in

Judaea, the Procurator and the tetrarchs are at one another's throats like dogs over a bone; Herod's progeny hate one another and are ready to resort to poison and murder of their brethren. And over all hovers the sinister shadow of the distant Caesar, an insane tyrant. The news of the sanguinary prescriptions which are enforced in Rome by his orders provokes a savage, uncontrollable hatred in all who hear of them. In Caesarea the Greeks have attacked our people more than once. Apparently there have been conflicts in Alexandria and Antioch. I learn that in Rome, at the news that the Pretorian Guard had arrested Sejanus, the mob attacked the Jewish quarter. Everywhere there is war, blood-letting, murder. Yet it is not so long since the Roman quill-drivers were announcing the 'golden age and the era of everlasting peace.'

I have a presentiment that some evil is imminent. At such a time a man wishes to feel free to observe whence the danger will come. Instead, all my attention is concentrated on Ruth's illness. I'm like a man who is carrying so heavy a burden that he can hardly see where to set his feet.

We are on the eve of some great event. What do you think it can be, Justus? Do you really expect that some day He whom we call the Messiah will come? The Sadducees have long since ceased to believe in His coming. They have stuffed their heads with Greek philosophy, and they regard Him simply as a symbol, and smile contemptuously. In any case, what do they need the Messiah for? All they are concerned with is the existence of the Temple, that all Israel should offer sacrifices in that Temple, and that they, and they alone, should be the intermediaries between man and the altar of the Lord. We Pharisees are far from wishing to deprive the people of their belief in the Messiah. We talk of Him often; in numerous homilies we tell what His coming will be like. But although I have written and spoken so much about it, I admit that I cannot rid myself of the rather disturbing thought that all these promises sound rather too good to come true. Messiah the king, the conqueror of Edom, the Lord of the world and Nature, which on His coming is to grow more bountiful than ever before – does it sound at all likely? Who are we Jews? A small people, surrounded by dozens of other races, and, like those others, fettered to the Roman chariot. And we at conflict among ourselves. Who would the Son of David need to be, to change all this? An ordinary man, or a demi-god? But demi-gods walk the earth only in the Greek legends. I do believe that the All Highest performed miraculous deeds of old. But today everything has grown quite ordinary. I have never seen anything at all resembling a miracle. The world around us is governed by rancour, hatred, pride, arrogance, passion. To master such a world, one would need to be even more evil, more filled with hatred, pride, and passion than the rest. War is the only thing that brings victory in this world. The Messiah would need to be a leader capable of leading us against all our enemies – and their number is legion. Anyone who could gather together our handful of youngsters and lead them on to conquer the whole world could hardly be regarded as a man of flesh and blood. Unfortunately, though I hate everything that derives from the Sadducees, I find myself beginning to think like them. I can't help thinking that the Messiah is only a kind of ideal conception of all the virtues; and if we were able to live up to it even in part, our life would be better, happier, finer. And I'm sure I'm not the only one with such thoughts. But nobody is prepared to express them aloud. And nor do I. I write about them only to you, and talk of them to Joseph.

As you know, he is neither a Pharisee nor a Sadducee, but holds to a philosophy which declares that honestly earned gold is the fundamental sense of human life. My Pharisee friends hold it against me that I am friendly with him, and that we are in trade together. Because he has relations with the non-Jews they regard him as defiled. At bottom Joseph is, I fear, a great sinner. But I have a weakness for him. Despite all his multiplicity of interests, which keep him always busy both in Jerusalem and in Arimathea, he's the only person who takes some interest in Ruth's health, and finds time to visit her and bring her presents. I don't understand how a man who does not observe the prescriptions of the law can possess so many good qualities. And yet but for him . . . I have already experienced moments of complete breakdown. I have felt like blaspheming, cursing, seeking oblivion in sin. At such times the insincere words of consolation which my Pharisee brethren say to me make me feel like vomiting. But Joseph's simple words, some joke which he makes to rid me of my despair, brings me back to sanity. I never needed human friendship more than now. But how hard it is to find that pearl, especially when you seek for it!

Through my partnership with Joseph my wealth is steadily increasing. I am almost as rich as he is. We are regarded as the most affluent men in all Judaea. How many pleasures I could provide for Ruth, if she were well! But she is indifferent to all I do. She doesn't like to offend me, so she wears my gift of a precious ring or bracelet for a moment or two, and says: 'Yes, they're very pretty.' Then: 'Take them away.' She stretches herself out and gently nods for me to depart. A spasm clutches my throat when I see that gesture, and even when I write about it.

I have always considered that the wealth which the Most High has permitted me to accumulate was given me as a mark of commendation on His part. And sometimes, as I con one of my homilies, I think I must have found favour in the eyes of the Eternal, since He allows me to write so well. So why has He afflicted me with this illness, like a thorn thrust into a labourer's hand? Why is He crushing me to the ground, when so many sinners go unpunished? What man knows and understands the meaning of health until disease enters his house as a guest? Who knows how love can suck out all a man's strength when he suddenly loses all power to help those he loves?

I can't help thinking that I am more susceptible to pain than most men. And yet I have to admit that all the world is filled with horrible sufferings which affect everybody, and every man is deserving of sympathy to some extent. Perhaps the truth is that each of us lives in a prison, and when we gaze at another man's house and envy him, his happiness, in reality we are looking only at another prison? If that which is to come is really to bring about a change it must provide an answer to the meaninglessness of life. I have written 'meaninglessness,' and although I feel that the word is inappropriate I cannot strike it out. You know me, Justus, and you know that I shall always remain faithful to the All Highest. I could never renounce the hope that in the end He will desire to help me. For that matter, I would not dare to let Him go, hope or no hope. What would become of me then? I am a true Israelite, one of those who are condemned to bear witness to Him. To my way of thinking either all my labour is service for Him or it begins to repel me with its senselessness. Then why does He acquiesce in this disease?

So now, dear teacher, you have the state of my soul, as you asked. As you see, it has changed since the days when I sat at your feet and listened to your instruction. At times I feel that I have aged greatly, though I know I should not say that, in view of your own venerable years. Write to me, and I shall write again about myself — and Ruth. O that I might be able to tell you, 'She is well again.'

DEAR JUSTUS,   SECOND LETTER.
The sight of Ruth's suffering makes me ready to do anything for her. Maybe that is only my unconscious way of attempting to escape from despair. Let it be so. Better to imagine, though vainly, that I am helping her than to stand with helpless hands and watch her face daily growing paler, or listen to her breathing, which is almost a groan. O Adonai! Job lost his children, but it is not written that he had to look on at their torments.

So when the Pharisaic Grand Council sent Hosea, Eleazar, and Samuel to observe at first hand the activities of John, son of

Zachariah, I went with them. I was not moved solely by curiosity. Our sacred writings are filled with records of prophets who healed and resurrected. I remembered the widow of Sidon: she was a heathen, compassionate, truly, but alien to our blood and our faith. But I am a Judaean, a faithful adherent of the Law, a Pharisee. I am not niggardly with alms, I don't mix with the heathen, I observe the rites of cleanliness, I keep the fasts and say the prayers. I don't want to boast, but I think my work is of some value. I teach, and I know that my teaching is listened to. The homilies I have written speak of the greatness, power and glory of the Eternal. I have just written one: 'As he was going his way a certain rabbi met an angel, who was carrying a bow. It was a narrow place, and neither was ready to step out of the way. "Step aside," said the rabbi, "I am occupied with thoughts of Him." But the angel would not. "What are you detaining me for?" the teacher grew impatient. And he was a very wise rabbi, knowing all the secrets of heaven and earth. Then the angel said: "I shall make way for you if you tell me what He is like." The rabbi smiled: "You have come to the right man. Only I can explain that to you. He is like the lightning: he falls with thunder on the sinner and strikes him to the ground." "But what does He do to the righteous?" the angel asked. "You carry His bow, and you don't know that? Sometimes He strikes him too with His arrows."

' "But why?"

' "He does it when a man grows too high."

' "So you consider, venerable master, that he is afraid of man?"

' "Sh-sh! Say not that, that would be blasphemy. It should be put differently: there is a secret weakness in Him, and when a man discovers it he grows equal to Him in strength. But only the wisest know that secret." And the angel stepped out of the path.'

Do you like my parable? That is just what I think: He is almighty, but there is some weakness in Him. One has only to discover the right adjuration. Our forefather Jacob must have known it, for he did not yield to Him. Unfortunately, I don't know the word.

Ruth's sufferings are frightening. It is impossible to think of glorifying the All Highest when I hear her groan and see her parted lips quivering with pain. You ask what the doctors think of it. They have no advice to give. At first they were self-confident, diagnosing the disease even before anyone had told them about it. But when their medicines proved ineffective they grew taciturn and mysterious. They left my questions unanswered, and became more and more exacting, though they no longer made any promises. In the end they began to stay away. As they departed they assured me Ruth would get well again. But how, and when, not one of them would say. They advised me to wait patiently. None of them admitted that his knowledge had proved false. They rather tried to ascribe the blame to my importunity.

Will you be annoyed when I tell you that in my grief I thought of seeking the help of the priest's son who lives in the wilderness? The belief is growing that he is a prophet. A great word, that. For many years now there has been no prophet in the land of Judaea. But this man does really remind one of Elias: he lived for years alone among the rocks between Hebron and the shore of the Dead Sea. When at last he came to the ford outside Bethabar, the people were troubled. He is tall, black, with unkempt hair; he dresses in a camel skin, and has eyes like two burning coals. They say he doesn't speak so much as shout. He is always crying: 'Repent, repent, repent of your sins.' He plunges people in the Jordan, pours water over their heads, and tells them how they are to behave in future. He is attracting enormous crowds. We had hardly got outside the city gate when we came upon great throngs of people pouring out from all the side roads and paths. And almost as many coming back from the Jordan. These had serious faces, they almost seemed a little frightened. They told us how this man was thundering against the priests and the Pharisees. The news has already reached Jerusalem that although John comes of the priestly line, he is filled with fury against the Sadducees. And quite rightly, too. But what can he have against us Pharisees? We honour the prophets, and we, too, call on the people to repent. Many of our brethren voluntarily do penance for the sins of the unclean mob. Any prophet who came to Judaea would find support only among us Pharisees.

As we walked on the day grew hotter and more stifling, and the road even more crowded. At noon we rested in a place where the white- and brown-coloured hills drop down into the plain surrounding Jericho. Here the vegetation, which had been rare, was thick like a mossy carpet. On the hill the city stood out white with its houses and the splendour of its palaces. Beyond a dense clump of balsam trees and tall grasses the Jordan flowed swiftly at the bottom of its ravine. The people were streaming down to it like innumerable torrents. Everybody was there: unclean boors, city craftsmen, hucksters, customs officials, loose women bedaubed with carmine, wealthy merchants, bankers, Levites, temple servants, soldiers, expositors of the Scriptures — even priests. I heard people talking Galilean, Canaan, Syro-Phoenician, Greek, Arabic. The chosen people were making their way down to the ford over the Jordan: Judaeans, Galileans, arrivals from the Diaspora, even Samaritans and Edomites. Many of them stepped into the foaming water to cross the river, but there were boats and rafts for those who didn't want to get wet. The crowds gathered on the banks reminded me of the pilgrims encamping under the walls of Jerusalem during the days of Passover or the Feast of Tabernacles.

The day was drawing to its close when we reached the river bank. The sun hung, a glowing ball, over the hills of Judaea, their sharp, serrated outlines stood in sombre and menacing shadow against its light. It was too late to cross and talk with the prophet, so we had to wait till morning. We found a spot some distance from the hubbub, where we could keep apart from the unclean. We observed the prescribed purifications and sat down for our evening meal. The prophet must have gone away, for the people on the farther bank were scattering. The mountains of Moab rose like a rosy cloud above the twilit ravine. But almost at once they began to fade, and as they turned grey they descended from the clouds to the earth. We said evening prayers, wrapped ourselves in our cloaks, and stretched ourselves out on the ground. From the depth of the ravine the sky did not seem so high as usual, it was like the shallow vaulting of the temple. Suddenly the stars shone out.

As I lay I thought of Ruth. The sight of illness is provocative of thought, even more, perhaps, than the sight of death. Death is the end of something; illness ends nothing. Illness comes unexpectedly, runs its course, passes off, and then, just when you think it has gone for good, it comes back again. We clench our teeth and wait for it to pass. Then, at last one day we feel we cannot stand it any longer. We have only strength left for today, or perhaps for tomorrow. But the days pass, several sabbaths elapse after that 'tomorrow,' and everything is still the same: perhaps a slight improvement, and then once more the illness returns.

At first I had energy and to spare, but now my energy is exhausted; now I think of myself as a wrestler who knows that his only way of overcoming his opponent is to outlast him. Ruth's illness is like a hump, to which one grows accustomed. Formerly I could not eat or sleep. Now I sleep more and more soundly, almost as though in self-defence against the inevitable awakening. It is not that I have ceased to fight. But I feel as though I have betrayed the cause. But I don't know when or how.

It was long before I could get to sleep.

We were aroused by the early morning hubbub of the mob. We saw a group of priests and Levites coming towards us. They were walking with a serious step, leaning on their sticks, their long robes dragging over the damp sand. Several lads sent the people scattering before them, so that they could pass without being touched by the throng. I saw that their leader was Jonathas, the son of Ananias; he was wearing the ephod, so he was acting in an official capacity as a representative of the Temple. Because of this we bowed to him first, though not one of us Pharisees can stand the man. This son of the former high priest, and brother-in-law to Caiaphas, the president of the Sanhedrin, is a loathsome Sadducee, who sneers at belief in resurrection. He has grown so like a Greek that it is really impudence on his part to wear the ephod.

He answered our bow with such a friendly smile that you would never have thought he once called us 'moles who burrow under the Temple.' 'Greetings, estimable teachers,' he said, 'may the Most High be with you.' We waited to see what would come next. Still smiling amiably, he told us where they were going. Apparently even the Sadducees can no longer pretend to be unaware of the crowds making their way down to the ford. And Pilate the Procurator also has sent a messenger to ask what this gathering at the river means. The Little Sanhedrin discussed the subject all day two days ago. One of them remembered the ancient custom which ordains that every newly arrived prophet must inform the Temple of his mission. So it was decided to send a deputation to this man John, to ask him to explain why he had come. The fact that Jonathas himself was at their head shows how seriously the priests take the matter.

'So we shall find out who he is before long,' Jonathas ended. 'And he won't get away with words. If he is Elias,' he smiled malevolently, 'we shall demand a sign of him. Let him work a miracle. If he can, of course,' he chuckled, stroking his beard. 'And then . . .'

The Sadducees don't believe in miracles, so they obviously thought this a wonderful trap. Yet they are justified in seeking to reduce the importance of this man. The Romans are suspicious, they smell conspiracies everywhere. The fight for our liberation may break out some day, but I don't think John's the man to lead the people in it.

Jonathas proposed that we should go with them to the

prophet. 'It will be better if you teachers also ask him questions,' he declared. 'If he fails to give satisfactory answers and is confused, so much the worse for his reputation.' When they want to flay the skin off some unclean clod, the Sadducees can manage perfectly without us. But when it's a question of convincing the people of something they prefer to act in concert with us. We deliberated for a moment or two over Jonathas's proposal. But in the end we agreed. John is not one of us, and there is no reason why we should take his part.

We crossed to the other bank in two large boats. A solid mass of people stood in a half circle right down to the water. We heard a voice coming from the middle of the crowd. It's quite true that this man doesn't speak, he shouts. The Temple boys made a way for us, and we walked sedately through the expectant people. I caught sight of John, standing bent over some men in the water. He is a lean and swarthy giant. Beneath his beetling brows he has the eyes of a dreamer, sorrowful and greyish blue, like the sky of early spring. But for his growth of hair, which made him look old, he would have seemed very young. But his movements and gestures are feverish. When he saw us he came to meet us. For a moment I felt quite anxious, for he looked as though he was making ready for a fight. He stood opposite us, leaning on his long staff. A look of disillusionment seemed to cross his face, almost as though he had been expecting to see someone else. Jonathas stepped forward and said in a loud voice, for all to hear:

'John, son of Zachariah! We have come from the high priest and the Sanhedrin. As ancient custom dictates, we wish to question you. Will you answer us?'

'Yes,' he said curtly. 'Ask on.'

'John, son of Zachariah. . . .' Jonathas began with the utmost gravity and unction. The people crowding around us were silent, for they wished to catch every word. 'Who are you? Are you the Messiah?'

The priest had hardly uttered the word when John exclaimed:

'No, no! I am not the Messiah.'

That reply seemed to me to dispose of all the danger. If John had proclaimed himself the Messiah he would not have needed to answer any further questions. The Messiah is higher than the Temple. But a prophet must keep his peace with the Temple. Truly, Jeremiah . . . But that is an old story.

'Then perhaps you are Elias?'

The answer came as swiftly as before.

'I am not.'

I saw that this reply took Jonathas by surprise. It did me, too, for the crowd identify John with Elias.

'Then are you a prophet?'

'No.'

I stared in astonishment into those grey-blue eyes, which seemed to be gazing into space. I noticed that those eyes were encircled with tiny furrows, like the eyes of desert nomads, or of mariners who are accustomed to looking out over great expanses. And simultaneously he seemed to be listening for something.

'Then who are you?' Now there was a note of contempt in Jonathas's voice.

He replied in the words of Isaiah:

'I am the voice crying in the wilderness . . .'

Now I joined in the questioning.

'Then why do you baptize?'

For one moment his gaze returned from space and rested on me. I discerned a painful, feverish tension in his eyes.

'I baptize with water, but He is already here who was before me, but will come after me . . .' His lips quivered. Gazing once more into the distance, he spoke with great tenderness, almost like a woman speaking of her beloved man:

'I am not worthy to unlace His sandals . . . He will come and baptize you with fire and the Spirit.'

The grey, pleasant eyes suddenly acquired a terrible look. The dreamy gentleness vanished from them.

'You generation of vipers! Do you think you will escape the

anger of the Lord? The rotted tree cannot escape the axe. So you have come to question me?'

Jonathas fell back; but the giant followed him, thundering angrily:

'I have only one thing to say to you: Repent! Repent in dust and ashes. Like Nineveh! Do you think you are any different from these?' He swung his arm around in a half circle. 'Don't think you're free from sin because you are the sons of Abraham! Look!'

He bent down, snatched up a handful of small stones, and thrust them right under my eyes.

'If He wishes, the All Highest can raise new sons of Abraham from these stones.'

I was seized with such a trembling that I could not answer. You can well imagine that one has good reason to be afraid when a furious giant of a man begins to threaten you. Then I realized that I was alone. My companions and the Sadducees had slipped into the crowd. I alone of all that embassage was standing confronting John, and he was shouting at me. The crowd must have enjoyed the sight, for I heard whispered sneers.

'He is coming,' he began again. 'Go, for maybe He is already approaching.'

The voice of thunder died away, his gaze passed over me as though I were wretched grass. I realized that this man lives on the verge between two worlds, so to speak; a world of dreams and a world of anger. When he focused his gaze on things close at hand he exploded; when he gazed into the distance he dreamed.

'He has a winnowing fan in His hand, and He will separate the wheat from the chaff. He will store the grain in the granary, but He will burn the chaff with unquenchable fire.'

Now some of the crowd began to question him: 'What shall we do? John, what are we to do?'

He shifted his gaze to them, but he did not storm at them. He replied:

'Have you two cloaks? Then give one to the poor.'

I hadn't noticed that a customs officer, an unclean fellow, had come within less than seven paces from me. John turned to this man and said:

'Take only what is due to you.'

And when a soldier wearing Herod's insignia asked: 'What am I to do?' he answered, 'Serve for your pay. Watch and guard what is entrusted to you, but don't flog, don't kill, do no man any wrong. . . .'

Among the crowd was some unclean peasant or fisherman from Galilee, so I judged by his dialect. He was stout, and had a broad, coarse face. His small eyes were sunk behind swollen cheeks. His hands were huge and rough. He stepped out of the crowd with an air both timorous and insolent. The sort of fellow who picks a quarrel with his host, is the first to raise his fists, and the first to run away. He had been pushed forward by several other Galileans. He muttered something, falling over his words, then bawled so loud that he frightened himself:

'What am I to do?'

John halted in front of him. He laid his hand on the man's shoulder, and his eyes rested on the Galilean's face for quite a while, concentrating all his gaze on those dull features.

'Leave your nets . . .' he said. 'And wait. . . . Wait!'

He passed on to some other men who were pressing towards him. Moved by some unconscious impulse, I followed him. I found myself among a group of people coming down to the water to be baptized. The Galilean fisherman tore off the cloak covering his sunburnt chest. It was an absurd thing for me to do. The Jordan must be thick with the sins of the unclean clods who do not observe the Law. I hadn't come to John for purification, but to have Ruth restored to health. Yet I, too, went down to the water, winding my robe round my arms as I went. Though it was not at all called for, I was prepared to submit to this baptism if it enabled me to plead with the prophet. As I passed him I raised my eyes and said almost humbly:

'What am I to do, rabbi? My . . .'

He interrupted me; but there was no anger in the gesture with which he laid his hand on my shoulder. He said: 'Go on serving to the best of your ability, but learn to renounce service. And wait!'

Strange words, don't you agree? He said 'wait' to me in the same tone as he had used to the Galilean. Perhaps he says it quite frequently, for after all, he appears to regard himself as the forerunner of another. But I don't understand his remark about denying myself in the least. What am I to deny myself?

The river water, warm and soft, flowed over me right up to my shoulders. John says it purifies, but I felt that really it soiled me. I withdrew into the crowd, ashamed of what I had done. To think I had allowed myself to bathe in the same water as customs officers and whores. Fortunately, my brethren had disappeared. I concealed myself among the riverside bushes and, sitting on the ground, reflected on the stupidity of my behaviour. I had gained nothing from this purification, since it appears that John does not heal. He repulses those who bring him the sick. 'My task is to prepare the way,' he says. 'When He comes . . .'

I remained sitting by the river all the rest of the day. Evening came in, and John stopped baptizing. The crowd dispersed along the bank. Fires were lighted, the hucksters shouted their wares. Not far from me I noticed the group of Galileans who were with the stout fisherman. They sat in a circle, said prayers, and began to eat. Then that fisherman talked and talked in a booming voice. Among his own people he lost all his shyness, in fact, he struck me as rather too noisy. Right opposite me was sitting a man with a boyish face as handsome as a girl's. I heard him turn to a fellow with his back to me: 'I didn't see you with the prophet, Nathanael?' I could not catch the other man's reply, but he pointed to a tall figure seated a little farther from the bank. 'You're always dreaming,' the young man said with a laugh. Dreaming! What can such people dream about? But the tough specimen (the others call him Simon) remarked: 'There's nothing to dream about. The prophet John said quite clearly that He will come at any moment. He told us all we had to do was wait.' Just imagine, Justus! He was talking of this Someone just as though He would step out from the bushes even while you looked. I went on listening, for their conversation amused me.

'Who will He be?' one of them asked.

'The Messiah, of course!' Simon laughed. 'He'll come in armour, armed with a sword and surrounded with soldiers. Or He'll come on a horse, like the Roman centurions.'

'And do you think there'll be a war, Simon?'

'Who knows whether it will be necessary? Quite possibly the very sight of Him will make everyone flee.'

'But what about us?'

'We shall follow Him,' Simon shouted fierily.

One of the others laughed and asked in all sincerity: 'Will He need such as we?'

'Well, John, what do you think?' they turned to the lad with the beautiful, girlish face.

'I think,' he replied calmly and slowly as before, 'that although we are poor and sinners we shall serve Him. What if He doesn't even see us? It will be a pleasure to serve the Messiah, even at a distance.'

'At least they're not conceited,' I thought as I lay gazing into the sky. Then I thought of Ruth again, and of the Someone whom John had foretold. And the two lines of thought converged in my mind.

I was a long time getting off to sleep, but I awoke rested and refreshed. The Galileans had gone; I expect they had joined the crowd surrounding the prophet. I, too, went back to him, with the idea of taking another look at him before setting off homeward. I made my way through the throng.

John was standing in their midst. They were plying him with questions, and he was answering. But his eyes gazed over the crowd. He seemed even more restless, if possible, than yesterday. He knitted his brows in his concentration. But as I stepped out of the crowd into the inner ring I saw his eyes, dilated with fiery feeling, apparently fixed on me.

I dropped back, for I thought he was about to break into a new storm of anger. But then I realized that his gaze was fixed not on me, but on someone close to me. His lips began to quiver as though he were terribly agitated. I turned my head. A tall man with darkly golden hair was at my side. His face was unforgettable: the face of someone you have met before, but cannot remember where or when. There are faces which remind one of a bird or a beast; but his face was reminiscent of all other human faces. Yet there was nothing common in it. It was as though all the pleasant expressions of all human faces were concentrated in this one face. He walked slowly towards John and John came to meet him. When they were face to face the prophet halted and said in a deep, choking, trembling tone:

'So You have come?'

He bent as though about to fall to his knees. But the man stepped forward and took him by the arm, saying:

'I have come to be baptized by you.'

'By me?' John exclaimed. 'Never! Why, it is You . . .'

'Let it be so,' the man said with calm resolution.

I would have liked to see John baptize this man. But the people closed around him in a solid ring, the Galileans among them, for they had fought their way through with their elbows. I did not feel like pushing among them. I decided to return home. I crossed the Jordan. As I stood on the farther bank I thought I heard thunder. I looked back. The tall man had just stepped out of the water and was wrapping himself in his robe. John was saying something, pointing to him with one hand. But the crowd seemed to be rather indifferent. I turned away. I was possessed with an inexplicable sorrow, as though something had passed by and I had not been able to halt it. I've wasted my time in coming here, I thought. I climbed heavily up the hill, over the loose stones. I wandered all day through a chilly rain that pierced to my bones.

I have more news for you. This time it is not about John the
son of Zachariah. Another man has eclipsed his glory. As
formerly the people hurried down to the Jordan, so now they
are flocking to see the newcomer from Galilee who has arrived
in Jerusalem, surrounded by his brothers and friends. The
people call him a prophet, though he does not prophesy. In
past days prophets subdued the hearts of kings; they shook
thrones and even the Temple. He has not addressed himself to
the king (in which he is wise, for only a fool would recognize
the libertine of Tiberias). Nor to the Sanhedrin. It appears he
wanders about the country continually, talking to unclean
clods and the mob, even including whores, customs officers and
beggars. He doesn't insist on outward respect for his teaching,
he just sits under a tree at the wayside or on some jutting rock
in a shady spot. What does he talk about? Until I've heard
him I cannot tell you. Everyone tells a different story of what
he has heard. Some find his remarks incomprehensible, for
others they are too wise; some he scandalizes, others he moves
to raptures. But everybody agrees that he speaks well, in
homely language. He has a pleasant voice, and there is an
underlying strength in his gentle words. If anybody tries to
argue with him, he catches fire, and his words fly like lightning. From what has been told me about him I at first thought
he must be one of Hillel's disciples who is repeating the old
master's doctrine. Apparently he has more than once expressed
a thought that Hillel was in the habit of uttering: whatever
a man wants others to do to him, he must first do to them.
But I quickly decided that he is not a disciple of Hillel. As a
true Pharisee, Hillel taught by expounding the Scriptures.
But this man speaks out boldly, not always appealing to the
Scriptures. His sayings convey the independent note that dis-

tinguishes a prophet. And in any case he could not have known Hillel, for he is my own age or even younger.

Then I thought he might be a disciple of John, for he, too, baptizes. But it transpired that it is not he who baptizes, but his disciples, and in any case they have stopped doing so now. If he ever was a disciple of John he is an ungrateful follower, for he has eclipsed his master just as surely as one blows out a candle with a single breath. The flood of people rushing down to the Jordan has dried up like the brook Cedron in the month of Iyar. That may be why John has left the Jordan and gone to Tiberias, where he stands outside the palace and fulminates against the tetrarch. The first person Antipas met on his return from Rome was the prophet John, who prophesied him an infamous death in a distant land because of his incest. Antipas cannot make up his mind what to do: they say he sits huddled up to Herodias and trembling with fear. And that's the man who wants the Romans to make him ruler over Judaea!

To return to the prophet from Galilee. His name is Joshua, Jesus. A name as bold as his words. I haven't been able to discover his father's name. He never mentions him. When speaking of himself he calls himself the son of man. As though we weren't all sons of men! Formerly he was a carpenter in Nazareth, a place which even the Galileans regard as a hornet's nest. It appears he was a good craftsman. One day he left everything, just like that, and went off to teach. He could have lived quite well on his honest earnings. But he preferred to be a vagabond, living on what people give him. Extraordinary, don't you agree? As we get older we grow more and more attached to a quiet, secure existence. He was just the reverse: when he reached mature age he gave up his quiet life for one menacing with unexpected event.

What else can I tell you about him? He doesn't fast, he is not a Nazarite, he doesn't abstain from wine. But he works miracles. That has won him a great crowd of followers. Ignore if you like three quarters of what the people say about him; but it can't be rejected altogether. I myself have talked with men whom he freed of fever with a single touch, whose sight he has restored, whose abscesses he has healed. Don't be surprised to hear that I have talked with such people. Ruth's illness has driven me to these extremes. I haven't mentioned her yet in this letter, for what is the point of it? Far from getting better, she seems to grow worse every day. The last doctor said to me as he went: 'We must confide in the strength of youth. Youth works wonders. . . .' But even if her youth were the sole remedy possible, every day diminishes its value. Instead of her youth consuming the disease, the disease is consuming her youth. Her chariot dashes ever faster down the hill, and yet it may go on running like that for a long time. I should say: fortunately. But I can't write that word and mean it. As I have already written, I am like a city which has surrendered but the enemy has not accepted its defeat: he orders it to fight on.

I am ashamed to say that to end this torment I am ready to go to the Galilean and ask him for help. Don't condemn me, Justus! It is said that he worked a remarkable miracle in Galilee. It was at Cana, a little place on the shore of Lake Gennesareth, where a young couple had just been married. He was invited among other guests. That's exactly like him! He went to drink wine and eat honey cakes among the Galilean peasants, who, as you will know, have simple habits and are always ready for a drunken brawl. How can a man keep himself clean among such people? They're not concerned in the least with prayer or fasting, the gathering up of the fragments, or the prescribed washing of utensils. No Pharisee would mix in such company. This Jesus fellow not only sat among them but, when they ran short of wine, turned water into wine! If he really worked this miracle I can only say a priceless gift has been entrusted to irresponsible hands. A prophet should be exalted; he may give bread to the hungry, but not wine. My servants carry out a basket of bread to beggars every day, but supposing instead of bread and a summons to prayer I gave each a flask of wine and encouraged them to make merry!

But the value of this deed needs to be estimated from another aspect also. He turned pitchers of water into wine for the people around him, but what has he done for those who have never fallen in with him? With such a great gift at his command, should he not seek out those who are most worthy to receive? Wouldn't it be fairer if he cured my Ruth, for instance, rather than flood the house of some Galilean peasant with wine (apparently of very good vintage)? If he were to do that I should be really grateful.

A little time before the Holy Days he came to Jerusalem. I decided to see him. Learning that he was sitting in Solomon's Porch, with his disciples and others listening to him, I made my way there. He was surrounded by a crowd stinking of garlic, onions, and stale olive oil. All of them unclean: peasants, small traders, craftsmen. I walked past them slowly, as though sunk in thought. But I observed them curiously from under the turban drawn well down over my eyes. And, by the brow of Moses! Now I shall tell you who this Galilean is. He is the tall man whom John greeted so ardently, and whom he baptized in the Jordan! I'm sure I'm not mistaken. He has a face one can never forget. As I told you then, the face of all humanity. I seek in vain for a new description. He is tall, well built, with features expressive of perfect harmony. Now I'm stuck again! In any case his face is fitting to his figure, his voice, his words. It is tranquil, but not dead. On the contrary, I would say it is too vivacious. Only, the word 'too' is not in accordance with the facts. In that face there is nothing too much, nothing too little. It is just what the human face should be. Those infamous Greek sculptors whom Antipas has brought to the country would be delighted to have him as their model: they would see in him a statue for the circus at Caesarea. But could even the most talented sculptor transfer such a face to stone? Every man's face has some detail which dominates all the rest. If, for instance, I wanted to represent you (forgive the impious thought!) I should show a thinking brow above eyebrows drawn in thought. The rest of the face would be unnecessary. But the Galilean's every feature is important. His brow thinks, his nose quivers with restrained feeling. His mouth . . . his mouth expresses love. I cannot put it in any other way. The lips, whether speaking or still, always seem to be expressive of love. And the eyes too. They are as black as a bottomless well, attracting and alluring with its depth. I shan't try to describe him further to you. In any case you won't get any idea of him from my words. But I cannot describe him otherwise than I have done: my stylus slips impotently over the tablet.

Well, so I passed by him, and he was talking to his crowd of followers. I feigned a momentary curiosity, and halted. He took no notice of me, but went on talking fervently, with conviction, with many gestures: 'The kingdom of God is at hand . . .' he said.

'What is this kingdom you're speaking of, rabbi?' I asked despite myself.

I called him 'rabbi' only in courtesy. He gave me a swift glance and replied:

'The prophets before John proclaimed the Law. He who knows it, knows it is the kingdom; he who denies it knows nothing. But the Law remains. Earth and heaven will pass away, but not one letter of the Law will change . . .'

Those words express him completely. He appears to be talking quite ordinarily, in the harsh tongue of the unclean clods. His words seem to be clear, even naïvely simple. The depth is not before them, but lies beyond them. It is just like taking a torch into a cave: as you go it continually reveals the further path. How has this small town carpenter come to know the Scriptures so well? However, he turned back to his teaching. He began to tell a parable:

'A certain king wished to take his brother's wife. So he sent his own wife back to her father and gave instructions to tell him: "I don't like your daughter, she doesn't sing well, nor does she go out of her way to do me pleasure. She's quarrelsome, and her tongue twists in her mouth like a spinning wheel. Nor did I receive a sufficiently munificent dowry from you for her. Take her back." But the father ordered the messengers to tell the king: "You have done evilly. For when you took my daughter you knew whom you were taking, and she wasn't a bad wife to you so long as you didn't lust after your brother's wife. But now you are adding injustice to injustice. Restore my daughter to favour, and give your brother back his wife, lest we both assemble forces and each of us punishes you because of his woman, and we hand your kingdom to another." For I say to you: he who leaves his wife to take another commits adultery, and he who marries the deserted wife is also guilty of adultery.'

Beyond those words, too, lies an abyss. He seemed to be referring quite openly to the dispute between Antipas and his father-in-law, Aretas; but then his thought seems to start up from the ground and fly. This kingdom which he says someone else will take, and the other kingdom which he says is approaching—are they not two images of the same thing? I wanted to question him on this point; but I left them, for it is not seemly for such as I to stand among a crowd of unclean men.

I thought, and I wrestled with the thought: but supposing he were to succeed in curing Ruth? I told you once that this illness is like a hump: if it were to disappear life would grow incredibly light. At times I think that then nothing would be lacking to complete my happiness.

I couldn't resist the desire to ask him for help. Obviously I had no wish to push myself in among a crowd of unclean men. The simplest course would have been to send my servant to him and invite him to my house. But I preferred to avoid that. The members of the Grand Council and the Sanhedrin speak with contempt of the Galilean prophet. What would they think if I were to invite him home? I would be covered with ridicule in their eyes. They might even regard it as an unclean act. But it occurred to me that I might see him surreptitiously, by night. The one difficulty was to know where to look for him; he is like a bird, which tucks its head under its wing on a different branch every night. So first I would have to arrange an appointment with him. But there is no way of approaching him quietly. He is not alone for a single moment. The crowd surrounds him all the time, even when he is eating.

But after some days I found an opportunity. Among the prophet's disciples I saw a familiar face: that of a little Bezethan merchant who comes from Karioth. I have bought things at his shop from time to time and have had talks with him. He is by no means a fool, and though young he mixes with many people. He's nothing much to look at: small, sickly, always coughing. He has restless, slippery, always moist hands. He was not a success in trade—but who in Bezetha could hope to compete with the Levites, who ply Ananias and his sons with gold? His creditors stripped him of everything. I lost sight of him. Now he has turned up again in the prophet's company. He follows him, listens to him, and when the throng jostles too much he reduces them to order, all with the air of being his master's most confidential servant. I managed to draw him apart. I thrust a few shekels into his moist palm. He promised to arrange a nocturnal talk with the prophet for me.

Yesterday he came running to me with the news that the Galilean was going to spend the night in a small house in the Ophel district of the city, and if I went there before the second watch I should be able to talk with him. That was not a very attractive prospect. Ophel is a colony of scum, and it's not safe to plunge at night into its labyrinth of stinking mud hovels. But I realized that it was my only chance of having a talk without causing a scandal. I cursed in spirit at the thought that I, a member of the Sanhedrin and the Pharisaic Grand Council, was planning to meet by stealth with a prophet of the unclean. But there was no alternative. And I was driven on by thoughts of Ruth's white face and her black eyebrows knitted with pain.

Wrapped in a black cloak, I set out last evening. The moon was almost at the full, and when it was not obscured by wind-

33

driven clouds it spread a clear light over the city. I was accompanied by two servants armed with swords and sticks. We went down the steps to the gloomy depths of the lower town. Over us extended the arches of the aqueduct. From the dignity of the palace quarter we descended into the abysm of the teeming mud hovels. Here live the poorest of the poor, and here during holy days stay pilgrims who cannot afford better quarters. Fortunately, the holy days were past, and the visitors had departed. A repellent stench pervades the whole district. Here everything stinks; the smell of filth and misery belches out from every dark opening.

We should never have found the house in which the Galilean was staying if the sound of our steps had not brought Judas out from some dark alley. Evidently he was waiting for our arrival.

He led us over disintegrating steps, through narrow, repulsive alleys, past horribly soiled walls. I felt my anxiety steadily increasing as I plunged deeper and deeper without hope of ever finding my own way back. I had never imagined that such a disgraceful morass existed in Jerusalem, almost at the foot of the Temple, for I had never been here before. Judas led the way nimbly and swiftly, like a rat among ruins. He appeared to know every little corner.

At last, close to some half-withered fig tree creaking in the puffs of the wind, he halted. Before us was a wall, and in the wall a low opening. He signed to us to wait, and slipped inside. The tree creaked, and the rustle of its withered leaves was like the tinkle of small change. Though I was wearing a thick cloak I felt cold, a shiver ran down my spine. My men looked about them fearfully.

From the darkness Judas's voice reached me:

'Come, rabbi! The master is not asleep, he will gladly talk with you. Let your men wait. . . .'

I parted from my servants reluctantly. With my hands stretched out in front of me I entered into the darkness. Judas put his hand on my arm and led me. We seemed to be walking along a corridor which appeared to go on and on for a long time. But it ended suddenly, and the darkness with it. Quite unexpectedly I found myself in a small room lit by a tallow lamp, and containing two benches and some wretched furniture. On one of the benches the Galilean was sitting with his head in his hands, lost in thought, perfectly still. Now I could observe him from the side, his profile showed up clearly against the wall: sharp, almost angular, yet amazingly soft and gentle in its lines. A long, hooked nose, distinctive nostrils, broad but delicate mouth, a resolute chin. And eyes expressive of gentleness and sympathy. Once more I noted that incomprehensible contradiction: his eyes seemed to enchant, but his lips, so one would judge, are shaped to command. They suggest strength and inflexible will. A thirst for power, perhaps? But I doubt it. Passions are like fever: they burn, but behind the heat lurks weakness. But this man might well desire something to the point of frenzy, yet never reach after the object of his desire with feverish hands.

Rather abashed, I halted at the door. He raised his eyes to me. They were calm enough, not menacing, rather pleasant, yet astonishingly piercing. I felt that he was looking right through me, knew everything already, and it wasn't necessary for me to say a word. Judas had vanished; there were only the two of us in the room. Suddenly he smiled. It was like a gleam of sunlight which clears the sky in a trice. I responded with a smile. Stepping into the room, I said:

'Greetings, good rabbi.'

He calmly indicated that I was to sit beside him on the bench.

'Why do you call me good?' he asked. 'Only the Almighty is good.'

His question could have only one significance. Did I regard him as close to the All Highest, or, as his opponents declare, did I consider him an instrument of Satan? I hesitated. For what do I really know about him? But I realized that if I did not show him respect I should not get his help for Ruth. And in any case it wasn't so easy to tell a man to his face that he is a servant of Belial. So I said:

'I'm sure you come from Him, rabbi. Nobody would be able to work such miracles without divine assistance. . . .'

I sat down on the bench and waited for him to speak. But he turned and fixed his eyes on me. He said calmly:

'You are sure . . . Then believe me, any man who wishes to see the kingdom must be born again . . . And completely. . . .'

I concentrated my thoughts. This man speaks of himself and this kingdom of his as though they were identical. Not as if he were a prophet or a guide to this kingdom, but the very kingdom itself. But what is this kingdom, since it doesn't exist at all, really? A man must be born again? That sounded absurd. Does it mean that a man has to die and come back to the world? Or that the old man becomes an infant and returns to his mother's womb? I expressed this last thought aloud, possibly with a touch of contempt. He had lost stature in my eyes. At times his words are irresistible, he carries you away; then he seems to withdraw, and everything seems a delusion. I confide to you my discovery: he could be a tyrant, but he has no wish to be.

He went on in a serious tone:

'Believe me, nobody can enter the kingdom who is not born of water and the Spirit. Flesh is born of flesh and is itself flesh. You are right, the old man does not return to his mother's womb. But the Spirit also gives birth, and gives birth to everlasting life. Why be surprised when I say you must be born again? Do you hear that wind?'

He stretched out his hand – it still bore the traces of heavy labour – to the shutter rattling in the wind.

'You hear its sound, but you don't see it. You don't know where it has come from or where it is going, but you know Him who holds it in His hand and commands it to blow. So it is with rebirth of the Spirit: you did not see it, yet it is accomplished. . . .'

'How?' I exclaimed. 'How is it accomplished?'

'Don't you know?' he said with gentle irony. 'You, who are a teacher, learned in the Scriptures, an expositor of the law, a writer of homilies? I tell you what I know and I testify to you concerning what I have seen. But you don't believe me. Shall I ever find belief on this earth?'

Pain and doubt sounded in those words. The hands fell helplessly, his face wore an expression of grievous questioning. For one moment I had the feeling that I was confronted with a beggar exposing his misery to the passers-by. He was speaking into the darkness, into the city invisible beyond the wall of that room, into the wide world.

'When I speak to you of earthly things you don't believe. So how will you believe when I speak to you of heavenly things? The way to heaven is known only to Him who came down from heaven: the Son of Man, who is.'

I felt a shiver down my back. He wasn't speaking to me, he wasn't even looking at me. His words were like a challenge to someone invisible, the conclusion of some incomprehensible dispute. I took a stealthy look at his face. I still had no idea what he was talking about, and I don't know whether anybody else would understand him either; his thoughts grow beyond the power of words. He talks like a sage or a madman. A man must be born again? How? Does he mean that something has to be understood? Discovered? I felt that my remark about the old man turning into an infant had been very stupid. Evidently he is referring to some exalted spiritual mystery. Possibly he is an Essene, or a Zadokite? Has he, perhaps, had revealed to him the adjuration which leads to the great mystery?

'But first, One must be lifted up, as Moses raised the brazen serpent on a stake at the foot of Mount Horeb. And whoever looks on Him and believes will not perish. He will be born to everlasting life. For the All Highest loved the world so much that He sent his only Son to it. He did not send Him as a judge, but as a witness to mercy and love. Not to condemn and punish, but to save and forgive. Whoever turns from Him has condemned himself. But every man who turns to Him shall find salvation.'

I have no idea how long he went on talking. I lost all sense of time. I completely ceased to understand him. But the conviction was born in me that the secret which he was announcing must be profound, one of the deepest mysteries in the world. The kingdom is to come with miracles, and among these the greatest, though invisible, is goodness. But 'goodness' fails to convey the least idea of this quality of the All Highest. If the Almighty is good, He must be the best too. I can conceive of absolute justice, but what does absolute goodness mean? Justice has its measure, goodness has none whatever. There is only one true justice, but the world of mercy is boundless.

The bench shook beneath me, the clay ceiling seemed to be falling on me. The world was divided into two, severed by this conversation. Before it I had been a man of balanced thought, with a firmly based view of life, and knowing no doubts. Now I was sure of nothing. Everything was disintegrating around me.

As I rose from the bench I trembled. But with an impetuous movement he went to the window and threw open the shutter. The light of dawn poured in together with the last puff of wind, and dimmed the faint light of the lamp.

'Light has come into the world,' he said.

For a moment I thought he was talking of the new day. But he was still pursuing his thoughts.

'But the people are afraid of the light, and feel better in the twilight which conceals their evil deeds. The light calls them, but they turn from it. The sun seeks them, but they prefer the shadow.'

He raised his hands to his face for a moment, then leaned on the window frame. Outside was the greenish white wall of Ophel, gleaming in the sunlight. The dying wind rustled the branches. The shadow cast by this man with his outspread arms was like a man crucified. From the Temple above us came the glassy sound of the silver trumpets with which the Levites were greeting the morning light.

He didn't turn round. He stood like a believer repeating the morning prayer, 'Hear O Israel,' with his face to the Temple. In a quiet voice he ended:

'The day has only twelve hours, and then . . . then.' I again caught a note of pain in his tone. 'And then . . . high . . . high, so that all men . . .'

I left soon after. I did not mention Ruth to him. I could not.

I had hardly reached home when I regretted my omission. In face of this illness everything else grows senseless. It is like a thorn in the foot, only vexatious at first, but then becoming hell. I had wasted my opportunity. What had this conversation brought me? I had listened to incomprehensible, possibly insane words. I had learnt that I should be born again. What has Ruth's illness to do with this unintelligible counsel? O Justus, why do these things come about? I serve the Eternal all my life. Everything in my life is service to Him. Yet He has sent me this illness, which is slowly crushing me. Instead of striking at His enemies, He strikes at his most fervent devotee! The miracle of goodness which the Galilean spoke of is surely a painful jest? Since that conversation my despair has increased. Before it I could be reconciled with the world. But not now, not now!

DEAR JUSTUS,   FOURTH LETTER.

There has been no change since I last wrote.

The prophet has gone back to Galilee. I haven't seen him since our conversation in the hovel of Ophel. I know he spent some time in Judaea, until the news arrived that John had been imprisoned. Urged on by Herodias, Antipas has flung him into the castle of Machaerus. I have been there once. It stands on a cliff, with the wild, precipitous side facing the sea. The other sides are flanked by deep ravines overgrown with a wild, entangled undergrowth and filled with hot wells which give off a musty smell. You could be sure to find the marks of Satan's talons everywhere there. I can well believe that a whole horde of unclean spirits are bending over the prophet as he lies in the dungeon. They are fond of singers and dreamers like him.

When the news spread among the people that John had been dragged off to Machaerus, Jesus disappeared from Judaea. And with good reason. When prophets perish, they perish one after another. Example is infectious. Hardly was John in prison when the Sadducees began to say that the prophet from Nazareth should be shut away too. We of the Grand Council regard him with a certain indulgence. He hasn't given us much trouble so far, and he may yet be of use to us. We have no reason to complain because he fulminated against the Sadducees.

So the prophet has returned to his Galilee. And there he is working miracles. I often think of him. I clutch eagerly at every scrap of news that people bring from those parts. There has been no change in Ruth's condition. And by comparison with that all else seems only a play of shadows. They may seem important, but they have no depth whatever. She is the only important thing. I see her behind everything. I eat, drink, talk, smile at people, or plunge into meditation – but it is all as fragile as a dream. It is a dream; the only reality is this illness.

Disease lurks deep, possibly in man's very soul. The doctors try to entice it out, but it is not to be taken in like that. It rarely feeds on feeble, wretched bodies, and when it does, it is only to administer the contemptuous *coup de grâce*. But a body young and in the full bloom of health – now that's a real prize. To transform a child's fresh shoulders into bone with scaly and festering skin stretched over it: that is disease's greatest triumph.

Doctor Sabbatai says diseases are the vapours of hell blown about the world by devils. Maybe he's right. But I happen to think that there is nothing in the world which was not created by the everlasting Adonai, and so there is nothing that does not bear His mark. Diseases also were created in those six days. Satan makes nothing of nothing. All he does is try to overturn the work of the Most Highest.

But the prophet of Nazareth does overcome diseases. And he does it with amazing freedom, almost casually. I don't know the final truth of what people say about him, but I will set down for you the details of three miracles which several people have told me about. Hardly had he reached Galilee – and just think, he went by way of Samaria, stopped in Sychar, and spent some days talking with the Samaritans – when he went to Cana, where he changed the water into wine on a previous occasion. While he was there one of Antipas's noblemen came to him – a man half Greek and half Arab, and not very honest, so they say. He insisted that the prophet should go with him to Capernaum and heal his son, who had been suddenly stricken down with disease. He distributed some coppers among the rabble, to get them to shout: 'Help him, rabbi! He's a good man, heal his son!' Jesus stopped and looked at them, then said: 'Must you have signs and wonders? Cannot you believe without them?' As if he didn't know that that is the only reason they follow him, because they want miracles! Then the boy's father stepped out of the crowd and began to whine: 'Come and heal my son, sir. Come quickly, for he's dying.' Jesus interrupted him: 'Return home, your son will live.' And he went his way. The man was dumbfounded. He ran after the Nazarene, stammering something and trying to seize his robe. Then he stopped, scratched his head, called to his man and dragged back home. He came back to Cana the very next day. His son had been restored to health at the very time Jesus was saying: 'Your son will live.' Think of that, Justus! He healed him with only a word, without even going all the distance from Cana to Capernaum. He uttered no spells, he did not touch the boy. He just said: 'Your son will live,' almost impatiently. Why, when I saw him in Ophel he could well have said: 'She will live,' and Ruth would have risen from her bed. Without my having to ask him to my house. But would I be able to confide in him? I passed him by and returned empty.

The second miracle took place as he was passing through a town. A leper came out to meet him. Jesus advanced towards the man as though he didn't see him. The leper cried out: 'Rabbi, make me whole! Rabbi, make me clean! I was a sinner, but I have suffered a long time now. If you wish you can make me clean. At first Jesus seemed not to hear these cries. But at last he halted. He looked at the man, stretched out his hand, and touched him: touched him, a leper! 'Yes, I do wish it,' he said. The white skin on the man's hands turned bronze, as though a shadow had fallen over it. He raised his hand and tugged away the rag covering his face. The furrows of the sores filled with flesh, the spots vanished as though washed away by invisible hands. 'Rabbi!' he cried, and fell to his knees. Tears, laughter and whines struggled together for mastery, he could say not a word more. The prophet bent over him. 'Go in peace,' he said. 'Take two sparrows, cedar wood, a crimson thread and a branch of hyssop. Go with these to the priest. Get him to declare you are cleansed, and then go and offer up a sacrifice as the Law commands. But sin no more, and tell no man who healed you.'

Here again you get that touch almost of negligence. Just the words: 'I do wish it,' and the most terrible of all diseases left the man. And then that 'Tell no man.' As though he were saying: 'It's nothing, there's no need to talk about it.' But if healing disease and assuaging suffering are nothing, what is the true significance of his works? I've already told you that this man's words open up an abyss. They sound quite ordinary, human words, but once they're uttered they don't die away; on the contrary, they grow in volume of sound. And so it is with his deeds; He healed one man – very good! But when he heals many the deed becomes like an avalanche starting down the mountain side. You can say 'tell no man' as much as you like, but the rolling stones themselves cry out.

Now to tell you of the third miracle. At Capernaum (his favourite town since he was driven out of Nazareth — I'll tell you about that in a moment) the prophet went one Sabbath to the synagogue. When the reader had finished reading the psalms and turned to the congregation to point to the one who was to read the prophets, Jesus raised his hand. He went boldly to the stand. The synagogue official handed him the roll of the prophets. He was about to read the first verse when a loud cry arose from the midst of the congregation. It came from a man possessed by a devil. The people shifted away from the man, who was tossing about, rending his garments, and howling through foaming lips. 'Go away! Go away!' he shouted. 'What have you come here for? Do you want to destroy us? I know who you are. . . .'

'Hold your tongue!' Jesus exclaimed.

The man's eyes started from his head, a white saliva dribbled from his lips, his voice rattled in his throat.

'Come out of him!' Jesus calmly ordered.

The man cried out so frightfully that the people were terrified and began to flee from the synagogue. He fell face downward on the pavement. His writhings slowly came to an end, and he lay motionless, as though dead. There was a deathly silence, the people stood frozen with fear. The man suddenly raised himself on his hands and fixed his eyes on the Nazarene standing with the roll of the Scriptures in his hands. 'O, master!' he whispered, in the tone of a man recovering from a long illness. He crawled to Jesus and pressed his lips to the healer's hand. The crowd broke into cries of amazement and wonder.

Can you fathom all the power that is in this man's very words, Justus? To say 'I wish it' and heal someone, to cry 'come out' and expel a devil, involves a power such as we have never known before. You know our doctors' delusions that sooner or later they will find a herb or an adjuration which will cure all weaknesses? The prophet from Nazareth has discovered something of the kind. He strikes at the very heart of the trouble.

But perhaps not every disease is a punishment? Of late I frequently read from the book of Job. But whose guilt has brought on Ruth's suffering? Not her own, that is sure. Then mine, perhaps? The All Highest is my witness that I strive to serve Him with all my strength. If I, a Pharisee, am not clean enough, then what of the common unclean man, or the heathen? And why does someone else have to suffer so much because of my neglect, when the greatest of sinners enjoy such excellent health?

The stories of these miracles are running all through Jerusalem. Most of them have been told to me by Judas Iscariot, the man who conducted me to the prophet at night. He arrived in Jerusalem the other day, possibly sent by Jesus to find out what the people of the Temple thought about him; or possibly Judas himself is not sure what to do: to stay with the master or return to Bezetha. The man's an amusing fellow. He's sick with love of money. Over a couple of coppers his cheeks flush crimson, and his eyes glitter feverishly. He hates the Galilean fishermen who follow the prophet around. He thinks they're fools. But for the master he has fear mingled with admiration. He confessed to me that in his view the power which Jesus possesses is greater than his ability to use it. With such a power, he declares, one could do much more than just talk to the stupid Galilean peasants about the need to love one another. But seemingly even he doesn't know what the prophet ought to do. Or perhaps he doesn't want to tell me. I get the feeling that his heart is eaten up with hatred. It's a mystery to me why he has chosen to follow this prophet of compassion in word and deed. He hates the other merchants who helped to ruin his business; he hates the Levites and Sadducees who oppressed him with their gold; he hates everybody who is powerful, wealthy, and happy. And at the same time he hates beggars such as himself. His humility is only a cloak which he will throw off at the first opportunity. I sometimes think this unsuccessful huckster is possessed with desires out of all proportion to his wretched figure.

It was Judas who told me how Jesus was driven out of Nazareth. Nazareth has the reputation of being a town of adventurers, rogues and tricksters. It's difficult to imagine that Jesus spent all his childhood and youth there. Possibly if he had lived elsewhere his extraordinary capacities and powers would have come to light earlier. But when he returned to his native town he was received with incredulity. Nobody likes to admit that one has overlooked something which is perfectly obvious to others. When they assembled in the synagogue they were agreed on one thing: that this carpenter, whose brothers and sisters were living among them, and whose mother was standing among the women on the farther side of the grille, would have to show them no small wonder. They brought several sick people to the synagogue door. When he arrived with his disciples he passed through them as though he hadn't noticed them. He entered the synagogue. When the time came for the reading from the prophets he rose from the bench and went to the stand. The reading for that day was from Isaiah. He began:

'The spirit of the Lord is upon me. He has sent me to bring good news to men that are humbled, to heal broken hearts, to bring freedom to the captives, to open the eyes of the blind, and to proclaim to all the year of forgiveness and mercy.'

He stopped and gazed over the roll at the congregation. Then he added, with great emphasis: 'And now are the Scriptures fulfilled in your sight.' At that there must surely have been a profound silence in the synagogue. Now, the people thought, now we shall see the miracles we've been waiting for, and the prophet will manifest his power more than ever before. But he spoke with growing passion:

'You are blind! Blind and deaf! Spring is coming, but you are not going out into the fields to sow the seed; the rains are imminent, but you will not gather the ripened ears from the fields. You are blind! You seek a sign, but you don't see the sign. You look for miracles, but you haven't seen the miracle. You have just heard words which you have been listening to for hundreds of years. But still your poor are weeping with hunger and cold. Your prisoners are still suffering in chains. And the sinners? They sin more from ignorance than malice. And the year of forgiveness? Is the grain left in the field for the poor to glean?' The Nazarenes listened humbly enough. They even nodded appreciatively at the beauty of his speech. They were still waiting for these words to be followed by miracles. But when he cried: 'You are blind! You wait continually for a sign, but the sign was given you long since,' they fidgeted impatiently. They felt they had listened long enough. One of them exclaimed:

'Enough of your talk! Work us a miracle!'

Others took up the demand: 'Work a miracle! You've talked long enough!'

He looked at them coldly. No, that's not the word; he never has a cold look for anyone. But when he is called on to give something he is not willing to give, his gaze turns glassy and fixed, as though he were forcibly restraining his tears. They shouted louder and louder:

'Work us a miracle! No more talk! Work a miracle!'

He stood confronting the mob. If he has any knowledge of human beings he must have known that in such a situation the artist has to give way. The honour of Nazareth was at stake. Let him work a miracle, and then he could reproach them again for their lying, their turpitude, their heartlessness. They would have listened to him humbly. But he told them what he thought of them, and wasn't prepared to work a miracle. Perhaps he couldn't. Often when he heals someone he says: 'Your faith has made you well.' Perhaps before he can do a man any good the beneficiary has to show some readiness to receive the gift; and if he doesn't the good may turn to evil. He was inflexible. They began to stamp and roar:

'A miracle! We want a miracle!'

He stood silent on the stand. At last he raised his hand to indicate that he wished to say something. They were silent at once, confident that they had won the day. They waited for

46

him to ask indulgently: 'Well, what do you want me to do?'
But he said:

'You demand a miracle of me. You shout: "You healed
strangers, now heal your own people. The news of your activities has reached us from Capernaum and Cana. Do something
even greater for us." But I tell you: the prophet's worst enemy
is his own country, his own house, his own family. Remember
that in the days of the famine the care of the prophet Elias
was entrusted not to an Israelite widow, but to a Phoenician
woman of Sarepta. And Elisha didn't send leprous Israelites
to wash in the Jordan, but the leader of the Syrians . . .'

I can almost hear the howl that shook the synagogue as he
said that. He had touched them to the quick. The crowd swayed
like a forest shaken with the wind, and rushed at him. It is said
that every Nazarene is a born murderer. The prophet would
have to pay with blood for his audacious words. He was seized
by dozens of hands, dragged out of the synagogue and through
the town, to the accompaniment of yells and catcalls. They
took him to a steep place just outside the town. If they had
thrown him down it he would have broken his arms and legs,
and might even have been killed. But although so far he had
made no resistance, now he shook them off, like autumn leaves
when you shake the trunk. He scattered them and passed
through the midst of them. Not one tried to stop him. Then
he looked back. His face had that look which I can only describe as 'filled with cold.' Then he walked away unhurriedly.
His shoulders were hunched as though he were carrying a
burden. From the top of the rise he could see all Nazareth
spread over the hillside like bones in the grass. There he had
spent his years when he was a nobody. Now that other towns
are opening their gates to him, his native town rejects him,
expels him. Yet he felt not anger, but compassion. He raised
his hands to his face, his shoulders heaved. Can you imagine
it: he wept! What was he weeping over? Judas told me he
wept for quite a time.

So he cries sometimes. He, who can do so much, cries when

47

he sees others suffering and crying. There would seem to be two beings in him: the one knows he can heal, but isn't at all in a hurry to do so; the other seems to filch the miraculous power from the first, in order to do something against all justice. For apparently justice consists in not healing and not betraying the superhuman power. . . .

Jesus didn't heal any of the sick Nazarenes, though everybody there was sure he would work the greatest of all his miracles just for them. In other places he made people well without being asked; here they expected him to heal, and he passed by indifferently. But perhaps not indifferently. I expect you've noticed how often I have to correct myself. But while our judgement of other men is often excessively simple, our judgement of him is always simplified. I should have said, 'passed by feigning indifference.' But even 'feigning' is unjust. He never pretends. He is extraordinarily impulsive in his actions, and yet no other man could exert so much command over his will as he does. There would appear to be no human weakness which he doesn't suffer from. But it's only weakness. Don't you think that only too often we consider weakness is the same as sin? We think of virtue as a state of non-weakness. Yet between human weakness and human sin there is a bound like the bound dividing illness from death. Not every illness ends in death. There is always a moment of crisis. But virtue is sometimes to be found on the very edge of the bound. Just where it is most difficult for it to be demonstrated.

So, you see, the prophet of Nazareth is no longer in Jerusalem. He is wandering about Galilee, healing, casting out devils, preaching his doctrine of love and forgiveness. But I am left with my sick daughter and the anxiety which I feel at the thought that he could cure her, and I didn't ask him to.

But supposing I were to go to Galilee to see him?

For some days now I have been playing with the idea of going to find him and ask for his help. Surely he wouldn't refuse me? I spoke to Judas about it yesterday. He was quite importunate in his attempts to persuade me to make the journey. I don't know what he expects to get out of it, but he was unusually insistent.

But supposing I go, and he does nothing for me? Yet he cannot refuse. He has done so much for others. And always without the least effort, apparently, so let him cure Ruth. Then . . .

What is his method of healing, I wonder? He is not a doctor, who regards healing the sick as his vocation. He heals people almost despite himself. As though he were giving a sign. What sign? But what does it matter? Let him heal Ruth. All my life depends on her being restored to health.

DEAR JUSTUS,

I am writing this letter in the house of Helego, son of Aram, a Pharisee of the town of Capernaum. I have carried out my plan and am in Galilee. I'm sitting outside my host's house, in the shadow of a sycamore, gazing at the lake below. The sun is flowing like a stream of heated resin down the steep slopes of the hills, which here rise straight from the water's edge; and it is glittering over the lake surface to the farther shore, which rises gently, in changing colours like a carpet. It is beautiful here. Back in Judaea the days are still cold, and the greyish green of the olives is only just beginning to show among the house walls. This is a luxurious season here, for the snow-capped summits still give off a pleasant cool, and the sea breathes warmth like a pleasantly burning fire. It is speckled with coloured patches, for it reflects everything: the high azure sky, the golden sunlight, the green of the hillsides, the white houses, the orange cliffs. The triangles of sails slowly pass through these patches, like clouds floating over the sky. The fishermen are returning from their night's labour.

So I have come to Galilee. Perhaps I should have come earlier. But illness has the effect of both repelling and restraining you; it sets in motion an endless series of hopeful influences, and an equally endless series of ebbs of courage and desire for the struggle. Symptoms will appear which so often before have been the forerunners of improvement; Ruth smiles and begins to take an interest in life. But then a dark cloud of deterioration in health overcasts her. And as she lies passive, silent, sorrowful, my hands drop to my sides. O Adonai! At such times I feel like fleeing to the end of the world in order to avoid seeing that sight. Or at least, to close my eyes and forget it all. But what is the good of closing one's eyes? I expect when you were a child you, too, were afraid of a robe hanging in the dark corner of a room. And you screwed up your eyelids, and covered your head with the blanket. But you couldn't sleep, for you knew the apparition was still there. So it is with me: I often close my eyes. And then I don't see her mournful eyes, or the reluctant movement of her emaciated hand. But I know, I always know what she looks like and can see her hand feebly beckoning to me, scornful of my impotence.

I have the feeling that Jesus is a very good doctor. From the very first words he said to me . . . But I'll deal with that in a moment. Let me first tell you all that has occurred during the past few months.

The winter passed, and I was still hesitating whether to go and see him or not. At last the rains stopped; the Holy Days were approaching. I told myself he would be sure to come to Jerusalem, so there was no point in searching for him in Galilee. And he did come. But he remained so short a time that I knew nothing about it until he had gone again. He arrived with a crowd of Galilean pilgrims, and went back with them. When he's here in Judaea he is not so bold, possibly he is afraid of meeting the same fate as John. Yet just before he left he did something which all Jerusalem is still talking about. I really don't understand the man. He is cautious, and at the same time full of audacity; he is prudent, yet he has a tendency to commit the maddest of deeds. You know that every year, during the period of the high holy days a miracle is worked at one of the sheeps' pools at Bethsaida: the water suddenly begins to seethe and bubble, and the first sick person to enter the water is restored to health. Of course, you will want to know why I haven't taken Ruth there. But remember: these porticos swarm with wretchedness and beggary. Every disease in the world can be picked up there. Every stone is soaked with pus, sweat, and urine. The flies hover in clouds and cling to the mouth, the nose, the eyes. When the water begins to move everybody rushes down, pushing and jostling. If I could purchase access to the water I shouldn't hesitate. I think I have more right to a miracle than many of those lying around the pool, who must be some of the worst of sinners. But I can't fight for it. Nor could I be sure of protecting Ruth from contact with these sick people. If you want the benefit of a miracle at Bethsaida you must be prepared to stake everything on one throw. And I don't like the element of risk. I prefer to act with moderation and prudence.

Well, Jesus went along to the pool. He always goes wherever the crowd is the filthiest and most repulsive. He walked among the suffering wretches and halted beside a man who, it appears, had been ill for years and had tried vainly again and again to get down to the pool. He asked the fellow: 'Do you wish to be well?'

Naturally the unhappy wretch began to pour out his troubles: 'Of course; who wouldn't? I've been lying here for years. But I never get down in time. I haven't the strength. Someone always beats me to it. Now if you, rabbi, would care to remain with me and carry me down . . . But I know you wouldn't want to . . .'

Jesus interrupted him curtly, as though bored by these complaints: 'Pick up your bed and walk.'

And the man got up. Just like that! He flung the blanket on which he had been lying around his shoulders, and walked away. He didn't even stop to thank his benefactor, and Jesus vanished in the crowd.

But as the man went through the city with his blanket the Pharisees and scribes stopped him in great indignation. For it was the Sabbath. They reproached him for carrying his blanket, but he explained that the man who had made him well had told him to pick up his bed and go home. Once more I can't help thinking that this Nazarene has more power than sense at his command. What made him heal the man without being asked, and on the Sabbath above all things! Couldn't he have waited till next day? And was this man the most deserving of all who were lying there? Jesus makes enemies quite unnecessarily. For my own Pharisee brethren are now beginning to speak of him hatefully. All our order is concerned with observing the prescriptions for purification, and anyone who violates them is bound to have us against him. He does something quite good in principle, but spoils it by the way he sets about it. As it happened, that evening the healed man met Jesus at the Temple, and began to shout: 'Look, this is the man who made me well. The great prophet!' Jesus was soon surrounded with people, and among them Pharisees and men learned in the law. One of them, Saul of Hebron, said to him:

'You have committed a sin by healing this man on the Sabbath. And you have added to your sin by ordering him to carry his bed home on the holy day.'

Possibly if they had searched the Law and the Commentaries together they would have found some formula to cover this deed. But in a voice calm yet as cutting as a sword, he said:

'My Father is always working, and I work . . .'

You can guess what the reaction was to that! None of the prophets had ever dared to call the All Highest his Father. It may be that this man is indeed proclaiming the teaching of the most holy Adonai. But what arrogance, to think that he is closer to the Eternal than any other mortal man! Someone exclaimed:

'That's blasphemy!'

He went on as though he had not heard the remark:

'For the son should imitate the Father in all things. The

Father loves his son so much that he shows him how He Himself works. And you will see even greater things, and be astonished. As the Father resurrects the dead, so will the son restore life to whomsoever he wishes. The Father has given the son all His authority, that you may do him reverence as you do the Father. And the man who doesn't worship the son doesn't worship the Father who sent him. He who believes my words believes the Father's words, and will gain everlasting life. Before long now even the dead will hear the son, for they, too, can live. The Father has given all authority to the son and entrusted His judgement to him, because he is human. Of myself I can do nothing. When I judge, I judge by the will of Him who sent me. And when I witness to myself, it is not I who witness, but my Father who witnesses to me. You wanted me to tell you who I am. I have a better witness than John, though he was a torch burning with a great flame. My deeds testify that my Father has sent me . . .'

'He's blaspheming,' they said. And if I had been there, I expect I'd have said the same. Saul of Hebron retorted:

'We haven't heard His word testifying to you.'

'You haven't heard?' Jesus raised his eyebrows and gazed at him with a challenging, yet appealing look. 'Search the Scriptures' (he pointed to the rolls which the scribes were carrying). 'Search them, and you will find mention of me. But you don't search, because you don't have the love of God in you. Others come in their own name and seeking their own glory, and you listen to them. But when I come in the name of my Father and seek His glory you don't wish to believe me. If only you would believe even Moses, for that matter! He wrote of me and foretold me. But you don't believe even him. So how could you believe me?'

Our brethren stood silent, choking with anger and hatred. I heard them reporting the incident in the Grand Council, and hatred foamed from their lips like the smell of garlic. As for me, I just don't know what to make of all this. You in your wisdom recognize that there are two kinds of truth. One is truth exclusively for the reason. We accept it or reject it, we allow ourselves to be convinced, or we create our own counter-truth against it. When we cease to think, when we eat, sleep, indulge in light conversation, or when we love, that truth is a matter of indifference to us. But there is another truth which it is not sufficient to accept with the mind. It must be accepted with all one's being, for until we accept it thus it is a revolt and a pain within us. Who knows: perhaps it is some such truth that this Jesus proclaims, and that's why his words cause such turmoil within me? I don't hate him. Why should I? At times I think it would be very fine if a truth existed so complete, one which so completely filled life, as that which he proclaims. Does that upset you, Justus? You devoted so much labour to inculcating in me the dispassionate attitude of the sage for whom not life is important, but truth. But this man says life is important, because it comprehends the truth. For him life and truth are not separate conceptions. As for myself . . . I don't know.

Next morning, everybody in the city was talking about this conversation. And they ran to look for Jesus. But he had slipped out of Jerusalem during the night, and didn't return. I realized then that if I wanted him to place his power and knowledge at Ruth's service I must go after him.

So I went. I followed the bank of the Jordan, to avoid contact with the Samaritans. I fell in with many people, especially pilgrims returning from Jerusalem after the Holy Days.

Among them were two young men with whom I travelled. In the evening I learned that they were two of John's disciples, and were going on a mission from him to Jesus. I tried to discover what it was. They wouldn't tell me, but they talked a great deal about their master. After going for years on end without even a home in which to take shelter from the weather, he is now shut away in a narrow and noisome dungeon. That must be a real torture for him. Even in those days he did not live in the present, but in extraordinary visions. You will understand that that sort of thing has the effect of plunging a man into two simultaneous worlds, of which one is the contradiction of the other. Every man has something within him that links him up with the land beyond the horizon. And yet he has to live the ordinary life at the same time. Unfortunately, we never succeed in giving such complete expression to our yearnings that the rapture drowns the consciousness of our weakness. I recall the Greek story of Tantalus. He suffered, and never ceased suffering. Just as I suffer because of Ruth. Even if she were not dying in my sight I should still be torn in two. It's just as though someone beside you is shouting. At first you take no notice. But then the shout more and more dominates you, until at last you don't even know whether it's someone else or yourself shouting. And willy nilly you, too, begin to shout. Then you concentrate all your will in trying not to hear it. And yet you know that it's something highly important to you. And you're ready to give anything just to hear it again.

I found Jesus in Capernaum. If you happen to enter a town when he is teaching in the vicinity you don't find a living soul at home: they're all out listening to him. As soon as he halts the crowd flocks round him and stares at him with eyes starting out of their heads. When he begins to speak they sit down on the grass, and are ready to listen to him all day. He is certainly worth listening to! He reminds me of a singer; only his song is incredibly mature in its expression. He reminds me of the blind Greek who out of nothing conjured up a war over a city and the homeward return of one of its conquerors. But the Greek's songs are the revelation of a dead world. In the Nazarene's song the beauty of the world is a living beauty. I heard him say: 'Look at the lilies of the field . . .' And when he said 'lily,' though you couldn't see the flower you could catch its delicate scent and almost touch its petals. And he added: 'Solomon in all his glory was not arrayed like one of them.' Others can compare the regal purple with a flame, its gleam with the glitter of jewels. He chooses an insignificant white flower. He reveals the beauty where we have ceased to see it.

Then, when he sets off again, the crowd parts before him and forms a narrow, endless lane. They lay the sick, the maimed, and the unclean along the sides of that lane. The sufferers stretch out their hands to him, call to him. And he bends over them, sometimes he touches their forehead or shoulder, and says quietly, always in the same tone: 'Rise, be clean . . . be no more sick. I wish you to be well.'

That was how I found him. He came through the people towards us where we had halted in a less crowded spot. He was distributing health as though it were alms which a modest man thrusts surreptitiously into a beggar's hand. John's two disciples stepped forward and barred his road.

'What do you want?' he asked.

'Rabbi,' one of them spoke up, 'our master, John, son of Zachariah, has heard in prison about you. He ordered us to seek you out and ask: "Are you He who was to come, or are we to go on waiting?"'

So that was the mission on which they had been sent. It was not surprising that doubt had assailed John in his gloomy dungeon. But perhaps there was something more to the question? The unction with which the messenger asked it had a strange ring. Every prophet must bear witness to himself. We as emissaries of the Sanhedrin had gone to John to demand that he should reveal his mission to us. The Sanhedrin has not sent anyone to Jesus. So perhaps John was doing what needs to be done when a new prophet arrives to proclaim the Almighty's word: he had sent men to ask him, in all seriousness, who he was.

'Go and tell John what you see,' he answered. 'The blind see, the deaf hear, the lame run like the hart, the dumb speak, the leprous are cleansed, the dead rise from the tomb, the poor have heard good news . . .'

Simple words enough. Nothing unintelligible in them. And yet, if he took John's question as a challenge to reveal his mission he couldn't have made a better reply. The emissaries made an obeisance and drew back into the crowd. Their faces were flaming. After they have told John what the Nazarene said I feel sure they'll come running back at once to Jesus.

They departed. But he turned to the crowd around him.

'Who is John?' he asked.

Of course, they did not answer. He went on:

'Is he a reed shaken by the wind? Or a courtier dressed in fine clothing? Or a prophet? Yes, and more than a prophet!' With the freedom which always characterises his appeals to the most obscure of the prophetic texts, he quoted Malachi: ' "I shall send an angel to prepare the way for you." No man born of woman was greater than John. Why didn't you accept his baptism? You scorned the aid which God Himself sent you. Like imprudent children, when you saw that John neither ate nor drank, you cried out: "Don't listen to him! Satan is in him." But now that you see the Son of Man eating and drinking, you again cry: "Don't listen to him." '

'And yet,' he ended unexpectedly, 'John is less than the least in the kingdom of heaven.'

That I cannot understand. Why is John to be so little in this kingdom Jesus is always talking about? As though to increase my doubts, he went on:

'There were prophets who prophesied before John. He is the last . . . But you killed the prophets and deny the kingdom. You all seek to do it violence. But it would be easier for heaven and earth to pass away than for a single word to be changed in the Lord's prophecies. Do you believe that Elias is to return? But you have had Elias.'

Does that mean that John is Elias? But he himself denied it. Yet no other prophet prophesied the immediate future, as he did. They prophesied things to come after decades and centuries. But if John has to be followed by something new, this something must surely be what Jesus calls the kingdom of heaven. Then his mysterious remark that John is the least would make sense. John has remained on the further side. But surely these two bounds are already in contact with each other? What is the significance of this cleavage in time, which the prophet of the unclean proclaims with such inviolable self-confidence? A kingdom? I still don't understand.

Suddenly I noticed that he was looking at me. He looked as though he was expecting me to speak, to ask him something. Did he recognize me, possibly? It is said that as a boy he questioned the learned doctors in the Temple so wisely that he amazed them. He still asks questions. But even more he demands to be questioned. I yielded to his gaze. I asked him:

'Rabbi, what is this kingdom? How can we get to it?'

'You have the commandments,' he replied. 'Surely you know them? You're a learned man, an expositor of the law.'

So he had recognized me.

'Yes, I know them,' I answered. 'But . . .' I was about to say that I didn't know keeping the commandments led to any kingdom. But I stammered: 'Which one, rabbi? Which commandment is the most important in order to find your kingdom?'

He smiled and fixed his kindly, pleasant gaze on me.

'You ask which is the most important? Is it not: "Thou shalt love the Lord thy God with all thy heart, and with all thy soul, and with all thy mind, and with all thy strength?" And the second is similar: "Love thy neighbour as thyself." '

I felt a sudden shock. I expect you know the feeling that you have discovered the thread which links together thousands of already-known thoughts and makes them one. I think I understood at once what he was getting at. There is not one of the ten commandments which would not be superseded if love existed. People are evil because they don't love. What though Caesar sends us sacrifices in his name, if his soldiers hate us? What of it that the Temple servants gather gifts for the Temple, when the unclean crowd is filled with hatred and anger? He is right: the people must be taught to love. It is a beautiful thought . . . But how delusory! His kingdom will not be overpopulated!

'You have said well, rabbi,' I commented. 'The Eternal has

to be loved with all one's strength, and our neighbour as one-self. That is more than all the burnt offerings and sacrifices.'

With his gaze still fixed on me, he said slowly:

'You are not far from the kingdom . . .'

Was that intended as praise? In that case, definitely not fulsome praise! If I, a Pharisee, am only 'not far,' where are all the bawling, unclean clods who surround him? But it wasn't praise. He didn't say it in that tone. I don't know, but I have the feeling that his words had little connection with mine. I am almost inclined to think that he has assigned me a place 'not far from the kingdom,' and that he sees me, or wishes to see me, just there and not elsewhere.

He went on, and I followed him.

So for some days now I have been wandering over the fields, sitting on the grass to listen to his teaching, marvelling at the miracles which he works every day. His is a simple life. He usually spends the night in the open, wrapped in his cloak, beside a campfire. He eats modestly, whatever comes his way, and sometimes forgets to eat altogether. During the day he is never alone. But while the casual listeners are always changing, the small group of disciples are his permanent and inseparable companions. He treats them as his closest friends. But what a lot they are! Apparently he himself chose them. He must have been blind! There are twelve altogether. The majority are local fishermen, simple and uncultured men. I saw some of them down at the Jordan twelve months ago. I remember the tough giant with coarse features and a voice that thunders like an Arab drum. He's fond of talking, bragging, exalting himself above the others. But the others are no better. They seem terribly proud of the fact that he has chosen them as his companions. Yet they fight among themselves to further orders. Each of them thinks he's better than the rest, each wants to be the first after the master. Through their familiarity with the master they expect some incredible glory for themselves in the future. What taste, to make friends of such a rabble!

The fisherman with the thundering voice is Simon son of

Jonas. His brother, Andrew, is with him. Then there are the two other fishermen brothers, James and John, whom the master has called 'the sons of thunder.' John is still a youth and has a face as beautiful as a girl's (I think I remember seeing him, too, down by the Jordan). But his hands are already roughened with hauling on fishing tackle, and his speech is as hard as that of the others. Then there's Philip, a lad who seems always astonished and is always hot and bothered, but when the master tackles the trouble he breaks into naïve delight, clapping, shouting, and singing. Nathanael comes from Cana; for some reason he regards himself as wiser than the others: he's a typical village braggart. There's another Simon who also comes from Cana: a former Zealot, thrown out of their brotherhood for petty theft or something of the sort. He too thinks himself no end of a fine fellow, because he once took part in an attack on some drunken legionaries. Thomas is a craftsman, another impulsive sort like Simon, and just as senseless in his impulses. Matthew is exactly the opposite: the most miserable wretch you ever set eyes on! The others are just boors, but he is, or was, a customs officer into the bargain. He served the unclean Romans, he collected taxes for them. He hardly ever says a word, and only looks around fearfully to see whether anyone is picking up a stone to throw at him.

Two others are the master's brothers, not his blood brothers, but the sons of his mother's sister or his father's brother. James is rather like Jesus: tall, good-looking, with meditative eyes. He speaks slowly as a rule, and never quarrels, but is a know-all. He always knows exactly what should have been done, and he is the only one who takes the liberty of criticizing his brother. He says: 'You shouldn't have done that,' and smiles. The other brother, Judah, is taciturn and meek like Matthew. He walks behind, says nothing, and gazes at the master with the eyes of a startled goat.

The last is the merchant from Karioth. A man dreaming of revenge, but quick-witted, experienced, and even with some knowledge of the Scriptures. I find him easier to talk to than the others. He's contemptuous of his comrades and says the master was very stupid to choose such disciples. And he thinks it's the Nazarene's fault that these Galilean peasants have had their heads turned. Not only has Jesus made friends with them, but he has even taught them to heal people and to drive out devils. I write 'taught,' but that is hardly the right word. Judas declares he has taught them nothing. He simply said: 'Go and heal.' And they have succeeded more than once in healing a man or driving out a devil. Fancy putting such a power into such hands!

However, they don't try out their powers when he is around. He's the only one that heals then. And not only heals! A few days before my arrival he brought a man back from death. He was on his way to Nain when he saw people carrying a bier, and a woman following it. A common sight: a mother mourning her young son, wailing, screaming, tearing her hair, rending her garment. He went up and touched the bier (he is quite regardless of the prescriptions concerning cleanliness) and stopped the bearers. He said briefly, as usual: 'Young boy, I tell you to get up.' And the boy sat up. Of course, there was a scene; the men carrying the bier let it drop and fled like madmen. It was surprising that this resurrection didn't end with several more deaths, for in the excitement people could easily have been trampled to death. But all ended well. He had every right to tell John's emissaries: 'The dead have risen from the grave.'

So now I'm following him around, but I haven't yet spoken to him about Ruth. I listen to his words, and am more and more convinced that if he does anything for me he will demand a very high price in return. Or maybe he won't, but all the same I shall have to give it. While I think this out I am letting the days pass.

I would like to summarize for you the essence of the Galilean's teaching. Though I don't know whether I shall be successful. If you were to ask me what Jesus is really after, I could easily answer: he wants everything. For that is the truth. Of course, you'll raise your eyebrows and tell me you don't understand what I mean. I agree; but you see, it isn't easy to understand him, either. The truth he proclaims is so simple in its details that a child could understand it. But as a whole it seems to go beyond human understanding. He speaks easily and transparently, as though leading you along a smooth road. But suddenly the road comes to an end and you feel you are tumbling into an abyss. And then he says: 'Give me your hand, lean on me, trust me . . . And close your eyes.'

Recently some of John's disciples came to see him. They're wandering about like lost sheep, and when they don't decide to follow Jesus they turn against him, as though jealous that he should be free while their master is still in the 'black fortress.' They asked him: 'Why don't your disciples fast?' He replied: 'It's not the time to fast when the young master is at the wedding. But the days will come when he will go away, and then they will weep and be sorrowful. No one patches an old garment with a new patch, or pours new wine into old leather bottles.' Those words would seem to have no connection with one another; but think about them, and you may draw the same conclusions as I did. The teaching he has brought has not come to complete or to add to anything; it subserves nothing. It is complete in itself. Any one who wants to accept it must throw away his old cloak and get rid of the old bottles. He must win a new cloak and new wine-skins.

Some days ago, surrounded by a multitude of people, he was walking in the fields outside a town. The day was pleasant, as always in this district. A single cloud passed over the sky, looking like a great handful of down. Below lay the emerald lake. Beyond it, indicated by several white lines above the greyish horizon, rise the heights of Ante-Lebanon. The crowd sounded like a mountain torrent. Suddenly it came to a halt. At this point the hills end in the steep wall of a bare cliff. The Nazarene swiftly climbed to the top and rose above us, a white form against the blue sky, his hair burnished with the sun. The crowd, who know his ways, at once guessed that he was about to speak, so they sat down below him. The grass, the cliff, were hidden under the mass of human beings. When they were settled down he raised his head to gaze up to the sky and seemed to be saying something, inaudibly. He often prays. But always briefly. He says a few words, then returns to the earth again.

He usually begins with a parable: there was once a king, a husbandman, a father. The people listen, and the cleverly hidden truth steals unperceived into their hearts. But this time he had a different way of beginning:

'The blessing of the Most High is upon those who are simple, believing, trusting, and poor in spirit. They shall receive the kingdom of heaven . . .'

He said this so seriously that he reminded me of a second Moses coming down from Mount Sinai and proclaiming the commandments he had been given. It was also rather like a rescript at Caesarea, in which the persons to be admitted to the ruler's favour are specified. He went on:

'The blessing of the Most High is upon the quiet and humble. They shall gain the earth. The blessing of the Most High is upon the poor, the weepers and the hungry, the sick and the prisoners. Their sufferings will end and change to joy. The blessing of the Most High is upon those who are wronged and those who have been denied justice. They shall receive the Almighty's justice.'

I pricked up my ears. Now we shall learn everything, I thought. He spoke clearly, as though reading a legal codex. But the prescriptions he proclaimed were strange: they said nothing of guilt and punishment. Yet they spoke of virtue and reward. 'The blessing of the Most High is upon those who are wronged!' So people who suffer injury are blessed? And they will be granted justice into the bargain? You might think from this that there is no greater boon in life than to be wronged. And who knows why a man weeps? It might quite well be because he had received justified punishment. But Jesus makes no distinction. According to him, every one who weeps receives a blessing, and every man's weeping will be changed to joy. Don't you agree that this is too great a simplification of the complex problems of life? And then he went on:

'The blessing of the Most High is upon the merciful. They shall be shown mercy. The blessing of the Most High is upon those whose hearts are not troubled with desires and are clean. They shall see the great Sabaoth. The blessing of the Most High is upon the peacemakers, who render good for evil, bread for a stone. They shall be called the children of the Lord.'

By now I felt sure he was proclaiming a kind of second Decalogue, the basic tenets of his doctrine. Undoubtedly a fine selection! But how naïve! What is the point of saying that the blessing of the Lord is upon the merciful and the upright, if there is no simultaneous proclamation of punishment for the egotistical and the thieves? We have to be sensible over these matters: the world is full of evil. Beside the few who have chosen to serve the Eternal there are thousands of unclean people who are breaking the commandments and prescriptions every day; and beyond them are multitudes without number of heathens and idolators. Fine teaching should be guarded like a precious jewel. And he who confesses it should be under the protection of the law. But according to Jesus the good are plunged into very deep water. They have a blessing, and that is to be sufficient for them. It doesn't protect them against evil. You will have noticed that he puts the good and the unhappy into the one class. 'The blessing of the Most High is upon those who weep.' That's an extraordinary viewpoint. I can understand ransoming one's guilt with tears and so gaining a

64

blessing. But when you've been blessed you shouldn't need to cry any more. What good would the blessing be if it were followed by tears? He seems to regard virtues and misfortunes as something equal to one another. The blessing of the Most High, he says, is upon the beggars, the prisoners, the maimed, the sick. There's only one blessing the sick can receive: and that's health! But I have gone too far. It's not so simple as that. Why can't I obtain a blessing for my Ruth? I have offered everything to the eternal Adonai. If there is no blessing for me, for whom can there be one? For a beggar, just because he is a beggar? But I give alms, I pay tithes, I am not niggardly with my sacrifices. Even Job did not give more. The blessing of the Most High is upon those who weep. But do you think, Justus, that I never weep? On the contrary, I cry like a little child, with a hard sob in my throat. And am I to have no right to justice? Or Ruth to health? If what he says were true, I should have been blessed already! And if I had been Ruth's illness would have left her. But it hasn't, and now I cannot even imagine what life would be like if it did suddenly disappear.

He is right: anyone who wishes to accept his teaching must dress himself in a completely new garment. No patches will be of any use. One has to change all one's ways of thinking, one's way of looking at the world; one must call prudence what formerly seemed frenzy. I don't know why I am following him, what I am waiting for. The new bottle is doubtless the same as being born again, as he put it that night. But a man can't change his skin like a snake. A man must remain himself. Nor is he to be changed so fundamentally by threats or summonses. I still think he demands too much.

He ended his teaching:

'The blessing of the Most High is upon those who suffer for righteousness' sake. They receive the kingdom of heaven. And you receive His blessing when you are hated, when you are thrown out of the synagogue, when you are falsely accused, when you are persecuted in my name, just as they persecuted and killed the prophets. Rejoice then, and be glad, and wait. For you, too, the reward will come . . .'

Is that all, you will ask? Yes, I get the impression that he has put all his teaching into this song of blessings. I call it a song because it was a song, like one of the psalms of degrees. You asked me to describe his teaching. Instead I have quoted his words. Are you satisfied? I doubt it. I, too, would prefer to hear something different, something with more substantial foundations, and rather less bewildering.

I must admit that I am frequently troubled with doubts as to whether he is not after all intending to overthrow the Law, as the Sadducees declare. By the old bottle he may even mean the Torah. But he himself assures us that that is not his intention:

'So long as heaven and earth exist, so long not one letter of the Scriptures will be changed. The man who respects and preserves the Law will find his place in the kingdom of heaven, though it be a low, and possibly the lowest place. But the greatest in the kingdom will be he who fulfils the Law.'

Here I don't think he has in mind simply the ordinary fulfilment of the prescriptions. For him to 'fulfil the Law' means to find in it some secret, inner sense. For instance, he takes the ancient prohibition from the Tablets: 'Thou shalt not kill,' and explains: 'The man who is angry with his brother has already in a sense killed him. The man who says to his brother: "You fool!" will go to Gehenna.' Or he recalls the commandment: 'Thou shalt not commit adultery,' and adds: 'But I tell you it is sufficient to lust after a strange woman, and you have already possessed her. Your wife is your body. But when you cast her off, remember: you will be guilty if you give that body to another.'

At times he says decidedly disturbing things. Once he remarked: 'You have heard what Moses said: "A life for a life, an eye for an eye, a tooth for a tooth, a bruise for a bruise." But I tell you: if someone strikes you on the cheek, turn the other to him; if someone takes your cloak, give him your robe too; if someone forces you to go with him, go with him even further; if someone asks for and insists on a loan, give it to him, even though you know you are really giving alms.'

Rather too exacting, don't you think? But listen to something still more provoking. He said it only this morning. Among the crowd were relatives of some of the Galileans who were killed by the Romans during the last harvest festival. Someone mentioned this, and, of course, at once there were tears and lamentations. Jesus was moved by their crying. When he hears of suffering he seems to suffer even more than the person telling him about it. 'I lost my son,' sobbed some woman with a withered face ploughed with furrows like sunburnt clay. 'I lost my husband,' said another, a young, beautifully built young woman, in the hard and colourless voice with which one smothers grief. His lips quivered. He sighed.

'Do you think,' he turned to the people around him, 'that her son and her husband were greater sinners than any of you?'

There was a silence born of astonishment and uncertainty.

'No,' he shook his head. 'Yet if you don't repent, you will all perish.' The words sounded like a stifled cry of despair. But then a new thought appeared to take shape in his mind. He threw his arms wide open, as he always does when he is speaking to everybody and about everybody:

'Do you remember what is written in the book of Leviticus? "Don't desire your brother's blood, don't store up hatred against him, don't seek to take vengeance upon him, love him as you love yourself." But I tell you . . .'

His voice gathered strength like the Jordan in the rainy season:

'Love your enemies and pray for those who persecute and hate you. What reward do you expect if you love your brother, or a man who loves you? The heathens do the same. But you must be different: you must be perfect, as your heavenly Father is perfect.'

When I heard that, for one moment I felt like leaving him

at once and going back to Jerusalem. What pleasure is there in dragging after a man whose words are like a stone in the mouth? Who could love a sinner, or a man who plans to kill you? And even if you do adopt such an attitude to your enemy, can you do any good at all by it? I say: the world is full of evil; good will not defend itself. But he doesn't see that. He imagines that truth must prevail just because it is truth. Unfortunately, the truth always has to be assisted. It had to be imposed on the people.

If you were to pay any attention to him you'd have to give up teaching and only behave as you wish others to behave. Yet I must admit that that is precisely what he does. Now that I am watching him close up I know and feel that he loves us all equally: me, and any unclean member of the crowd, any Arab, Roman, Greek, and who knows whom else. Not only that. He loves a stranger as much as he loves his closest relations: his mother, his disciples, brother, or sister . . . His love appears to be boundless. I can't imagine his rejecting anyone. The people demand miracles of him as though they were loans which they have no intention of repaying. And he gives them miracles. He gives as though he is anxious for his actions to be in full harmony with his words. All the miracles he performs every day are, so to speak, visible demonstrations of this truth. 'Look,' he seems to be saying, 'this is what Adonai is like. I have made you well; now you know what you can expect from Him. This is a sign that you should believe in Him.' But supposing there are some who don't need this sign? Some who have faith in the Everlasting without the testimony of a miracle? This thought occurred to me only today, and it is beginning to trouble me. I seem to see a trap opening under my feet. You have been given health, I am thinking, in order that you may know that the Lord is merciful. But if you already believe that, what then?

By what right does he speak in the name of the Eternal? This audacity always repels me. I cannot stand his arrogance. A few days ago we were with him in the little town of

Chorazin, close to Capernaum. The people gave him a great welcome, as they do everywhere in these parts; they brought out their sick and tugged at his cloak, for they believe that the very touch of his garment, even his shadow, can bring them health. They listened to his words, beat their breasts, and scratched their heads like men who have decided to deny themselves something. But when we returned to the town some days later the first thing we met was a wedding procession which had escorted the young bride to her betrothed, and was now returning with drunken revelry to her parents' house to continue the merrymaking. He stopped and let fly at them. You never know what he will do or say next, whether he will smile at a horde of the unclean or shout at them impulsively. At times he speaks quite sharply, as though cracking a camel whip.

'Woe unto you, Chorazin!' he cried. 'For if Tyre and Sidon had seen as many miracles as you have they would have repented already in sackcloth and ashes. And so I tell you it will be easier for the cities of Phoenicia than for you in the Day of Judgement.'

He immediately turned to face towards Capernaum, the town which he seems to like so much that the people have even begun to call it his town.

'And as for you, Capernaum, do you exalt yourself to heaven? No, Sheol draws you down. You are worse than Sodom! I tell you it will be easier for the people among whom Lot dwelt than for your people, when the Day of Judgement comes.'

We stood dumbfounded. Only Peter drew a little to one side and looked down his nose. The sons of Zebedee raised a shout: 'Quite right too! They deserve punishment. Fire will fall on them from heaven!'

I gazed at the Nazarene's face. During this outburst it had an expression of offended dignity, as though the drunken brawling had been a personal insult. But now the flash in his eyes faded. Now they were like the surface of a deep well, which glazes over with cold or throbs with heat. What he said sounded like the rebuke of a mother speaking to a disobedient child. He turned back to the people of Chorazin.

'Come to me, all of you who are suffering and who work hard. Take my yoke and bear it as I do, humbly and quietly. If you do you will not lack joy. For my yoke is not a burden, it is a pleasure.'

A pleasure? That is like his blessing on the weepers. It's almost saying: you're happy because you weep. No, Justus, this philosophy is not for me. I weep, and I'm not at all happy. I serve the Lord, but that doesn't bring me happiness. What does Jesus offer? Instead of pain coming from outside us, pain which we can bear within ourselves. That's only word-spinning. When my head aches I can't change the pain for toothache, even though the headache seems to be the worse when you have it. Fasting also is the infliction of pain on oneself. But why cannot my fasting take the place of Ruth's suffering?

The blessing of the All Highest is on those who are merciful, on the peacemakers, the weepers. And he himself is the criterion of that. He is merciful when he bends over the sufferers and seems to be instilling his own strength into them. He is a peacemaker: in all this disorderly band of Galilean rabble there is never any fighting among themselves. He weeps; he must weep often. He is poor, and he suffers persecution. Everything that he says is the sign of blessing and happiness is his. And we, too, are conscious of that blessing. It is like an aureole over his head as he stands in the sunlight. Not that he is anything extraordinary. And yet something incomprehensible, intangible yet incontrovertible, radiates from him. No man has ever spoken as he does.

He speaks with such great confidence in the Eternal that it almost sounds like blasphemy, yet he himself must possess such confidence, none the less. 'Take no thought for what you shall eat or drink or what you will wear,' he has said more than once. 'Look at the birds; they don't gather grain to store and don't torment themselves with thoughts of what may happen. They have trust, and so each of these sparrows which are sold for a couple of coppers is in the hand of God. Don't worry about tomorrow. There's enough to worry about today. Seek above all the kingdom of God; seek it persistently, without relaxing, and all the rest will be given you. Your Father in heaven knows quite well that man cannot live without bread.'

That's his life exactly: that of a bird, without care for the morrow, though not without thought for the morrow. But it's expecting too much from people like us, to demand that they shall become perhaps even rather thoughtless. We see too much in anticipation. Already today we're concerned with troubles to come tomorrow. If they don't come we don't even notice it, we're too occupied with a further lot of troubles. How many lies we create, in our belief that it will be better so, more prudent so. Sometimes I tremble at the thought of what will happen if Ruth's illness lasts another year or two. How much we torture ourselves!

But he knows nothing of all this. Though he only smiles, his quiet smile is more pleasant than another man's noisy laughter. His voice often has a note of sorrow, grief, almost of despair. But even more one hears in it a note of joy. It is a strange joy, like the gurgle of water at the bottom of a deep rocky cleft. We have to strain our ears to hear it, but it is always there. And there are moments when the spring spurts up into a fountain and sparkles with all the colours of the rainbow in the sunlight. Once he exclaimed: 'Ask! Knock! Every one who asks will receive, to every one who knocks it will be opened. If you ask for fish you will not be given a serpent.' At such times there is a note of rapture in his voice. He appears to have only one sorrow and one joy: sorrow that people can be evil, and an all-engulfing joy that the goodness of the Most High is greater than all human evil. Recently, as we were passing through Capernaum, seven elders of the synagogue came and asked him to heal the servant of the Roman centurion who commands the force guarding the frontier between the two tetrarchs, Antipas and Philip. Apparently this centurion is very well disposed to the faithful and, having himself joined with those 'who fear the Lord,' he has helped in the building of the synagogue. 'Take me to the man,' Jesus briefly replied.

We passed along the cypress-lined road at the lakeside. Gennesareth lay bathed in the sunlight, a level expanse at the bottom of a cauldron. The fishermen were standing in the water, hauling in their net ropes with all their strength. Of course, Simon and the others were attracted by the sight, and began to shout advice. Their hands itched to get hold of the ropes. They were following Jesus, but all their being was with the boats and nets. They would never have agreed to abandon that life if he hadn't spoken to them one day in a manner that would not take no for an answer. John, the son of Zebedee, told me how it happened.

'It was before the rainy season,' he said. 'The teacher was speaking to the people; and to get away from the crowd he climbed into our boat. When the sun was dropping down behind Mount Carmel and the people departed, he said to Simon: "Cast out your nets." We had been out on the sea all night without catching anything. There had been a storm a day or two before, and we knew we would never catch anything in such conditions: the waves were breaking too heavily against the shore. But Simon said: "Since the rabbi commands, we'll sail." We cast off. The first black patches of dusk were shifting over the lake surface when we dropped our net. We knocked with sticks on the bottom of the boat. "The floats are dancing, the fish have come," Simon shouted. We snatched up the ropes. Though there were four of us the net wouldn't budge: it might have been anchored to the bottom. Fortunately a boat belonging to a fisherman acquaintance was in the vicinity. We called to them to come and help; they seized hold of the net on the farther side. But even then we weren't able to shift it at first. Andrew shouted: "The ropes are breaking." As he strained at the rope, Simon groaned: "We shall lose the net." That would have been terrible, for we could never have bought another. "It's coming," James suddenly cried. And the water between the two boats began to seethe. Suddenly a silvery mass of fish emerged from the black waters like a rock rising from the sea. I have never seen anything like it, rabbi. We could never have got the catch to shore if other boats hadn't come to our aid. When the stones scrunched under the keel we saw the teacher standing on the shore. Simon pushed through us. He jumped into the water and took great leaps to the land. He flung himself at the teacher's feet: you know how impulsive he is. "Leave me, rabbi," he cried, "for I am a sinful man."

'But the teacher smiled and rested both hands on Simon's shoulders. "From now on you will catch men," he said. And then (John smiled a melancholy smile) we left everything.'

As we were going to the centurion's house we saw a horseman galloping towards us. He saw us and reined in his horse. He was a Roman soldier. Standing at the roadside, holding himself erect, he waited for the Nazarene to draw level with him. Then he swiftly bent his knee and knelt down. Jesus halted.

'This is the centurion we spoke of,' the synagogue officer whispered to Jesus across his shoulder.

The soldier rose to his feet, but he kept his head still sunk on his chest, and stood with folded hands.

'Don't bother to come further,' he said. 'I heard you were coming and have ridden out to meet you, to tell you I am not worthy that you should be my guest. Rather should I serve you. I know you have only to say the word and my man will be healed. You are like the tribune, who orders a soldier: "Go there," or "Do this," and the soldier obeys.'

For a moment there was silence. The centurion stood with his head still bowed. Jesus looked at him, his piercing black eyes almost expressive of anxiety, I would say. He seemed to be waiting tensely for something.

'Go then,' he said abruptly. 'You have believed, and so be it.'

Even now the centurion did not raise his head. With a stiff, soldierly movement he bent his knee, and made a low obeisance, as though wanting to kiss the master's garment. Then he rose. His youthful face beamed with joy. He had taken the word as the deed. Raising his hand, he saluted the master in military fashion, as he would a superior officer. He hurried to his horse and sprang on to its back. Turning round, he raised his hand. Then he galloped off to the dry clatter of hoofs on the stones of the road.

When at last the horse and rider merged into the distance, Jesus turned to us. I have told you before of his joy. I have never seen it so strongly marked as it was at that moment. He gently shook his head, as though astonished at or not altogether believing something, and said quietly, perhaps only to himself:

'I have not found such faith here . . .'

Then he raised his eyes and gazed out across the lake, at the fallow hills of Gilead, at the varied green of the Galilean shore.

'Truly,' he said, 'I tell you that many shall come from the east and the west and carry off the kingdom . . .' The joy in his voice was like the ringing of sheep-bells in the still air of noonday. But then it was veiled with sorrow like the mist accompanying the first rains:

'But the sons of the kingdom will be lost in darkness.'

We were at a loss to know what he was talking about. He passed between us and went down to the sea. As we followed I was thinking: you might say there are two beings in him. One rejoices in the coming of strangers, the other weeps because the sons of the inheritance may be deprived of their heritage. He wants it all ways. That struck me like lightning striking the calm mirror of the lake.

He wants it all ways. That is the essence of his teaching concerning the blessed who are happy and weep, the kingdom which is full of his own people and strangers too. Really, I don't know why I go on following him around.

But I have to tell you that the Roman centurion's servant recovered his health at the same hour in which Jesus said: 'So be it.'

This time I must say I don't know what to write to you. What I have seen has changed all my views of him. I've assured you more than once that he's quite an ordinary sort of man. Today I must say: 'I don't know who he is: a man, or some other mysterious being only pretending to be a man.'

If I were not seeing him every day, and seeing him eating and drinking like the rest of us; if I hadn't seen him one day enter a carpenter's workshop and succumb to the temptation of the saw, the planes, the hammers and gimlets and begin to work up a block of wood, with every movement revealing that he knew exactly what he was doing; if it were not for the tears which I have frequently seen in his eyes; if it were not for the sorrow which sometimes tones his words, I should perhaps cease to believe that he really exists. But he is a man; his feet leave traces in the sand, and the grasses bend under them. When he is tired you can see it in his face. And at such a time he may lean against any rock or side of a boat, and go right off to sleep. He dropped off just like that one night when we were out in a boat: he slept the sleep of a workman who is dog-tired. But I'll tell you about that incident later.

He rarely spends more than one night in the same place. We wander along the roads and paths of Galilee, though the year is now at the full. Everything has ripened, the harvest is almost all gathered in, any day now it will be possible to pick the dates. The ponds and the smaller streams are dried up. The Jordan has abated and now runs, a silver thread, at the bottom of the ravine. The vegetation which covers the slopes is kept alive only by the incessant efforts of the Galilean farmers. Hermon's white cap has melted, its grey-green summit rises to the sky, barely dominating the extensive ridges.

Wherever he goes, as soon as he stops he begins to teach. He speaks in the synagogues, but he prefers the open sky. I've noticed that of late there has been a change in his manner of speaking. Formerly, when he told a parable, he at once explained what it meant. Today he still tells his stories, but he hardly ever explains what he has in mind by them. Only to his disciples does he explain them later, if they haven't understood.

Possibly this change is due to the opposition he has met with of late. The common people still flock after him, listening to everything he says and in raptures over his miracles. But the Nazarenes are not wasting their time: they have spread slanderous stories concerning their fellow citizen all over the country. They have drawn the Temple's attention to him. It is growing more and more common for priests, Levites and scribes to be found among his audience. And Pharisees too. They have turned to me to ask me what I think of this new teacher. They have tried to catch him out in his words and actions. He has spoken harshly about our brethren. Not one word has been forgotten.

'Haven't you noticed, rabbi,' they asked me, 'that he doesn't remember to wash before eating, and he picks up his bread with unclean hands? One mustn't sit at the same table with him. And he doesn't respect the Sabbath. We ourselves saw him one Sabbath walking with his disciples through the cornfields, and they plucked ears, husked them in their hands, and ate them. When we drew his attention to what they were doing, do you know what he replied? He reminded us how King David of blessed memory took the shew bread from the Temple and ate it. He actually compared these unclean clods with our great king! And he added: "There is someone who is greater than the Temple." It was blasphemy to compare himself with the Temple like that. Then he said: "The Son of Man is lord of the Sabbath." Whom is he calling the Son of Man? Daniel uses this phrase to refer to the Messiah. Is he then daring to call himself by the name of him who is to come? That's blasphemy. The Almighty alone is lord of the Sabbath. And when we told him that Baal Zebub was casting out devils through his agency, he cried that we were vipers, and possessed not by one but by seven devils. Have you heard what the people say of him? They say he is of the line of David. That's blasphemy! He's only a common carpenter. Herod burnt the genealogical records, may he be accursed, and now any beggar can claim to be a descendant of the kingly line. Rabbi, you must contradict him. You're wise, you know the Law. There is a homily which says the dignity of one learned in the law is greater than that of an angel. Order him to hold his tongue. The days of prophets are ended. Order him to be silent, rabbi.'

Their eyes glittered beneath their turbans, their fingers plucked angrily at the fringes of their talliths. They hate him. They want me to oppose him. They were insistent, they tempted me with flattering words: such words have a more murderous effect than a sword set against the throat. But I thought: if I oppose him, who will save Ruth? I know he blasphemes and violates the prescriptions. But there is something in him that renders me impotent. Perhaps he cast a spell on me when he told me I was not far from the kingdom? In any case I cannot oppose him. I told them it was too soon, we must go on listening to what he says. They retorted: 'He's said quite enough already. Censure him, rabbi, and order him to hold his tongue. If he spoils the people nobody will want to listen to our teaching.'

But I knew I couldn't. I must see more of his deeds and hear more of what he has to say. We argued till late in the night. When they departed in dudgeon one of them said: 'It's a great outrage that you listen to him and say nothing.' But what can I do? If he would only see to it that his disciples scrupulously washed their hands and respected the Sabbath nobody could find fault with him. His teaching is free from error. The miracles he works appear to testify that the Almighty is with him. So why is he so imprudent? Why does he make things so difficult for me?

Possibly he talks in parables because he knows his enemies

are waiting impatiently to catch him out. One day he related:

'The kingdom of heaven is like a man who went out to sow. Some of the seed fell among thorns, which choked them; others fell by the wayside, and were trodden underfoot. Yet others fell on stones, and the sun burnt them; others on soft ground, and they germinated swiftly, but they withered just as swiftly. But some of the seed fell on good ground, and grew to bear heavy ears, returning the farmer more than all he had lost.'

'The kingdom of heaven,' he said on another occasion, 'is like seed which a man sows, and it grows day and night, and the sower hardly notices the moment when the ears are ripe for gathering. And the man is amazed, for the grain and the soil, the rain and the sun have done everything, and all he has to do is gather in the harvest.'

In this district the people are starting the second sowing of the year, and all his parables have reference to field work. He never speaks of things which the people listening to him cannot see with their own eyes, or at least cannot imagine for themselves. In his stories you never find doctors learned in the law, or angels, or devils, or a voice from heaven. There are only ordinary people, unclean individuals like those to be seen around him. But then, that is exactly how the great Hillel said we were to teach: to bring the Law nearer to the common people. So he speaks well. But it is just as certain that the teaching on purification came down to us by way of Joshua through the prophets, to the doctors, to Shammai, and then to Hillel, and it became more sacred than the Law itself, because we voluntarily took this duty on ourselves to glorify the name of the Presence. So why is there this contradiction in him? If he would only understand! For one cannot treat him as one would some self-appointed know-all deceiving the people with empty talk which is contrary to the doctrines.

He is always followed by an enormous crowd; you wouldn't think it was the season for field work. They wait on his every word, and lay the sick down in front of him. And he never rejects anyone. Of late his disciples have tried to drive people away so that he can have time for food and rest. But he noticed that they were preventing a crowd of women with their children from coming to him to ask a blessing for their little ones. And he said: 'What are you sending the children away from me for? The kingdom of God is theirs.' But he seems to be growing more and more exhausted. As soon as he is given a moment's peace he drops his head on his arm and is still. Yesterday I heard him tell Simon: 'Make ready a boat; we shall go for a sail this evening.' I realized that he was anxious to get away from this crowd of admirers, who weary him. I decided to ask him to take me with him; I thought it would be easier for me to get him to help Ruth when we reached the deserted shore of Decapolis. So I did ask:

'Rabbi, allow me to sail with you and your disciples to the farther shore.'

He raised his head and looked at me. With the heat and his labours his cheeks have sunk in, and a violet veil seemed to be spread over his face. He has a beautiful face. He wears the tallith only when he enters the synagogue, and he never wears the phylacteries. But for the fringes on his cloak you might take him for a heathen. He fixed his weary eyes on me. He always looks as though he can see right through you, can see things you yourself know nothing about.

'Come if you wish,' he said. 'But remember: the foxes have holes, and the birds have nests; only the Son of Man has no home in which he can shut himself away . . .'

I thanked him, and was about to go when one of his disciples, Thomas, came up with his hair matted and sprinkled with earth. It transpired that he had just heard of his father's death.

'Rabbi,' he sobbed, 'I must pay my last respects to him who gave me birth. I shan't sail with you, but will go and see to the burial and the funeral feast.'

To my astonishment the Nazarene shook his head.

'Come with us,' he said calmly as usual, more asking than commanding, and yet in a tone that could not be gainsaid. 'Let the grave-diggers see to the dead.'

What is one to make of such a remark? The commandments tell us to honour our parents, and many of the prescriptions deal with the son's duties to his father. Who should bury the father, if not the son? But he says, leave it to the grave-diggers. A further rejection of all our teachings. How can I justify his conduct when he says such things?

We gathered on the shore late in the afternoon. Simon and Andrew had prepared a boat. All the twelve were going. Thomas was not absent. His hair was combed and oiled. He showed no sign of mourning. What a tremendous influence this man's words have on these unclean louts! A crowd of people assembled on the shore. 'You'll come back, won't you, rabbi?' they asked anxiously. He nodded. He was so tired, he swayed on his feet.

I had already noticed that Simon, Andrew, and the sons of Zebedee were standing a little to one side, having an earnest discussion. I caught the words: 'But it was roaring in the Great Chest . . .' 'The teacher said we were to sail today . . .' 'Warn him . . .' 'He knows everything . . .' 'But supposing . . .'

I felt uncomfortable. The 'Great Chest' is the name given to the cliffs between Bethsaida of Galilee and Capernaum, and the local fishermen say that when a storm is approaching from the west you can hear the roar of the Great Sea there. I looked at the sky rather anxiously. The weather seemed set fair. But evidently the disciples were not the only people who had heard the warning signal, for voices called from the crowd: 'Don't sail today, rabbi. They say a roar can be heard in the "Great Chest." There may be a storm.' He appeared to pay no attention. The head of the local synagogue, Jairus, the man who had persuaded Jesus to heal the Roman centurion's servant, stepped out of the crowd. Folding his hands under his tallith, he said:

'You'd better not sail today, rabbi. They say there's going to be a storm . . .'

Jesus seemed to make a last effort to overcome his weariness; he replied:

'You can tell the weather by the sky. Why can't you discern the hour which has come?'

A cloak was spread and a cushion placed for him in the stern. The western wind was not yet blowing, so the fishermen took to their oars. I got into the boat without any enthusiasm. I even wondered for a moment whether to remain behind. I was sure I could read anxiety in the disciples' faces. But I thought I ought to go for Ruth's sake. The people on the shore called farewell wishes for a safe voyage. Hardly was Jesus on the boat when he dropped heavily to the cushion. Before I could look round, his breathing grew slow and regular, the rather sibilant breathing of a sleeper.

I looked at the sky anxiously again and again; the first stars were beginning to shine. Ahead of us the peaks of the hills were still burning, but their rosy gleam faded rapidly. There was no wind, the sail hung limp. My fears began to die away. 'They were only trying to keep the teacher with them,' I thought. So long as I could see the shore I was comforted: we could always flee back to it if a storm blew up. But now darkness descended over everything, there was only the faint light of the stars. We could not see the bank, we could see nothing at all around us; we moved as though canopied with the tents of Kedar. I was not even sure that we were moving. It was just as though the water had turned to stone and held us fast in the middle of the lake. I could barely discern the teacher's outline. He lay huddled on the bench. Some of the disciples were rowing, the others were dozing, leaning against one another. Nobody talked; the splash of oars was the only sound that disturbed the silence.

My fears began to grow again. I could not sleep like these others. If a storm should come up, would we be able to flee before it? Would these fishermen, who had shown alarm at the very possibility, be able to face it? I tried to direct my thoughts in another direction: my mind turned to Ruth. But that led to gloomy thoughts, as black as the night around us. I imagined I was talking to her, and my lips writhed, and my voice broke in a sob. But she was silent. What does she think of as she lies listening to the cruel rhythm of the disease consuming her body? All I have done for her is as nothing. O Adonai! Eliphaz was right in saying that the sky itself is not clean enough for Thee, nor the stars, nor even the angels. None the less I must converse with Thee. Thou shalt tell me why she suffers so much. For what sin? And whose? O Adonai! If he heals in Thy Name, why hasn't he himself offered me her health? Others don't have to ask, yet they receive. I beg in silence. Doesn't he see that?

I don't suppose you know how unexpectedly the western wind blows up over the Sea of Galilee at the dead of night. It was as though an enormous, invisible fist had torn out of the darkness to strike at our boat. The mast began to crack, and the sail bellied out with a terrible roar. The wind carried us away and up to the crest of the wave, then flung us from a tremendous height down into the sombre, roaring cauldron. The stillness flew away like a startled bird, leaving place for a thousand sounds. The black, petrified surface of the lake came to life. It turned to a tossing mass of white foam. We flew upward again, to be buried in the bottomless depths. A hissing noose of foam flew over our heads, plunging us into water. I saw the sons of Jonah fling themselves on the sail. They tried to lower it. But it tore out of their hands like a living creature. The gathering waste of water bore us upward again, and then beneath our feet there was an emptiness, into which we fell without end. Staggering and waving their arms, the fishermen struggled with the sail. They mastered it at last, they crushed the deafening flapping of the ribboned canvas. But the roar of the sea continued like a thunderous music. The waves struck us violently, like rocks leaping out of the water. The blows came at us from all sides. We seemed to be writhing like a man under the lash. Suddenly, out of the darkness a pillar of water rose right under our bows and hurled itself upon us. Now we were standing up to our ankles in water, clinging to the gunwale and the benches, wet through, deafened and shattered by the whistling wind, which thrust the breath deep down into our chests. A second pillar flew over the right gunwale. At the same moment some invisible force plunged us to the very bottom of the lake. The water flooded over us, and reached half-way up our calves.

I suddenly gathered that someone next to me was whispering in what seemed a terrifying whisper. But it was a shout. Simon, I think it was, bawled: 'Bail out the water!' Clinging with one hand to the bench, I squatted down and helplessly tried to bail out the water with my hand. I was wet through. Again I heard a human voice, before it was carried away by the wind: 'Bail out the water! We're sinking!' At that moment the boat leaped as though the waves were flinging it against the pillar rising from the lake. The bench slipped out of my hands. I sat down on the bottom. I looked up convulsively. The foam was like snow on reeling mountain heights. But still higher, in a shifting scrap of sky the stars shone calmly, as though gazing with blind eyes, indifferent to the things happening below.

I tried to scramble up. Someone sprang across me. I heard yet again a voice which the wind first silenced, then allowed to sound out with all the strength of despair:

'Teacher! Teacher!'

Then I remembered him. He had been in the boat asleep only a moment or two before. I tried again to get up. Another stream of water poured over me. Clinging to the side, I shuffled along on my knees. A gigantic form towered above me. It must have been Simon. Away at the stern, despite the roar and the whirling darkness, I saw a quiet form, still huddled on the bench. The storm had not awakened him. He was sleeping in the sinking boat as though on a couch in a warm room.

'Teacher!' Simon's hoarse voice shouted. 'Teacher! We're perishing.' The others shouted too. And I shouted.

We were tossed about once more. I clung to the firm arm of a fisherman to avoid falling. Now there was so much water in the bottom that it swept me off my feet. I strained my eyes into the darkness where the sleeping man was alarming in his immobility. But at last he stirred. Suddenly, through the uproar of the sea I heard his voice, unbelievably calm, weary, almost sorrowful:

'Where is your faith? Why have you no trust?'

Something pierced my breast, as though I had been wounded by a knife thrust. Like the echo of a song which reaches our ears belatedly, I recalled the words of Job in which I had prayed before the storm broke: 'Whatever may come, I will trust Thee.' How boundless is his trust, I pondered, and what boundless trust he demands in turn! This storm seemed to be tearing the world to shreds. All the world, not only our immediate surroundings.

A slender white form stood before me. He had risen to his feet. I heard him speak, but now it was in a different tone, not the wearied, sorrowful voice of a teacher whose instruction is in vain. Now it was lightning amid lightnings, thunder against the roar of the wind and the sea. He spoke; he didn't even shout. But that ordinary, yet commanding voice reached up to the stars and down to the bottom of the sea. It began as a sound lost in the chaos of the storm; it ended as a call in a night as quiet as stillness itself. All that had been a moment before: the thrashing of the wind, the water, and the darkness, suddenly ceased to be, as though it never had been. Do you follow me? A second before, the waves had been pouring over the stars and washing the sky. But the whistle of the wind broke off like a note from a snapping string. Once more the sky extended spaciously above us, and, as before, the stars dropped to the sea and lay in safety on its gently furrowed surface. If we hadn't been wet through, and worn out with struggling against the wind, if there hadn't been the water in the boat, we might have thought the storm had been no more than a dream.

He dropped back on to the bench, huddled up, and was still. Had he fallen asleep again? Simon muttered to us to bail out the water. As we worked our eyes were fixed on the teacher. And now, whatever we did, all our thoughts were concentrated on him. We could not understand how, after all that had happened, he could go off to sleep again.

But that didn't end the story, Justus. In the morning we drew close to the shore. Before us rose precipitous cliffs. There was only one spot where it was possible to land: a point where the water had washed away the cliff and broken it into great jagged rocks. Jesus woke up and told Simon they would land here. We sailed cautiously between the rocks, sounding the bottom with our oars. The water gurgled around the rocks, but the sea which he had stilled was so tranquil that we could safely leave the boat and step out on to the shore. There was a cleft in the cliff, and a gentle slope led up to a plain covered with luxuriant grass and trees. We saw a town not far off. 'That's Gerazim,' said James, who knew the district well. A great herd of pigs was grazing in the shade of spreading oaks, and several half-naked youngsters were watching over them. The lads stared at us inquisitively. Suddenly one of them shouted to us and pointed, as though to warn us against some danger. As we turned to look we heard a savage, terrifying shriek.

At first it was difficult to tell whether the form running towards us was man or animal. It was an enormous brute, naked, but covered with curly hair, mud, and congealed blood. A piece of broken chain hung from one wrist. We realized that he was a lunatic, and obviously dangerous. Simon ran back a few paces, then cried out: 'The teacher!' and he and Thomas hurried to guard their master. Jesus stood perfectly still, and showed no sign of alarm. The man made no attempt to attack him, but fell headlong, writhing and howling. He beat his head on the stones until blood spurted from his forehead. He tore up the grass with both hands and flung it over himself. Spittle dribbled from his lips in a thick white stream. I began to catch words among his incoherent ravings:

'Go away! Go away, Son of Him! You have nothing in common with us. Your time has not yet come. Go away!'

A shiver ran down my back. Evidently Satan had taken possession of this madman. I know the spells for adjuring Samael the father of Cain, and for Asmodeus born of incest. But I was so badly shaken that I forgot them. Only one thought ran through my brain: this was how the father of lies must have writhed before the Eternal, when he had to admit that he had failed to overcome Job. Suddenly Jesus spoke:

'Come out of this man!'

Calmly and firmly, as always. Just as he had said 'Be still!' to the storm a few hours before. There was no agitation in his tone. It was a command which could not but be obeyed.

The madman howled even more vociferously than before. He cried hoarsely:

'Why, why? We are not afraid of you! There are many of us.'

'What is your name?'

'Our name is Legion. Do you hear? Legion. A whole day would not be long enough for us to tell them all.'

'Then come out of him, every one of you!'

The man cried out as though being tortured. He dug his teeth into his arm and tore away some of the flesh. Mingled with the snarling and bellowing we heard more and more clearly the sound of sobbing. 'What do you want of us? Why are you tormenting us?' he whined. He sat up suddenly, and a timorous smile appeared on his filthy face and bloodstained lips. 'Where shall we go?' he asked. 'You know what we have to endure *there*. Allow us to remain here.' He pointed to the houses of Gerazim. 'Let us share it between us. You there, we here. They don't want you here, we tell you. They prefer those herds of pigs to you . . .'

'Then I permit you to enter those pigs. Go!'

The man threw himself back and writhed convulsively. Something resembling a puff of wind flew past us. We heard the herdsmen shouting, and the dogs howling as they ran off with their tails between their legs. The swine began to run round in circles, grunting furiously. Then, quite suddenly, they tore like a black avalanche across the field towards the sea. They poured over the cliff without a halt. Every one, to the very last, fell through the air, awkwardly waving its little legs, and plunged into the sea. Not one came up again.

Then Jesus pointed to the man lying on the ground and said:

'Take care of him.'

He went off to a great rock and sat down with his head in his hands. Praying, or weeping? The man slowly came back to life. He dressed in a robe which he himself found nearby. He washed his hands and face. When we went to join the teacher and have our morning meal he also came up. His eyes were expressive of his admiration, fear, and gratitude. Jesus shared out the fish and bread we had brought, and nodded to the man to join us. At first the poor wretch seemed unable to take in that there was food for him too. At last he knelt down and awkwardly held out his hand, and Jesus gave him some bread. He did not get up, but squatted on his heels and gulped down the food. Then he gulped down the words which Jesus said to us:

'Were you frightened by the storm? I tell you there will be even greater storms, and the Son of Man will be taken from you. But don't be afraid, little flock: your Father has decided to give you the kingdom. And the fact that with His spirit I cast out devils is a sign that the kingdom is already at hand. Fear not. Whatever may happen, I am with you. I shall not reject anyone who has not rejected me. And though a man lose his life, he shall gain it.'

We were listening so closely to these amazing words that we failed to notice a great crowd of people coming out from the town. When they drew near I saw that they were staring at us fearfully. Several old men with grey beards, and wearing long cloaks, were at their head, together with herdsmen with black skins round their thighs. They were obviously heathens.

They halted a few paces away, evidently afraid to come any nearer. One of the old men stepped forward, bowed very low, and said in Greek:

'Sir, we ask you, who have destroyed our herds, to leave us. You must be a powerful magician, for you have restored this madman to his senses. We don't want to offend you, but please go away. Go back to your Jewish people. You have done us much injury, though we had done nothing to you. We have lost herds of great value. But we don't hold that against you. We only ask you to leave us. You are too mighty to remain in our parts. So go back.' He bowed humbly.

The others supported him, making deep obeisances. I felt sure Jesus would say something to them. But he rose and made his way back to the shore without uttering a word. We followed him. He climbed into the boat, and we took our places. Then we saw that the man who had been freed of the devils was standing on a rock close to the boat. He set his foot irresolutely on the gunwale, and gave the Nazarene a pleading look. For the first time since his tormentors had left him he spoke:

'Take me too, sir . . .'

But Jesus shook his head.

'Stay here,' he said. 'Go back home and tell your people about the mercy of God. Tell them everything,' he said with emphasis.

The man drew back. There was a look of sorrow in his eyes, but he obeyed. Simon pushed the boat off and we floated out between the rocks. The man stood erect above the water. And above him we saw the inhabitants of Gerazim, gazing after us. Suddenly the man cried across the water to us:

'I shall tell everything. Everything.'

By the third hour we were back in Capernaum. A crowd came running to greet the teacher as soon as our boat neared the shore. Among them I noticed Jairus.

At Capernaum he worked another amazing miracle. But I shall have to leave the telling of that to a later letter. Somehow I must order my thoughts and reach some conclusion: Who is this man who can still a storm, and drive out a whole legion of devils, yet sleeps worn out right through the howling of the wind?

Quite unexpectedly I have left him. I am on my way back to Jerusalem. Yet I feel that I haven't settled the question of his identity, or what he really teaches, or what he wants of me. On the other hand, I have taken on a heavy burden.

A few days after our return from Gerazim, early one morning we were all on the same hill which he mounted to proclaim his beatitudes. The side of the hill is cloven with a deep channel which divides the summit into two humps. Through this gap one can see Lake Gennesareth, looking like the enormous arena of a Roman circus. That morning a solid mass of yellowish-grey mist lay below us, and the sun struggled vainly to break through it. We had spent the night in the cliffs; one frequently does that sort of thing when wandering about with Jesus. I slept badly, and woke up again and again. Whenever I raised my head I saw that the master was not among us. He had gone off to the top of the hill in the evening, and remained praying there till the morning. When we scrambled to our feet he called down to us:

'Come here! I have something to say to you.'

He seemed to wait for us impatiently, as though he were in a hurry to share his thoughts with us. Standing at the cliff edge, he put his hands affectionately on John's and Simon's shoulders, and said:

'Listen, children! I want you to scatter over the land of Galilee, to tell the people that the hour has come and every man should repent . . .'

He stopped, and gazed at us as though trying to see what impression these unexpected words had made. But his disciples avoided his gaze, and took stealthy glances at one another.

Their faces revealed their astonishment, distrust and anxiety. These boors feel sure of themselves only when they are in a crowd. He had hardly said these words to them when they lost all their self-confidence, their braggadocio, their naïve dreams of 'ruling in the teacher's kingdom.' Simon scratched his nape with his great fingers.

'What about you, teacher?' he asked. 'Aren't you going with us?'

Jesus smiled and shook his head. Apparently he had foreseen all their objections, and was now calmly waiting for them to utter them in order to turn them down.

'No. You'll be going by yourselves, in twos . . .'

'When, rabbi?' one of them ventured to ask.

'At once,' he replied, gently but firmly.

They began to fidget and look at one another questioningly. Possibly they thought that after his all-night vigil he was a little confused of mind. They were particularly bewildered by the smiling way in which he was telling them. James the Little (so called to distinguish him from James the son of Zebedee) pouted his lips contemptuously. He clearly did not approve of his 'brother's' idea. But Philip forestalled him. Twining his finger into the hair above his ear, he barked:

'We must first go to a town and buy food for the road. And not one of us has decent sandals.' He looked triumphantly at his fellows, as though he had found a well in the desert. 'We couldn't get far in these clouts.'

'We haven't a copper,' Judas observed, opening the money bag and shaking it. The teacher had put him in charge of the small sums which people contributed to the support of their little fellowship.

They all looked at Jesus interrogatively. But he was still smiling.

'You don't need anything,' he said persuasively. 'Neither money, nor food, nor even a purse. Go in your worn sandals and the clothes you are wearing. Go just as you are, providing yourselves with nothing. The harvest is waiting for you. Go and reap. Don't visit the heathens and the Samaritans, seek rather the sheep which have been lost from the flock of Israel. Tell them the hour has come. And as a sign, you will heal the sick, you will cleanse the lepers and drive out devils. Accept what you are given, like a labourer who doesn't argue over his pay; but you are not to demand anything. You have received freely from me; now give as freely.'

He stopped and looked at them expectantly. But they went on staring at one another and did not move. Instead of encouraging them, his last words had filled them with even greater alarm. It was one thing to heal or to drive out devils when he was at hand; but it was quite another to use such powers when he was far off. In the silence James said bitingly:

'You're sending us to the sheep, but where there are sheep there are always wolves wandering around.'

'Very true,' he admitted. But he went on just as cheerfully: 'I am sending you as sheep among wolves. You must have the trust of a dove and the cunning of a fox.'

'But if the sheep trusts the wolf, the wolf takes advantage of it,' Simon remarked.

'The sheep worried to death is not afraid of the wolf,' he replied. 'And you, too, must fear only that which can retain power over you even after death. What if they kill the body? What if they haul you before the judge? Yes, all this will happen,' he said in a completely different tone. His glittering eyes faded: they seemed to be searching the horizon. 'I have come to bring peace. But my words will bring war. Because of them a house will be divided against itself: brother against brother, wife against husband. Because of them brother will betray brother, the son his father. I have brought love. But because of it they will hate you. They hate me, so why should you expect different treatment? That is the fate of disciples. You will be hunted like me, you will hide, and never find a city of refuge. I tell you: even before you are caught you will have to bear on your shoulders the cross of presentiments, doubts, and fear.'

91

For a moment he stopped speaking, and his eyes returned from their distant journey and rested on the little, terrified group of disciples. He smiled again:

'But remember what I told you that morning after the storm: I am with you. Whoever loses his life for my sake will gain it; whoever carries his cross for my sake will find me. And whoever gives you shelter during your wanderings will be giving me shelter, and not only me but Him who sent me. Bless every man who listens to you. But now, go! When a month has passed, we shall meet together again on this hill. I shall be waiting for you. Go quickly: the grain is white and ready for your sickle. You must not let it be spilt on the ground.'

They looked at one another once more. The mist had vanished completely from the lake: the air was transparent and glassy. The heat drank up the last traces of moisture on the grass and our cloaks. The disciples began to sort themselves out into pairs. Simon nodded to John: 'You come with me.' (I think he was afraid John might remain behind with the master.) Judas selected Simon the Zealot as his companion. The two taciturn ones, Judah and Matthew, linked up. But not one of the pairs wanted to be the first to leave.

At last Philip remarked: 'Well, we ought to go without further delay. It will be hot before long.'

But he made no attempt to move. Every one of them seemed to have something urgent to do: they tucked up their robes, or tightened their sandal strings, watching the others surreptitiously. They might never have set out if he hadn't said:

'Go now, children; go now! Shalom aleichem. Peace be with you.'

'Aleichem shalom,' they answered. Judah, the master's brother, and Matthew, were the first to go. The shingle scrunched under their feet. Two by two the others bowed to the master, and disappeared round the cliff. In a few moments only he and I were left standing on the rise. Their voices and the tap of sticks on stones floated up to us from below. For some time they were lost to sight, and when they reappeared they were like a string of white patches along the track crossing the green field. The teacher gazed after them. I have told you before that he seems to make no distinction whatever in his love. You would have thought that that group of unclean boors was more precious to him than a child is to its father, that he thought of them not even as children born of his flesh, but as his creations; as the Almighty must have thought when he picked up man as a handful of clay from the earth, and set him down a living creature.

Only when they were lost to sight did he raise his eyes and whisper a brief prayer to heaven. 'This is the moment I've been waiting for,' I thought. There were only we two now, and I realized that it was a case of now or never. I sought mentally for words. I must admit that after all I have witnessed during the last few weeks I cannot talk to him as formerly. I have the roar of the storm in my ears continually, and the outcry of the crowd when Jairus's wife ran out of the house. I haven't told you about that incident yet. But there is so much to tell you, with so much happening every day. He resurrected the child of Jairus, the president of the synagogue.

When he went to Jairus's house the people told him: 'There's no point in your going there, rabbi. She's dead already. Can't you hear the weeping women?'

But he refused to be deterred. He shook his head: 'You're mistaken; she is asleep.'

And he didn't even hurry. On the way he stopped because some woman touched his garment and was healed without his assent. I could tell you much about that incident too. When he went into the house he took only John, Simon, and James with him. The lamentations stopped almost at once. Through the silence a woman's piercing cry sounded. Jairus's wife ran out of the house. She had tears on her scratched cheeks and a smile on her lips. Panting and stammering, she exclaimed: 'She has revived. He said: "Wake up," and she opened her eyes. She's eating and laughing.' Then she ran back into the house as swiftly as she had come.

Usually I feel that it's best to be silent in his presence. But I knew that if I went away without speaking now I should never obtain his healing power for Ruth. So I began to stammer:

'Rabbi, I . . .'

He looked at me again with a look which might be interpreted as an astonished query: 'Why don't you ask me?'

'Is there something you want of me?' he asked.

His challenging gaze made my task easier. And yet: I was true to myself. After all I didn't mention Ruth.

'Rabbi!' I whispered. 'What have I to do to gain the kingdom? The life which you said . . . that it must be born a second time. You remember?'

I could tell by his eyes that he understood.

'But you know what the Law demands,' he said, 'and the commandments which Moses brought down . . .'

'I do.'

'And you know which is the greatest of the commandments. So what else do you wish to know?'

I flung out my hands helplessly.

'I have never ceased to fulfil the commandments.' I got out the words with difficulty. 'From my earliest years. I have always taken pleasure in being in the Lord's house, I have always loved the splendour of His Temple . . . I have served Him with all my strength . . .'

'And none the less . . .' he commented.

'Yes,' I exclaimed. 'None the less I lack something.'

'But you don't know what?'

'No, I don't,' I replied very quietly. I could feel my heart beating.

He was silent; he seemed to be meditating.

'Then I shall tell you,' he said at last. 'You have too many cares, too many anxieties, troubles, fears. Give them to me. Give them all to me, Nicodemus, and come and follow me.'

'But how can I give you my cares, rabbi?' I asked. My voice

94

quivered and I was profoundly moved, for I felt that he had reached right down to the wound in my heart.

'Give them all to me,' he repeated gently. But he did not explain. I began to be afraid that he would say again: 'You are learned, you know the Scriptures, you should know . . .'

What if I am learned? I don't know; I really don't. I timidly raised my eyes to him. But the sight of his face filled me with comfort: it had the same look of warm sincerity that I had seen as he watched his departing disciples. I confessed:

'You know that I don't understand you, rabbi . . .'

He did not chide me, didn't sneer. He said in a kindly tone:

'I want you to give me all that fetters you. I want you to take your cross of cares and fears from your shoulders and take on mine. Shall we exchange crosses, Nicodemus?'

I was a little repelled: this was rather distasteful. The cross is an instrument of heinous execution, and even to mention it is unpleasant. Only the rabble of the cities enjoys watching crucifixions. Fortunately, Pilate has recently issued a proclamation that this repulsive punishment is to be applied only to the faithless and dishonourable.

'Why talk of a cross, rabbi?' I objected. 'That's a shameful death. Do you really mean that you want someone to accompany you in a difficult trial?'

'Yes. I want someone to accompany me in a difficult trial.'

I hesitated. My thoughts and feelings wavered to and fro within me. It occurred to me that perhaps he had an inkling of the growing dislike he's provoking among the Pharisees. Perhaps he was looking to me to help him in that direction? At the same time I realized that it would be very indiscreet to promise him my help. How was I to know what he would yet do or say? I raised my eyes to him cautiously . . . How can you ever realize what it meant to me to discover that this man loved me? To have come upon such a moment in the days of our youth would have sent us into the seventh heaven of delight. But how much greater joy must come to a man when he finds love well on in his human span? A boy seeks love, but he doesn't know what he is seeking. The man who has crossed the mysterious bound of forty years knows how valuable is such a prize. And for that reason he desires to have the love of another more than ever before.

If you only knew how he looked at me! The crowd can be bought with miracles, but only thus can they be won over. That must be the secret of the devotion which these unclean boors feel for him. Even they have felt it through their thick skins. And when someone has offered us such love, can we tell him we are not prepared to promise him something? I am soft-hearted, and I often come to regret the many promises I have made. Maybe I shall regret this one too. I don't know what else this man will yet demand of me. He said: 'Give me your cares and fears.' All of them? Including my anxiety over Ruth? He can divine human thoughts, so he must know about her illness. He wants to take it all from me. But what does he give me in exchange? He called it a 'cross.' I was only a lad when the soldiers of Coponius surrounded Sephoris with a ring of crosses. The Scriptures rightly declare: 'Cursed be he who is hung on a cross.' I simply didn't know what answer to make. Then I had the impression that his face was again veiled with sorrow. Yet the sorrow did not obscure his love. And at that I could resist no longer. I said:

'If you wish it, rabbi, let it be so.'

But even as I said the words I was seized with terror – a fearful, strangling terror. I felt that I had walked into a trap. As I gazed at him my terror increased. In his eyes I thought I read a sentence. I realized that now I could not ask him for help as Jairus had done, nor could I even venture to steal power from him, like the woman with the issue of blood. In return for that gaze I had surrendered Ruth. Jairus saved his daughter; the woman of Nain recovered her son. But I? The trap clashed fast behind me. O Adonai, have mercy!

I am writing this at night. Perhaps I am too fearful for Ruth after all: perhaps everything will be as before. But can it? When I think of the worst that can happen, I think that anything would be better than that. Let the disease go on for years! But I know that when I return and see her suffering I shall repeat in despair: this must end somehow! It simply must!

So Jesus and I have reached a kind of agreement. I left him standing on the hill. I am on my way back to Judaea. I shall try to defend him against the accusations which are pouring in to the Sanhedrin. I am not his disciple. I have nothing in common with these fishermen. Our agreement concerns only him and me. Really, it's quite absurd: I have given him my cares, which all the same I still have, and have promised something which fills me with incomprehensible fear. A cross is infamous, and I can't understand why he mentioned it.

DEAR JUSTUS,   NINTH LETTER.

I really don't know how to thank you. The young doctor from Antioch whom you recommended to me has visited Ruth. I like the man: he has an open mind, and although he's a Greek, he understands our customs. He said she should get well. May it be so. Unfortunately, all his predecessors have said the same. I have heard it so many times. Your Luke is certainly more honest than the others. His promises are not merely mysterious remarks with nothing to them. I feel sure he'll not give up the fight until it's finished. But will any of the tests he has promised bring any result? And is there time to apply them all?

Jesus alone could restore her to health. But he has passed me by as he passed the sick Nazarenes. He punished them. But why is he punishing me? Me, who agreed to take up what he called 'the cross'? I have a disturbing feeling that his words conceal a danger more threatening than I could foresee at the time.

A dry heat is withering everything here in Jerusalem. The

grapevines have turned grey, the grass is parched, the palm branches droop low, the figs have ripened in their heavy bunches of leaves. All the priestly community and everybody who has the money have left Jerusalem for their summer residences. I would have been at my villa in Emmaus long since, but Ruth's illness holds me back.

So far I have not had occasion to talk with anyone about Jesus. Of the Grand Council members I have seen only Joel bar Gorion. He is a little man and goes everlastingly with bowed shoulders: he declares that he carries the sins of all Israel on his back. I found him repeating a prayer for sinners. He was standing with his arms stretched above his head, knocking his brow against the wall. At last he turned round and pretended he had only just noticed me. He welcomed me with great heartiness, which I can't help thinking was put on.

'Oh, whom do my eyes see? The great rabbi, the wise rabbi Nicodemus. So you've come back already, rabbi? How glad I am! Is it true that you've been in Galilee? I have been told you were there. People say, though I cannot believe it, that you stood among a crowd of unclean boors and listened to the words of some charlatan who is telling the Galileans all sorts of nonsense for their comfort. I told Jochanan bar Zakkai— may the great and wise rabbi's name be held in honour—to ignore the liars. I said our rabbi Nicodemus would never touch an unclean person, any more than one of our brethren would touch a corpse or a pig.'

I had to thank him. Then I asked:

'What have you heard about the prophet of Nazareth, then?'

Joel's little eyes glittered. They dart from side to side like two black mice. He pulled a face, as though he had taken a bite at a bitter lemon.

'He, he, he! The great and wise rabbi is jesting. A prophet? What prophet? Of Nazareth? Only thieves, drunkards and madmen come from Nazareth. There has already been talk about that liar in our assembly; more talk than necessary! We know all about him!'

He pursed up his lips; but after a moment he rubbed his palms together and broke into a laugh.

'He, he, he! It's good that the great and wise rabbi has returned. Galilee is a land of darkness.'

I have also seen Jonathas, son of Ananias. In fact the high priest sent him to me. He and I are to act as the representatives of the Sanhedrin during the celebrations which Antipas plans in honour of his birthday. The idea doesn't please me at all: I hate Herod's bastards. But Caiaphas strongly urged me to agree, and in order to reconcile me to the idea he even sent me a basket of fine fruits for Ruth. Antipas knows that no Israelite with any self-respect would go to Tiberias, because he built it on a cemetery; so he is arranging for the celebrations to take place at Machaerus. They're to be on a very grand scale, partly because he wants to show off Herodias to everybody: she has completely enslaved him. But it is said that the chief reason for all this is that Pilate the Procurator is expected to be present. Antipas has had many quarrels with him in the past, and now he wants to win his favour.

So I told Jonathas I would go. I took the opportunity of his visit to ask him, too, what he had heard about Jesus. He laughed merrily.

'You ask me what I've heard about him? It is I who should ask you. For everyone says he's a Pharisee. Someone has told Caiaphas that he is repeating Hillel's teaching; others say he makes up parables on the principles laid down by Gamaliel. Confess, Nicodemus! He's one of your brethren. But, speaking seriously, it wouldn't matter at all that he talks rubbish about resurrection, angels, and other marvellous phenomena, if he didn't stir up so much excitement among the common people. I want to be frank, so I'll tell you: we've decided to draw Antipas's attention to him. You Pharisees are fond of talking nonsense that irritates the Romans. In our view, the more we ourselves do to eliminate everything that annoys them the more the Romans will trust us, and the more we shall be able to obtain from them. Don't you agree, Nicodemus? You doctors

99

are fond of supplementing the Law with various doctrines of your own. There's nothing bad in that (of course, this is between ourselves) so long as the unity of the Cult and the Temple is preserved. But you know quite well that there is an end to all doctrine, faith, and morality when some brigand from the wilderness starts to imitate Judas Maccabeus. And Sephoris lies on the same hill as Nazareth.'

That's quite true: it's on the farther side of the hill. The crosses which Coponius raised twenty-five years ago must have cast their shadows over Nazareth.

During my stay in Galilee I have grown rather unused to the feverish life of Jerusalem. Up there a man thinks slowly, and slowly absorbs hardly audible sounds amid the silence. But here there's no time for anything. Here you have to shout in order to be heard, and nothing is heard except a shout. It's a stupid existence, but one which it is impossible to get away from.

When I left Jesus, instead of returning straight along the river Jordan I turned aside to Nazareth. You often used to tell me that if you want to know a man really well you must go and see the place where he came into the world. Nazareth has an evil fame. But I reflected that even the general opinion may be erroneous: I must see everything for myself.

Nazareth is like many another little Galilean town. It is half surrounded by hills, and it nestles on a slope amid them like a kitten in a child's arms. It's a scattered handful of small white houses among black cypresses which form almost a small grove. At the foot of the hill is a spring surrounded by a stone barrier. I halted beside it, weary and thirsty. For a long time there was nobody to speak to; only women carrying pitchers on their heads came down to draw water. Then some Levite arrived, and he greeted me courteously. I asked him to conduct me to an inn where I could spend the night. Beyond the hill, Mount Tabor raised its white brow. Jesus must have had it frequently in sight when he was a lad. As we approached the town I noticed the synagogue, also surrounded with cypresses. The inn was situated just before the first houses, I thanked the Levite, and before departing he called out the innkeeper and commended me to his care. The Levite and I had chatted as we walked along, and he had discovered who I was. The innkeeper was very hospitable. I was pleasantly surprised, for I had expected coarseness and discourtesy. He brought me food to eat in the shade of a fig tree. I stood up to say a prayer. As I was about to eat I heard someone shout:

'Rabbi, don't eat!'

I looked up in amazement. Several men had entered the inn yard. By their dress I judged that they were elders of the synagogue. My Levite acquaintance was leading them. They all had prayer-shawls round their shoulders and phylacteries fastened to their brows. They looked to be pious and worthy men. One of them, evidently the president of the synagogue, sternly asked the innkeeper whether the food and utensils set before me had chanced to be touched by unclean hands. But there appeared to be no reason for alarm. The president turned to me and gave me a very ceremonious welcome, expressing their joy that I had deigned to visit their wretched little place. Then he said:

'Forgive me, reverend rabbi, for shouting as I did; but you can never be quite sure of these common people. They allow women to touch everything. Forgive us, and please eat now in confidence.'

I was quite astonished by the friendly spirit he showed. I invited them to share my meal. The heat of the day had passed, a wind was stirring the fig branches above our heads. When we had eaten we stretched ourselves comfortably on benches which the innkeeper set under the tree for all the guests.

'May we be allowed to ask, revered rabbi, what has brought you to our town?' the president asked at last. 'Nazareth is a miserable hole, and we have nothing to rejoice the eye of so eminent a visitor. And an evil fame is attached to it. But quite unjustly, believe me, rabbi. Of course, we have had all sorts of people living in our town. But what city is without a sinner?'

'I have no doubt you are right,' I replied. 'And as I listen to you I realize that all that is said about the Nazarenes is false.'

'The great rabbi's words are like a plaster of oil on a fresh wound,' one of them observed.

'Would you be willing to comfort our ears in the synagogue tomorrow with your words of wisdom?' the president asked. 'It is long since we had anyone so famous in our town.'

I felt that I could not resist their honied speech. I am accustomed to respect, but their words captivated me.

'Be so good as to offer us a small portion of your wisdom,' they pleaded. Without doubt they thought my silence indicated my reluctance to agree. '"Spare not bread to the poor, nor the word of God to the desirous," said the great Hillel.'

'Nobody ever visits Nazareth. It's years since we heard the teaching of a great doctor from Jerusalem. They all say the same . . .'

'Except when someone dares who . . .'

The man broke off in the middle of the sentence, transfixed by the others' looks. I guessed that he was thinking of Jesus's speech in the synagogue.

'I suppose you were about to mention your Jesus?' I asked.

There was a dead silence. My guests sat dumb, giving one another sidelong glances.

'Yes,' the president said at last. 'Simon bar Arak was referring to that accursed sinner. We don't like talking about him. We excluded him from the synagogue because of his blasphemy. We have set a curse on him. He ought to be stoned,' he ended resolutely.

'Rabbi Jehudah is right,' one of the others assented. 'That man has brought shame on our town. It's because of him that people speak evil of Nazareth.'

'But he comes from Nazareth himself, doesn't he?' I asked.

'Unfortunately,' the president admitted.

'He grew up among us like a wolf's whelp among dogs,' the Levite exclaimed with hatred in his tone.

'Nobody suspected him . . .'

'Unfortunately,' rabbi Jehudah repeated. He sighed. 'Though to tell the truth, we could disown him. He wasn't born in Nazareth.'

'No?'

'No. Our family registers, which my predecessors managed to conceal from Herod's men – may Sheol never be pleasant to him! – don't mention his birth. His father was a Judaean. The royal line has fallen low,' he added through clenched teeth.

'So it is true that he comes of the line of David?'

'So it is written. But a mistake could easily have been made. However, it is in the wisdom of the learned such as yourself, not in the blood of David, that our salvation is to be found.'

'But it is said that from David will descend the Child of Righteousness,' the Levite objected.

'There are those who interpret the passage thus,' rabbi Jehudah said in a superior tone. 'But the doctors most learned in the Scriptures' (he looked at me, inviting me with a smile to support him) 'say that it is those who are pure who are the true descendants of David. And one must not take every word of the prophets literally . . .'

'Quite so,' I admitted.

'The rabbi has spoken,' he said in a tone which ended all argument. He drew himself up triumphantly, and went on:

'In the days when the whole country was visited with a terrible earthquake – because of the sins of Herod, no doubt – Jacob, the son of Matthan, a carpenter, arrived in Nazareth from Judaea. He settled among us, and worked. Then he had a son Joseph. This Joseph took himself a wife from Jerusalem, the daughter of a weaver named Joachim. Not long afterward the Romans – curse them! – ordered the sons of Israel to be numbered, despite the Law of the All Highest. As the prescriptions required, Joseph went to Bethlehem, to his family home, taking his wife with him. She was just expecting a child. They rode off, and did not come back. Nobody knows why not. Women who should know said the child would be born before the time, that it was conceived before the bride came to dwell in the bridegroom's house. When Joseph did return with his wife, they brought the child with them. It is said they had wandered as far as Egypt.

'Joseph was a carpenter like his father, and he taught his son the trade. His wife was a sempstress; she spun, wove, and sewed. They didn't have any more children. Then Joseph fell ill and died. Now his widow had to work still harder, to make ends meet. Their son went to school. He was much younger than I, but I remember him sitting among us, shouting the words of the Torah. They must have been very poor, for I never saw sandals on his feet, and his cloak was made from his father's old robe. Then he, too, began to work, and he, too, had plenty to do. He reached the age when a man is free to speak in the synagogue. But he never raised his voice. He stood at the door with the poorest of the poor, and only listened. Until, suddenly one day . . .'

'He left the town,' the man who had first referred to Jesus exclaimed.

'He went off without a thought for anyone,' said another. 'He left his workshop, his home, he took no steps to care for his mother.'

'And if she hadn't worked,' rabbi Jehudah harshly confirmed, 'the community would have had to look after her.'

'He's a bad son, a bad son,' the Levite shook his head.

They all spoke at once, growing more and more excited. They obviously felt a deep hatred for Jesus. After a moment or two rabbi Jehudah noticed that I was astonished at their outburst. He drooped his head and said with a smile:

'Forgive us, revered rabbi. We were carried away. That man has brought shame on our town among all Israel. But he is an unclean fellow and not worth wasting our breath on. Forgive us! The man who possesses the wisdom of the Lord takes no notice of the barking dog.'

'Please forgive us,' the others took him up. 'We were speaking of someone who is not worthy to trouble your ears.'

But their eyes still glittered with excitement. And they could

not think of any other subject to turn their minds from Jesus.
As for me, he was the only subject I was interested in. I asked:

'But what was he like when he dwelt among you? You say
he is a bad son. Was he always so? Has he ever done anything
to earn this general dislike? I wish you would tell me about it.
I find it of some interest . . .'

I looked at each of them in turn. They bit their lips to sup-
press a further outbreak. They waited for Jehudah to speak.
After a moment he remarked:

'Well, he never did anyone any actual wrong . . . In
fact . . .'

'But how about his parents?' I asked relentlessly.

'By all accounts Joseph was a good craftsman,' the president
muttered.

'And his mother?'

'Oh, she's a good woman.'

'She helped others,' came the reluctant remark. 'And there
are many who bless her.'

Jehudah placed his hand palm downward firmly on the
table, as though anxious to put an end to the turn the talk
had taken. He said with cold passion:

'But she's his mother.'

'It's all through her.'

'But . . .' I felt that if I asked another question I should
be hated as deeply as Jesus himself. 'But if you say he did
nobody any wrong, why are you . . .?'

'If he were prepared to work honestly,' rabbi Jehudah interrupted, 'nobody would have any complaint. He was a skilled
carpenter, he helped others, he knew the Scriptures . . .'

'Then why are you so hostile to him?' I asked.

The president drummed his fingers on the table. 'Hostile?'
he said contemptuously. He looked at the others. 'Hostile?' he
shrugged his shoulders. ' "The sinner is the enemy of the Lord," '
he quoted. 'We are not his enemies. "An unclean fellow is not
deserving of either the smile or the contempt of the wise man," '
he quoted again.

There was a silence. The conversation dried up. They departed in some dudgeon.

Next morning I called to a small boy who was watching my asses being groomed, and asked him:

'Do you know the house of Jesus son of Joseph, the carpenter?'

'Yes.'

'Take me there and I'll give you a shekel.'

He ran on in front enthusiastically. The sun climbed up from behind Mount Tabor like a child who has been hiding behind a haystack. We went almost to the top of the hill, beyond the main group of houses. Under a smooth rocky cliff we came upon several clay hovels clinging like birds' nests to the stones. I passed them and stood on the spacious, grassy summit. On the farther side the slope dropped gently down to the valley of Jezreel. A little place I noticed on the right of the slope must be Sephoris.

We went down and back to the hovels. The boy jumped about joyfully, in expectation of the silver coin he had been promised. Suddenly he stopped and asked:

'D'you want to see where that lunatic lived?'

'Yes,' I answered. 'But why do you call him that?'

'That's what everybody calls him,' he replied. But then his eyes glittered cunningly: 'But others say he's a great miracle-worker.'

We stopped outside one of the hovels. The old, heavy door was fastened by a wooden bolt. I went inside. A chill struck me: the place looked as though nobody had let a single ray of warm sun into it for a long time. I saw a wretched interior, typical of the poorest huts of Galilean peasants: a few household articles, a mill, a hand press, a bench by the wall. The clay floor was carefully swept, the carpenter's tools were neatly arranged on the wall. Two stone tubs by the door were filled with water to the brim. My eyes took in detail after detail, eager to learn some new feature of the people who lived there. There was not a single shaving on the bench. A small cross, shining with the brightness of freshly planed wood, lay on it. Another cross! He must have crosses on his mind!

There was nothing else of interest to be noted. I went out again, and asked the boy:

'Doesn't his mother live here any longer?'

'No. They say she's gone to Bethsaida to live.'

She wanted to be nearer her son, I thought. But in any case why should she stay in Nazareth, when they hate him so much? I gave the boy his shekel, and went back downhill. I was filled with such indignation against the local people that, instead of remaining and giving instruction in the synagogue, I set off at once on my journey to Jerusalem.

So he is of the line of David after all. And he was not born in Nazareth, but in Bethlehem. I may go and see what I can find out there.

Bethlehem . . . That reminds me of the prophecy of the prophet Micah: 'Bethlehem . . . reckoned least of the towns of Judah: from thee will come the King of Israel, he who comes from ages untold.' He seems to be favoured by the prophecies!

You know, your doctor from Antioch tells me that the Greeks, too, have a presentiment that someone, or something, is coming . . . We certainly live in interesting times.

DEAR JUSTUS, TENTH LETTER.

I have just arrived home from Machaerus. There is much to tell you of events there.

Antipas organized spectacles such as we haven't seen since his father's frenzied orgies. The castle was decorated with coloured linens, and each evening it was illuminated like Jerusalem on the first day of the harvest festival. The wild and lonely mountain gorges echoed all the week with the noise of Arab drums, zithers, harps, and pipes. A true son of Herod, he tried to please everybody; there were horse-races and wrestling matches; there was wild music, dancing girls for the Arabs, and for the faithful there were devout songs sung morning and evening by Levites brought from Galilee.

Everybody was there. First and foremost were the tetrarch's estimable kinsmen: his brother Philip, his nephew Alexander (the son of Alexander), Agrippa, who came from Rome, and Herod king of Chalcis. Philip is the most respectable of the lot: he is a quiet and peaceful sort of man, and seemed bored with all the noise and excitement. Besides Herod Antipater's family there were a number of petty Arab kings and princes. They smacked their lips appreciatively and pretended to be delighted when Antipas looked at them. But they hate him really.

Julius Pontius Pilate arrived as expected for the celebrations. This was the first time I had ever seen him close to, and I had an opportunity of talking to him. Of recent years he hardly ever shows his face in Jerusalem. My first impression of him was that he regarded all the world with philosophic impassivity. But as soon as he began to speak I changed my view. He's a mercenary, completely lacking in manners and culture. It is said that he's really the son of a leader of a tribe known as Gauls, and was sent to Rome as a hostage when he was a child. There he was Latinized so completely that he changed his name, became a tribune, and distinguished himself in battle. But if he had ambitions, nothing much came of them. Caesar appointed him to the post of Procurator of Judaea six years ago: that was pretty well equivalent to banishment. He had hardly landed in Caesarea when he tried to show us that he intended to rule with a rod of iron. You will remember how he brought the Roman military standards into Jerusalem by night, and the votive tablets which he ordered to be hung on the walls of Antonia. But he had to withdraw both these affronts because of our inflexible opposition. Since then he has lived mainly in Caesarea. He comes to Jerusalem only during the high holidays, and his arrival is always a harbinger of bloodshed. We prefer him to remain in Caesarea. Relations between him and the Sanhedrin have tacitly been organized on the basis that he remains there and doesn't interfere with us, while we ensure order in the city. The arrangement would be excellent but for his voracious greed. He insists on being paid, and paid well, for everything. I hear about this from Joseph, who negotiates with him on behalf of the Sanhedrin. The sons of Ananias do the same in the name of themselves and their father. He shamelessly sells them positions and closes his eyes to their extortionate demands on pilgrims. Through him the Sadducees have greatly increased their power, though everybody hates them. Fortunately, we, too, have some influence with him, through his wife, who is semi-proselytized.

He is of average height, broad-shouldered, with great, shapeless hands, muscular arms, and a bald head flecked with the last traces of auburn hair. He has the heavy roll of a bear, likes to clap people on their shoulders, and goes off into peals of senseless laughter. He and Antipas spent some time walking and conversing in the garden: they are just like two dogs sniffing suspiciously at each other.

When they returned, Pilate came up and greeted the guests standing by the wall. He wore a vacuous smile, like that of a tribune reviewing recruits. He gave one of the Arab princes a jovial smack on the belly, and tugged another's beard. The Arabs responded with a laugh that sounded like sheep bleating. But I must admit that he behaved less unceremoniously with us. He exchanged greetings with Jonathas as an old acquaintance. 'How are you, Jonathas?' he said with a twist of his lips intended to indicate his amiability. 'And by the way,' he added as though he had remembered something, 'when do you propose to bring me the money?'

'We're collecting it,' Jonathas replied as he bowed.

'Well, go on collecting!' Pilate broke into a coarse guffaw and screwed up one eye. 'You can't take me in like that! All you have to do is put your hands in the Temple treasury. You've got plenty there. Get a move on, I tell you.'

As though anxious to distract the Procurator's attention, Jonathas introduced me: 'This is rabbi Nicodemus, a learned man and a Pharisee, and the Sanhedrin's representative.'

'*Salve!*' Pilate negligently offered me his hand. 'A Pharisee?' he asked in a tone of amazement. 'So you're one of those people who know all about life after death, and talk of rewards and punishments, and spirits?' He snorted with laughter. 'How very amusing! So you think spirits fly, like this?' He set both hands to his temples and waggled his fingers. 'My wife's terribly fond of that sort of thing. She has Pharisees to visit her and tell her all about the spirits. But we know what to think of all that, don't we, Jonathas?' He put his hand on Jonathas's shoulder and roared with laughter again.

The drunken revelries grew more licentious with every day. The banqueting went on day and night. At one stage I saw Pilate, with a dancing girl on either side of him, talking across the table to Herodias, who was reclining on a couch. Despite her age, that woman still knows the art of captivating men. She has retained a magnificent figure. When she rests her black, glittering eyes on Antipas with a look of anxious solicitude, it is difficult to believe that she has defiled herself by associating with one of her own uncles, and betrayed and abandoned him for Antipas, another uncle. A girl, still physically undeveloped and slender, almost lanky, was sitting at her feet. I thought she was one of Herodias's servants, but I found out that she's the daughter of Herodias and Philip.

I listened for a while to Pilate's talk with Herodias: she was trying to persuade him that her present husband wishes to be his most faithful friend. 'You'll find that out when the time comes. If you are in need . . .'

'I shall never have need of anything from him,' Pilate said boastfully. 'But if you say it is so I'm quite prepared to believe you. By Hecate, you have beautiful arms, Herodias,' he added, while stroking the arms of one of the dancing girls supporting him.

He leaned across the table and talked quietly, so I could not catch his further remarks. She listened to him with a smile. 'You're quite right, Procurator,' I heard her say at last. 'There is far too much in the Temple treasury.' She clinked glasses with him. 'I'll take up the matter myself,' she added as they drank.

I didn't know what to make of this interesting remark, so I decided to mention it to Jonathas. But he only shrugged his shoulders: 'Oh, we know what he's after. He's already given us to understand more than once that we should use some of the Temple funds to pay for the construction of an aqueduct from Siloh to Antonia. A good idea, of course! But not using our money! We haven't refused him outright; we simply pretend we don't know what he's hinting at. Now he's seeking Herodias's support. The fool.'

A moment or two later I saw him talking gaily to Pilate. I'm beginning to suspect that the Sadducees have the Procurator more under their control than we think.

The banqueting had quickly passed into an orgy. The Arab and Nubian dancing women tried to surpass one another with their dances, then went and joined the guests. The Arabian petty kings rolled with them on the floor. The servants brought in endless amphoras of wine, and helped those who wanted to ease their overloaded stomachs to find the vomitorium. I grew more and more disgusted. Pilate bellowed away merrily at one end of the table, but Antipas sat more and more gloomy. The ill-feeling between him and Pilate had not been dissipated at all. Herodias's attempts to bring them together were fruitless. They are still as isolated from each other as two trees on opposite banks of the Jordan. Antipas appeared to be the more recalcitrant: clearly he did not put any trust in the Procurator's noisy familiarity.

One early morning, when the guests, exhausted with their all-night revelries, were snoring on the couches, I slipped out into the garden for my morning prayers. As I was coming back I ran into Antipas: he was alone, trudging along moodily with both hands behind his back. When he noticed me he made straight for me, took me amiably by the arm and led me deeper into the garden.

'I suppose all these goings on are an affront to you, rabbi?' he said as we walked along a shady avenue. 'You're a Pharisee, a clean and devout man. But you mustn't take offence. I have to do all this for these uncircumcized (he said this as though he had observed the Law all his life, but in fact he has only just agreed to have his sons circumcized). If I didn't try to live in friendship with them they'd destroy me. Pilate's a scoundrel; in order to ingratiate himself with Tiberias he's ready to tell I know not what lies about me. Agrippa would like to undermine my position too, and Alexander as well, only he's too stupid. I've got enemies all around me. I have to be on my guard all the time. But envious and wicked people are to be found everywhere. Take your Sadducees. They fawn on the Romans, they intrigue with Pilate. Is it possible to remain honest in this world, when everybody else is dishonest? Tell me, rabbi, since you are so wise: can a man go on fighting everybody when he gets no support from anybody?

'Tell me!' he insisted. But he did not wait for my reply. 'I've got enemies everywhere! Pilate, Vitellius, Tiberias, Agrippa, Alexander, Philip, Aretas, the Sadducees. And you, too, are not friends of mine. You think I'm impious. Yet all I want is peace and a little happiness. Herodias loves me and looks after me. Nobody has ever done that before, nobody has ever loved me before. In past days I never knew when I might be handed a poisoned cup. I couldn't trust even my wife. That's why I sent her back to her father. But Herodias would follow me to the ends of the earth. What does it matter that she was Philip's wife? She didn't want him, and he didn't want her.

'Why does he bring it up against me?' he broke out as we turned a second time into the avenue. 'I respected him, and still do. He's a wise and holy prophet. I adore him just as I would adore Elias or Isaiah if they were to return to the earth. I shan't condemn him to death, though Herodias wants me to. But why does he say such terrible things about me? What have I done to him? He says I've done worse than David did with Uriah's wife. But I haven't sent anybody to his death. I only love Herodias, and she loves me.'

His words made me think at once of John. I had completely forgotten that the prophet was incarcerated in a dungeon under this very castle. This fool had flung him into prison, but he was still afraid of him. Herod had been a cunning wolf, but a brave one. But this Antipas is only a fox, as Jesus said, capable of burrowing by night, but not of making a bold stand in the daylight.

'John is indeed a holy prophet,' he assured me feverishly. 'I'm always ready to talk with him. I listen to him. I'd do all he says. But I will not put away Herodias. I love her, and she loves me. And I need her. In her presence I can be good, just, and gentle . . . For a king to be good he has to be loved. I expect you Pharisees remember the prescription that a bill of divorcement can be given for any cause. Philip will give her such a bill. I shall make him! But John won't hear of it. You can't talk to him about it; he starts to shout and utter threats at once . . .'

He walked me up and down for an hour, and all his conversation ran on this theme. Finally, in order to get away I told him I would talk to John, and maybe I could convince him that Antipas's association with Herodias was not to be condemned so harshly. Antipas was highly delighted. He at once sent for the commander of the guard and ordered him to conduct me to John's dungeon.

That is how I came to see the prophet of Bethabar on the Jordan again (though I could have seen him without Antipas's help; the dungeon's barred window looks out on to the court-yard, and he can talk with his disciples through the bars). I went down slippery stone steps. At the bottom a man was lying on straw. I recognized him at once, though he had changed greatly during the past two years. He had grown thin and aged, and his tanned skin had taken on the yellowish-grey colour of an old clout. He was not fettered, and a basket of excellent provisions stood on the ground beside his litter. Yet for such a man as he nothing can atone for the torment of imprisonment.

He did not stir when I went in. He did not even raise his head. He lay with his face in a patch of sunlight, letting the rays caress him. When I stood over him he slowly opened his eyes and sat up. The guard left us together. My eyes gradually grew accustomed to the contrast of total darkness and the sloping shaft of dazzling light. He sat a pace away from me, resting his head on his bent knees. Then he raised his head, and I saw his eyes. They had changed least of all; they were still dreamy, the eyes of someone who is seeking and waiting for something. His anger with all that was close at hand had departed from them. I heard a voice, hoarse and quiet, but still the same voice that had thundered over the river:

'Have you come for me at last?'

'Rabbi,' I began. I had no idea what he meant. 'I've come to see you. I don't suppose you know who I am. I came to you once at Bethabar . . .'

'Maybe,' he assented, as though wishing to avoid the pain of trying to remember. 'You're a Pharisee, aren't you?' he asked.

I nodded. I expected him to question me further. But he sat silent: possibly he had sailed off again from the shore to which I had recalled him.

'On that occasion, rabbi, you ordered me to wait,' I began again after a moment. 'And you said I was to serve; but I was also to be able to renounce service . . .'

He raised his head again and fixed his gaze on me, as if I had said something extremely important, something that revolves in the mind slowly but importunately.

'Yes,' he said slowly, '. . . to renounce . .

'Renounce . . .' he said once more, like a man who has yielded his beloved to his friend and now stands rejoicing in the other man's happiness. 'To perform one's task and vanish. To burn oneself out like a lamp down to the last drop of oil, and have no regrets . . .' He raised his face still higher; the sunlight flooded over his thin cheeks and firmly compressed lips. But after a moment the dreamy expression changed to one of grief or irritation. He abruptly, though reluctantly, demanded:

'What have you come for? What do you want of me?'

'Rabbi,' I tried to explain diffidently, 'in those days you said and you taught . . .'

'In those days,' he exclaimed, 'things were different. Then I was the Voice. The Voice of one crying in the wilderness. Today . . .' He ran his fingers over his thin, bare chest. 'Who am I? Nothing! My tongue has been torn from me. I am silence. Go to him, ask him . . .' He bowed his head to rest his forehead on his knees, and he panted violently.

Now I thought I understood. His cup was running over. Another had arrived and had taken his disciples from him; and he himself was in prison. His body seemed to be shaking with the ague.

'What are you standing here for?' he said again without raising his head. 'I tell you: go to him. He will grow, but I shall diminish, until at last when they come for me it will be as for a child. Go . . .' His irritable impatience changed to a gentle persuasion: 'Go! What do you expect from me? I am only a withered tree. He is putting forth his green shoots.'

He straightened himself up, seemingly with great effort. Now he was breathing calmly and deeply.

'He is life,' he went on. 'The blind have seen, the lame have run, and the scabs have dropped away from the lepers, the wretched have heard the good news. Go to him. He knows everything. He has come from heaven. He speaks the truth. My disciples have gone to follow him. They are wise and prudent. I alone cannot follow him . . .'

I could not refrain from asking:

'You follow him? But it was you who baptized him, not he you!'

He smiled almost indulgently at my slow-wittedness.

'The mother suckles her son; but when the son grows up he surpasses his mother,' he said. 'He wanted the rain to fall from heaven first on to the human hands, and only then to the ground. He wants our singing, but when we lack the voice he ends the song for us, more beautifully than we had begun it. The human spirit has its limits. Only he knows no limits. The Father has given him everything. And whoever comes to him gains everything . . .'

'So you think, rabbi, that he is the Messiah?' I asked as I squatted down beside the straw.

He replied in the words of Ezekiel: ' "Vain visions and flattering hopes Israel shall know no longer." The blind have seen, the dead have risen, the poor have heard the word of consolation. You ask if he is the Messiah,' he said, as though he had not answered my question already. 'He is the one who had to come. It was for him that I trod out the road. It was he I foretold. He has come and brought salvation. Follow him! Leave me.' He raised his voice, as though there were many beside me in the dungeon. 'Follow him. I can serve no more. I have nothing with which to serve. I am not needed by him . . .'

I once wrote to you: 'Sad is the fate of prophets who have lived to see the fulfilment of their prophecies.' John's words sounded pitiful. Yet one could say he was almost envious of his disciples who have gone off to follow the teacher of Nazareth. I remember Jesus himself once said that John is less than the people of the kingdom. These two men appear to share a secret which I cannot penetrate.

'But you are a great prophet,' I said, in the attempt to comfort him.

'I am not a prophet,' he contradicted me, as he had when we questioned him in the name of the Sanhedrin. 'I am the Voice which is silent . . . There is no longer any need for a Voice,' he exclaimed.

His face lit up, he spoke fervently, his eyes were fixed on the shaft of light with its whirling, glittering motes of dust.

'Now everything—men, trees, the stones, the stars—must speak. He doesn't need a voice . . .'

'But not everybody is following him,' I remarked.

He gently nodded and smiled.

'I know. You don't accept him. But he will call you, each in his own time. And me too. He will have need of me yet again. Once more. For the last time . . .'

I could hardly anticipate that that would be my last talk with John, and that his life would come to its end so soon after.

Antipas's guests were wearied with six days of incessant banqueting. But that evening the flagging diversions were given new life. Antipas, or rather, Herodias, who I think was determined to bring about a *rapprochement* between Antipas and Pilate at all costs, ordered the guests to be provided not with wine, but with an intoxicating liquor made in Syria from maize grain. This she did to raise them again to a state of frenzy. It had immediate effect: the revellers ate and drank, they drank and ate; they bawled, they belched, they hiccuped, they hugged the dancers and serving girls. The orgies became a real debauchery, like those of the loathsome Phrygian celebrations in honour of their divinities. Jonathas also took part. In the light of the lamps festooned with azure streams of smoke from burning incense, under the garlands of flowers, amid the nauseating stench of sweat and attar of roses, wine, and sauces, I saw a mass of half-naked bodies intertwined and tossing as though in fever. I stood to one side, looking on, filled with disgust, waiting for a convenient opportunity to slip away.

Through the crowd I saw Antipas. He was sitting on his throne, with Herodias leaning over him. As the tetrarch listened he put his arm round her, but she loosened his hand from her waist. She seemed to be trying to convince him, or at least persuade him, of something. Then she tossed her head as though she had taken umbrage at his remark, and rejoined the guests. Antipas called to her, but she did not look round.

Someone shook me so violently that I all but fell. I looked

up angrily, and saw Pilate. He was swaying on his feet, his little eyes were half closed, a streak of ruddy hair hung over his sweaty brow.

'Have I shaken you up?' he said in a challenging tone, as though determined to provoke me to a scene. But then he laughed: 'So it's you, Pharisee?' He laid his great paw on my shoulder. 'Don't get angry. I suppose I've defiled you with my touch? But don't get angry. You can wash. Washing's necessary. And for that you need water. Listen, Pharisee! I expect you're terribly rich?'

He waited for a moment with a smile on his face.

'I like rich men. Haven't you ever had any business dealings with me? Why not? Why don't you come and see me? I'd like to get to know you better. Listen . . . I want you to come and see me. But we need water . . . I tell you . . . You wash yourself, I bathe myself . . . Ha-ha-ha!'

He staggered off to the table. But as he passed Herodias's couch she seized him by the tunic and stopped him. He bent over her. I saw him run his hand insolently along her arm right to the shoulder. She smiled and gazed into his eyes. I thought she was drunk and was about to fling her arms round his neck; if she did Antipas would be quite capable of killing her. She rested her finger against the Roman's smooth cheek. He tried to sit down beside her, but the girl, Salome, was already sitting there. Herodias ordered her daughter to get up. Then she said something to her, pointing to the middle of the hall. The child raised her arms uncertainly, as though she were trying to defend herself against her mother's insistence. Then Pilate spoke to her; his words had the effect of causing her to walk away with an air of dignity. The Roman laughed and stretched himself out at Herodias's side.

I looked across at Antipas. He was still sitting on his throne, but he was watching Pilate closely. If Herodias was genuinely anxious to establish a friendship between these two men she had gone quite the wrong way to work. The tetrarch's eyes were flaming; his hands clutched the base of his heavy goblet as though he felt like throwing it at Pilate. But he controlled himself, though he took great gulps of wine.

Meanwhile Salome was standing in the centre of the hall, where the Libyan girls had been dancing. At first I felt rather sorry for her: she looked so innocent, and strangely out of place in this scene of revelry. She turned slowly on her toes, gazing about the hall as though examining it inquisitively. Nobody took any notice of her. I turned to watching her. She raised her thin arms above her head with a gesture of boredom and circled round again on her toes. The Arab musicians were still playing their melody: the drums rattled, the pipes sounded shrilly. She twisted faster and faster in time with the rhythm. She rose to the points of her toes, the silver bangles round her calves jingled against one another. Though she seemed to be dancing the same dance as the grown women had performed a few moments before, her dancing had a more mature quality to it. She appeared to have a better understanding than they of the significance of these body writhings, the belly movements, the play of her legs. She had passed from her first diffident turns to more and more elemental movements. And she began to attract attention. At the sight of her spinning in the middle of the floor the musicians played faster and more emphatically. Now the girl was oblivious of her surroundings, and succumbed completely to the call of the music. Her movements accelerated in rivalry with the wild bedouin music, the unfastened robe flew apart to reveal her slender body. Her long and supple thighs quivered and gleamed, her breasts swelled like bunches of mulberries in the spring rain. One could hardly doubt that she knew exactly what she was doing. I would never have allowed Ruth . . . And yet, wouldn't it be better if she could dance like this child?

The guests rose to their feet and formed a ring around the dancing girl. They began to clap the tempo with their hands. Their eyes flamed with passion as they watched her. I, too, felt that, against all my inclinations, the more I watched this dance the more I was possessed with a fearful rapture. There are times in a man's life when he forgets all the homilies and pre-scriptions. We are weaker than our bodies. A more than usually expressive movement on the part of Salome caused a sound like the howling of a wolf in a moonlit night to rise from the ring of men. From time to time there was a burst of tense, nervous laughter.

Someone pushed violently through the ring to the innermost circle. It was Antipas. His cheeks were pale, he panted, his lips were twisted in a brutal grin. He watched the girl closely, but occasionally he looked at Herodias. She had risen from her couch and, supported by Pilate, was standing on the opposite side of the circle. In this group of men flaming with passion the tetrarch and his wife were sensuality incarnate: the girl was the concentration of all their fury of desire, love, and hate.

But now for some unknown reason Salome's ecstasy faded. A look of fear and confusion passed over her face. She sud-denly stopped dancing. She sped round the ring like a frightened animal seeking a way of escape. She ran to her mother and hid her head under Herodias's elbow.

The guests broke into shouting and laughter. They turned couches, driving the dancing girls in front of them like goats. back to their orgies; the Roman tribune hugged one of the girls and she screamed. The Arab petty rulers returned to their But Antipas shouted for all the hall to hear:

'Salome, dance again!'

The girl peered out from behind her mother and dived back under Herodias's arm.

'Salome . . . give us another dance!' he ordered. He went to her and added: 'If you'll dance I'll give you a pair of beautiful earrings. And a bracelet. I'll give you a slave, I'll give you a bunch of corals, pearls, a couple of rings . . . You can choose whatever you wish from the treasury. If you'll dance again.'

Instead of replying the girl hid still more behind her mother.

'Dance!' he commanded, in a savage and domineering voice. 'Dance! We, the king, ask you to.' He swayed drunkenly on his legs. 'Dance! D'you hear?' he snarled. 'If you don't obey . . . Order her to dance,' he turned to Herodias.

'Don't you see she's too bashful?' the mother replied, gazing fixedly at her husband.

'Bashful? But she has danced!' he stormed. 'She must dance for me now. D'you hear? She must. She wasn't dancing for me before. So now she must. I didn't know she could dance like that. You concealed her from me because you wanted to show her off to . . . You . . . !'

'Antipas!' Her voice had a cold ring; her eyes gazed at him resolutely. It is said that a woman can love a man to the point of frenzy. But Herodias's love was of the kind that controls frenzy. The Edomite, whose father had mercilessly murdered the ones he loved most deeply, yielded before her gaze. He answered moodily:

'Let her dance . . . Tell her to dance for me. I'll do anything she asks. She can have everything she wishes. Up to half of my kingdom.' He turned to the guests and shouted: 'Listen! If Salome dances for me I'll give her everything she demands. Up to half of my kingdom.'

Pilate snorted with laughter.

'Ho, ho! That will be the end of the tetrarchy. I must write to Caesar to inform him we have a queen of Galilee now!'

But Antipas took no notice of the remark. In his excitement he danced and beat his fist in his palm.

'If Salome will dance for me I swear by my royal word that I'll give her whatever she wishes . . .'

Herodias bent down and whispered to her daughter. The child slowly nodded and went to the centre of the hall; a circle quickly formed around her. The musicians struck up their savage melody. A look of fear crossed Salome's face. She fixed her eyes on her mother as though seeking her support. Herodias smiled at her daughter, and the child smiled back. And now her small, bare soles began to tread the floor again, slowly at first, as though she were treading out grapes, then faster and faster, until she was whirling rapidly. I again saw her slender body revealed in the midst of the flying muslin, her wide open eyes, her parted lips, the thin arms swiftly undulating and waving. I tried not to think what that dance conveyed. I tried to remember that I was watching a child. How can one speak of justice in a world where a child in the full bloom of health is made to pander to the debauchery of grown-ups? The guests clapped furiously, and their loud, hissing breath was as furious as their clapping. Antipas clapped too. Joy, pride, and lust shone in his face. I mastered the fever of excitement which was increasingly taking possession of me, and turned to go out, thinking this was a good moment to slip away from the banquet. But with a last filthy gesture Salome stopped dancing. She curtseyed to Antipas and ran to her mother. If she hadn't stopped at that moment I believe the watching men would have done her some wrong; as it was they stretched out their hands to take hold of her.

Appreciative shouts and chuckles broke from the ring. But the voice of Antipas rose above them all:

'Come here; come to me, my beautiful one, my dove. You danced marvellously . . .'

He set his hands on her shoulders and, blinking with emotion, kissed her on the forehead.

'Tell me, you did dance only for me, didn't you? And now say what you would like. I swear in the presence of all this gathering that you shall have whatever you wish. Gold, slaves, a castle: it shall all be yours. Speak up so that everybody can hear.'

There was a great silence. The child looked up at her mother. Herodias nodded gently. Salome slipped neatly out of Antipas's embrace and fell back a step.

'If you wish to reward me,' she said in a low, quivering and not at all child-like tone, 'order a soldier to bring me this minute the head of the false prophet whom you hold in prison . . .'

Then she ran and nestled against Herodias. The silence grew

even deeper: so deep that I could hear the buzz of the mosquitoes around the candelabra.

'You want the head of the prophet, John the Baptist?' he said slowly, as though he could not believe his ears. He looked from the child to Herodias. In his eyes there was a mortal terror. 'Has the wine robbed you of your wits?' he cried in a shrill, almost falsetto voice. 'That man is holy . . .' His voice rose still higher. 'Do you know what may happen if I raise my hand against him? It's you who have told her to ask for this!' He squatted down to bring his face on a level with the girl's. 'Salome,' he said, 'I'll give you everything you wish. Don't listen to your mother. I'll give you gold, pearls, silks, slaves, horses . . . Now tell me what you yourself would like . . . Quickly!'

She said again, in a muffled voice:

'Give me, my lord, the head of the false prophet.'

'Curse it!' he snarled. He turned to his wife: 'You've tricked me. I never intended to let you have that. I'll give her anything but that. Don't you know that the king who kills a prophet loses his kingdom for ever?'

'You're behaving childishly,' she said calmly. 'I've told you again and again you must choose between me and him. What can happen to you when I am watching over your welfare?' She raised her voice, so that all could hear: 'You said you would give the child whatever she wished. You have pledged your royal word.'

'I've pledged my royal word,' he groaned. All his fire had left him. He looked round the hall at the guests as though they were strangers. He must have noticed Pilate's sneering smile, but he showed no reaction. Yet suddenly, like a man clutching at any straw, he exclaimed:

'The Roman Procurator will not be pleased at this execution . . .'

All eyes were turned on Pilate. He was still smiling, but now it was a smile of courtesy.

'You are the king,' he replied. 'And he is your subject.

He appears to have been stirring up the people. Do as you wish.'

Antipas looked back at Herodias in desperation. 'I can't kill him,' he exclaimed.

'So you intend to break your word?'

Slowly, like a parrot, Salome added:

'O king, give me the head of the false prophet.'

'You'll bring disaster on us,' he groaned to Herodias. There were tears in his eyes. All his passion was spent and dead.

'I am at your side,' Herodias quietly said.

'But why kill him? He cannot say anything more: he's in prison,' he argued with her.

'So long as he's alive he can always be set free. And then you'll have revolts, war . . . The Romans will have an excuse to intervene,' she said even more quietly.

'He's a prophet, a holy prophet . . .'

'You are a king!' she interrupted impatiently. 'And besides, the important thing isn't what's to come, but what is.'

'What did you tell her to dance for?' he wailed.

'You wanted her to.'

'Give me the head of the false prophet,' the girl said again.

'Let her have it!' Herodias said in an imperious tone. 'You heard what the Roman said? He'll think you're trying to protect someone who has stirred up the people of Judaea to revolt.'

The tetrarch sighed. Clutching his head in his hands, he went slowly back to the throne. He sat down. There was a deathly silence in the hall. He called the commander of his guard:

'Proxen!'

The officer presented himself.

'Go and cut off the head of rabbi John and bring it here on a tray . . .'

Proxen bowed and went out. Nobody said a word: everybody was filled with horror. The girls huddled together fearfully. Suddenly from the depths of the palace came a muffled cry. The guests breathed more heavily: the air was heavy as though in anticipation of a thunderstorm. All the passion and frenzy of the orgies had passed. We all waited, not daring to move from the spot.

Then we heard footsteps. They drew nearer, grew louder, louder; and each step struck at our hearts and aroused an echo. At last the soldier appeared in the doorway. As he passed me I saw the head on the tray. The flaxen hair streaked with grey was imbrued in blood. The eyes were wide open, staring. They gazed up at the flower-garlanded vaulting as though at the rising sun. Proxen halted before Antipas, and held out the tray. But the tetrarch covered his eyes with one hand and thrust away the tray with the other.

'I don't want it,' he exclaimed. 'Give it to her.'

The officer carried the tray to Salome. The girl took it from his hands and, walking on tiptoe, bore the severed head to her mother. Herodias nodded calmly. Someone laughed, but it sounded like the grating of a well crane. Pilate was the first to master his feeling of horror. He said impassively:

'Rebels have to be crushed.'

'Very true, Procurator,' Herodias supported him. 'Then they will be a lesson to others.'

'There's another man already going about Galilee . . .' a guest remarked.

Wailing like a madman, Antipas cried:

'It's not another man. It's John. I've killed him, but he's already walking again. It's impossible to kill him. He himself said I would be reduced, I would perish . . . It's he!'

He flung his cloak over his head; but the sound of howling and sobbing came audibly from under it. Herodias went to her husband. She put her arms round his shoulders; but he huddled against her like a terrified child sobbing its heart out.

I fled from Machaerus that very same night. And not I alone. Almost all the guests fled too.

Well, I have done as you advised. I decided to set off early in the morning, and rose before dawn. But the weather was not encouraging: a wind had been blowing all night, and a heavy, cold rain mingled with snow was falling. When I went to the housetop I shivered all over in the keen breeze. Everywhere was white. I heard the rumour of the melting snow flowing down the walls. Then I remembered that someone had told me the weather had been just as wretched on that occasion, years ago, when they arrived at the royal city. And it seemed obvious that if I wanted to find it exactly as it had been that night I, too, must go through the snow and the cold under this lowering sky. You taught me that to discover the truth of truths one must not act like an onlooker from a distance; to get to know someone properly you must set your feet in his footprints not when the sun is shining, but when the imprint is deep and filled with snow-water.

So I took a stick, wrapped myself in my robe and, after prayers, set out. The streets were deserted; only the wind tossed about them like a homeless dog. My feet were frozen long before I reached the palace where that monster, Herod, had resided. You will remember that Augustus ordered Cyrene, the Legate of Syria, to look into the affairs of Judaea, to ascertain the state of the country under Roman rule. And Cyrene ordered a census of the people without even consulting the king. As you know, when other censuses were ordered, later on, the people revolted, and were suppressed with bloodshed. But on that first occasion they were taken by surprise, and each man went to his native place to be registered. The time of the year was about the same as now; the snow-covered hills emerged from a milky mist, the roads were dissolving into icy, slippery mud. Caravans of men wandered through the countryside, cursing the Romans and Herod. There were not many women among them; the census did not apply to women, and in such filthy weather only a woman who would not or could not be left behind accompanied her man.

Yet those two set out together from Nazareth. I thought of them continually as I passed the Joppa gate and journeyed along the Hill of Evil Counsel. The cold pierced to my marrow. Patches of snow lay on the northern slope of the hill, and streams of black water poured from beneath them, like serpents deserting their nests. The road slowly climbed upward. The wind beat icy drops into my face. I could not feel my toes, and my shoulders ached with stiffness from the manner in which I had to carry my head. At times a blast of wind beat the breath out of me.

That could not have been a pleasant journey for a woman who was to give birth the same night. I don't know whether she rode an ass, or whether because of their poverty she went on foot, leaning on her husband's arm. But whether she walked or rode, she must have overcome her weakness. She was to be the mother of a great miracle-worker, so perhaps she, too, could work miracles? I know the people of Nazareth declare they all three lived quite normal lives for many years. At first I found this difficult to believe, but I am coming to understand it. If a prophet — I cannot bring myself to call him the Messiah — has to enter on that role as a mature man he must conceal himself and his mission until he comes to maturity. That calls for strength. Possibly she did not feel the wind lashing her face, or the pain that comes over a woman in wave after wave. In her case suffering and poverty may have been only a cloak concealing the future glory. Any people they passed must surely have wondered whether these two would reach the nearest village before nightfall. But she must have known that she would not fall as she trudged along that road, she would manage to reach a spot where she could bring forth her child in relative comfort. But even if she was weak, she knew that no harm threatened her. And one does not fear even the worst if one knows that all will end well.

I reached the highest point on the road. Here it was almost impossible to make headway against the wind. But now the way had begun to run downhill. Before me stretched a long, broad valley, lost in the grey distance. On the farther side was Bethlehem. The town squatted between the rocky outliers of the hills like a criminal between guards. When I had gone a few yards the wind grew lighter. But snow began to fall. The air was filled with white flakes which floated down slowly and heavily, vanishing as they touched the ground.

When I reached the town I was exhausted, frozen to the marrow, and hungry. My only thought was of sitting by a fire; I had lost all desire to follow in anybody else's footsteps. What had I dragged myself away from my work for, from my meditations on the Scriptures? Instead of wasting time and health in wandering through the bitter cold to a town of the long dead past, I would be better employed sitting beside a fire and seeking to understand the words of the Eternal. I felt an increasing anger with Jesus, as though it was he who had commanded me to travel that filthy morning to the place of his birth. If he were the Messiah, I thought, he should make the way easy for anyone seeking to follow in his footsteps. That would be a sign that he was what he claimed to be.

The inn was the first building I came to. It was an ordinary sort of place: a walled courtyard, with an open gallery round the walls. It was completely empty. The central, open area, where the pack animals are tethered, was like a pond, with mud and dung emerging here and there. Under one gallery a fire was burning, and a man was dozing over it. Evidently he was the innkeeper, for when I went in he jumped up and greeted me courteously:

'May the All Highest be with you.'

'And may He always watch over you,' I replied.

After the usual exchange of formal greetings I sat down by the fire and began to feel pleasantly warm. The innkeeper offered me wine, bread, cheese, and olives. When I removed my cloak and he saw that I was a Pharisee he called me 'rabbi.'

My ill humour passed. Now I felt glad I had come and that at last I would get to the very source of the truth.

'Listen!' I said. 'Have you been innkeeper here long?'

As I expected, the inn had belonged to his father, and to his grandfather before him.

'Have you ever by chance heard of Jesus of Nazareth?'

He nodded. 'Yes, rabbi; I've heard of him. He's a prophet. There were two of them. But the tetrarch had John put to death.'

'Is it true that Jesus was born here in Bethlehem?' For some reason my voice trembled as I asked.

'Yes,' he answered. 'It was here, in this inn.'

Without waiting to be questioned further he plunged into a long story. Years ago—it was before he was born—two wanderers had arrived at the inn in the late afternoon. The inn was full to overflowing, and there was no place for them. At first his father wouldn't even let them enter. But at once there were signs that the new arrivals were remarkable miracle-workers: the walls of the inn expanded so that everybody could be accommodated; the snow and rain stopped falling and it turned as warm as if it were the month of Tammuz; an extraordinary star with a tail appeared over the town, and its tail pointed straight down to the inn. Of course, the strangers were allowed to enter at once, and they were given the best places by the fire. The innkeeper and the guests all hurried to wait on and do honour to them. The woman was pregnant. She gave birth to a son that same night. All the women in the place waited on her and bathed and swaddled the child. It was the most beautiful child anyone had ever seen. It was able to talk at once. One could tell immediately that a great prophet had entered the world. The child grew swiftly, like the youthful urge of a mulberry sapling; by the time it was twelve months old it knew more than the average boy of fifteen. It was always working miracles. When the child saw his mother had to bring water up from the spring at the bottom of the hill he struck his foot against a stone and water gushed out of

E

the cliff. And when they decided to return to Galilee the child touched the chain barring off the courtyard and coins sprinkled down from it. His parents were able to buy a whole caravan of asses and return to their own parts in comfort.

'That's all lies,' I heard a voice.

I had not noticed before that an old woman with a pitcher on her arm had come up.

'You're lying,' she said harshly, pursing up her lips till they were ringed with tiny furrows.

'What do you want, mother?' the innkeeper muttered reluctantly.

'I want what I want,' the old woman snorted. 'But don't you tell lies. You're always lying.'

'So what your son has just told me isn't true?' I asked. 'Could you tell me what did happen?'

I am not in the habit of addressing an unclean woman directly, but my curiosity would not let me rest. She must have been astonished at my speaking to her, for she did not reply at once. She stood with the pitcher still in the crook of her arm.

'If you will allow me, rabbi, I'll tell you,' she said irresolutely. 'It wasn't in the least like what my son said. He thinks he amuses the guests with his lies. But he's a fool . . .'

She cleared her throat. Her gown hung loose around her, so I could see her thin, toil-worn feet covered with a red crust of mud to above the ankles.

'It was like this,' she began. 'A day just like this. Snow was falling, the asses and camels shivered with cold. A great number of people had arrived, because of the census. By the evening the courtyard was filled with animals, and men were lying side by side under the roof.

'I was terribly tired, all but dropping with weariness. But my husband shouted to me again and again to fetch water, and to help tend the camels. I only sighed for night and for all those people, who talked and ate as if they'd never stop, to lie down and go to sleep.

'Just at that moment a man pushed his way through to me.

His cloak was wet, he had obviously come straight from the road. He quietly asked whether I could take him and his wife. He explained that they'd only just arrived, they were terribly tired, and his wife was expecting at any moment.

'I was almost mad with tiredness myself. I shouted at the top of my voice: "No, I haven't any room. Go somewhere else. Can't you see we're full up?"

'He tried to tell me they'd tried everywhere in the town, but nobody wanted to take them in. "If you would be good enough to find some corner for my wife," he said. "I can remain outside."

'That made me even more furious. My baby, Judah, was beating his fist on my breast, for it was time to feed him. Through the hubbub I heard my husband calling: probably he wanted me to run to the well yet again for water. And at that thought I was almost frantic. I shouted as though the man had done me some evil: "Clear out! Get out of here! There's no room for you or your wife. Clear out!"

'I must have shouted very loud, for my husband heard me and came up. Of course he was delighted at the hubbub, his chats with the travellers, and the opportunity to collect and retail gossip. "What are you shouting at this respectable traveller for?" he asked. I began to be afraid he would order me to give up my bed for this man's wife.

'I burst out: "They can clear off. There's no room here for them. D'you want me to look after every beggar that arrives? I don't suppose this fellow can even pay for his night's lodging!" The look on the man's face when he heard this convinced me that I was right. "Throw him out!" I said. "Let him and his woman go elsewhere."

'My words had their effect: the courteous smile vanished from my husband's face. But he must have felt sorry for them, for he took the man aside and had a talk with him. The stranger insisted and pleaded, pointing to the woman behind him. She stood leaning against one of the roof poles. It was this very pole, rabbi. Her feet were covered with mud. She had her hands pressed to her chest, her face was earthy, her eyes were faded; she was biting her lips. You could tell her hour was near. But I began to shout again, for I thought my husband was giving way and would order me to give up my bed. He shrugged his shoulders and scratched his head. I felt no sympathy whatever for the woman, but my husband nodded to the inn gateway. "Come; I'll find something for you," he muttered. The woman staggered along, bent almost double, clinging to every roof pole. My husband accompanied them to the gate, pointed, and said something to them. The man went out with his arm solicitously round his wife's shoulder.

'It was a long time before I could get to bed. I had to wait on the guests, to bake bread for them, to bring water, and feed the camels. I wept with helpless despair. My Judah fell asleep, unfed, in my arms. But my husband moved among the guests, accepting their wine, whistling merrily, and jingling the coins in his leather wallet. As he went past me once he said: "I've allowed that couple to put up in the grotto with the manger. There's less draught there." I flung at him through my teeth: "You ought to drive them away. Set the dogs on them! The shameless beggars!" He smiled benevolently. "Poor wretches! The woman may quite likely drop tonight. You ought to go out to her." "Wouldn't you like to!" I stormed. "Let her fend for herself. I'm not going to run about after any beggar!"

'The guests didn't stop eating and talking and lie down to sleep until late in the night. My husband slept in my bed. He didn't remain on his own couch: he gave it up to a guest, for a good reward, of course. When he came to me he stank of the wine he had drunk. And when he dropped off to sleep he took up all the bed, and I was pushed out on to the bare earth. I was mortally tired, but I couldn't sleep. I lay shivering with the cold, listening to the camels grunting and coughing.'

'So the walls of your inn didn't expand?' I asked impatiently. 'And there wasn't any star pointing it out?'

She shrugged her shoulders. 'Women like me haven't time for that,' she said. 'It's a man's job to look at the stars.

'But I did hear later on,' she said after a moment, 'that there was said to be a star. Symcha, son of Timmaeus, told me so. Apparently they heard voices and singing too. I met them as I came out of the grotto. I only went there because I couldn't sleep. I remembered the hard time I'd had with my own child. I took a mug of warm water, a little oil, and some rag. I could hardly make my way to the inn gate because of the sleepers everywhere. The grotto was where we kept our animals: goats, yoke-oxen, and a she-ass. A faint light came from the entrance. As I went in I heard a baby crying. The woman was kneeling over the manger – it was carved from a tree trunk – whispering something quietly to the child. Do you think it strange that she was able to move immediately after giving birth? But we women who work hard get strength from somewhere or other when it's necessary. Her husband had lit a fire in one corner. But there was no draught, and the grotto was filled with stifling, pungent smoke.

'When she saw me the woman was alarmed. Possibly she thought I'd come to throw them out of the grotto. But when she saw I wanted to help her face lit up with joy. It was a good job I'd come: she was young and inexperienced. I had to show her everything: how to wash the child, how to give it the breast, how to wrap it in the swaddling-band. The smoke got into the child's eyes and throat. It didn't stop crying. I sang it the songs I was used to singing to my Judah. At last it sobbed itself off to sleep, and I laid it back in the manger. Then I milked a goat, so that the mother could have a drink of warm milk. As I was going she said: "Thank you, sister." She put her arm round me and pressed her cheek to my face: her cheek was wet with tears. She was smiling through those tears. "Thank you," she whispered; "he'll repay you." I thought she meant her husband. My head was aching, but when I went out I freshened up in the breeze. I leaned against a rock. The night was at its end. I knew that the coming day would be just as horribly exhausting. And yet, instead of hurrying back and snatching a few moments' sleep, I stood leaning against the rock, breathing in the fresh air.

'It was then that old Timmaeus, with his sons and several other shepherds, came up. They looked sinister with their sticks and the knives stuck in their belts.

' "Is that you, Sarah?" he asked. "Is it true that a child has been born in the grotto where you stall your cattle?" My voice refused to come to my lips. Timmaeus is a quiet sort of fellow. But I thought I caught a threatening note in his voice. What did these shepherds want with the child of a couple of beggars, a child born in a cattle shelter?

' "No, no!" I cried, thinking the lie would stop them. But they went on to the grotto as though they didn't believe me. So I stood in their path. "What do you want of them?" I demanded. "They're poor people. I won't let you do them any harm. If it's money you want, here are a couple of coppers."

' "You're a fool, Sarah," Timmaeus said contemptuously, pushing me out of his way.

'He and his companions went in. Only his son Symcha halted for a moment and hurriedly said something about a star, voices, and lights. But I didn't believe him. I hurried after them. I found them standing at the entrance. By now the daylight was streaming in. At the sight of them the woman had started to her feet in alarm, and was standing with the child pressed to her breast. But to my amazement Timmaeus knelt down and gave the woman a white ball of fresh cheese, as though it were some priceless gift. The others knelt down too. The young mother didn't seem to understand even now what these fearful-looking strangers in sheepskins had come for. But if someone smiles at a woman's child she has to respond with a smile. She took a step forward. She held out her son towards the shepherds, like a priest showing the sacrifice to the people before offering it up.'

'Was he really so fine and healthy?' I interrupted.

'A child is always beautiful,' she answered. 'But this one

wasn't very healthy. It cried often, and when it cried the mother cried too. It seemed rather small, like a child born before time. The mother lacked milk, so it was often hungry. They had to spend several days in the grotto before the inn emptied and we could transfer them here.'

'Your son said he grew swiftly, more swiftly than an ordinary child,' I observed.

She shrugged her shoulders. 'He grew like any other boy would in his place. There was nothing extraordinary about him.'

'But why didn't they create better conditions for him? They could work miracles, couldn't they? And so could he, if he brought water out of the cliff simply by stamping his foot.'

'My son was lying, rabbi. I had his delicate little feet in my hands more than once. His mother had to go down to the valley for water like the rest of us.'

'But what about the money that fell from the chain?'

'That's a lie too. When they left our house his father brought us one denarius and said he couldn't give any more. But if I liked, he would make me something for the house, as he was a carpenter. I told him to make a table, and he did. There it is, rabbi, just behind you.'

I looked at it. It was heavy, like those found in richer peasant houses, only fashioned more expertly.

'And so that's all you know about the birth of this Jesus of Nazareth?' I asked.

'That's all, rabbi.'

'Has he ever been back here?'

'No, rabbi. I've heard that he goes about Galilee, teaching.'

The evening was drawing down, so I decided to spend the night in the inn and return to Jerusalem next morning. The woman went off to attend to her domestic tasks. The innkeeper, evidently abashed by his mother's exposure, sat down and said nothing. After dark a little caravan of merchants travelling from Hebron to Damascus arrived. I kept myself apart, for they looked unclean. The dark, dank evening spent in this lonely place filled me with mournful thoughts. I saw the old woman come out of the inn, and asked:

'Are you going to the grotto? If so, would you let me see it?'

'Come then, rabbi.'

The wind was blowing again, the sky was partly clear of cloud, and stars were shining. The woman carried an oil lamp in her cupped hands. She led me to a rocky cliff, with a small opening in it. We went in. The grotto stank of animals and damp straw. She raised her lamp. A manger hollowed out of a trunk was supported on two trestles. A white ox was breathing over it.

'This is the place,' she said.

'So this is the place,' I repeated. It was littered with rotting straw and dung. Only a terribly poverty-stricken wretch could have been born in such a den. It was not fitted for the birth of a descendant of David, a prophet, the Messiah.

I felt even more sad and depressed, as though the low roof were pressing down on my head. The ox chewed noisily; the saliva dribbled from its muzzle into the manger. I took another glance around and went out.

We returned without exchanging a word at first. But when we had gone some paces I thought of a question which required an immediate answer.

'Listen,' I said. 'You said you had a child then. That isn't the man I spoke with, is it?'

'No,' she replied. She went on for a moment or two without speaking, then added thickly: 'Judah's dead.'

'Did he die then?' I asked diffidently. The events of those past times were slowly forming into a single picture in my mind. It must have been about then that Herod the monster ordered all the little children in Bethlehem to be murdered. It was strange that Jesus had escaped the assassins' swords.

'Yes,' she replied. 'The king's soldiers killed him when they were searching for the infant Jesus.'

'Searching for the infant Jesus,' I repeated. Now I thought

I had found a new piece in the picture which was slowly emerging from the gloom of time. 'So they searched for him?'

'Yes. They asked after him. But his parents had gone away with him the previous night. The soldiers wouldn't believe it. And to make sure he wouldn't escape they murdered all the male children.'

'So because of him you lost your son,' I said through my teeth.

She made no reply. I again felt a growing dislike, almost hatred for the man whose truth I had come here to discover. I said angrily:

'In that case they repaid you well for your efforts on their behalf. I should think you're sorry you didn't drive them away.'

'No,' I heard her say. The reply was low and quiet. 'I'm sorry I was so merciless to them . . .'

I halted. I flung into her face almost spitefully:

'But your child perished because of them. Or didn't you love it?' (She sighed.) 'If they hadn't come to you the children of Bethlehem might have been spared. He was saved, but many other children had to pay for it with their lives. Did it have to be so?' I went on, as though arguing with someone other than this old woman. 'Why does he raise some from the dead and make others well, while he allows others to perish because of him? If I were you I should hate them!' I turned to the woman.

I walked back to the inn, with her at my side. We were not far from the gate when she spoke again: 'I am only a stupid, unclean woman. What can I know? But why should I hate them? I was unkind to them. But they didn't remember it against me. They were so good. Nobody has ever smiled at me as that mother and baby smiled. My Judah might have died in any case. He might have fallen into the well, or caught a fever. The will of the All Highest is in everything. You say our boys died because of him? But now it seems he is making people well, raising them from the dead, driving out devils, saying beautiful things. It's just as though my Judah made it possible for all this to happen.'

What answer could I make to that? I returned to the inn, flung myself down on my couch, and tried to sleep. I saw the stars come out above the roof. Once more my excitement turned to sorrow. Once more I had failed to discover the one thing that might bring me happiness and peace. Who is this man, I ask, Justus? Why does he sometimes work miracles and sometimes not? If his victory could be my victory, Ruth's victory . . . But this victory looks more like defeat: mine, Ruth's, and his too.

DEAR JUSTUS, TWELFTH LETTER.

The winter has passed, and the spring; and summer is here. Dry, hot, and as unbearable as ever. But I don't see it. I don't droop in the noonday heat, like a palm. I see nothing of what is going on around me. I live as though I had no life: I am nothing but pain.

You remember that I have often written that I didn't think I could stand these continual fluctuations in Ruth's illness much longer. Today I think of those times as almost happiness. It is all now a thing of the past. The illness has passed into a new phase: there is never any improvement now, only steady deterioration. I have to tell myself frankly that nothing can help any longer: she will die.

That's a terrible word: the very sound of it makes me shiver. If she were to die . . . But why must she? She didn't die when the epidemic was carrying off hundreds and thousands of people. The All Highest brought her through safely, like the Israelite youths whom Nebuchadnezzar flung into the fiery furnace. Was I not grateful to Him for that? Evidently He doesn't need our gratitude. He saved her then in order to kill her now. No: I take that back. She is still alive, and she will live! I trust in Him, indeed I do.

I continually repeat the psalm: 'The Lord is my refuge and my fortress. He covers me with the feathers of His wings. With Him I do not fear the terror by night, nor the enemy's arrow which flies in the darkness, nor the disease which strikes down in broad daylight . . .'

I close my eyes, and say with all the conviction I can muster: 'I trust, I trust; only let it be that when I open my eyes she is better.' I don't even pray that she will be well. But then I open my eyes, and there is no change. I never thought I could love anyone so much, with all my being. She is departing . . . She alters more and more, is more and more remote. She is fading like a dream that the day erases from the memory. O Adonai!

I haven't seen Jesus for a whole year. He did not come to Jerusalem for the harvest festival, he didn't come for Chanukah, he didn't show himself during the week of Passover. I can guess the reason: he is raising up more and more enemies against himself. The Sadducees have grown rather colder in their anger, but now the entire Grand Council is burning with desire to get him in their clutches. They grind their teeth as they listen to the stories told by the men they send after him. He seems to be seeking war with us. Apparently when someone asked him why he and his disciples didn't observe the purification prescriptions he replied by speaking to the Pharisee brethren in the crowd: 'All these rules and regulations are your own invention, and you have set them above the Lord's commandments. It was of you that the prophet Isaiah spoke when he said that there are some who reverence the Eternal only with their lips, while their hearts are fettered to riches, glory, power and knowledge. Not with loud prayers is the Most Holy Presence worshipped. And it isn't sufficient to wash only the outside of the body or the pot. Dirt does not come from outside, and it doesn't stain. It is the heart that pours out impurity covering the whole of the man. Why don't you teach the people to cleanse themselves of this kind of impurity? Did you encourage them to go to John? No. You want them only to come to you, to proclaim only your glory. You demand to be reverenced, to be called "rabbi," though there is only one true teacher, the Messiah; or you order them to call you "Father," though there is only one Father, He who dwells in heaven. And so you are accursed. You locked the door and threw away the key so that nobody could enter. You are accursed because you do wrong to the widows, you are exact in weighing out a sacrifice of cumin seed, and are miserly in the sacrifice of the heart. You are accursed, you are whited sepulchres, and though you be washed with lime you will go on stinking. You are accursed, you who glorify the prophets, but have not remembered a single one of their teachings. Blind leaders of the blind! You are accursed, for you cannot see the camel, though you can see a gnat.'

A terrible imprecation. It needs to be said only once to be tantamount to a declaration of war. Now there can be no other feeling but hatred between him and the Grand Council. Apparently he has even said of us: 'Listen to what they say, but don't imitate them!' And the crowd agreed. He cannot hope to escape now.

And yet I still cannot regard him as an enemy. I should hate him. But I know only too well the falsity and sinfulness of many of our brethren. But why does he say these things aloud? He wants people to have pure hearts as well as clean hands. But who is to say whether the enforced observance of many prescriptions doesn't incline the sinner towards virtue? He always seems too unpractical to me. Even if a Pharisee keeps himself clean only outwardly, isn't he better than an unclean boor who is as sinful in his heart as he is filthy in his body? And on the other hand, he cannot really get any satisfaction out of allowing all the scum, the fishermen, customs officers, street girls, to come to him. Where is the logic in his behaviour?

I was sitting writing this letter to you when I heard the rustle of sandals at the door. I turned, and to my surprise saw Judas Iscariot.

'What are you doing here?' I asked. 'Have you all come to Jerusalem?'

I still cannot stifle the hope that he will come and restore Ruth to health. But Judas shook his head. He ran an uneasy glance around my room: as though he wanted to be sure nobody else was there. He reminded me more than ever of a frightened rat. But when driven up against a wall this rat is prepared to bite. He laid his finger to his lips. I couldn't be sure whether he had come to talk to me or threaten me. Then it suddenly occurred to me that the teacher had been imprisoned. Forgetting Judas's gesture, I exclaimed:

'Have they caught him?'

'Sssh!' he hissed. 'What are you shouting for, rabbi? I don't want all the household to know I'm here.' He stood confronting me, filled with fear and anger. 'No, they haven't caught him yet. But they will tomorrow or the day after. Now he can't escape. This is the end . . .'

'The end of what?' I asked, even more astonished at his behaviour than at his words.

'Of everything.' He flung out his hands in despair. 'Of our hopes . . . He's a traitor . . .'

'A traitor?' I was still more astonished. 'Whom has he betrayed?'

'Us,' he burst out. 'Us, the people, everybody . . .' Now he was speaking with the touch of exaggeration he was wont to use when accusing his neighbour of dishonest competition. 'He's become a coward.' (Like all cowards, he accused another of cowardice.) 'He doesn't want to fight.'

'I don't understand a word you're saying. Sit down and tell me everything from the beginning. You can speak without fear; nobody will come in.'

Despite my assurance he looked around again. He sat down on a stool with his knees wide apart.

'Good! Then I'll tell you, rabbi.'

He struck his fist several times on his knee.

'Haven't I always told you, rabbi, that if he wished he could do anything? He has a power which no other man has ever possessed. Have you heard how he fed thousands of people?'

I had heard some incredible tale that he had fed an enormous number of heathens at Decapolis: but it hadn't occurred to me that it might be true. I remember he had said: 'Don't go to the heathens or the Samaritans, go to the sons of Israel. The Son of Man has come to find what has been lost among the chosen people.' And he also taught: 'Take no thought for what you shall eat . . .'

'Do you mean when he is said to have fed the heathens at Decapolis?' I asked.

'That was another time. Before that he had given bread to the faithful. He was staying not far from Bethsaida at the time. An enormous number of pilgrims were travelling along the road on their way to Jerusalem for the Passover. But when they saw him they stopped to listen to his teaching. He talked to them all day, and healed too. When evening came on we said to him: "It would be better to stop now, for it's late. They've been listening all day, and they must be hungry. Let them go off to the neighbouring villages to buy food for themselves." He replied, just as though he were angry because we had interrupted him: "You give them something to eat!" He knew quite well that there were no shops nor even a stall in the vicinity. And besides, think of the quantity of food we would have had to buy to feed them all! As usual, we hadn't a copper. We stood there, not knowing what to do. And he just went on teaching. You know, rabbi, how he likes to put you in difficulties, and when you're completely at a dead end to know what to do, only then does he find some quite unexpected way out.'

'Yes,' I muttered. 'I know about that.' It was a very sound observation on Judas's part.

'At last he stopped talking and called us over to him. "What have you got to give the people?" he asked. It sounded just as though he was poking fun at us.

'Andrew boomed: "Mark has five griddle loaves and two fishes in his basket. But that's not even enough for us."

'He said, just as though he hadn't heard that last remark, "Tell the people to sit down in fifties, so that the food can be distributed more easily."

'I was determined to avert this disaster: I was sure it would have a bad end. "Rabbi," I intervened, "let them fend for themselves. Five flat loaves are nothing among such a crowd. They'll laugh at you."

'He repeated quite firmly: "Tell them to sit down."

'Simon, who does everything Jesus demands, at once began to bawl at the people. I felt like running away. I was sure we wouldn't get out of this trouble without cracked heads. He's a great miracle-worker, but who would have credited him with the ability to work such an incredible miracle? He took the basket of bread and fish. You remember, rabbi, that whenever he eats he shares his food with his friends? Now he broke up every little griddle cake and gave the pieces to us. And he told us: "Break the pieces up and hand them round." And it was marvellous: when I broke up my little piece I realized that I could break every little piece I had again and again, and yet again, without end. The bread simply grew in my hands. When we gave the people the pieces they turned into whole cakes again. At first they didn't realize that something quite un-heard-of was happening. But gradually a murmur of aston-ishment and admiration rose from the seated multitude. But their amazement was nothing compared with ours. I was as though struck by lightning. I realized that now at last he had revealed all his power. Now, I thought, what we have been waiting for must come about. He can multiply bread without end, so he will also be able to multiply gold, land, and weapons. And who will be able to withstand him? We shall overcome everybody. The people's shouting increased, and it turned to a roar when he ordered the fragments to be gathered up, and we collected twelve baskets, full.

'When everybody was crammed with food he sat among us

on the hillside and ate too. He seemed tired, but satisfied. When the people jumped to their feet and began to cheer in his honour an anxious look appeared on his face.

'He called us round him. "Go to the boat and cast off at once," he ordered. "And make haste."

' "But how about you, rabbi?" Simon asked.

' "Don't worry about me. Go to the boat, quickly."

' "We're not going to sail away now," I protested. "You've worked the greatest of all miracles. So we and the people wish to do you reverence as is fitting."

'He shouted as though in despair: "Silence! Set sail at once!"

'But the others also began to object: "Let us stay, rabbi. The people wish to worship you."

'He looked mortally frightened; a crowd of people was coming towards us, shouting and cheering. "Have I got to tell you twice? Go this minute!" he ordered. I had never seen him so worked up. We submitted, and reluctantly walked away.

'We went down to the stony shore and unfastened the boat. The people surrounding him looked like a great white patch of snow above us. Their shouting echoed over the lake and back from the hills.

' "Perhaps we ought to go back?" Thomas said.

' "Yes, come on, we'll go back," I supported him. I felt that such an opportunity would never occur again. "The people will proclaim him king. He'll turn one sword into a thousand. We shall take revenge for our wrongs."

' "Let's go back, let's go back!" the others took me up. I was confident I had won. But Simon, with a powerful thrust of his oar, pushed off the boat.

' "The teacher has ordered us to sail," he shouted.

' "You're a fool!' I cried. "He'll be grateful to us one day for forcing him . . ." Simon's oar whistled over my head.

' "It's you that's the fool," he roared. "Do as he says, and don't try to be clever!"

'What could I do? He's as strong as a bull. And nobody dared say another word about going back. We sailed away.

'I almost cried in my rage: "You're fools, fools! If we had forced him to he might have revealed himself to the world. Tomorrow we might have been the rulers of Israel. You're fools and cowards!".

'They breathed heavily, but no one answered. I was beside myself, and beat my fist against the side of the boat.

'Meanwhile, darkness came down over us. We couldn't see the hills and that patch of thousands of robes. But their shouts followed us, until, as we sailed on, they gradually faded away. What was happening back there behind us? Was he promising to lead them as soon as dawn came, and telling them to rest now? But why had he driven us away? We alone have been faithful to him from the beginning. I sank into a gloomy reverie. A wind blew up more and more. The boat began to rock violently. The foam dashed over the sides. You remember, rabbi, that night when the storm all but sank us? This time the wind was not so strong, but it blew steadily, and increased in violence. At last we were no longer making any progress: by rowing with all our strength we managed to avoid being blown back. Those of us who were not rowing began to bail out the water. With my heavy exertions, I no longer thought of what might have been. Sweat poured down my face, my robe and cloak were wet through. The only sound to be heard between the howling of the wind was an occasional shout from Simon and the panting breath of the rowers.

'I was so busy bailing that it was not till the others cried out that I looked up. At first I noticed nothing unusual: it seemed that the moon had risen and was casting a quivering, gleaming path over the water. But then I realized that the moon couldn't be right down at water level, and certainly couldn't be coming towards us along that silvery path. Then, as what I had taken to be a shining disc approached, I saw that it was a gigantic human form, which was walking, or rather floating, or flying, above the water with amazing tranquillity and indifference to the waves tossing around it. We began to shout with fear: some of us covered our heads with our cloaks, others fell to their knees. The apparition came on as though it hadn't seen us. It went right past us. The rowers dropped their oars, so that one or two were carried away by the sea. The waves all but capsized us, and we were near to being drowned. But at that moment death was less terrifying than the spectral form.

'Then right beside us we suddenly heard a human voice. A voice so well known. His words were stronger than our fear. We peered timorously over the side. It was he standing on that quivering, silvery path. Our fear fled, it was changed to a wild and rapturous joy. Suddenly Simon jumped to his feet and with one bound leapt over the side. We were struck dumb again. But he walked towards the teacher with his arms outstretched, uncertainly, like a man who is trying out his legs for the first time after a long illness. He had almost reached Jesus when a great wall of water rolled towards him and hung right over the path. He cried out . . . and immediately he began to sink in the water. He came to the surface again, struggling desperately. The teacher bent down, took him by the hand, and said something to him. And then the master came walking lightly towards the boat, as though that tossing sea were a stretch of soft grass, dragging Simon behind him, half immersed in the waves. Simon clung tightly to Jesus's hand and the teacher helped him to scramble into the boat before he, too, climbed in. We fell to our knees around him as he stood among us. And then the wind dropped, the waves stopped tossing, and there we were in broad daylight, right off the shore. In front Capernaum was awakening to the kiss of the first rays of sunlight.'

As he said this Judas shook himself as though trying to get rid of some unpleasant touch. The look of disillusionment and despair returned to his face. He laughed curtly.

'So you see, rabbi,' he pulled a wry face, 'at that moment everything seemed sunny and joyous even to me. But he . . .' He shrugged his shoulders contemptuously.

'But what you've just told me is amazing, Judas. What is this man?' I was so shaken by his story that I asked him the question as though he were not a petty merchant from Bezetha but a learned doctor.

'What is he?' he repeated slowly, as though chewing over each word. 'Wait until I've told you all, rabbi. When we stepped on to the shore we had an answer all ready to that question. That afternoon he told us to go with him to the synagogue. I expect you've seen it, rabbi? It's a fine building, only recently built. It must have cost a lot. Money can be found for everything, but not for us. The place was full. Many of those he had fed miraculously were present. They surrounded him in the vestibule, and wanted to know how and when he had crossed the sea, for they had been looking for him. But he wouldn't tell them.

'He said, harshly, as though they deserved the reproach: "You've been searching for me because you were given bread. Seek other bread, and when you eat it you will never be hungry again."

' "Where can we buy it?" they asked.

'He said: "Believe what I tell you, and you'll be given it."

' "Show us a sign that your words are true," the people asked. "Moses sent our fathers manna from heaven. Work us another miracle with bread."

'I quietly encouraged them. "Quite right," I said. "He can do it. And he will do it; you've only got to ask him."

'But he didn't seem to like what they said, and brusquely replied: "It wasn't Moses that sent the manna in the wilderness, but your Father. And today He is again giving you bread, only this time it is the life of the world."

' "Then tell us where to look for it," they exclaimed. "Is it the bread you gave us yesterday? If so, give it to us again."

'I saw him compress his lips and screw up his eyes. "I am that bread," he said firmly. The people started back, for the remark was quite unpleasant, even repellent. But he went on as though determined to upset them even more: "The man

147

to whom I give myself will never be hungry again." They looked at one another and shrugged their shoulders. "I see you don't want to believe me," he cried. "Yet that is the reason why I have come down from heaven: so that not one of you should perish."

'They started to shout: "What is he saying? He comes from heaven? Does he think we don't know who he is and where he comes from? We all know he's the son of Joseph the carpenter. His mother is still living in Bethsaida. What is he calling himself bread for? Has he gone mad?"

'He silenced them with: "Cease your murmuring! No one will find his way to me whom the Father has not first given me. But you have the words of the Father, and you should know your way to me. I tell you: the man who believes in me has found everlasting life. Yes, I am the bread. Your fathers ate manna, but they died. Whoever eats of me will not die!"

'Now the crowd were jeering angrily and indignantly: "You're talking bosh! What are you trying to put over us? Whoever heard of eating human flesh? You're mad! Would you prefer us to eat you raw, or cooked?"

'The admiration and respect they had felt for him after that last miracle crumbled down like a wall of clay. My presentiment had been sound: that moment had been unique. Now it was too late. They sneered and laughed at him. And this was in Capernaum, where he had always been listened to readily. The President of the Assembly vainly tried to defend him. But he didn't want anyone's defence.

'Instead of holding his tongue, he said again with a desperate fervour: "I tell you: if you don't eat my body and drink my blood you will not rise again from the dead. For my blood is the only true drink and my body is the only true bread."

'Anywhere else, these words might have led to his being thrown out of the synagogue. But in Capernaum he has Jairus and some of the elders on his side. So the people only spat down at his feet and left him, commenting: "We've heard enough of this rubbish. Who can understand what he's raving about?"

'The only people left standing by him were we disciples and the few who regularly accompany him. But as if it were not enough to have frightened off the ordinary people, he turned to us: "Are you offended too?" he asked. "But then what will happen later?" He shook his head. "It is the spirit that quickens, not the flesh. But my words are spirit. Even among you there are some who do not believe."

'I looked around those who were left. One or two shrugged their shoulders and walked away. The few left with him were like a handful of snow set on a stone in the sun. What made him behave like that? What is he after? Does he want us to believe in him? I believed, and I still believe, that if he wished he could bring about great changes. But he doesn't wish it. I tell you, rabbi, he's become a coward; he's betrayed the cause. But even now you haven't heard all. Listen to the end, and you'll see that I'm right.'

He was so excited that he was shouting, forgetful of his caution when he had first entered my room.

'When we left the synagogue only we twelve were with him. He walked in front with his head bowed, sad and silent. Perhaps then he realized what he had done by his imprudent words. Suddenly he turned to us and whispered: "Come!" We left Capernaum at once, without telling anyone where and why we were going. He hurried us to the heathen parts around Sidon. We were lost among the unclean like needles in a haystack. I feel sure he realized that he had failed, and he fled in fear of the dangers threatening him. Possibly only then did he realize that dangers lay in wait for him everywhere. All these years we have shifted from spot to spot like hunted animals. But this was a flight in terror.

'We always spent the night in the open, and when we moved among people it was only to buy bread, or rather, to beg for it, for we had no money. But we rarely succeeded in begging: the Syro-Phoenicians can't stand us Israelites. So we went hungry most of the time. He turned on his tracks and twisted this way and that, as though trying to put a hunter off the scent. He worked no miracles; the only one he performed was when he healed a child of some heathen woman who wouldn't take his "no" for an answer. After wandering about for several days we returned to Galilee. But we slipped past the towns secretly, not showing ourselves in public. The heathens of Decapolis heard that he was near at hand and came out in a multitude for him to heal their sick. He worked many miracles, talked to them, and finally fed them miraculously. The unclean heathens were filled with seven loaves of bread, and four baskets of fragments were picked up afterwards. But we went about with empty bellies! He hasn't a ha'porth of common-sense. He feeds strangers, and lets his own people starve. Then we took a boat and we sailed to Bethsaida. There he only saw his mother and healed some blind wretch. That was the last miracle he worked. The thought occurred to me that his powers were beginning to leave him. Previously a single word of his had been sufficient to heal people and even raise them from the dead. This time he had to spit into the man's eyes as though he were some magician; and when he asked if the man could see, the fellow had to confess that he couldn't see at all well. Only after Jesus had touched his eyes did he see properly. I was filled with more and more gloomy forebodings.

'We didn't even spend the night in Bethsaida; he drove us northward that very same day. We wandered along the path beneath the cliff by the Jordan side. He talked to us a great deal, but I noticed that he didn't tell us anything new. He repeated his old homilies and parables, explaining them all over again. Now I felt sure a change had occurred in him. He was like a man who knows he has to die, and so spends his time only in consolidating what he has already succeeded in doing. We came to the deep ravine where the Jordan flows in a thin, silver torrent over the black rocks. Here at last the teacher slowed his steps. He allowed us to rest in the plentiful grass or to sit on the stones above the foaming river. He himself went off alone for hours on end to pray. He prayed more than ever before. He seemed troubled and very sorrowful. It's those disciples of his that are the cause of it all. It's through them that he's become a nobody. Now Zion will go on being run by the rich, the priests, the Sadducees . . .'

He stopped suddenly: I'm sure it was only to avoid saying: '. . . and the Pharisees.'

'We passed through the forest and skirted Caesarea. Outside the town there is a lofty cliff, with water flowing from its foot. In the cliff is a deep, gloomy hole, which leads to the depths of hell. The heathens throw flowers into this hole and say they are paying tribute to their gods. We approached the cliff with loathing, fearfully. But he must needs decide to stop just there. He hadn't said a word to us all that day. Now he called up around him, and asked: "Whom do the people say I am?"

'We looked at one another. The people are saying such different things about him, these days. Antipas's servants declare he is John risen from the dead; and apparently the tetrarch himself believes it. Others say he's Elias, or Jeremiah or Hezekiah. We told him these things, but he listened with his head bowed, his eyes fixed on the water gushing out of the cliff. Suddenly he raised his head. He looked at us as a man looks when his fate depends on the words he is about to hear. I rather felt that he turned to me first. He asked sharply, firmly, like a man testing the strength of some instrument: "But whom do you think I am?"

'As I say, I had the feeling that it was me he was really asking. After all, I'm the only one of his disciples who has some understanding of life and has seen the world. But what could I reply? If he'd asked us immediately after the miracle of the bread I shouldn't have hesitated: he convinced me then that he was the Messiah. But the Messiah will not turn weak before victory. The Messiah cannot know defeat! After all that had happened could I say he was a great miracle-worker? He had worked two marvellous miracles. But apart from miracles, what is he? No one, nothing. I thought his question was rather uncalled for. The others didn't know what to say either.

'But suddenly Simon bawled as though he hadn't noticed the things that had happened during the past few days: "You're the Messiah and the son of the All Highest." '

Judas cleared his throat, and stroked his scanty beard with the fingers of both hands. I was all ears. I was rather astonished to note that my heart was beating violently.

'There was a dead silence,' Judas continued, 'for none of us had made such a declaration before. I hadn't the least idea how Jesus would react to this injudicious remark. His eyes rested on Simon's face. The son of Jonas stood with mouth gaping, smiling foolishly in his confusion. Suddenly it seemed as though all the fears, anxieties and sorrows I had seen in the teacher's face during the past few days vanished completely. It lit up with joy. And when he smiles, everything seems to smile.

'He raised both hands above Simon's head. "The blessing of the All Highest," he said slowly and seriously, "be upon you, Simon. It was not you who confessed what you have just said, but my Father who told you to say it. But for this reason I give you today a new name: henceforth you will be called Cephas, and upon this rock I shall build my church, my kingdom, and the gates of Gehenna shall not prevail against it. And I shall give you the key of the kingdom, and you shall open and close everything with that key. What you open on earth shall be opened in heaven; and what you close on earth shall be closed in heaven." '

'What a promise!' I exclaimed. 'And fancy making it to him!'

'You're right, rabbi!' Judas assented. 'He has made that fool, that unclean boor first after himself. It will be a small church that he wants to build, in any case. If he were to die there would only be twelve of us left to build it – and not even twelve. I wouldn't remain a single hour under the leadership of Simon Cephas! Some rock! A man who's a fool and a sinner!'

'I suppose Simon's grown unbearably proud now?' I asked.

'I see you know him, rabbi,' Judas laughed bitterly and maliciously. 'In fact he at once upset the teacher . . . But I must finish. We had hardly recovered from the shock of hearing Simon thus exalted when Jesus sat down on the grass and began to say that he had to go to Jerusalem, and that there the scribes, priests and elders would kill him . . .'

'Kill him?' I exclaimed. 'I think he exaggerates. But he may be right. Everybody here hates him since he healed that man at the pool of Bethesda. Even the beggars.' (I don't think I've mentioned before that since he worked that miracle the water has not been troubled again. The people have lost all hope of any further miracle there.) 'But if he feels that he is in danger of death he shouldn't come here.'

'He says he must, and that it is necessary for him to suffer. He said: "What if a man should gain the whole world, if he loses himself in the gaining of it?"'

'He must be mad!' I cried. 'If a man perishes he will gain nothing.'

'You see now what has happened to him!' Judas raised his hands above his head and shook his fists. 'Even that super-wise leader Cephas realized how senseless it was. But he's now very proud and he drew the teacher aside to direct his attention to the nonsense he was talking. But as soon as Jesus heard what Peter was saying he shouted angrily: "Be gone! Get behind me with your temptations, Satan." Then he seemed to recover himself, and added: "You don't know what comes from God and what from man." He turned to us and said: "Listen, children! Any of you who wants to follow me must take up his cross and carry it as I am carrying mine . . ."'

'So he's talking of a cross again!' I said more to myself than to Judas.

'He's always talking about a cross. A fine symbol for a church! True, he says he'll rise again. He even said we shan't die until we have seen him coming in glory.'

'A poor and uncertain consolation!' I muttered. I was experiencing what Judas, too, must have felt: a terrible sorrow that robbed one of all desire to live. My despair over Ruth returned, rendered all the more intense by this feeling of sorrow. The world seemed as gloomy as if it were the depths of winter.

'And what did the disciples say to that?' I asked at last.

'They lost heart. They fidgeted from foot to foot, and looked at one another in perplexity. Yes, it's poor consolation to have to wait for a miracle when his power has vanished and may not come back. I wondered whether I ought not to go off and leave him altogether. I assure you others of us were thinking the same.

'He noticed that, and asked: "And do you, too, wish to desert me?"

'Then Simon spoke up, humbly and diffidently: "But where shall we go? And to whom shall we turn, since we have believed that you, rabbi, are the Messiah?"

'He rested his head on his hands and seemed sorrowful and agitated again. "Yes," he said quietly, "I have chosen twelve to be my followers, but one of them is a devil."

'Simon must have heard that remark as I heard it, for he hung his head. I'm sure he realized that the teacher was thinking of him.'

'So you went away and left him?' I asked.

'No. If they were to leave him now they really wouldn't know what to do with themselves. Nor have I left him. I shall go back and see how things go. Who knows, he may recover his power. But if he does I shall seize him by the hand . . . Those fools won't stop me a second time.'

He slipped out of my house as he had come: quietly, cautiously. He returned to his master, of whom he has such doubts, and I turned back to the illness before which I am impotent. The world is still like a gloomy, rainy day, so far as I'm concerned. For if he has lost the power to restore people to health, where can I look for help for Ruth?

154

. . . For the first time I saw a look of utter apathy in her face. She was not interested in my return. She gently pouted her lips, as though blowing me a kiss. But nothing interested her: neither my talk nor what I had brought back with me. I shall always remember her as I saw her at that moment: her black hair scattered over the pillow, one terribly thin arm half raised in the attempt to wave to me.

Yet that same evening I felt that hope had returned. 'I don't believe things are quite so bad,' Luke assured me. 'She's very weak, but . . .'

I clutched hungrily at his words. In order to get through the night, I tried to believe that the thing I dreaded was not coming yet . . . How can one sleep when one is sure that the morrow will bring that? I tried to swallow down the doctor's words as though they were a sleeping draught, so that I could close my eyes and not wake up until . . . it was all over. I was utterly exhausted. I dropped into a heavy, dreamless sleep.

I was snatched out of that sleep by a cry. Not for one moment had I any doubt what it meant. I started up trembling, sober, but ready to face anything that came. I was called to her. The time was early morning; it was grey and cold. I dressed carefully, as though about to go on a journey. I was almost astonished when I was told that everything seemed to indicate the end was near, but there was no certainty yet. Instead of sending a servant for Luke, I went myself. I walked along as though in a dream. The early morning mist was thick and clinging. My mind functioned; it registered impressions: what a lot of people were about so early in the morning! Surely not all of them had a dear one dying? But of course not: they were craftsmen going off to work, or merchants seeking goods, or beggars, or customs officers. Jerusalem is full of such people. In the daytime you hardly notice them. But why should I concern myself with them? Or with the world at all, for that matter? Ruth was dying. Dying? I had been watching her die for three years. What good would life be without her, or even without this constant anxiety for her health? Yet perhaps everything would come to an end with her death? Perhaps I would die too? What tie with life would I have then? My work? My homilies? Footling things: I had wasted my life. I should have spent all my time with her. No, no: I had to defend myself. I must be sensible. Man isn't created for that sort of existence. Every one of us has some work to do. My homilies had their purpose. If the All Highest hadn't wanted me to write them He would not have directed my life so inexorably along a single road. Could I have been other than I am? Yes, and no. I could have been if I had found something else in life. Even a little satisfaction . . . But every joy I had was changed to bitterness. I had had Ruth, and Ruth was dying. Fame, recognition, esteem, were all distant echoes, of which I could never feel certain. Wealth? How often I had thanked the Eternal for giving me wealth! Yet what had come of it? I hadn't been able to save Ruth.

I dreamed of arms embracing me, and of weeping out all my sorrow in that embrace; of palms that would ease the pain with their touch.

In vain! I was alone, alone with my grief and my faith in the Eternal. O Adonai! Never before had I realized what a terrible test His Invisibility is to our hearts. Only tangible arms, only the genuine touch of a hand could have rid me of my sorrowing despair. Though even then I did not really despair. Despair is the rejection of hope. I had not rejected hope, it had left me of itself. It had left me in a wilderness in which there was no place even for revolt.

A paralytic was brought to Jesus one day. There was a great crowd of people around the house; it was impossible to get near him. But the afflicted man's kinsmen were determined to obtain the teacher's aid. They carried him up to the roof, tore a hole in it, and let him down at Jesus's feet. He was not in the least surprised; he looked at the man as though he did not see his complaint, or perhaps saw some other complaint invisible to anyone else. He said: 'You are freed of your sins.' But then he said something more, and the man got up.

I did not tear open any roof in order to let Ruth down at his feet. On the contrary, when everybody else was seeking his aid and his strength I agreed to share his weakness. He said then: 'You have too many cares . . . take my cross on yourself . . .' How could I know that his cross was also every man's cross, and that when I thought I would free myself of my cross by giving it to him he would turn to me with his cross? This is his Truth . . .

The sun rose over the hills and the Levites sounded the trumpets. I halted to repeat: 'Hear, O Israel . . .' But the familiar, daily prayer died on my lips. Instead of saying: 'Hear, O Israel: the Lord our God is one God,' the cry broke from my heart: 'Adonai! Give me back my Ruth!' I stood there repeating those words endlessly. But suddenly an unknown force closed my mouth, stifled that cry. I felt myself going numb; I thought I was going out of my mind. I was dying and I could not die. The pain which had been circling around me like a hungry beast of prey now sprang on me and fastened all its talons in my heart. Vaguely, as though through mist, I realized that there was only one word more I could say, one word I must say. It was my only hope. With lips that knocked against each other like two pieces of wood I whispered: 'If it is your demand, come and take her . . .' I felt that I was disintegrating like a sunbaked roof under the blows of sticks and feet. It was not that I was carrying her through the roof down to the room where he was teaching: I myself was the house, and it was through my lacerated body that he accomplished his deed.

I ran upstairs. I ran swiftly, but my thoughts ran more swiftly. Ruth was sitting up. But that was because she was being supported. Her eyes had fled under her upper lids, her mouth was not closed, I saw the teeth between her lips. I saw everything: thousands of details which I had never noticed before. Then they allowed her to fall back. That was no longer Ruth. It was a small, crumpled integument. I touched the hand, not yet cold. It was no longer her hand.

Where is Ruth? Where are you? It cannot be that you do not exist. I know that you do . . . I know, I feel that . . . But where? I always wanted to go before you, to clear all dangers from your path. Now it is you who have gone first . . . The wailing women are screaming round your body, the musicians are beating their drums and playing their piercing pipes. I know it is so, but I hear nothing. I, too, have died.

No. I have not died. I am suffering, so I am still alive.

That paralytic man went away healed. Nothing will ever repair the roof of my body. I am a house left wide open to the rain and the sun.

DEAR JUSTUS,   FOURTEENTH LETTER.

Forgive my long silence. It was difficult for me to write. Time passed, but I remained outside it, like an island which the current speeds past. But no, I did not remain outside it. The current bore me along as if I were a piece of dry wood. And now autumn is coming to its end. The heat is gone, and only the dry, cloddy or dusty earth retains the memory of the summer torment. Clouds are gathering in the sky, and every day they are heavier. But meanwhile the air is dry and stifling. Of an evening the wind raises clouds of crimson dust, shakes the fig trees; it flies into the city and rustles the withered leaves of the boughs used for the booths during the Feast of Tabernacles. All the gardens, yards, and squares are littered with them. The festival has arrived and for two days all the men have been sleeping and eating outside their homes. Yesterday evening the city flamed with thousands of fires, and there was a great dance in the Temple courtyard. Many pilgrims have arrived: the streets are filled with people laughing, singing, waving branches of lemon, palm, willow, and myrtle, and crying, 'Hallelu Hoshiannah!'

I cannot be merry. My lips do not utter the words: 'I thank Thee, for Thou hast heard me and become my salvation. Praise the Lord for He is good.' This festive joy irritates me. This cheerful festival of the harvest could equally well be called the festival of death. Choked with the heat, the earth is panting like an ass worn out with labour. The dried up torrents are a miserable sight. Everything is dead: only man has remained alive. Why cannot he lay down his head and die too? And not be wrested from sleep each morning by the same, constantly reviving cry in the heart.

Ruth is no more: life has remained. I hate it! Not only because it pricks my breast, but because, after months of struggle, when it seemed that the hand of death was laid on my life too, it is beginning to rise up and revive. Though I do not wish it, hopes are beginning to quicken within me. I cannot stand this intermingling of life and death! Man should live only so long as he wishes to. We are like trees: we die, but then the rains come and the cold, and after that the spring and the sun, and we must blossom again. Every weeping is followed by joy. But I don't want it. Ruth will not revive. I want to remain till the end with my sorrow, my open wound. What if it does heal over? To what end? Is someone envious even of my pain?

Now I don't care whether I see Jesus again or not. And yet my heart beat more violently when John the son of Zebedee called to see me, the day before the Feast of Tabernacles. I should hate every memory that has any link with the time when I followed the teacher like a dumb beggar who implores compassion. None the less, I was glad to see John. Something assuaging and soothing (though simultaneously wounding and troubling) has passed from the teacher to his disciples. Their simple faces, their awkward movements seem to retain a fraction of his power. Besides, John has an attractive face: hand-some, and even thoughtful. I have more than once asked myself whence this common unclean youngster derived this delicacy of feature. He bowed respectfully, and I greeted him warmly. I invited him to sit down, and ordered bread, fruit, and honey to be brought. He broke the flat cakes of bread with his hands in just the same way as the teacher breaks bread.

'What news have you brought?' I asked. 'What is Jesus doing? You must warn him that his enemies in Jerusalem are far from diminishing . . .'

He replied in a rather mysterious tone:

'The teacher is coming to the city for the festival.'

I expressed my astonishment. Such thoughtlessness would have a bad result. Though Jesus had not been in Jerusalem for eighteen months, hatred for him was still growing. His life might be endangered. And who would defend him? The crowd? An unreliable ally! But what had happened to his power? Was it true that it had grown feebler since the two great miracles of the bread?

'Yes. The teacher hasn't worked a miracle for a long time,' John admitted. 'These days he avoids people, and only has us with him. We, too, thought he shouldn't come. When his "brothers" said he ought to go to Jerusalem and let the world see who he was he replied that he would not, because his time was not yet come. But after they set out, he told me and Judah to gather the women: his mother and mine, Alpheus's widow, Joanna the wife of Chuz, and to go and celebrate the Feast of Tabernacles in Jerusalem. He said no more; but I know that when he sends his mother anywhere he will be following her soon after. I am certain he'll come.'

'So you've brought her here?'

'Yes, rabbi. And I have to ask you something in connection with her arrival: would you take the teacher's mother and her sister into your house? The city is so crowded with people that it's difficult to find a suitable place where she can stay. She doesn't want anything special, but I can't find anything for her.

And she's his mother. She would be comfortable in your house, rabbi . . .'

'Very willingly. The house is large, and empty. Bring her along, and she will lack nothing.'

I felt like adding: if he comes he can stay here too. But I stopped myself. If I had put him up and the news had leaked out that he was sheltering in my house the consequences to myself might have been serious. I would have drawn part of the hatred for him upon myself. And perhaps I'd rather not see him here. He didn't seem to understand when I wanted him to cure Ruth. Now it's too late his presence would be hardly bearable.

John brought both the women to my house the same evening. I had been curious to know what Jesus's mother looked like. But when she came in I was amazed. She is altogether different from what I had imagined. There is nothing at first sight to distinguish her from any ordinary unclean woman in the crowd, with her face sun-tanned and wind-burnt. One feature is striking: she gives the impression that she is still a maiden. A woman who has a grown-up son, and who has had to work hard all her life, too often looks like a worn-out old crone. She has retained the full bloom of youth: a flower which has blossomed and has remained immaculate in its blossoming. Her sister is younger than she, but she looks old enough to be her grandmother. Mary has vivid black eyes, and smiles cross her face like sunlight over fields. There is a great likeness to her son. But her face is womanly, and expressive of devotion and trust. She seems to be continually listening and waiting for something. Every woman waits for love, and the fruits of love. But she has both these behind her. So what is she still waiting for?

Her voice is pleasant, but it has a note of resolution. She doesn't talk much, and her tone is low. She must be fond of children, for as soon as she appears in the street she is surrounded by a throng of black-haired, half-naked infants, who talk to her as though they had known her for years. She is a true matriarch: she should have lots of children and grand-children around her. One son is too few for her.

She was smiling as she entered my house, and with her arrival the sorrowful atmosphere was lightened somewhat. She is very amiable, yet she is by no means free of anxieties. I feel sure she lives in constant fear for her son. Yet she seems to be quite free of any feeling of bitterness or irritation, anger or reproach.

The morning after their arrival I went on to the housetop at dawn and turned my face to the Temple, to say the 'Shema.' I was astonished to find that she was already there. She was standing gazing at the view extending before her. From my house you can see the Temple and the city in all their splendour. The Mount of Olives presented a compact mass of black olive trees beneath the high, light blue sky. Over its crest runs the road to Bethany. The rampart of hills rises level with the height of the city wall; the white and gold Temple towers above the crowded houses on the slope. Through the colonnade above the Tyropeon valley one can see the courtyard, barred with a low, inner wall, the steps leading up to the Sanctuary, and the enormous façade throwing a rosy shadow over the Temple roof. The brawl of the Levites' silver trumpets sounded four times. I bowed my head and, drawing the tallith down over my brow, prayed concentratedly. After my prayers I was about to go down again, when something made me speak to her. She has that same evocative quality which her son possesses: she, too, seems to be saying, 'Ask, and I can answer you.'

'How are you, Mary?' I asked. 'Have you rested well after your journey?'

'Thank you, rabbi,' she smiled her pleasant smile. 'I came up before dawn to see the first ray of sunlight falling on the Temple. It is beautiful, isn't it?'

'You don't often visit Jerusalem?'

'Not now. But I lived in the Temple for years.'

'Why, what were you doing there?'

'I was among the children dedicated to the service of the All

Highest. I was only a few years old then. I was my parents' first child, and they had lost all hope of having children. They wanted to show their gratitude to the Lord, so they presented me to the Temple. It brought me great happiness.'

'And then the priests gave you in marriage?' I asked.

'I went to the house of Joseph the carpenter,' she replied.

'But your husband is no longer living, is he?'

'No.'

I caught a note of sorrow in her voice, and a shadow slipped over her face. In this respect, too, she is like her son: in their lives sorrow and joy seem to be intertwined like wild vines. But perhaps it is that sorrow is only another aspect of joy, and joy another aspect of sorrow?

'No,' she repeated. 'He has not lived to see the great day . . .'

'Death,' I said bitterly, 'lies in wait most of all for those we loved the best.'

She raised her head, and I read anxiety in her glance. When someone mentions death I think of Ruth, but she undoubtedly thinks of her son. She said emphatically, like someone dispelling a presentiment with words of reason:

'He will overcome death . . .'

'Who will?'

'The Messiah,' she whispered.

I went closer to her (though I still observed the prescribed seven paces).

'He will overcome death?' I asked. 'Is your son then the Messiah?'

The sun rose higher, casting a pleasant, autumnal warmth. She laid one hand on the stone balustrade. She did not look at me, but seemed to be meditating over her reply. She said slowly, with many pauses:

'I'm only a woman . . . You, rabbi, should know. You know the Scriptures, the prophets. I . . .' She hesitated, as though uncertain whether to put her thoughts into speech. 'I have gained so much . . . He has done the greatest of things for me. For a simple maiden like myself. All Israel was entreating what I asked for. I shall never understand why He chose me . . . Perhaps you understand that, rabbi? I can only rejoice and sing that He is great, merciful, good, exalting the humble and visiting the poor.'

She was silent, but her words must have flowed on in her thoughts. The words I had heard were like sparkles on a river surface, which betray the course of its current, but tell you nothing of its depth. Her gaze slipped past the Temple and was fixed on the black mass of the olive trees.

'You haven't answered me,' I said. 'Is he the Messiah?'

'It's you who should know,' she repeated. 'I know only that some day all people will say of me: "Blessed is she, and filled with the grace of the Lord." ' (She said these words confidently, yet with a hint of shame in speaking thus of herself.) 'But before that my heart will be pierced with seven swords . . .'

There's no denying that his closest and most intimate friends are an extraordinary lot. When I ask them if he is the Messiah they seem to agree, but they do it as though his Messianic mission were only a part – and that not the most important part – of the truth concerning him. Do they regard him as the Messiah or don't they? Yet he blessed Simon when he declared he was the Messiah; but almost in the same breath he spoke of torture, death, a cross . . .

'But surely he has told you what he thinks of himself? He's your son . . .'

She shook her head. 'I've never asked him,' she made the amazing confession, 'and he has never spoken to me about it. Who am I to ask? I only gaze at him and link everything I see and hear in my memory, like olive stones on a string.'

'But during all the years he was living with you . . .'

'During all those years he was only my child. The most beautiful child in the world, as the firstborn always is to its mother. I have often felt like deciding that what happened in the beginning was only a dream from which I awoke to life. But today I think it is life itself that is the dream. And the reality was in the beginning and now is again . . .'

'So you say the years you spent with him were different?' I asked, increasingly inquisitive. 'They had nothing miraculous about them? They were just ordinary?'

'Very ordinary,' she agreed.

'And how do you reconcile yourself to the present-day reality?' I exclaimed.

She sighed quietly. 'If I didn't have these few stringed stones,' she said, 'I don't know how things would go. One may receive a gift from heaven, but it doesn't last a lifetime. It hardly seems enough.'

'He works many miracles,' I remarked.

'Yes. But one miracle must suffice for each. The kingdom comes into being only once for each . . .'

'I have never seen him in that light,' I muttered. My sorrow returned as I thought of the days when I had followed him around, but hadn't found words to ask him to heal Ruth.

'Have you heard, rabbi, his parable of the kingdom: how it is like a seed dropped into the soil, which sprouts and grows day and night, while the farmer is busy with other matters? Perhaps what we are waiting for has already come to pass? That was how it was with me. Before I could even utter the words: "Let it be as you have said," he was living within me.'

'What do you mean, Mary?' Her words seemed like the gleam of a lamp suddenly lighting up a great, gloomy palace.

She bowed her head. A flush spread over her swarthy face. She replied in a quivering voice:

'I'm thinking of when the angel Gabriel came to tell me he would be born . . .'

'You saw an angel? Tell me all about it, will you? I believe in angels; I shan't laugh at you,' I hastened to reassure her.

She smiled at me gratefully.

'I saw him as clearly as I see you, rabbi. It was morning, and the sun was just rising above the hills of Gilead. It was the month of Adar. I was standing at my loom. I am a good weaver,' she said proudly. 'That morning the work went even better than usual. Suddenly I felt that there was someone in the room with me. I was seized with fear; I cried out, and looked up. There he was standing in front of me: a shining figure, with wings. I knew at once who he was. My heart beat so fast I pressed my hand to it. He appeared to bow to me, like a servant to his master. I couldn't believe it. It was I who should have bowed down to him, to thank him for allowing me to see him. But I couldn't move. I heard his voice: "Greetings, woman who art filled with grace, and blessed among women . . ." I didn't know what to say. For a moment I thought he had come to punish me. I was about to fall to my knees. But I was terrified to see him kneeling before me.

' "Be not afraid," he said. "You will bear a son, and you shall call him Jesus. He will be your son and the son of the Most High. The Lord will give Him the throne of his father David, and his kingdom shall never have an end."

' "How can this be?" I whispered. "I have asked Joseph, and he has agreed . . ."

'He held out his hand as though to stop me. "Say but the word, and it shall be. Is there anything He cannot do? But today all His power depends on your word, Mary."

'I felt as though the earth were shaking under my feet. I knew I could accept or reject the gift offered to me. He asked, he did not command. I was sure that if I said "I dare not," I should find myself standing alone at my loom and the time of waiting would continue. But if I were to say, "Yes," from that moment the stars and the sun would shine differently, the grass would grow differently, the age-old promise given to our father Abraham would be fulfilled. The time of waiting would come to an end. Was I to know that the miraculous transformation would be achieved so imperceptibly, as though nothing had happened? But even if I had known I should have spoken in accordance with His will. For it was His will. And so it was that even before I said to the angel: "So be it," it was accomplished.'

'Then whose son is he?' I asked in consternation.

She bowed her head, like a dutiful wife subject to her husband's will.

'He is His . . .' Then, smiling with a pride that was nigh to rapture: 'And mine . . .'

'But what of your husband, Mary?' What she had said opened new, dazzling horizons. Even the sun seemed less bright, and the Temple less magnificent, in that light.

There was a tender and sincere look in her eyes as she said: 'Dear, good Joseph . . . But I couldn't tell him even then, though I knew how much it would cost him when he found out. He loved me with the true love that demands nothing. He had agreed to all I asked. But how could he foresee that the place he resigned would be occupied by someone else? He had agreed that he would be no more than my protector. He had renounced me . . . And he was justified in expecting the same sacrifice from me. I did not make that sacrifice. An even greater renunciation was demanded of him than he had made. The terrible moment arrived when in his eyes I read that he had discovered the secret. My throat was choked with a sob, but even then I could not tell him. How could I confess to receiving such unjustified grace? How much I would have given to press his head against my breast and tell him that to me he would always be as he had been. But I could not. His eyes filled with suffering, he dragged himself to the next room. I couldn't get to sleep for a long time that night. I thought I could hear his weeping. I lay filled with regret that I could do nothing to help him. At last I fell asleep.

'In the morning, when I awoke, sorrow and anxiety awoke with me. I got up slowly, and slowly set about my tasks. I delayed the moment when I knew Joseph would enter the room. I trembled at the thought that I would see him suffering, and I be unable to help. I heard his footsteps, and my heart beat faster. He came in. I looked at him, ready to despair . . . and I was suddenly possessed by a tremendous, rapturous joy. He stood there kind, joyful, renewed in spirit. He hummed as he went to the bench. I heard the brave swish of his plane, the grinding of the drills, the ringing tap of the hammer. He was absorbed in his work. When it was finished he gave it a close scrutiny, as though he regretted having to part from it. Then he raised his head. I saw the look of triumph change to one of pleasure. He caressed the smooth surface of the wood with his palm. He asked in a careless tone, as though concerning something long since known: "So your son is to be called Jesus?"'

'And he never desired you as wife after?' I asked.

'No,' she replied. 'He could keep his own counsel. I know it wasn't easy for him. Believe me, rabbi, we remained just two ordinary people. The kingdom grows slowly, imperceptibly in such as we. In Joseph it grew like a grain of mustard seed, which develops into a tree. When he died . . .'

'Then he told you what he had felt, I suppose?'

'Why should he have talked about that? The kingdom is in no need of words. He turned his eyes to him whom he called his son. He beckoned me over with a nod. He whispered: "I haven't taught him how to make wheels yet, Mary. And he's not too sure with the plane. He won't be able to earn a living at once. You will have to work . . ." That was his one anxiety when he died.'

Have you, Justus, understood the significance of her words, which I have tried to set down for you as faithfully as possible? If it is all true, who is this man who was born in a woman's pain and weakness, but was conceived by an incomprehensible gesture of the Almighty? I don't know; and I shall never learn. Was he, indeed, destined to be someone greater than man? I do understand that she is the way to the incomprehensible. If I'd known her while Ruth was still alive I should have been able to ask her. But must I again reproach myself for not doing something I could have done? No! I shall go mad if I go on doing that. She is the road which leads to the Unknown. Like the Golden Gate, which is the quickest route from the valley of Cedron to the Temple courtyard. They say that at one time it was walled up, and the prophet Ezekiel said that the Most High Himself would open it. And now, one might say that the prophecy has been fulfilled: the road is opened from the valley of dry bones to the Lord's altar. At times the old stories can be given strange interpretations.

That evening she said: 'I'm strangely excited. He has arrived in the city.' And, in fact, John came under cover of darkness (I have forbidden him to hang about near my house in the daytime) with the news that the teacher is in Jerusalem. What will come of this, I wonder? I am amazed at his thoughtlessness.

DEAR JUSTUS,   FIFTEENTH LETTER.

Judas was right: this man is challenging fate. What does he think he can achieve by it? Why does he deliberately provoke everybody? I have already told you, I think, that the Grand Council has taken the harshest of decisions in regard to him. And yesterday it was all but put into operation. The decision took me so completely by surprise that I was unable to do anything in his defence. He was saved only by an accident. He emerged from the crowd on the last day of the festival, like a cloud which appears unheralded in a clear sky. I was standing among the throng which had gathered in the synagogue to listen to instruction while waiting for the procession to set out, when I heard his voice. I would know it among a thousand. He unrolled the roll, and a whisper ran through the congregation: 'It's the prophet from Galilee. The one who has healed, has raised from the dead . . . The one they want to kill.' So even the common people know that he is threatened with death. But he didn't seem in the least disturbed. He began to read the psalm slowly, giving each word its due emphasis:

'Thou who art amazing in justice, hear us!
Thou art our salvation,
The hope of the earth and the waters,
The builder of the mountains girdled with strength,
The sea rages at Thy touch . . .'

He handed the roll back to the synagogue official, and looked at the people, whose eyes were fixed on him feverishly.

'Amazing in justice! But do you know what is the justice of the Most High? There was a farmer who went to the market-place early in the morning to hire labourers to pick the grapes in his vineyard. And he agreed to pay them one penny a day. But when the sun was high, about the third hour the man went again to the market-place and hired more labourers, promising to pay them a just wage. And he did the same at the sixth and the ninth hour. Late in the afternoon, at the eleventh hour he went to the market-place yet again, and finding men who had been standing about without work all day, he said to them: "Come to my vineyard." And they went. But when evening came and he had to pay his labourers, he summoned them to come to him. He began by paying those who had arrived last. He gave each of them a penny, so they went off blessing him and singing for joy. Then he paid those who had been hired at the ninth, the sixth, and the third hour. Each received a penny. So those who had worked all through the day expected to receive more. But they, too, received a penny. And they began to grumble.

'The man was astonished, and asked them: "What are you grumbling at? Have I done you any wrong? Didn't we agree on one penny?"

' "Yes," they answered. "But why did you give each of the others a penny too? We have toiled all day, and each has filled a barrel. And those others have hardly done more than press out a bunch of grapes. That's not fair!"

' "But I promised you a penny, and you agreed. A penny is a good wage for a day. Don't you agree?"

' "Yes," they admitted; "it's excellent pay."

' "Then why don't you take it and go away singing like the others?"

' "Because, after all, it isn't right that they should have had a penny too. They worked for only an hour. That's not fair."

' "Do you mean I'm not fair because I treated them well?"

the man asked. "Can't I show a kindness to the man who came last? Do you forbid me to do as I like with my own? Envy has stung you like a scorpion. I give every one of you good pay. And it pleases me to do so. So take your penny and go in peace. Go before I get annoyed with you."

'That is the justice of the Most High. It is a merciful justice in which the first is the last and the least — even those who have been searched for and compelled to come in — are the first. But why is it that these last are grateful, while the first, who have been in my Father's house all the time, feel no gratitude whatever?'

Someone jogged my arm. I looked round, and saw Judas. There was an angry expression on his face. It was almost as though he took the teacher's parable to his own heart. 'Now, you see, rabbi, he's really . . .'

The rest of his sentence was lost in the hubbub that arose. Not all the listeners had understood the story, but it aroused general admiration. The people nodded and said to one another: 'He's wise, he's learned. He's a true prophet. Where did he learn all this? Whose pupil was he?'

'Are you amazed at my teaching?' I heard Jesus say. He was still standing on the dais, as though he had something more to say. 'You ask who was my teacher? But this is not my teaching. I have a Teacher. The man who seeks his own glory speaks from himself. But I am not concerned with my own glory. I seek the glory of Him who taught me all things and who sent me. I speak His words. But you know that my words are true. For Moses also said so when he delivered the Law. But none of you wish to obey it.'

'None of us?' the cry broke from my lips. Others took it up indignantly. 'Do you say we don't want to obey the Law?' Cries of protest came from all sides. 'What right have you to say so? Who gave you permission to judge us? We observe the prescriptions . . .'

'You do not obey the Law,' he silenced them sternly. 'And so you wish to kill me.'

There was a moment's silence, then several shouted: 'We want to kill you? You're mad! Who wants to kill you?'

But I noticed that many were silent, evidently recalling the threats which had been made against him.

'You,' he said inflexibly. 'And why? Because I cured a man on the Sabbath two years ago? But circumcisions are performed on the Sabbath, and you justify that by the desire to win a new soul for Israel. But isn't a man's life important enough for you?'

The synagogue was filled with hubbub. Everybody was shouting.

'What's he saying? He's mad. He's always breaking the Sabbath. They said this man would die if he came to Jerusalem. But here he is speaking openly, afraid of nothing. Drive him out! Stone him! But he's the Messiah. Only the Messiah could work such miracles. Some Messiah! The Scriptures say the Messiah will come no man knows whence, but we all know this fellow comes from Galilee . . .'

His voice rose above the tumult like a bird calling through a storm: 'You know quite well who I am and whence I come. Have trust in me, believe in me. I do not speak from myself and do not proclaim my own teaching. I have brought you the words of Him whom you know not. But I know Him, because I have come from Him.'

'D'you hear that?' a voice cried. 'He says he comes from the Most High. He's blaspheming.'

I noticed that there were Pharisees among the crowd; they took up the shout and called: 'He's blaspheming. Crucify him! The blasphemer!'

I felt Judas's hand on my arm again. 'Didn't I tell you, rabbi?' he whispered feverishly. 'He wants them to kill him, and us with him! He's lost his courage; he's fled from his power. He's betrayed us. He called me a rich man . . .' In his excitement he squeezed my arm painfully. 'I, a rich man!' He snorted. 'That's the way he repays faithfulness to him.'

I failed to make sense of his further remarks, they were lost in the shouts of the crowd.

'Drive him out!' some were crying; evidently they did not wish to see bloodshed.

'You want to drive me out?' I heard him say. The crowd grew quiet, anxious to hear what he was saying. 'I shall not be much longer with you. But when I go away you will seek me in vain; for where I go you will not be able to follow. You will die in your sins . . .'

'Where is he intending to go to? Is he thinking of killing himself?' a voice asked, and it sounded to me like Judas.

'Perhaps he intends to go to the heathens,' someone else suggested.

'To give them more bread, I suppose!'

Suddenly a man pushed up to the dais and roared right into the teacher's face: 'Who are you?'

I recognized him, and felt a shiver of foreboding run down my back. This fellow was one of the senior guards of the Pharisees' Grand Council. A man named Gadi. And I noticed that several other watchmen, with sticks in their hands, were close behind him. Now I felt sure our brethren had decided to act swiftly and ruthlessly. I had little doubt that the crowd in the synagogue would not do anything to defend Jesus.

'Who are you?' the man repeated impatiently.

There was no look of anxiety or uncertainty on the teacher's face now. Was it that he didn't realize the danger threatening him? He fixed his deep black eyes on the man.

'I am the beginning,' he said. He raised his head and looked around the crowded synagogue. 'But you have rejected this beginning. Only when you lift me up will you be convinced that I am who I am, and my words are the words of my Father. For I always do as He desires. But He will never leave me.'

The crowd had stopped shouting. They stood with staring eyes and gaping mouths. They didn't understand a word he said. The guard scratched himself behind his ear in perplexity. 'What is he getting at? What is he talking about?' I heard whispers. I myself would gladly have asked what he meant. It suddenly flashed through my mind that by the 'beginning' he must mean the beginning of something new. The world I lived in before I met him was old. He brought something new. It began with him. So perhaps that's what he meant? Yet in that case he was foretelling something or someone who had yet to come.

'Then who are you?' the guard asked yet again. But the teacher made no answer. He raised his hand above his head, like the priest who a moment or two later would be carrying a silver pitcher of water through the Golden Gate. He began to speak in his tone of fervent appeal, the tone which might be a request, or might be a command: 'If any of you are thirsty, let him come to me. I shall give him drink . . .'

Through the walls of the synagogue came the sounds of trumpets, flutes, and pipes, and the first words of the hymn:

> 'Hallelujah!
> Praise Him, all ye servants of the Lord.
> Praise His Name.
> May it be blessed and honoured for ever and ever . . .'

The crowd fidgeted impatiently. It was time to go and join the procession. But the teacher held them fettered by his words:

'If any of you are thirsty, let him believe in me and he will not suffer thirst any longer. A river of the living water will flow from his heart. Don't you remember Ezekiel's promise: "When that stream comes, every creature will revive!"?'

But the crowd was attracted by the music and singing, and they began to leave the synagogue. Only a small group remained. I saw the guards whispering to one another and looking about them. I grew anxious, for I suspected they would attack him at any moment now. But they only nodded to one another and went out. I felt relieved. I, too, could go now. I didn't stop to hear him to the end, but went thoughtfully towards the entrance.

Yet I still felt a weight on my heart. I felt sure that there was a good deal of truth in what Judas had said. Jesus does genuinely seem to be courting danger. Formerly he spoke simply, gently; now he speaks as though determined to upset everybody.

I decided that as soon as the solemnities were ended I would go to the Grand Council to see what was being plotted against Jesus. I went out into the sunlight and joined the procession as it made its way down the hill towards Siloh, waving branches and singing:

'Behold the Gate of the Eternal!
Behold the Gate of the Just!
We thank Thee that Thou hast been pleased to hear us,
And hast deigned to save us.'

In the Grand Council I found a large gathering of all our most worthy brethren. They were standing round Jonathan bar Azziel, who was shouting something at a man huddled on the ground at his feet. I recognized the man as Gadi.

'You fool! You dog! You unclean lout!' the learned doctor was shouting. 'Didn't I tell you exactly what you had to do? You'll soon know what reward you have gained. We shall wipe you out, and all your family with you. Is this how you repay the kindness we have shown you?' He kicked the man in the face. 'I'll teach you to disobey! Don't you know who we are? There's not a man in all Judaea who could escape if we decided on his death! You were dying of hunger when we took you into our service, and you'll die of hunger when we throw you out!'

The man tried to press his lips to rabbi Jonathan's sandal. But the rabbi kicked him in the face again.

'Forgive me, most reverend rabbi!' Gadi groaned.

'You ask forgiveness, you dog? Then tell all this assembly why you didn't bring him here as we ordered.'

'I couldn't, great rabbi. I couldn't.'

'You couldn't? Why, did he set the mob on to you?'

'No. But we didn't dare . . .'

'You didn't dare? Did you hear him?' Jonathan turned indignantly to the brethren. 'They didn't dare! They were not afraid to disobey us. But they didn't dare to seize that accursed sinner and bring him to us!'

'Did you order them to do that?' I asked.

He turned and looked at me. I felt that some of the fury he felt for Gadi was directed at me as he said: 'Ah, so it's you, rabbi Nicodemus! Of course I did. And you would have done, too, if you had known what that man has just been saying. He expounded a homily. That is a speciality of yours, rabbi; you should be able to appreciate it. He said two men went to the Temple: a Pharisee and a customs officer. But do you know which of these two was the just man? The customs officer! Because he prayed humbly, while the Pharisee only boasted of his virtues. Everybody knows that's not true. So why does he say it? To spread hatred! To set the mob against us. He's not a prophet, he's an agitator! He's broken the Sabbath, he's violated the prescriptions in regard to cleanliness, and now he wants to set the common people against us. Are we to let him get away with that? Yes, I ordered the guard to bring him here. If the priestly officers were not in the hands of scoundrels he would have been locked away long ago. But they themselves betray the law. I gave orders for him to be brought here. And this fellow (he pointed to the guard) came back empty-handed. And now he says he didn't dare take the man prisoner. Why didn't you dare, you dog?'

'Oh, most reverend rabbi,' the man whimpered, 'nobody ever spoke as this man does . . .'

'Nobody? Never?' Jonathan said contemptuously. 'Not one of our worthy and reverend rabbis, for instance?

'Hey!' he called to the guard at the door. 'Take this fool away and beat some sense into him. Thirty-nine strokes. But not one stroke more. And then fine him ten denarii.'

'Mercy, mercy!' the man sobbed. 'Where can I find so much money? My children will die of hunger.'

'You'll bring up the next lot better,' Jonathan said coldly. The man was led out of the hall; Jonathan beckoned for a bowl and a jug of water. He washed the tips of his fingers diligently. As he wiped them in a soft linen towel he said through his teeth: 'He's slipped through our fingers. If it hadn't been for that fool we would have done with him. But we shall get him yet.'

'Were you intending to kill him, rabbi?' I asked rather naïvely.

'No, I only wanted to stroke him,' he answered slowly, staring at me through half-closed eyes.

'Our Law,' I said, 'insists that a man should be questioned and judged properly . . .'

He did not reply. But across his shoulder rabbi Joel cried: 'Don't you defend him! Did you become a Galilean yourself, Nicodemus, when you went about following him? Don't you defend him!'

'Rather than defend him,' rabbi Jochanan added, 'you should read in the sacred books. Remember that Judaea is the mother of the prophets. Only thieves have come from Galilee.'

The doctors fixed their eyes on me. Behind their pretence of goodwill I felt the chill of those eyes like the touch of knives on bare flesh. But I pretended to be indifferent, and left the hall without saying any more.

Next day Jesus was sitting in Solomon's Porch, surrounded by disciples and others. When I approached he gave me a friendly smile and said:

'Welcome, friend. May the Most High be with you!'

He had never called me friend before. And his smile seemed more intimate than usual. He smiled at me quite joyously, as though we were linked by some secret, an oath of friendship which nobody else knew about. But why should he feel joy? I have always suspected that he doesn't feel happiest when he is healing, but would be happiest of all if someone came to him without asking to be healed.

My arrival interrupted his teaching. I have no idea what he had been talking about, but his words must have been effective, for the people were sitting thoughtfully with furrowed brows, their fingers entwined in their beards or their heads resting on their fists. All the disciples were present; I thought I detected expressions of irresolution and fear on their faces. They were no longer the noisy boors I had known, unbearable in their conviction that through their master they would sooner or later become the rulers of all the world.

Simon was the first to speak. He asked timidly, like a man uncertainly sounding the bottom on which his boat has grounded.

'But then . . . if that is how things are to be arranged between man and woman, it would be better not to get married . . . wouldn't it?'

'No, Peter.' (It was the first time I had heard him call Simon by this new name.) 'There are some who are castrated even in their mother's womb; there are some who are castrated by the executioners; but there are some also who have castrated themselves, in order to find the kingdom. But don't be troubled. This will be understood by him to whom it is given . . .'

However, Peter did not seem reassured. In a tone that sounded rather like despair, he exclaimed:

'How can a man live without wife, without children, without love?'

'What new demand has the teacher made now?' I wondered. I don't like Simon. But his anxiety was understandable. To follow the teacher he had left home, wife, and children. But he had not renounced them for ever. True, Jesus once said that no man who had put his hand to the plough should turn back. But now he said gently:

'There are things which man cannot do, nor even understand. But there is nothing of this kind with the Eternal . . .'

His gaze passed from Simon's face, strained with the effort of thought, to the anxious faces of the other disciples. It ran over them like a musician's finger over the strings of a cythara, and rested on me.

'Believe me,' he said, 'that man will receive a hundredfold, and eternal life as well.'

The anxiety passed from their faces just as the nocturnal shadows vanish from a corner when the sunlight reaches it. They are thoughtless, and anything comforts them. But I admit that his words awakened an incomprehensible joy in me also. Yet at the same time my mind protested. Easy enough to say that one can give up everything and then have it all back a hundredfold. I don't want a hundred Ruths. If only she were to return . . . But she won't: this is all talk. So I told myself. But when I raised my eyes I saw that he was still looking at me, and smiling. And I could not voice my protest.

At that moment we heard the sound of shouting. I felt anxious: rabbi Jonathan's threats were still fresh in my mind. A crowd approached, led by several young Pharisees. But they didn't appear to have any guards with them. They were dragging someone along. The people around the teacher instinctively fell back behind him. But he sat unmoved, calm, with his head raised, and on his face the same challenging smile which I had seen an hour before.

The crowd halted right in front of him. One of the brethren stepped forward, and bowed ironically. I surmised that this was not an attack, but some plan to have fun at his expense.

'Greetings, rabbi,' the Pharisee said. 'Look whom we've brought before you.' The others pushed a woman forward. She was almost naked, and clutching a torn piece of sheeting convulsively to her breast. Though the rouge on her cheeks was smudged with blows, and her darkened eyelashes were leaving black streaks as her tears ran down her face, her crime was obvious at one glance. Her shoulders were heaving, a thread of blood was flowing from one ear, from which the ring had been torn. Her eyes darted in terror from one to another of the men surrounding her. At last her gaze rested on Jesus. At first she shifted it away: possibly she took his smile as just another jeer. But after a moment she looked at him timidly again. She didn't appear to recognize him, but something in his look must have affected her, for she lowered her eyes and huddled down with

179

her arms folded one around the other, as though she were trying to cover her nakedness.

'This woman is an adulteress,' the young Pharisee said. 'We caught her in the very act of sinning . . .'

'What do you want me to do about it?' he asked.

'We have brought her for you to judge. What shall we do with her?'

I still could not think what they were aiming at. But it was obviously a trap.

'What does Moses command you to do?' Jesus spoke calmly, and his smiling gaze rested on the woman. Her head drooped, and her arms twined round her body bashfully.

'Moses? Oh, we know the Law.' The Pharisee smiled confidently. 'The Torah says: he who commits adultery with another man's wife must perish . . . both he and the adulteress. This woman has committed adultery. It is usual to stone them. But what is your opinion?' He bent over the teacher sitting at the foot of the pillar. Now I thought I saw the trap. They knew his compassion. They hoped to show publicly that his behaviour was contrary to the Law.

'Stone her! She must die! She's infamous!' I heard a hateful voice right beside me. I looked round in amazement, for it was Judas's voice. He was standing with clenched fists. 'Let her die!' he cried hoarsely.

'So you agree that such a woman must be crushed like a dog?' The Pharisee was obviously disillusioned; he hadn't expected to hear the Torah confirmed. The woman trembled even more violently. She was on the point of collapse.

Jesus slowly rose to his feet. The gentle goodness in his face changed to a look of majestic authority.

'You have said,' he began slowly, 'that according to the Law the adulterer should perish with the adulteress. Therefore let any man among you who is free from the sin cast the stone at them.'

His eyes suddenly flashed lightning. He didn't flare up with indignation, but his gaze struck like whips at the Pharisees.

And they fell back. Some of them already had stones in their hands, but they hid them hurriedly in their robes.

He said no more, but bent down, and, stretching out his finger, wrote something in the dust of the stone pavement, right beside the woman's feet. The writing remained for only a moment, for the breeze erased the letters. But I succeeded in reading: 'You, too, have committed adultery . . .' Someone fell back into the crowd and vanished. It was the young Pharisee. The teacher wrote again. Once more I read: 'You have committed adultery.' Another of the men in the ring turned and slipped away. The long, thin finger wrote swiftly. The words came one after another. I couldn't always read them. But after each sentence another of the crowd slipped away, and others did not wait to read the accusation. The teacher went on writing. It was as though he were writing in water: the words did not remain, they were erased. But the moment of time for which they endured was long enough.

At last not one of the woman's accusers was left. Only Judas remained standing with clenched fists. Jesus did not raise his head, but went on writing. Then he looked up. His face seemed to turn grey. His eyes fell on Judas with a challenging look. But the disciple stood obstinate, filled with rancour. Jesus bent down and wrote again.

I failed to read that writing. But in Iscariot's eyes I saw fear: the fear of an animal caught in a trap. The clenched fists relaxed. He looked about him as though anxious to see whether anybody else had read those words. Then he quietly slipped away.

I wondered what would happen now. Jesus was still kneeling, with his finger on the pavement. But he didn't write. He slowly raised his head. Once more his face was pleasant and gentle. He looked at the woman, and she broke into a soundless weeping. She sobbed, her face twisted with grief, but she was unable to conceal her face, for her hands still clutched the sheet around her. Her head sank lower and lower, and the dirty tears fell into the red dust at her feet.

'Don't cry,' he said gently. 'No man has condemned you.'

She burst into a still more violent, unhappy weeping.

'Nor do I condemn you,' he added. 'Go, but don't sin again.'

She went on crying, more quietly. Then she slowly turned and walked away. He stood gazing after her. After a moment he stooped again and stretched out his finger to the dusty pavement. Very meditatively he described certain signs on it. When I looked more closely I saw they were words, which seemed to read: 'He said: "I will not go." But afterwards he felt sorry and went to do his father's will. But another said: "I am going," but didn't go. Why don't you go, though I have called to you so many times?'

Perhaps I only thought he wrote these words? But if I read them correctly, for whom did he write them? The wind had already blown them away. I don't know why, but I suddenly felt anxious. Yet it wasn't a nagging, but a pleasant feeling. I felt afraid of something which yet seemed to have all the radiance of hope. 'Why don't you go?' Whom had he written those words for, I wondered?

Without saying another word he rose and went away, followed by his disciples. I remained, like a man awakened from a succession of dreams. Perhaps he didn't write those words at all, I repeated as I stood by the balustrade overlooking the valley of Cedron. What an extraordinary man he is! He never says outright that he wants something, he never commands. He asks timidly, like a fearful beggar. Or he writes in sand words that are erased by the wind the moment they are written. And yet it is very difficult to refuse him what he asks!

DEAR JUSTUS, SIXTEENTH LETTER.

Although it is autumn, the sky is clouded, and the first rains have fallen, we have had a number of really hot days. But I don't mean only the weather, but certain events which have left the people in a state of excitement. The city is bubbling like a pot of boiling water. In consequence the teacher has been forgotten. That is just as well. But for Pilate's unexpected move there would certainly have been a further attempt on his life.

After the incident with the adulteress Jesus disappeared from the city for several days. In Bethany there is a family which always gives him a warm and hospitable welcome. The head of the house is a man named Lazarus, a weaver and gardener. He is a quiet, pious man, a Pharisee of lower degree. He is unmarried, and lives with his sister Martha, who is a spinster. She's an energetic woman, always bustling about with a cheerful smile; always ready to serve others and to help people in trouble. She is well known to the merchants of Bezetha, for she often goes there early in the morning with a cartload of vegetables, fruit, or woven materials. The beggars at the Dung Gate know her too, for she is generous with her alms. These two devout people have a sister who is known to all the world: but hardly for her virtue. Mary, the youngest of the family, an auburn-haired woman hardly more than a girl, has taken the wrong road. She troubled Jerusalem for a year or two with her profligate behaviour. Then she followed one of Antipas's palace officials to Galilee and acquired an unsavoury reputation in Tiberias, Magdala, and Kaim. I'm positive that if she had wished she could have had Antipas, and Pilate, and even Vitellius the Legate, for her lovers. But she wouldn't be tied down to any one man, not even to a king. She changed her lovers more swiftly than the fashionable ladies of the city change their sandals. There was not a man who could resist her charms. Despite her dissolute life she kept her beauty. I have seen her several times, and I shall never forget that magnificent, proud, and miraculously beautiful face. Her eyes are as changeable as a stone polished into innumerable facets. Her contemptuously curved lips seem to be challenging you to force them to smile submissively, if you can.

Lazarus and Martha must have suffered a good deal from their sister's ill fame. But I never heard that either of them spoke badly of her. Lazarus did say to me once: 'She isn't a bad girl, only . . . believe me, rabbi . . . She just doesn't understand . . .'

The evening after the teacher had arrived in the city for the festival a woman called to see his mother. Her head was wrapped in a shawl, and she wore a modest gown. But her movements were not those of ordinary women. A lock of auburn hair had slipped from under the shawl, and beneath her gown white feet with beautifully moulded toes were visible. I looked at her more closely, and was dumbfounded. It was Mary: the public sinner, the courtesan. But completely changed: there was not a trace of paint on her face, not one ring on her fingers, her feet were not shod in costly sandals, but were bare. When she saw Mary she fell to her knees. She put her arms round the older woman's legs with the gesture which the young wife uses to show respect to her husband's mother. They must have been long acquainted: they whispered together like people who have much to tell each other. What can his mother have in common with this woman? Jesus turns all the established orders upside down! I was shocked when he forgave that adulteress. But forgiveness is not the same as friendship. He frequently says the last will be first and the first last. But what could this woman do to earn so much as a pennyworth of grace?

I questioned Judas about it. He laughed outright, and his laugh sounded like a wheel grating beneath an overloaded cart.

'So you're asking about that girl from Magdala, Lazarus's sister? Of course . . . there's not a sinner trading in the human body whom he wouldn't forgive. According to him it's all our fault.' He laughed spitefully. 'We deceive them, and then we abandon them. But they're never to blame! I suppose you know who she was? Even in our sinful age such dissolute conduct is revolting. One couldn't count all the men she has given herself to. Of course, only wealthy ones! But then, one day, I stared and couldn't believe my eyes! Among the crowd asking the teacher for health I saw her. O, I thought, so your punishment has come upon you at last. So you've been stricken with disease! And you want the teacher to heal you so that you can tempt men to sin again.

'She flung herself at his feet, and cried: "Save me! Save me! Take from me my eyes, my hair, my teeth, all that men desire of me. Only set me free. And then I shall live only for you."

'The shameless hussy! But do you know what he answered? "I take all these, and you too. But as for you: come out of her!" The evil spirits flew out of her with a whistle, like air from a burst bladder. She fell in a swoon. Several days passed. We were staying with a certain Pharisee at Nain. Jesus was sitting at the table when this woman burst into the room. She ran up to him, and flung herself at his feet. She wept, and washed his feet with her tears, and then she wiped them with those red curls of hers. Instead of pushing her away, he praised her for what she had done. He said she loved more because she had been given more. And he smiled at her and said: "All your sins are forgiven you." The people around him were indignant. How can such a woman have forgiveness? She ought to be stoned.'

'But what is she doing now?' I asked.

'What is she doing? She's his most faithful servant. She sweeps the dust before him. She's ready to scratch out the eyes of anyone who might try to do him an injury. She lives a terribly virtuous life these days! And well she may! She's tried everything else, she may as well try virtue too!'

So Mary had changed from being a loose woman to one of Jesus's most devoted admirers. It's amazing. And he allows her to be with him, and to mix with the simple, but virtuous, women who accompany him in his wanderings! Rather imprudent benevolence on his part! He lays himself open to suspicion. At times Judas's rancour is amusing. But he's right in saying that there is no greater sin than that of Rahab. That was a dark stain on the royal line. But if he is descended from that line . . .

Evidently Jesus came to know Lazarus and Martha through Mary. He never spends the night in Jerusalem nowadays, but goes off to Bethany as soon as twilight falls. He seems to have a great love for this weaver and his sister. I write 'great love,' but the words are really meaningless. For he bestows great love upon everybody. In watching him one begins to understand his story of the labourers in the vineyard. That penny is like his love. He can give it to all and everyone, and commit no injustice. For it is of infinite value.

Although he has come into the city only infrequently since the festival, he has caused a further uproar in the Grand Council. One day, on his way to the Temple he passed a blind beggar sitting in the sun, a young lad known to all the city. His parents bought him the right to sit by the gate. As Jesus and his disciples were passing him Philip asked:

'Rabbi, you know all things. Did this lad sin, or his parents, that the Most High punished him with blindness?'

Philip is a fool. But Jesus stopped, as though to give greater emphasis to his reply:

'Neither he nor his parents. He was stricken with blindness that the work of the Most High might be shown through him.' He turned to look at the walls of the Temple, over which the tranquil light of the autumnal sun was flowing. 'This light will not shine for long now,' he added. 'Night is coming.' (I don't understand this remark, for it was quite early in the morning.) 'But when it comes, nothing will dispel the darkness. So long as I am here I am the light . . .' He bent down, spat, and mixed the spittle into the dust with his finger. Then he went to the beggar, laid the paste of mud on the boy's eyes, and said: 'Go and wash in Siloh.'

All the same, his miracles are not so remarkable as they were formerly. This lad had his sight restored only when he went and washed. Of course, as soon as people noticed that he could see there was a great to do. He was surrounded by crowds, and he had to tell his story again and again. At last a guard came and summoned him to the Grand Council.

It was about an hour later that I happened to go to the Council. I found rabbi Jochanan bar Zakkai questioning two obviously frightened, old people. The lad was standing at their side.

'So this is your son?' the doctor asked. 'See that you don't lie!'

'Yes, he's our son,' the woman said. But the man only nodded.

'And you say he was born blind?'

'It is as you say, most reverend rabbi.'

'Then how is it he can see now?'

The woman and her husband exchanged glances. She was about to say something, but he put his hand over her mouth. He stammered:

'We don't know, most reverend rabbi. Really we don't! How are we to know? I make pots, for I am a potter. I work all day. And my wife spends her day plucking feathers. How are we to know how he recovered his sight? We are simple, uneducated people. He is our son . . .'

'Yes, he is our son,' the old woman assented. 'And he was born blind.'

'But how is it he can see now?' rabbi Jochanan asked sternly.

'We don't know,' the man said, bowing again and again. 'How should we know? He is of age; let him tell you himself, rabbi.'

Jochanan turned impatiently to the lad.

'So you say you have been healed?'

The youngster nodded.

'Maybe, maybe . . . The Most High can do all things. You will make a sacrifice to the Eternal Presence for the grace He has shown you. It was He who cured you, not that sinner.'

'I don't know whether he's a sinner,' the boy answered sharply. 'But I know it was he who cured me.'

'How could he do it?' Rabbi Jochanan shrugged his shoulders. 'How can a sinful man work such a miracle?'

'I've told you twice already,' the lad retorted. 'Become one of his disciples and you'll know for yourself.'

'Hold your tongue!' Jochanan shouted, and stamped his feet. 'It's for such as you to be his disciples. He's the very man for sinners and beggars. The righteous have only one teacher:

187

Moses. He heard the words of the Lord and brought them down to men. Our fathers saw his glory. But no one knows where this man has come from.'

'I'm surprised you don't know,' the lad shouted back. 'You say he's a sinner,' he went on, ignoring his parents' gestures to him to be silent. 'But this sinner restores people to health. Could a sinner do that? The people say that only a man sent by the Most High could do anything like that.'

'Hold your tongue!' Jochanan's voice brayed like a trumpet. 'You scum, you ignorant, unclean clod! Are you trying to teach us? Get out! We shall expel you from the synagogue. You're accursed!' He raised both hands and shook them above his forehead. 'By the great Ha-Makom, whose Name may not be uttered, but which is written with forty-two letters, by the everlasting Sabaoth, by Michael the Archangel and the twelve other archangels, by the seraphim and the Throne, I proclaim you unclean. Get out! Soil not the threshold of this house! Keep far from the faithful, that they may not be defiled by you. May death and destruction be your lot. May you be swallowed up in Gehenna! May the devils take you into their hands. Get out!'

The boy flew out, driven into the street by the guards. His parents fell to the ground and beat their heads on the pavement in their terror. They, too, were taken out. Rabbi Jochanan drew the tallith over his head and prayed, his hands extended to heaven.

One of the brethren happened to notice me. He accosted me aggressively:

'You were seen with that accursed sinner today, rabbi . . .'

They all turned and looked at me. In their eyes I read anger and a challenging hate. My heart began to beat faster, I felt a great void in my belly. I felt like saying that I had gone to him only out of curiosity, and that I was not his disciple. But I said nothing. I left the hall.

At that very moment, when it seemed that if Jesus showed his face in Jerusalem again the result would be tragic for him, Pilate unexpectedly arrived in the city. As I have told you, for years now he has come to Jerusalem only at times of festivals. But this time he came long after the great 'Hallelujah' closing the Harvest Festival. The morning had broken grey and windy, my house was filled with whistles and creaks. A greyish gloom settled over the city. I was expecting to hear the deafening thunder of autumn rains at any moment. But instead of rain, I heard the thunder of hoofs as Pilate's armed escort rode in. I had a foreboding that some evil was at hand. And before an hour had passed I was summoned to a meeting of the Sanhedrin. I wrapped myself in my cloak, and went. The rain still hung in the air, not yet falling. The grey clouds were rolling across the sky like piles of dirty linen.

The members of the Sanhedrin had hardly assembled when Caiaphas entered. His face was pale, his black eyes smouldered moodily.

'Oh, most reverend rabbis,' he began. But he had only got out these words when he began to pant for breath. He clutched at his short, thick neck. 'Oh, most reverend rabbis!' he continued, recovering his breath. 'A great misfortune has occurred. That . . . that barbarian . . . that unclean foreigner, that Edomite, that . . . once more he has raised his impious hand . . .'

'Woe, woe!' all the assembly lamented and bowed their heads.

'Has he soiled the Holy Place again with his unclean signs?' rabbi Jonathan asked.

'Worse, worse!' Caiaphas tore at his fine black beard. 'That barbarian, that . . .' He was choking again with indignation. '. . . that Roman bootjack has dared to rifle the treasury,' he shouted, his eyes bulging as though the words were stones sticking in his throat.

'Rifled the Temple treasury?' many of the council cried out. 'He's laid his hands on the treasury of the Most High?'

'Yes.' Caiaphas banged his fists on the desk. 'The scurvy,

unclean barbarian burst in with his men and ordered us to
hand over a full three hundred talents.'

Through the roar of indignation that filled the hall I heard
rabbi Oncelos hiss:

'So he didn't take all the treasure: only three hundred
talents?'

The hall was suddenly silent.

'Every farthing in the treasury belongs to the Eternal,' one
of the Sadducees retorted.

'Three hundred talents is an enormous sum,' another exclaimed.

'Oh, I know, I know,' Oncelos admitted. 'But we would like
to know exactly what happened.'

'Why didn't he take four hundred?' rabbi Jochanan queried.
'He demanded three hundred . . .'

'Oh, how very kind of him,' rabbi Eleazar sneered. 'But what
did he want exactly so much for?'

'He wants to build an aqueduct,' Jonathas son of Ananias
replied rather reluctantly.

There was another eloquent silence. Our Pharisee brethren
looked at one another significantly.

'That's strange,' rabbi Jonathan observed caustically. 'A great
fuss is made. We are summoned to sit in council. The high
priest orders us to wring our hands over the Roman's sacri-
legious deed. And what do we learn? The barbarian comes
politely and takes three hundred talents from the treasury.
Exactly three hundred talents. Where would you find another
man who wouldn't have taken it all? But we know how it has
been arranged.' He pointed an accusing hand at the Sadducees'
bench. 'The Roman didn't steal the money. You gave it to
him!'

'How dare you say that?' the Sadducees shouted.

'Then deny it if you can!'

'You are insulting the High Priest.'

'You have stolen the gold of the Most High!'

'Now, now!' Jonathas, the president, tried to restore order.

'Stop shouting! Enough of these recriminations. I'll explain it all to you.'

'Good, let him explain,' rabbi Jonathan said, turning to us Pharisees.

Jonathas anxiously rubbed his hands together. Ananias's oldest son is more Greek than Jew. He reads Greek books, enters into disputations with Greek philosophers, and spends his evenings discus throwing and racing. He has a habit of sneering. But as he stood before the Sanhedrin he seemed more worried than sneering.

'The worthy rabbi Jonathan son of Azziel is not correct. We didn't give Pilate the money. It is true that for a long time he has been pestering us to give him three hundred talents to build an aqueduct . . .'

'So that he and you could have Roman baths fitted up in your homes,' a Pharisee shouted.

'I can fit up baths without the aid of an aqueduct,' the president retorted proudly. 'Pilate wanted to build the aqueduct in order to have water for his own use. We explained that gold from the treasury could not be used for this purpose.'

'You shouldn't even have discussed it with him. You shouldn't talk with foreigners. You Sadducees don't observe the Law relating to purity, and that's why these things happen . . .'

'Worthy rabbi Eleazar is getting excited unnecessarily. Someone has to talk to the Romans. If the Romans had only you to deal with there would be endless conflicts in the land, and crosses would be erected on all the hills . . .'

'The Most High would be with us in the struggle. We would conquer,' one of the younger Pharisees cried.

'The Most High aids the wise and not the madmen. Since the days of the Maccabees every rising has ended in defeat. What we need is peace. Someone must talk with the Romans. Someone must sacrifice his purity. We and the foreigners are both living on this earth. You are able to serve the Lord in your purity only because we have undertaken the care of the people . . .'

'By associating with the unclean! Because of that ten of Israel's tribes were lost!'

'And what will happen to the two which are left, if all men hate them? Can they fight all the world?'

'Don't you Sadducees believe in the Eternal?'

'We do, more than you do! But our faith is not that of the ignorant, unclean clods.'

'You are not concerned about purity.'

'That's what you say! You pot washers!' the Sadducees retorted.

'Quiet!' Rabbi Jonathas again stilled the hubbub. 'We shall not discuss such questions now. Let us consider what we are to do about Pilate.'

'What can we do, if he already has the gold?'

'We can do something.' Jonathas put on a conciliatory smile. 'We told him: "Take the money, for we haven't the strength to oppose you." But what will happen when the people get to hear of it? You all know he's afraid of riots, uproars, and conflicts. If the people take action he'll give the money back. I know him. All that's necessary is that the rabble of Ophel should start demonstrating. We have nothing in common with them. But you Pharisees have influence over them.'

'Our aim is to bring the Law closer to the people,' rabbi Joel said proudly.

'Precisely, precisely!' Jonathas took him up. 'A very laudable aim. And in that way you have gained influence over the common people. Tell them what has happened, and convince them that the Roman has committed sacrilege. Let them go to Antonia and make a scene. And if the soldiers do treat them rather roughly . . .'

'In short, you want us to provoke a rising?' rabbi Jochanan asked.

'A rising? Why use such words at this stage? We know Pilate. He's a coward. You don't need to start a rising. Let the people demonstrate, and he'll order his soldiers to kill a few of them. That's all. All we want is that the news of his arbitrary conduct should get to Vitellius's ears. He'll send a report to Caesar.'

'Hm!' Rabbi Jonathan coughed and looked at us Pharisees. 'We could try it. The people will do anything we order them to.' (He emphasised 'we.') 'But why should we pull the irons out of the fire for you? Why should we care if Pilate has taken gold from you?'

'Not from us, from the Temple.'

'But you are its guardians.'

'We won't go into that. All we are asking now is that you should help us. Possibly tomorrow we shall be able to help you in some way. Well, what would you want in exchange for this little demonstration?'

I cannot remember the Sanhedrin ever being the scene of such bargaining before. The Sadducees must realize that their power is nearly gone, if they seek an understanding with us. We Pharisees have been waiting a hundred years for the power to pass into our hands. And now I'm sure it will before long.

'What do we want in exchange?' Jonathan, Jochanan and Eleazar put their heads together. 'The Grand Council must think it over. But you shall have your demonstration. The crowd will be outside Antonia tomorrow morning.'

Now to tell you what happened next day. As rabbi Jonathan had promised, from early dawn a huge crowd gathered outside the gate of Antonia, shouting: 'Hand back the Temple treasure!' Our brethren organized the demonstration magnificently. The people were convinced that the Romans had committed a terrible sacrilege. The hours passed, there were two heavy showers of rain, but the crowd did not abate. Pilate didn't come out, the gate was closed and fastened, the Roman guards were withdrawn from the street to the walls.

We assembled in the Temple and waited for the Procurator to yield. On the last occasion, when we demonstrated over the introduction of the legions' standards into the city, Pilate held out for three days. The task of organizing the demonstration was entrusted to young Pharisees, some of whom directed the shouts, while others hurried through the city, to rope in anyone not already taking part.

Then we heard of the disaster. The mercenary has grown intelligent. Last time he tried to frighten the people with the flash of swords, and failed. This time he ordered his soldiers to wrap themselves in cloaks and mix unnoticed with the crowd. When their officer blew his whistle they threw off their cloaks and brought out cudgels. They laid about them mercilessly, as only Romans can. There was a panic, and people who had looked death in the face a few years before now fled like cowardly dogs. Many had broken heads, arms, and legs. Even some of the Pharisees were beaten up. Instead of songs of victory, groans and reproaches are filling the city.

We had lost. Pilate summoned our representatives to him and told them with a smile that he was grateful to the Sanhedrin for the gold it was offering towards the cost of the aqueduct, and he would see that the work was started at once. By the autumn the troops concerned with keeping order in the city would be able to bathe in pure, cold water. And a fountain would be installed in Pilate's own atrium. When Caiaphas heard this he bellowed like a bull being slaughtered. In their fury the Sadducees have broken off all relations with Pilate. And you can imagine the hatred the people of Jerusalem feel for the Romans now.

With all this happening in the city, Jesus has been forgotten. He never comes into Jerusalem. But I know he has not returned to Galilee. He is somewhere close at hand, like a man who has slipped out of his house, but is available at call.

Instead of profiting by the fact that he has dropped out of the public eye to lie low for a time, he is again courting danger. He came to Jerusalem for the feast of Chanukah. This year's celebrations were marred by the cold and rain. Rain and snow put out the lights which the faithful had lit on their house roofs. I don't think I have ever found the festival of the Dedication of the Temple so grey and joyless before.

The frozen inhabitants of Jerusalem gathered each day at the porticos. Someone saw him coming along with his disciples. 'Look!' he shouted; 'here comes the prophet of Galilee.' The people were gloomy and disgruntled. What if the day of the cleansing of the Temple from its defilement by Epiphanus had been celebrated for now almost two hundred years? Had there been any change since then? When years later the Roman commander defiled the sanctuary nobody bothered to purify the Temple with the due solemnity. But at least Pompey didn't carry anything off. Pilate has stolen the Temple gold and is building an aqueduct with it. Thus our people sink lower and lower, step by step. Will there ever be an end to our humiliations?

So it was not surprising that someone cried to Jesus:

'Listen, rabbi! How long do you intend to keep us in uncertainty? If you're the Messiah tell us so straight out . . .'

Jesus stopped. Possibly he would have gone by without a word if he hadn't been accosted. But he rarely leaves a question unanswered:

'I have told you so many times, and you have not listened to me. I have shown you by my deeds so many times, but you have refused to believe me. What else must I do? I have come to my sheep, just as the prophet prophesied. I have sought those which were lost, and I have called those which had broken away. I am prepared to give my life for them, just as a good shepherd gives his life for his sheep. But obviously there has to be judgement as between sheep and sheep. Evidently you are not yet my sheep. For if you were mine, nobody would wrest you from my hands. What the Father has given me nobody can take from me. For I and the Father are one.'

That was sufficient to drive the rancorous people to fury. Their misery found vent in anger. They raised sticks and fists, and one or two stooped to pick up stones.

'He's blaspheming!' they shouted. 'Stone him! He's a blasphemer.'

He asked calmly, as though unaware that death threatened him:

'What do you wish to stone me for? For which of the deeds I have done?'

'You're blaspheming!' they shouted.

'So you regard my words as blasphemy?' he asked sorrowfully. 'But what of my deeds? If you don't want to believe my words, then believe my deeds. Everything I have done is a testimony . . .'

He slipped into the crowd, and before anyone could throw a stone he had vanished. He must have left the city immediately, for he was not seen again. But this brief scene once more deflected the people's anger from Pilate and the Romans and focused it on him. These are two aspects of the same trouble. The people have had enough of the life they are living. They want to be free, and so they hate the Romans; and for the same reason they placed great hopes in Jesus. I am beginning to understand men like Judas, whose faith is beginning to turn to resentment, and who charge him with treachery. After the miracles he had worked they expected he would also work the miracle of victory over the Romans. But you would think Pilate and the Romans are as dear to him as his own brothers. I've already told you that he seems both glad and sorry that foreigners are to come and take over the neglected heritage. He presents one with a thousand mysteries. But people like Judas cannot stand mysteries. They always want to know everything.

Many people in Jerusalem are beginning to think on the same lines as Judas now. The local rabble talk contemptuously of Jesus. He must have thousands of adherents and friends in Galilee still. But here every man has looked to him to fulfil his own secret hopes and desires. Why didn't he remain among his own people? They would not have understood him, but at least they would have appreciated him, especially if he didn't set out to provoke our brethren unnecessarily. We Pharisees grant every man the right to speak on matters connected with the Most High. He could have done a lot of good yet by teaching the people love for the Eternal Presence. Meanwhile, he seems to regard his work as finished. What good has he achieved during these past three years? He has gathered around him a handful of disciples and a few people who are prepared to listen to him. But he could have all Galilee, Judaea, and Peraea behind him, yet he can achieve nothing without Jerusalem. Our doctors are right in that respect: a prophet can survive only in Zion. Meanwhile, here in Jerusalem he has upset everybody, both high and low. He has lost all the appreciation he once had.

'If he keeps coming back to Jerusalem I'm afraid that he'll be killed sooner or later.'

So I said to Lazarus's two sisters, who called on me one day, much to my surprise. If Mary had come by herself I doubt whether I should have talked to her. I don't want anything to do with women who have lived in sin. The fact that he receives such sinners and even talks to them, even accepts food from their hands, doesn't attract me in the least. He goes too far in his goodness. There would be no Law if there were no punishment for sinners.

But I didn't want to offend Martha. Certain of our doctors declare that woman was the last thing the Most High created, and opine that she is as to half the work of Satan. I've given up all belief in this since his mother came to stay in my house. But Martha, too, is a whole and complete being. She doesn't exist for herself alone. If someone convinced her that all the world needs is cooked food she'd stand by the hearth for the rest of her life. There's no end to her goodness.

I've told you that she is always cheerful and friendly in spirit. But when she called I noticed that her eyes were screwed up painfully. By the way, these two sisters are quite unlike each other. Martha is not beautiful; she looks like a big, good-natured child. But beauty radiates from Mary like perfume from a flower. No rouge or black could add to it. She carries her head proudly, and her gaze seems to rest on passing people only under compulsion. Her eyes seem always to be seeking someone above your head. She has a look rather like that of John son of Zachariah.

They came to me to consult me in regard to their trouble. Their brother had suddenly fallen seriously ill. At first they thought the fever would pass, that it was simply caused by the changeable winter weather. But it didn't.

'If it goes on much longer he's sure to die,' Martha said quietly.

'How can I help you?' I asked. I knew they had no need of money. They had always had sufficient from their industry.

'We want your advice, rabbi,' Martha said. 'You know' (she smiled despite her sorrow) 'that if he were here, he'd heal Lazarus with a single word.'

That remark was like a sword thrust into my heart. Hadn't he been in Jerusalem during Ruth's illness? Once more that terrible question arose before me; I shall never find any answer to it. Or rather, I have tried to tell myself that he didn't help me because he regarded me as someone close to him. A feeble explanation, I know. But it has given me some peace. Now Martha's words robbed me of that peace.

'Yes,' I said, 'he's your friend, so he'd help if you were to ask him. But he isn't here. And I don't even know where he is.'

'I know where he is,' Martha said quietly. 'He has gone into the wilderness near Ephraim.'

'Then send someone for him.

They both started to their feet, and Mary, who so far had let her sister do all the talking, exclaimed:

'But if he comes they may kill him. They wanted to stone him the last time he was here.'

Stroking my beard, I meditated over my answer.

'Yes,' I admitted; 'he's in great danger if he comes to Jerusalem. He has enemies among the priests, among the doctors, even among the people.' I felt tempted to add: 'You're right, it would be unwise to send for him.' I don't wish Lazarus any ill. But I had a terrible desire that he should get well without the teacher's aid. And besides, I thought, Jesus had shown no concern over Ruth's health and life; her death had been a matter of indifference to him. But if Lazarus were to die . . . Lazarus is his friend. If Lazarus died, Jesus might realize what a man feels when he gets no aid from anywhere whatever. He didn't take any notice of my despair then. Will he take any notice of these women's despair now? The moments passed, but I still didn't know what to say to these sisters.

'If there is any danger to him,' Mary suddenly remarked, 'it would be better for Lazarus to die.'

That struck me as perfectly cruel. I looked at my visitors in some anxiety. 'You don't seem to have much love for your brother, Mary,' I commented.

'You mustn't think that!' Martha spoke up, and tears appeared at the corners of her eyes. 'She's very fond of Lazarus . . .'

'Don't defend me, Martha,' Mary interrupted. 'What the rabbi says is quite true: I don't love you deeply enough, I don't love you as you and Lazarus love me. And I'm so terribly afraid for him.' Her deep, melodious voice broke. 'If Lazarus were to die I should weep for all the rest of my life. I should never forgive myself for repaying his goodness as I have. But if anything were to happen to Jesus all the people, even the stones, would have to . . . No,' she cried, 'that simply mustn't be allowed to happen.'

I stroked my beard again, endeavouring to order my thoughts.

If Ruth were still alive, and if I felt sure that he could heal her, I shouldn't hesitate for one moment. I gazed at Mary as though seeing her for the first time. Her eyes were expressive of blind fidelity and fervent devotion. Her face is extraordinarily beautiful. It betrays not the least trace of her former sinful life. I turned my eyes to Martha. I understood her better. She would never be able to choose so resolutely as her sister had. I, too, though I expect and await so much from this teacher . . . 'expect'? The word came of itself from my stylus. What can I expect from him? Ruth is dead. His kingdom is one of only words and dreams. He is not the Messiah. Martha and I are ordinary people, and we know the cost of pain.

'How can I advise you?' I muttered. 'I think that in any case you should do what you can to save your brother. The teacher may possibly be in danger if he comes to Jerusalem. But if he only visits you at Bethany who is to know? Ask him not to show himself in the city.'

'You are wise, rabbi,' Martha exclaimed. She smiled through her tears. Mary said nothing. She sat with drooping head, like someone who has already said all that there is to be said.

'I don't suppose you have anyone you can send,' I said. I was beginning to feel some compulsion to act despite myself, despite my thoughts, despite my regrets. 'If you like I'll send my servant Ahir to Ephraim. He'll find him and bring him to you.'

They bowed with gratitude and respect.

A full week passed before Ahir returned. He was travel-worn, his feet were encased with dried mud, his cloak was dirty and damp. Ahir is a faithful servant; his father served in my father's house. So I have no secrets from him.

'Did you find him?' I asked.

'Yes, rabbi. I found him, and he is on his way. If you wish to see him when he comes to Bethany hurry there at once. He should arrive late in the afternoon.'

'But you had to spend a long time looking for him?'

'Not so long, rabbi. But he had left Ephraim. He had gone to the farther side of the Jordan. And when I did find him he didn't want to come.'

'Didn't want to come?'

'He's a strange man. When I told him Lazarus was ill he only smiled. He said to his disciples: "This illness does not involve death; but through it glory will come to the Son of Man." And he said no more about going to Bethany. I didn't know what to make of it. He appears to know everything, and he acts as though he knew nothing. Two days later he sent for me. He told me to tell him more about Lazarus's illness. And then he said to his people: "Let us go to Judaea."

'His disciples pleaded with him not to go, because he was in danger of death there. But he said: "So long as it is day a man sees his road and doesn't stumble. But when the night comes he may fall. Let us go. Our friend Lazarus has fallen asleep. We must go and awaken him."

' "But if he's asleep," his disciples objected, "he'll get better."

'He shook his head: "Lazarus has fallen into the sleep of death," he said.'

'And then he set out at once?' I asked Ahir.

'Yes. His disciples made no further objection. One of them cried: "If the rabbi is going to his death we'll die with him." '

I smiled superciliously. Which of them had played the braggart now? Simon or Thomas? They're both liable to boast without stopping to think. But if they knew how much danger does threaten them and their master they would never show their noses inside Jerusalem again. Heroism is usually only thoughtlessness. At times I regret that I cannot be thoughtless in some ways. And yet I want to see him. I'm curious to know what he will say when they ask him: 'Why didn't you come earlier, seeing that you've dared to come at all?'

'Go and summon Dathan and Hepher,' I told Ahir. 'Tell them to bring my stick, cloak, and sandals. They will be going with me to Bethany.'

The house of Lazarus was a house of mourning. The weeping women and funeral players had departed, but the scent of burnt incense still hung about the rooms, and a crowd of mourning guests was sitting round the table. Martha and the servants brought food and waited on them. Her eyes were red, her lips compressed. All the same she thought of everything, had an eye to everything. She stifled her pain with labour. She seemed to be bustling about more energetically than ever.

Mary was sitting by herself in a quiet part of the garden. When she saw me she started to her feet and ran to meet me. A fold of her golden hair fell over her forehead and cheek like a brazen serpent. She panted, a burning impatience glowed in her dilated eyes. 'He'll be here any moment now,' I told her. She drooped her head and sighed heavily, like a runner who flags as he comes up to the post. She went back to her seat. Martha had the face of someone who has experienced defeat, but has succeeded in bearing it. Mary's face didn't reflect defeat. One would have thought she was still fighting . . .

Ahir had reckoned well: the sun was beginning to sink behind the Mount of Olives when someone hurried to the house crying: 'Martha, Mary! The teacher is outside.' Martha flew out at once. I went after her. He was just entering the gate in the low wall. He was exactly the same as always: calm, and smiling pleasantly. Martha ran and flung herself at his feet. As she lay there I could see that her shoulders, which had been so strong to bear the burden of the domestic tasks, were slender, feminine, quivering. She wept at his feet. At last she raised her eyes to him. Her voice, which she had kept under control in front of her guests, shook and broke:

'If you had been here, rabbi, Lazarus would not have died,' she sobbed. 'But I know,' she added, mastering her tears, 'that even now whatever you ask the All Highest for He will do for you.'

He nodded as though to confirm her words.

'Your brother will arise,' he said.

'I know he will,' she said humbly. 'The reverend doctors tell us so. And so you have taught us, rabbi. We shall arise on the last day . . .'

Gently but firmly he put his hands on her shoulders. He pushed her back a little as though he wanted to look into her eyes.

'I am the resurrection and the life,' he said. 'Anyone who has believed on me, even though he dies, shall live, and he who is living shall not die. Do you believe that, Martha?'

She gazed up at him trustfully.

'I believe, rabbi,' she answered. 'I believe you are the Messiah, the son of the Most High, who has come down from heaven . . .'

As though conscious that there was nothing to add to this bold confession, she rose and went away hurriedly. I recalled that Simon had used the very same words to him. 'Are these people mad?' I mentally asked myself. What is it they see in him? Of course he's not an ordinary man. He's a prophet, a teacher. But when they use such words of him they blaspheme. Yet he doesn't contradict them, doesn't rebuke them for saying such things. The son of the Most High!

He came towards me through the garden. I stood irresolute, not knowing whether to run away or remain and greet him. But at that moment a throng of people ran out of the house, Mary at their head. She, too, fell at his feet. And she greeted him in the very words her sister had used:

'If you had been here, rabbi, Lazarus would not have died.'

He passed his hand over her flaming hair. And, as though the touch had some magical effect, his face suddenly changed its expression. The calm and pleasant look yielded to a spasm of pain. For the first time I noticed something Judas has mentioned: he trembled. I had been thinking he was indifferent to suffering. But now I saw a face which pain overspread with its pallor. It was just as though some dam inside him, which previously had been holding back that suffering, had broken down. His face darkened like a sky overcast with a hail-cloud. He broke into sobbing: he was overwhelmed with sobbing like a child which has lost its mother. And in those tears could be heard the cries of thousands of people mourning outside the tombs.

'Where is he lying?' he asked.

'Come, rabbi, and we'll show you his tomb,' they said.

We went into the heart of the garden. He walked, still weeping, between the weeping sisters. His disciples and the guests followed. As I walked along I realized that I had not thought of him as loving Lazarus so much. If the penny paid by the vineyard owner represented his love, could anyone complain of injustice?

But if he loved Lazarus so much, why didn't he come in time to restore him to health? If he knew when Lazarus died, he must have known of his friend's illness before Ahir found him. He had healed so many people, couldn't he have healed Lazarus? It is a warped sort of friendship that finds pleasure in torturing those you love, and even yourself. But perhaps it was only because he was afraid? Perhaps he didn't want to heal Lazarus because he knew that any miracle worked in Bethany would be talked about all over Jerusalem before the day was out?

We halted before the cliff in which the tomb was carved. The stone closing the entrance was thrust into a narrow corridor with a steeply sloping floor. He wept without stopping. He seemed like a pitifully weak man crushed by pain which he lacked the strength to bear. What a contradiction between this present state of his and the words Martha had said! That weeping conveyed all our helplessness in face of death. I wept like that when they rolled the stone before Ruth's tomb. 'The end: this is the end,' I kept repeating to myself then. What had he come here for? To grieve over Lazarus? But beyond that stone lay only a decomposing body.

Then I heard him say:

'Remove the stone.'

I thought I hadn't heard aright. But a murmur of astonishment and terror from the others assured me that he really had said those words. I raised my eyes to him. He changes with the speed of lightning. He was no longer weeping. He was standing erect before the white stone wall. Like Moses striking the rock. (What made me think of that comparison?) The people fell back, leaving him and the two sisters standing before the tomb. Mary was gazing at him with wide, staring eyes: eyes that seemed to be crying out with hope. Martha's face was serious, with the seriousness of someone who has recovered her self-control.

'He's stinking already, rabbi,' she said. 'This is the fourth day since we laid him in the tomb.'

He interrupted her almost reproachfully:

'Did I not tell you to believe in me?'

She made no further objection. Four men seized the stone and with great effort rolled it away. A chill, the scent of incense, and the intolerably sickly smell of decomposition came from the dark opening. The teacher folded his arms and looked upward. That is always his manner of praying: swiftly, quietly, in an almost inaudible whisper. I didn't hear what he said, but I and all those present heard him call in a loud voice. I couldn't run away; but I shielded my eyes with my hands. Why is it that we are so afraid of the dead, even though they be our most loved ones? Perhaps it's just because that motionless body is no longer any part of them. It's only a body. I had my fingers over my eyes, but I did not cease to watch. I expect I cried out like the rest. In the corridor carved out of the rock appeared a white form, moving up to the mouth with awkward bounds. We all cried out, covered our eyes or fell to the ground. Above the hubbub I heard Jesus's voice:

'Unbind him!'

But nobody except the sisters and the teacher himself ventured to go up to that form. They bent over it. The cries died away. Possibly we were saving our voices to cry out at the sight we should see when the cloth fell from the dead man's face. But when we saw Lazarus's head between Mary and Martha not one of us cried out. There was no reason to. This was a living man, looking as though just aroused from sleep,.

smiling distrustfully, blinking and gazing, as though in astonishment at himself, his sisters, his surroundings. Then he raised his eyes to the teacher. What feeling was conveyed in that gaze? Fear? Amazement? Adoration? I cannot tell you. I saw joy in those eyes. Because he had returned to life? Because the first man he saw when he came back to life was the teacher? I saw him kneel down, and Jesus nestled his head against his chest. Then he called almost gaily to Martha: 'Bring him some food, he must be hungry.' The people who had seen all this stood rooted to the ground, filled with dread and wonderment. But gradually they began to pluck up courage. One after another they went to Lazarus and touched him diffidently. I, too, went up to him. He was a living man. The smell of decomposition had gone; the pallor, the chill, the rigidity had all gone. He smiled at us and stretched out his hands in welcome, like someone who has returned from a long journey. He ate the bread which Martha gave him. The silent wonder slowly changed to rapture. The disciples were the first to find their voices. They cried out joyfully, like drunken men who have no idea what they are saying: 'Hallelujah! Hallelujah! The great rabbi! The great prophet! The Son of David! The Messiah! The Son of the Most High!' The terms grew more and more audacious: 'The Son of the Eternal; The Messiah! Hallelujah!'

But I did not shout with the others. When the feast of mourning was transformed into a feast of joy I left Lazarus's and Martha's house. Though it was a cold and misty evening I preferred not to share their joy but to return to Jerusalem. I think you will understand why, Justus. He had resurrected Lazarus. But if I were to lead him to the rock where Ruth has been lying for almost a year, would he burst into tears and say as he has just said: 'Come out from the tomb!'? I don't believe it, I cannot believe it.

He once said: 'You need to have faith; and then at your command a mountain will hurl itself into the sea.' I would like to believe that. But I can't. So perhaps I am not worthy of such a miracle? That is one answer. Evidently I am worse than these unclean people, these fishermen, customs officers, street girls! He worked a miracle for Mary; he won't for me. I am worse, more wretched; weaker, more sinful. And I felt sure that I was better, cleaner. But he has turned the world upside down. He has given it to simple men like Simon, Thomas, and Philip. There is no place in it for me. I should have been born unclean, I should not have become a learned doctor, an expert on the Law, a writer of homilies and commentaries. But I am who I am. That is why Ruth suffered and died. She died as a sign that I don't belong to his world. In the former world I banqueted, and Lazarus was a beggar. Now the roles are reversed. But I don't want the scraps from anyone's table. I don't want to participate in other people's joy. I return to myself, to my loneliness, to my pain, to my memories of Ruth. If he had resurrected Ruth for me I should not have made any further demands of life.

I don't know who he is. It is certain that he is someone great. Maybe he is the Messiah, maybe he really is the Son of the Most High. But whoever he is, the joy he brings is not destined for me.

DEAR JUSTUS, EIGHTEENTH LETTER.
During the past few weeks I have been a prey to sorrow, bitterness, almost to despair. Never before have I thought of death as something to be desired. Nor had I ever been tempted to think that suicide might be a way out. I was always a lonely man. But today I feel that I have only now come to know what real loneliness is. Now that he has deceived me! I'm beginning to use Judas's language. And I know it is wrong. Jesus wouldn't even know how to deceive. He could be charged with anything rather than insincerity. It is we who deceive ourselves, by interpreting his words as we want to. What was it he said to me that time? 'Take my cross, and I will take yours.' Not

a word about Ruth. I only imagined that that illness was my cross, and that his cross was his difficulties with our brethren. The true meaning of his words is to be sought deeper, much deeper. Three years have passed since I first saw him, down on the bank of the Jordan. I thought that during these three years I had come to know him inside out. Nothing of the kind! I still don't even know who he is. He said recently that he is the beginning. He certainly has become the beginning for me. But the beginning of what? I am forty years old, I'm not a boy. I have achieved knowledge and a position of importance. They say I am the leading writer of homilies. I could say then that I had found my road, and should have gone walking along it till I died. That's the normal course of life. But Ruth's illness upset everything. I have stopped writing homilies. That doesn't mean that I can no longer write them. On the contrary, I feel an inner compulsion to write again. But I resist it. Formerly my writings came into being without pain, without effort, out of a joyous desire to serve the All Highest. Now I know that is all finished. What I would write now would be written not on wax but on an open heart. I must write, and yet I'm afraid of writing.

Listen, Justus! I'm beginning to discover what it is he wanted of me. I was right: it was a trap. He wanted me to write a homily about him. He cannot write it himself. Or perhaps he doesn't want to? But he insisted that I should become his stylus. That was to be his cross. I imagined that my task was to defend him, to save him. But that's not what he wants at all. He may be deliberately seeking death. But he wanted me to write a homily about him. I'm absolutely sure of that now. And that's why he didn't heal Ruth. Of course he knew of her illness. He read the despair in my eyes. He knew the moment of her agony. Possibly he even wept over her, as he wept at the tomb of Lazarus. But he didn't grant my wish. He allowed Ruth to die. And he hasn't resurrected her. He is merciless to his own. And to himself also. His miracles are for others. Judas is right in feeling that he has been tricked. He followed him in the belief that Jesus would be *his* master, *his* king, *his* Messiah. Meanwhile he is the Messiah of all those who reject him. But those who follow him have to share his fate. Surely he must be the Messiah. But different, not the one we were expecting. We've been deceived once more. Life is one continual deception.

He ordered me to write a homily about him. But why me? Just me? I'm a diffident sort of man, I admit it. I know my way about among things known, simple, hallowed by tradition. A homily about him would be a contradiction of all my being. Whoever had to write it would need to be prepared to struggle against the majority. People would regard a homily about him as an offence. If one wishes to gain recognition one should write about anything but him! I am a quiet man; I hate disputations. Everybody would become my enemy. I don't want that, far from it. Why has he chosen me? What did I go to him for? He said: 'You are not far from the kingdom.' And I felt at once that he was, so to speak, assigning me to my place of work. Every man has some consolation in this life. I have none. None! My ability to write homilies? That has become like a wound in my palm. What made me write that, Justus? I know very well the significance of a pierced palm. I'm shivering. Why did I write those words? How precisely everything he says comes to fulfilment! He said: 'I give you my cross.' I have my palm nailed to his homily, like a condemned man nailed to the crossbeam of a cross.

Dear Justus,　　　　　　　　　　Nineteenth Letter.

When I left Lazarus's house after his resurrection I felt sure I would never return. But now I find myself preparing to go there.

A lad has brought me a message from Lazarus. Martha's brother told him to tell me: 'Come to us for a feast. The teacher is in my house. We wish to see you.'

I was taken aback. Taken aback, astonished, and alarmed. I had let them know exactly what was decided at the Sanhedrin meeting and had asked them to inform Jesus. In any case it is becoming the topic of conversation elsewhere, and the readers have read out the proclamation of the Supreme Council in all the synagogues. Lazarus himself is in danger, especially as people are still talking about his resurrection and are even coming from distant parts to Bethany to see the man who died.

True, things are rather quieter at present. The holidays will begin in a few days and crowds of pilgrims are already pouring into Jerusalem. In such crowds it is easier to avoid the attentions of the spies. I doubt whether the Sanhedrin will take action against him during the present period. The conviction is general that the Galileans would defend their prophet; and we all know what they are capable of. But why court danger? Instead of thrusting himself right under his enemies' noses it would be better if he went off to the other side of the Jordan or to Trachonitis and remain there quietly for a year or two. Why this exaggerated fervour to come to Jerusalem for the holy days, when it appears that sentence has already been passed?

Now I am not in a position to save him even if I wished. I am not trusted in the Sanhedrin and the Grand Council, and they have concealed from me the steps they are taking against him. But quite apart from this, supposing the Most High requires his death? That thought never leaves me now. Subconsciously I have had the conviction hitherto that he is someone whom the Eternal has entrusted with a special mission. The teachings of certain prophets also seemed an offence and audacious insolence in their time. But the All Highest defended them. But him He condemns to death. And it is curious that he himself seems to be aware of this. He behaves like a man who is deliberately aiming at an end which has been indicated to him. But if that is so, there is a tremendous, and so far as I am concerned incomprehensible, mystery behind all this. If a man came to earth to be killed here by sentence of the Most High what sort of Messiah would he be? We expected a Messiah conqueror, leader, victor, not a Messiah persecuted by heaven and earth.

But of course you won't understand these thoughts. I must tell you all that has happened.

The very day after Jesus worked the miracle of raising Lazarus from the dead the Grand Council sent guards to Bethany to arrest him. But he had departed before sunrise, and the pursuit failed to discover him. The guards behaved mercilessly: they beat up Lazarus, struck Mary, turned everything upside down and smashed things to pieces, including Lazarus's loom. When they left they threatened that if they came again and he refused to tell them where the teacher had hidden, things would be even worse for them. And the Grand Council expelled Lazarus from membership.

Two days later I was summoned to a meeting of the Sanhedrin. It was to be a very solemn assembly, for Caiaphas had just been chosen as high priest for the fifteenth time in succession. Pilate has confirmed his election, though I hadn't expected him to, because of the tense relations that exist at present between the Sadducees and the Procurator. But evidently Pilate wanted to mollify the sons of Betus and Ananias, in order to have business dealings with them again. At present the only intermediary between him and the Sanhedrin is Joseph; but he has no personal ambitions whatever, so he cannot be drawn into the business of purchase of offices.

Dressed in the sacred robe of the high priest, Caiaphas entered the assembly. We rose and bowed to him reverently, and he blessed us. I don't like Caiaphas. No road to the acquisition of wealth is evil in his sight. All the merchants in the Temple precincts pay dues to him from their turnover. A man like Caiaphas could have achieved the highest position in the nation only in such times as these, when scoundrels and unbelievers perform the sacred functions in the Temple. Nobody likes him, he has enemies even among his own people. But everybody is afraid of him, for he is unscrupulous in the methods he employs. Like all the Sadducees, Caiaphas would like to pass for a Greek, but as he is not willing to do Greek exercises he carries around a belly that is far from Greek. And yet I must admit that when he stands before us wearing the sacred robe and ephod, with his brow shadowed by the golden plate with its inscription, 'Set apart for the Lord,' he looks completely different. Then one doesn't notice his greedy eyes, his covetous lips, his shaking cheeks and great belly. His dignity overshadows the crafty son of Betus.

Joseph and I were the last to arrive at the meeting. As I live next door to Caiaphas I usually am one of the first to arrive. But on this occasion the majority of the members were already in their seats. I suddenly had the suspicion that I had been deliberately summoned late so that before I arrived they could discuss something which it was undesirable that I should hear. I shared my suspicions with Joseph, and he admitted that he had the same impression. But he laughed at it: 'They're afraid of us: what fools!' Joseph is completely fearless, and he feels only contempt for the majority of the Sanhedrin members. He thinks they're fit only for intrigues, squabbles, and mutual slanders. But from the moment it occurred to me that they had been discussing something in secret from me I felt disquiet. I can't stand hostility; and concealed hostility always makes me fearful.

When towards the end of the deliberations Jonathas abruptly turned to me, I started and shivered.

'A few days ago,' he said, 'an amazing incident occurred right outside the city, at Bethany. I hope rabbi Nicodemus, who, so we are told, was a witness of this incident, will be good enough to tell us the truth as to what happened.'

The president's voice was courteous, so I mastered my uneasiness. In the last resort, what could they do to me? And why shouldn't I have been at Bethany when the miracle was worked? I rose, and gave a detailed report. The hall listened to me in silence; no one interrupted with questions or exclamations. But I felt that they were by no means indifferent. And I felt sure that the subject they had been discussing before I arrived was connected with Jesus.

'So you say he resurrected this Lazarus?' Jonathas asked, when I ended. There was a sneer on his face.

'Yes.'

'Hm, in that case a very unusual incident occurred.' I had the impression that the story more amused than disturbed Jonathas, but that for some reason he felt obliged to question me. 'Hm! But perhaps what happened was that Lazarus hid himself in the tomb in order to help his friend work this miracle?'

'No,' I objected firmly. 'That's impossible. Lazarus had been ill. When we went to the tomb we found the stone rolled over the entrance. And when the stone was removed there was a strong smell of putrefaction. And Lazarus came out swathed in sheets.'

'Well, all that could easily be fixed up,' the president laughed. 'He could have recovered. The entrance could be blocked easily enough, especially if there was access to the tomb from the farther side. And a living man can be wrapped up in sheets. Then all that remains to be done is to put a dead sheep just inside the entrance . . .'

'Have all these frauds been confirmed?' Joseph asked quite unexpectedly.

There has been a mutual dislike between Jonathas and Joseph ever since the time when Joseph remained in contact with Pilate, whereas Jonathas broke off all relations with the Procurator at Caiaphas's request. I surmised that my friend only wanted to plague the president, and wasn't really interested in the question at all. Jonathas replied with sarcastic courtesy:

'Oh no, they haven't been confirmed. Nobody has looked for them. On the contrary, as we've just heard, everybody's been completely overwhelmed by this . . . miracle. Evidently it didn't even occur to anyone that the whole business might be just a common fraud. Of course in all this I'm referring only to the ordinary unclean mob. I'm quite sure that rabbi Nicodemus retained his common sense and didn't succumb to this naïve belief that a dead man could be revived . . .'

'I am a Pharisee, Jonathas,' I broke in. 'I believe in resurrection.'

A murmur arose from the bench around me. From my own brethren I heard comments:

'What are you saying, Nicodemus? We believe in resurrection, of course. We Pharisees all believe that men will rise on the last day. But it will be the last day. And the Most High will resurrect them, not some sinner. He couldn't resurrect anybody.'

'And yet he did,' I turned to my own people. 'Nor was it the first time he's done so. But on this occasion I saw it with my own eyes.'

Jonathas smiled again, ironically:

'Well, as rabbi Nicodemus saw it . . .'

'It's not true,' rabbi Jonathan cried. 'Nicodemus didn't see it. I mean, of course he isn't lying,' he corrected himself. 'But without doubt he has been duped by an illusion . . .'

'Are all the people who have seen Lazarus in the temple and the market also suffering from illusions?' Joseph spoke again. 'I myself saw him only yesterday.'

'Yes, that's true,' Jonathan slowly said at last, like someone who has perforce to yield. 'Lazarus is going about telling everybody how he was resurrected. Maybe it was a trick, as our revered president suggests. But trick or not, this business must be stopped once for all! That Galilean has stirred up the people quite enough. I know what is being said in the city. Do you want war with the Romans tomorrow?'

'Of course we don't,' Caiaphas intervened. 'Rabbi Jonathan is talking sense. None of us wants war. Such a war would be the end of us all!'

'We must put a stop to this accursed sinner!' rabbi Eleazer exclaimed.

'Well said! We must put a stop to him!' Caiaphas turned back to our brethren. 'I understand you have caught him again and again teaching erroneous doctrine. So what could be simpler? Let someone sent by you throw the first stone. And let him take good aim. The moment blood starts to flow others will throw too.'

'That's no good!' Jonathan shook his head.

'Why not?'

'Our brethren have already picked up stones to throw at him more than once. Nothing came of it. He's slippery. And he has many friends.'

'Then we'll have him brought here, give him forty strokes, and forbid him to remain in the city. Let him go back to his Galilee.'

'It's too late for that,' rabbi Joel crowed. 'He's already taught the people to sin and despise the sacred purifications. He must die!'

'Yes,' rabbi Jonathan said moodily but resolutely. 'He must die.'

'I have nothing against that,' Jonathas commented, shrugging his shoulders. 'As you know, I have suffered great losses through him. But let us consider one point for a moment. If we wish to sentence him to death in the usual manner, our sentence will be subject to Pilate's confirmation. And he may take it into his head to spite us . . .'

'Then it would be better to arrange it through the Zealots,' Jehudah, Jonathan's brother, suggested.

'No, no!' Jonathan objected. 'He's quite capable of getting away from the Zealots too. He must be killed and his teaching wiped out. So he must be condemned and die an infamous death, in the sight of all . . .'

'But Pilate . . .' Jonathas repeated his reservation.

'Perhaps Joseph would arrange it for us,' someone suggested.

'You needn't count on that!' Joseph thundered. 'I'm not trading in any man's death. I'm a merchant, not a murderer.'

'I agree that Joseph should not be asked to arrange the affair,' the president assented. 'It would only draw Pilate's attention to the circumstance that we are anxious for the man's death. And we cannot hope to buy him over, for I don't suppose he's got rid of the last lot of gold yet.'

'Then what are we to do?' rabbi Jonathan asked. 'He must die,' he declared emphatically. 'Our agreement . . .'

'We haven't forgotten it,' Jonathas swiftly assured him.

'The president is only considering what kind of death this miracle-worker should die,' Caiaphas said in a soothing tone.

'But he hasn't been condemned yet,' I ventured to point out.

My words caused a ripple of agitation. But the president controlled it at once.

'Of course he hasn't,' he smiled at me rather ironically. 'First we must arrest and try him. Justly and properly. But before that we have got to find out where he is. We must proclaim in all the synagogues that we are seeking him. We'll offer a reward to anyone who indicates where he is staying.'

'But not too big a reward,' Caiaphas intervened. 'Otherwise the idea might get around that he is someone of importance. I suggest thirty shekels, the price for a slave who has been gored by a neighbour's bull.'

'The revered high priest is absolutely right,' the president observed.

'But what then?' rabbi Eleazar asked impatiently.

'We must think that over,' Jonathas said. 'It might be worth while arranging a little revolt . . .'

'Another revolt?' several younger Pharisees exclaimed. 'For all Jerusalem to be beaten up again?'

Rabbi Jonathan himself silenced them. 'Don't get worked up!' he said. 'A stick is a good teacher. If it weren't for their sticks our hatred of the Romans might grow rusty. We'll have to think over how to ensure that this accursed fellow dies. For he must die!'

'He must!' several of our brethren echoed him resolutely.

I was thinking this would mark the end of the session, when rabbi Jonathan unexpectedly rose again and turned to address Caiaphas:

'Your reverence, today you start a new year of your reign as high priest. Without doubt you are mindful of the privileges which have been conferred on you this day.' I was amazed at this formal speech, and above all at the respect with which Jonathan was addressing his enemy. But he went on: 'Today you can utter a prophecy with the aid of the sacred stones Urim and Thummim. We request and call on you to do so. Prophesy! Proclaim that this sinner must die.'

'Why ask that?' rabbi Eleazar jumped to his feet. I saw that others of our brethren were equally displeased with our leader's proposal. 'We know quite well that he's dangerous and must die.'

I, too, could not understand rabbi Jonathan's rather thoughtless suggestion. 'He is tempting the Most High,' I thought. I realized that if the prophecy was against Jesus's death nobody would dare to raise his hand against the teacher. Jonathan must have been carried away by his rancour. But he shook his head obstinately:

'Let the sacred stones speak. I ask you, venerable father, to act on my proposal.'

'Why call for the voice of the Most High on such a petty matter?' Caiaphas asked, obviously taken by surprise. 'Are you the only one to ask it, rabbi?'

'I support the proposal,' I cried, believing that this would be a way of saving Jesus. The Most High surely would not cast His verdict on the side of injustice? A crime was being plotted against an innocent man. I hate Caiaphas. But he would prophesy in his capacity as high priest. At such times the Eternal may speak even through the mouth of a sinner. Let Him speak! Then it would be clear to all that the teacher had been sent by Him.

'As you wish,' Caiaphas folded his arms. He yielded reluctantly. He had no desire to prophesy, and looked about him in the hope of being freed from the task. But the others did not know what to do. Caiaphas realized, of course, that whatever he prophesied would involve him in difficulties: either he would have to seek Pilate's assent to execution of the sentence, or he would be charged with watching over the life of a man whom he regarded as dangerous, but who then would be inviolable. But he could not withdraw now. If he is called upon to do so by two members of the Sanhedrin the high priest must prophesy. 'As you wish,' he said again. 'Pray that the Lord may send His answer through my hand.'

He folded his arms, bowed his head, and began to repeat the incantation governing the act of prophesying.

'O Adonai, Sabaoth, Shekinah! Give Thy sign to me, Thy high priest, whom Thou hast deigned to call into Thy service. Give me the sign and say: is it for the good of Thy chosen nation that this man shall die? Give the sign! I put my right hand into the sacred wallet. In my fingers I feel the two sacred stones, the Urim and Thummim. I know not which is black and which is red. But let the one I have taken be Thy reply. If it is Urim, it shall signify that Thou hast answered "no" to my question. If it is Thummim, Thou hast answered "Yes." O Adonai, Sabaoth, Shekinah! Sevenfold Holy! I call on Thee! I have chosen the stone. I draw it out now from the sacred wallet. Behold the sign of the Most High! Behold!'

He opened his hand. We all started from the benches and surrounded him.

'Thummim! Thummim!' they shouted. My breath stopped for a moment. 'Thummim! The Lord has spoken. He must die!'

What does it mean, Justus? So he should die? What unbelievable consequences that resurrection has had. I passed the news to Lazarus at once and told him to let the teacher know. Since then several weeks have passed. Our brethren are still discussing the best way of taking him prisoner. The proclamation calling for his arrest has been published in all the synagogues. And yet now he is coming to Bethany! And Lazarus has invited me to go and see him.

Yet I shall go. And as soon as I get back I shall write to you again. But tell me what you think of it all without waiting for my next letter.

I have been to Bethany and seen him. I returned feeling rather depressed. Two days later an incident occurred which was shattering. I have never experienced anything like it. It really did seem to me . . . and not merely seemed, for I was absolutely sure. I shouted, and hundreds of people around me shouted too. But with the evening there came a sobering of our feelings which was alarming. And today . . .

But to start from the beginning. Lazarus gave a banquet for the teacher and his disciples. Apart from them I was the only one present. I have told you that Lazarus was beaten up by the guards. I now learned that they broke his arm and several ribs, knocked out one eye, and mutilated all his body. The man who came back from the tomb full of masculine vigour is now a painfully twisted cripple. He could not rise to welcome us. But when the teacher went to him he caught at his hand and pressed it to his lips. I couldn't help thinking that Lazarus hadn't benefited much from his resurrection. Before, he was respected and esteemed. Now he is suffering injury and obloquy. When Ruth died, that was the end of her suffering. It looks as though resurrection is to be the beginning of it for Lazarus. But in that case, why did Jesus raise him from the dead? And why is Lazarus so grateful to him?

I was sitting musing in this fashion when I felt Jesus's eyes on me. I raised my head, and involuntarily asked:

'Do you want something, rabbi?'

'I want to ask you, friend (he always calls me "friend") whether you are fond of parables.'

'Oh yes, rabbi. I think the wisdom of life is revealed most clearly in parables and homilies. I have composed many myself.'

'Then listen to the one I shall tell you. A certain man went out to sow. And he cast the seed before him. Some fell on good, soft, moist ground, and they swiftly took root. But others fell on hard, barren, poor ground. And although they took root, and the stalks shot up, they were as weak as children learning to walk. But the farmer was sorry about the soil which had yielded miserable ears. So he set to work on it again, turned it over deeply with a spade, collected the stones buried in it, and watered it . . .

'And when harvest came the yield from the poor soil was as high as that from the good soil. And the farmer said: "I don't regret my labour, for now the soil into which I put so much effort is dearer to me. And it has yielded good fruit." What do you think of this parable, friend?'

'It's beautiful,' I said. 'I suppose what you mean is that by men's labour even the most wretched thing can be turned into something of value.'

'You have understood well,' he praised me. But his praise sounded like that given to a child which has understood as much as can be expected at his age. 'There is not a sheep in the flock,' he went on, 'which is not worth seeking by night among rocks and thorns. But only a good farmer goes out to look for it. And the Son of Man also waters the poor oats and goes in search of the lost sheep.'

I suppose he must have been thinking of his disciples, and was resorting to the subtle method of a parable to explain to me why he had chosen just them. I ran my gaze over their faces. Poor soil, demanding great effort. And as yet it's impossible to say what fruit it will yield. He was still looking at me, and seemed to be expecting me to question him further.

'But,' I commented, 'the farmer's labour is not always fruitful.'

'Not always,' he admitted. 'And yet the Son of Man is ready to go out and seek the lost sheep at any time, even in rain and storm. Like a woman who has lost a penny, but sweeps her room till she finds it. Like a farmer who manures, tills and waters the poor soil until it yields good results.

He bowed his head. Once more sorrow took charge of him

and bent him to the ground, just as too heavy a crop of fruit bears down the young apple tree. And suddenly the thought occurred to me: 'This man has deluded himself too.' He had expected victory. But, because he needed comrades, he had chosen them from the lowest of the low. That was a mistake – a serious mistake. He had been confident that he would be able to transform these fishermen, craftsmen and customs officers. But he hadn't. They had remained what they were. Now he was trying to console himself. Against all the evidence and his own experience he was maintaining that there was no soil so poor that it would not yield fruit. But no good would ever come from this unclean soil. He felt that, although he still resisted the thought.

Martha waited on us, watchful as ever to ensure that nobody was neglected. Mary was not in the room. I was astonished at this, for she doesn't leave the teacher as a rule: she sits close by, absorbing every word he says. I was wondering why she was absent, when she came into the room. She entered bowed, barefoot, her hair scattered over her shoulders, and clutching something to her breast. She looked more like a mourning woman than one welcoming a dear guest. She moved quietly along by the wall, as though anxious to avoid being noticed. She halted behind the teacher's couch. Under the hair which fell in strands around her face I saw her eyes, darkened, almost black, and half closed as though with suppressed pain. Suddenly she took her hands from her breast, and I saw she was carrying a fine alabaster flask. She neatly broke the neck, and a stupefying scent filled the room. It must have contained a precious and very expensive oil, the one called 'regal.' She allowed it to flow over Jesus's hair. She delicately gathered the drops on her finger-tips and rubbed them along the black strands of hair like a skilful friseur.

Conversation at the table stopped abruptly. During the evening Jesus had seemed sorrowful and taciturn, but his disciples had been more garrulous than usual. Now all talk died away, and they gazed at him and Mary in silence. By their attitude they all seemed to be thinking the same thought. And Philip gave expression to it:

'Ho, ho, ho! What a scent! Truly "regal." It must have cost a lot!'

'What an expense!' Simon the Zealot exclaimed.

'And why use oil at all?' Judas inquired. 'Only loose women use such perfumes. Instead of spending money on that sort of thing it should have been given to the poor.'

The words came as a slap in the face for Mary, especially as they were obviously meant for her.

'Very true, very true!' The others agreed. 'It would have been better to give the money to the poor. And the rabbi would have been better pleased, too, without doubt.'

The woman said nothing, but slipped to her knees. I saw her face, covered with a flood of auburn hair, right by the teacher's feet. Seeing her sorrow, he gently touched her brow and stroked her head.

'Why do you hurt her?' he asked quietly. 'She loves me and wishes to serve me. You will always have the poor with you, and may you never forget them! But I shall not be with you for long . . . She has anointed my body for death, for the tomb. I tell you, wherever there is talk of the gospel I have brought, all over the world people will remember this deed of hers.'

The disciples were silent. His words must have shocked them, for their joy departed from them at once. They looked at one another fearfully, and whispered: 'What is he talking about death again for?'

Philip spoke for them all; there were tears in his colourless eyes.

'Rabbi, we love you too,' he stammered. 'Why do you talk about dying? No harm will come to you if you don't go to the city. Don't go . . .'

The others took up his words. They chorused: 'Don't go!'

He shook his head slowly but resolutely, like a man who has long since taken a decision and regards it as irrevocable.

'I shall go, the day after tomorrow,' he said.

'But the priests and Pharisees are bound to hear of it,' Judas exclaimed.

He fixed his eyes on Judas calmly but sorrowfully.

'All the world will hear of it,' he said.

All the world did indeed hear of it.

I can still see the first incidents of that day. I made my way to the temple through streets swarming with people. I heard a shout coming from the valley of Cedron, but I took no notice of it. On the eve of the holy days the city is filled with shouting, singing, and hubbub. Many pilgrims arrive singing to the strains of a harp. I was lost in thought, and didn't realize that something unusual was happening. Suddenly someone called out my name in a voice which I recognized, but which sounded amazingly strange. I looked up and saw rabbis Joel and Jonathan. They looked even stranger than their voices sounded. They did not look like two doctors learned in the Law, and wholly absorbed in contemplation of it. They were excited, and were violently waving their arms. They demanded of me:

'Rabbi Nicodemus, what is he intending to do? You surely know. What is he after?'

'Who, reverend rabbis?' I asked, for I had no idea what they were talking about.

'Why, that prophet of yours,' rabbi Joel almost spat the words out. But in a tone not of contempt, but of terror.

'I don't know anything about it. He isn't here,' I answered, taken aback by their words.

'He isn't here?' they exclaimed in unison. 'He's marching into Jerusalem at the head of thousands of people. All the rabble have flocked around him. What is he after, Nicodemus? You're on good terms with him. He won't order them to kill, will he?' rabbi Joel stammered.

'He's marching into Jerusalem?'

'Can't you hear? Then look!' They seized my arms and dragged me to the porch. Through the columns I saw an enormous procession winding down the road from the Mount of Olives into the Valley of Cedron. 'Everybody's running after him!' rabbi Joel cried. 'All Jerusalem! And many even of our own brethren. They're waving branches, they're throwing their cloaks under the hoofs of his ass . . . I suppose you told him of the gloss on the prophets which declares the Messiah will come riding into Jerusalem on an ass. Do you hear what they're shouting? "Glory to the Son of David!"'

'He is the son of David,' I replied without thinking.

'Maybe, maybe . . . if you say so. But tell us what he's intending to do. Will he disperse the Sanhedrin and proclaim himself the Messiah?'

I listened for a moment to the shouts which rose from the procession. 'He wishes to establish his kingdom . . .' I answered.

'His kingdom means the rule of the rabble, customs officers and loose women,' Jonathan said with cold passion. 'Better that the nation should never regain its freedom than that it should have such a king.'

The shouts of the approaching people broke through the double archway of the Golden Gate. I was seized with a feeling of fervour and intoxication. I forgot all my afflictions, anxieties, and fears. At last! He has taken action. He has revealed who he is. All the past, his flights from the world, his fears, his prophecies of death, were only ways of testing his disciples. But the testing time was over, the time for victory had come. Now he would no longer be a wandering teacher, with every man hunting him. He had revealed himself, and all the nation believed in him. I had judged that he had lost all meaning for the people, had lost their sympathy. Nothing of the kind. This terrified rabbi Joel and impotently angry Jonathan were like leaves blown from the tree by the powerful winter blast. Of course, there were still the Romans. But at that moment they held no terrors for me. Nothing had any terror for me. The suddenness of the change in the situation filled me with unbounded confidence in the teacher's power.

He could do all things. He was the Messiah. Joshua had ordered the trumpets to sound, and the walls of Jericho had fallen. What of the Romans? They might agree to recognize him. But in any case he would manage all that, so why worry?

'The Messiah,' I said to Jonathan, 'will be the One whom the Most High sends us.'

With an equally challenging fury he replied: 'We don't want such a Messiah, even though the Presence Himself should send him!'

The procession was now pouring into the Temple courtyard. I had no wish to go on arguing with Jonathan. I ignored him as something of no importance. I broke a branch from a tree and ran to meet the procession. I heard Joel's shuffling steps at my side. So the great doctor evidently felt safer in my company.

It was not easy for me to make my way through to the teacher; he was surrounded by thousands of people shouting in his honour. It was a triumph beyond anything I could have believed, if someone had foretold it. The disciples surrounded their master like a guard round a king. Pushing through the crowd, I saw him dismount from his ass. Among the disciples was Judas. He seemed to be bursting with pride, running this way and that, issuing orders, telling some to get back, and allowing others to come nearer. When he saw me he nodded, but quite negligently: one would not have thought that I was a leading Pharisee and he a petty merchant of Bezetha. He was no longer a beggar concealing his spite beneath a humble smile, but the highest of the royal retinue.

'Come closer, rabbi,' he said graciously. 'But you get back!' he barked at some unclean fellow who was pressing too close. 'You stink! Get back, d'you hear?'

'Hallelujah! Hallelujah!' The crowd shouted and sang. 'Welcome, Son of David. Hosannah! Welcome to the king who has come riding on an ass. Hallelujah!'

'Ah!' I heard a scandalized whisper behind me. 'He shouldn't let them talk like that. That's a sin, a great sin!'

Joel said these words quietly, but the teacher must have heard them. He glanced in our direction. Despite the general rejoicing there was no look of joy on his face. The rabble surrounding him spread their cloaks under his feet as he walked towards the Sanctuary. But he stepped on them as though this tribute were unpleasant to him. He looked at Joel without halting, and the reverend doctor shrank under that gaze, like a toadstool shrivelling in the heat.

'If these people were to be silent,' Jesus said, 'the very stones would cry out.'

He went on, and I ran after him. But he suddenly stopped. As always on the eve of the Holy Days, the steps leading to the Temple were covered with stalls. Sacrificial animals were standing here for sale, and on the top step, right under the portico, twenty money-changers' tables were set out. The shouts of the people following the teacher mingled with the clamour of the hucksters, the jingle of coins, the bleating of sheep, the bellowing of cattle and calves, the cooing of doves. It is a revolting sight, this market, but we have grown accustomed to it. He must have seen it frequently enough in the past. But he stared at it now with flaming eyes, as though he had never seen it before. His features reflected his feelings of disgust, indignation, and anger. Anger, but not fury. With a slow, deliberate movement he unfastened the leather thong round his waist and folded it into a whip. The crowd instinctively halted. He went slowly towards the stalls, like a man going to perform an unpleasant but necessary duty. He walked through the crowd to the top of the steps, and went to one of the money-changers' tables. He struck the top solemnly with the whip, then sent it flying down the steps. A stream of gold scattered over the flagstones and among the feet of the crowd, the scales clattered down. The man behind the table started up and bellowed as though he were being flayed alive. He raised his hands to attack Jesus, but fell back abruptly as though repelled by force, changed his mind, and dived down at the people's feet to collect the money.

The teacher walked on, moving among the merchants, over-throwing tables, scattering cages, breaking down the animal pens. A roar and moan of lamentation arose. But nobody attempted to stop him. The merchants snatched up their goods wherever they could and fled down the steps, as though washed away by torrents of rain. Jesus remained standing alone, the thong hanging from his lowered hand. At his feet were scattered coins looking like pieces of amber, and greenish black heaps of dung, like seaweed left behind by the sea. A moment before Jesus had towered majestic and powerful; but now he stood hunched, evidently exhausted. But the crowd did not notice the change. For them he was the man who had smashed the priests' exploitation, he was the victor, the king and Messiah. They shouted with renewed fervour and enthusiasm:

'Praise to the Son of David! Glory and honour to the King who comes in the name of the Most High, Hosannah! Hosannah!'

His disciples surrounded him in a ring. I followed them, and heard him say something to them. What he said astonished and frightened me. He ended:

'I am filled with alarm . . . Have I none the less to say to the Father: deliver me? No, for that after all is what I have come for.'

He added something which I failed to catch. There was a sound as of thunder, as if lightning had struck very close at hand. I looked up, but could not see any clouds, save a few white fleecy clouds floating high in the sky.

But while I was still looking to see which direction the storm was approaching from, a shout arose:

'An angel has spoken to him. He is the true Son of David. Hallelujah!'

He did not contradict the shout. He turned and asked his disciples:

'Did you hear? That voice was for you.' In a solemn tone he added: 'And behold the judgement of the earth has begun. Now all that remains is for me to be extended on the cross, and I shall gather all men in to myself . . .'

'Don't say such things!' Simon exclaimed. 'Don't spoil our joy! The Messiah will not die. He cannot die. The Messiah lives for ever . . . You mustn't talk like that . . .'

But I felt that my feeling of joy and rapture were gone. He had smothered it with fear, as soldiers pour stones into their enemies' wells in a defeated country. Had he come surrounded by these exultant crowds only to steal surreptitiously away from the city and back to Bethany? He had well said: all the world had heard of his power. But, having lit the lamp, he at once extinguished it. Men like Joel have probably already recovered from their fright, and now hate him all the more because of their momentary weakness. As for the Sadducees, they must be in a fury at the way he drove the merchants out from the Temple. I can imagine Caiaphas at this moment!

What was the purpose of this triumphal entry, if it was not to bring victory?

And now we have seen today's incidents.

I spent some hours in the city, going from porch to porch. And I noticed that there were many young Pharisees in the crowd surrounding him. Evidently they were sent by the Grand Council to watch him. He must know that quite well, yet he attacked us all the more, as though contemptuous of danger. Hearing the people call him the Son of David, he asked our brethren in the crowd:

'In your view whose son will the Messiah be?'

'David's,' several answered reluctantly. 'So the prophets say . . .'

As though the reply were inadequate, he asked again:

'But what is meant by the words of the psalm: "The Lord said to my Lord, sit on my right hand, and I shall put all your enemies under your feet." In that case David calls his own son "Lord." How do you elucidate that?'

They looked at one another glumly, and went off without replying. He gazed after them with a look of mournful love, and said:

'O fools and blind! How often have I sent you my prophets, but you have stoned them and killed them! The measure of your crimes must be filled. O Jerusalem,' he cried, not in anger, but in a despairing sorrow. 'City that killed the prophets and those who were sent to you!' He stood with hands outstretched, gazing down at the hovels of Ophel below him, and the palaces of Zion. 'O Jerusalem, how often have I desired to gather up your children as a chicken gathers her chicks under her wing, but you did not want me to. O Jerusalem! You are doomed to perish. You will be as deserted as a house swept clean by the winds. But they, too, will not see me until they say: "Blessed is He who comes in the name of the Most High!"'

Great tears flowed down his cheeks. The people standing round him were silent. They were startled by this outburst, and fearful, though they did not understand his words.

He nodded to his disciples to follow him, and set off towards the Golden Gate. I went with him. Evening was coming on, and the serrated shadow of the wall covered the ravine as with a cloak, reaching as far as Absalom's Tomb. But the opposite slope of the Mount of Olives was bathed in rosy light. The air was still.

We passed through the gate and began to drop down into the valley. The teacher went in front, silent and bowed, as though still sorrowing over the city for which he had prophesied destruction. The disciples dragged after him, exchanging whispered remarks. All their self-confidence of the previous days had left them. Judas and I brought up the rear. He was once more a petty creature filled with concealed anger. As we stepped on to the bridge over the swollen torrent he said hurriedly:

'You see, rabbi, you see? He's drawing back again. He's not willing to . . . When he was willing he carried everybody with him. So he can if he wishes. But he doesn't wish. Why not?'

'I don't know,' I muttered.

'Why didn't he seize power yesterday?' Judas whispered feverishly. 'He could have done . . . But he betrayed us. He has betrayed the cause . . .'

'What cause?' I asked, not thinking much over my question.

He raised his bloodshot eyes to me. During the last few days he has grown thin and dark of face: it is almost as though he has shrivelled.

'The cause . . .' he began, but stopped short. He looked at me from under his brows, with a gaze that almost seemed hateful. 'You never will understand that, rabbi,' he muttered evasively.

He said no more, and I didn't follow up his remarks. How could I? Each of us was looking for something quite different in this teacher. But he hasn't come up to the expectations of any of us. Not because he's too small. He seems rather to be greater than anything we had expected. To all our demands he seems to give the one answer: 'Is that all you want?' But in that case what has he brought us? Does the sun shine any differently since he has arrived on the earth to talk about his kingdom?

We emerged from the depths of shadow and began to climb the sunlit slope. Our shadows extended before us, broken over the steps carved into the red, clay earth. The low and stunted grey olives sparkled in the sunlight. Jesus walked slowly, dragging his feet as though worn out by some tremendous effort. I noticed that again and again he raised his hand to wipe the sweat from his brow. Or possibly it wasn't sweat, but tears?

Suddenly he halted. He pointed to a small meadow extending along by a low wall of flat stones. He sat down, and we sat around him. There was a long silence. The city lay in a compact mass at our feet, girdled by the terrace of Moriah, and striped like a tiger skin with the sunlight streaming through the colonnade above Tyropeon. From this point we could clearly see people moving about the Temple courtyard. The sun sank lower and lower, its rays slipped horizontally over the roofs and the courtyard. But because of this the Sanctuary itself seemed even more magnificent and gigantic than usual, with its pylons, projected by their shadows, sharply delineated against the burning sky, so that it looked like an enormous step pyramid with its apex turned towards us. Straight ahead of us was the double gate leading to the women's courtyard. The courtyard itself was like a well, but, like a stone at the bottom of a well, through it shone the gold of the gate leading to the sacrificial altar. The marvellous edifice held our eyes enthralled. The sun shone through the columns, was reflected from the golden roof, and crimsoned the plume of smoke which arose from the altar, spreading an aureole of azure, purple, and gold over all things. The Temple seemed to be ascending into the air, like some unearthly phenomenon.

How beautiful is our Temple! Although I have spent all my life at the foot of its walls, I always gaze with rapture at its form, so light and yet so majestic. Herod was an infamous and faithless scoundrel, but undoubtedly this work of his has redeemed some of his crimes. I sometimes think that so long as the Temple exists, not even the worst of lots is altogether hopeless. Nor was I the only one to be moved by such feelings at this moment.

'Look, rabbi!' One of the disciples exclaimed. 'Isn't it magnificent?'

He answered in the same mournful tone he had used when standing outside the porch:

'Not one stone of it will be left on another . . .'

'What made you say that, rabbi?' several of us cried out. 'That will not be. That cannot be!'

'Not one stone will be left on another,' he repeated emphatically. 'But when you see the soldiers surrounding the city, flee! And let not one of you return for anything. For at that time the days of vengeance will be at hand, the days which the prophets have foretold. People will die of hunger and the sword, and the heathens will tread the ruins of the city. And so it will be without end, until the times are fulfilled . . .'

'But then?' I asked eagerly.

He went on without looking at me:

'Then there will be signs in the sun and the stars, and the people will be oppressed as never before. Fear will dwell among you, the fear of expectation, so that many of you will die even of that fear. But before then the people will turn against you. You will be persecuted, imprisoned, and put to death. You will be delivered to judgement, as criminals. Brother will betray brother, and father his son. In many hearts love will die. In those days remember what I have said to you: but when you have come up for judgement, don't consider beforehand what you shall say. The Holy Spirit itself will speak to you and tell you. You will be hated by the world because you were faithful to me. But stand fast! They will want to delude you. People will come and say to you: "We are the Messiah!" And they will work great signs, and will promise . . . Do not believe them! Do not listen to them! Wait for my coming. For I shall come. I shall not leave you alone and afraid, my friends. I shall come, and I shall shorten the terrible days for those whom I have chosen . . .'

We sat speechless, frightened and depressed. Prophets have frequently foretold things which did not come to pass. But he spoke in a tone of great certainty, as though not one word he had uttered would fail.

'I shall shorten those days,' he said in a more kindly tone. Possibly he saw how much he had depressed us, and wanted to comfort us. 'Don't be afraid. When these things come about, raise your heads confidently and boldly. I shall be close at hand. Only watch, to ensure that I don't find you sleeping or feasting. And pray often. Do not cease . . .'

'Tell us now when these things will be?' Philip asked.

He shook his head.

'No one knows the day of the end, except the Father. You must watch. The Son of Man will come like lightning, he will steal into the house like a thief by night, before the cock crows. Therefore watch and pray, that it may not be with you as it was with those in the days of Noah, who did not notice the oncoming flood. Watch as friends watch for the return of the betrothed from the wedding celebrations. Watch, but don't be afraid . . .'

Despite these comforting words, we sat overwhelmed by the horror of the vision he had opened to us. Simon's quivering voice broke the silence:

'But where will you be in those days, master?'

He smiled faintly. The sun fell on the serrated walls of the Temple, its fading rays streaked the sky. Now the Temple was a black mass. A wind began to blow up. It died away again.

His reply flowed like oil over the sea of our fears. Although it had reference only to Simon, each of us breathed more easily, vaguely feeling that it was also a reply to the alarm of his own heart. The words came quietly, yet quivering with such strength as though they would never fade into silence:

'I shall be with you, wherever you are, Peter.'

DEAR JUSTUS,   TWENTY-FIRST LETTER.

It has happened. What had to happen has happened. They have taken him. They may have killed him already. But it was what he wanted. He did all he could to concentrate the hatred of the priests and doctors on himself. True, he did not surrender himself to them. During the past few days he was in the habit of slipping out of the city each evening, going across the fields to Bethany, or spending the night in one of the vineyards on the Mount of Olives. But he remained in Jerusalem all day, and right up to the last he would not hold his tongue. Only yesterday morning he was talking at one of the porches, and entered into a lively dispute with men whom the Grand Council, Sadducees and Herodians all sent to him. He vanquished them. But it was only a verbal victory. Even though they did go away furious, panting for revenge, while the crowd laughed at them, the words he used were just as incomprehensible to the people who applauded him. What he says is always his own thought, and his words are different from the words of others. He appears to recognize no rules whatever. Even the most beautiful things in our life require to be contained within forms governed by law. Man must be obedient to certain prescriptions. One cannot even be good just how one likes. But he is different: he demands that every rule should be superseded by a single law which he regards as absolute, and which he considers must be observed at the cost of all others. That law is the law of compassion. Whoever fulfils the work of compassion has so to speak fulfilled all the other prescriptions. The Law gave us ten commandments. Our scribes have formulated large numbers of prescriptions. But he says, if a man doesn't love the Most High and his neighbour, there is no point in refraining from murder, theft or lust; there is no point in observing all the prescriptions relating to purity and the Sabbath. He has built his teaching on the Torah, but also above the Torah. That which the Torah regards as the end of human perfection is only the beginning for him. The Torah demands: 'Be an honest man.' He appears to teach: 'Since you are an honest man, you can become my disciple. But even if you are not an honest man, you can still be my disciple provided you only have love . . .'

Only love . . . But that simple teaching is the most difficult of all. Why is it that a man who demands only absolute, unyielding love is hated so much? The Temple guards arrested him an hour ago. What James told me has made me shiver. It's terrible, terrible . . .

I always seem to start my letters from the end: the events of his life are so devastating that the latest incident always tends to obscure all that has happened before. But I want to give you every detail. So I shall try to provide you with a narrative of events in their strict order.

This morning I ran into rabbi Joel. I was right: the devout martyr for the sins of Israel has completely recovered from his fright.

'Ah, whom do I see, whom do I see?' he raised his hands. 'Rabbi Nicodemus! It's ages since we last met.' (Four days, to be exact.) 'The worthy rabbi is never present at the meetings of the Little Sanhedrin . . .'

These words confirmed my supposition that meetings of the inner group of the Grand Council are being held in secret from me. The Temple staff have told me that the Sadducees' leaders are meeting each evening together with our leading brethren in Caiaphas's palace. Nobody has told either me or Joseph about these meetings.

'There's no need for me to be present at every meeting,' I observed calmly.

'Oh, of course not; of course not!' he hastily agreed. 'The reverend rabbi Nicodemus is working hard, doubtless? Writing his beautiful homilies? Oh, if I could only write like you! The Most High has put a great talent in your hands. With that talent you serve the Eternal, and gain glory for yourself. One day the whole nation will be learning Nicodemus's homilies. May he never do anything else, may he not squander his thoughts on unnecessary matters . . . I have been troubled of late to see that instead of writing you are going about with that man from Galilee. It's a waste of your time. I saw you running after him with a branch in your hand. I rather think you even declared he was the Messiah . . .'

I made no reply. I pretended I had not heard his last words. He did not press the point, but stood rubbing his hands.

'That man has laid himself open to great peril,' he observed. 'As if it were not enough for him to ignore the sacred prescriptions governing purity, he has now turned to sending the merchants packing. Possibly he was even right in doing so . . . But he has exposed himself to great peril . . . The Sadducees will never forgive him for that. They are plotting his death now. And any man who has Caiaphas for enemy must be prepared for anything. At any moment. Yes, yes,' he sighed, 'heavy are our people's sins, very heavy . . . He who has undertaken to do penance for them has much to suffer . . .'

He walked off, dragging his feet. I found myself wondering why he had told me all this. I came to the conclusion that he had done it because of the dislike he felt for Caiaphas. Joel regards the high priest as a festering ulcer on the body of the nation. He hates him like poison. Even his hatred for the teacher is feeble by comparison with what he feels for the high priest. I doubt whether he found it easy to agree to the alliance Jonathan has concluded with the Sadducees on behalf of our brethren. I decided that Joel was deliberately warning me that great danger threatens Jesus.

Having put this construction on Joel's remarks, I took a decision. Twilight was hardly falling when I mounted an ass and rode out through the Dung Gate along the road to Bethlehem. When I was a little way outside the city I turned along the side of the Mount of Olives to make my way to Bethany through the olive groves. I thought that this circumspection might defeat any spies who might be watching my movements.

Lazarus's house was wrapped in such quiet that everybody seemed asleep. I knocked at the door, but had to wait a long time before it was opened. At last I heard heavy footsteps, and Lazarus appeared. He makes shift to walk with the aid of two sticks. I must admit I feel something akin to terror every time I see him. Death has the effect of removing and exalting a man; but I can never forget that I have stood before this man's sealed tomb. I have never talked to him about it. But perhaps I should. He might be able to tell me something about Ruth. On the other side, perhaps, one can get to know a little about another? I have never dared to ask. In all probability the memory of Sheol has faded from his mind since his return to life. Surely it wouldn't be possible to go on living, possessing knowledge of what things are like there?

'The Most High be with you, rabbi,' he said. 'Come in. You have arrived late, and you must be weary. The teacher is not asleep, we are all sitting together. He spoke about you today . . .'

'There's something I want to tell him . . .'

'Then come in. Martha will bring water for you to wash.'

They were all in the one room. He was sitting in the centre, with his hands clasped round his knee. He was not talking, he was gazing into the fire. I was struck at once by the circumstance that his face was almost like that of an old man. For some days he seems to have been living a year in every hour. And yet, despite his seriousness, he is a young man, in the plenitude of health and strength. He could undertake the most exhausting journey without growing tired. But now his face reveals his exhaustion, his loss of energy; he seems to be bowed down under a load of cares. He was breathing heavily. He looked like someone who has lost all hope and is passively awaiting the coming of defeat. When he heard my steps he slowly raised his head. A faint smile passed over his lips, like sunlight strayed from an autumn day.

'Peace be with you, friend,' he said, and beckoned for me to go over to him. I felt his hot hands on my shoulders. Was he hoping I could save him? I instinctively tried to summon up freedom of action and energy: other people's weakness frequently has the effect of making us strong. But I could not. I, too, felt fear and despair beneath my skin. The thought passed through my mind that neither of us was capable of taking a serious decision. As I felt my breast against his breast I looked across his shoulder: the disciples and the women were sitting with bowed heads. They appeared to share the teacher's loss of spirit.

'I was thinking of you today, Nicodemus,' he said. He let me go, and I slipped out of his embrace. 'And I wanted to see you, very, very much . . .'

'Is there something you want me to do, rabbi?' I asked.

I expected him to shake his head gently, as he had shaken it so often when he was asked if he wished to eat, to drink, to sleep, to rest. But he raised a suffering look to me, the look of one among the many sick he had healed, and quietly said:

'Yes.'

'What is it?' I asked. Though I saw him in such a state of depression, I could not forget entirely those moments in which, in the twinkle of an eye, all human weakness had fallen away from him, to reveal an incomprehensible might. Nor was that my only feeling. I know he had not saved Ruth. But he had given so much to others that I, though I had received nothing, none the less felt indebted to him.

'What is it?' I repeated. 'Only tell me. I shall be at your service. I have come in order to save you. You are in danger. But early tomorrow morning I shall send you two asses, or even camels, together with a trustworthy and intelligent man. You will go far away. This spot is dangerous for you. The Pharisees and priests are plotting something, so I was told today. I think it possible that they may arrest you even during the holy days. But if you go away, when everything is quiet you may be able to come back.'

I felt the touch of his hand on my palm.

'Don't talk of that, friend,' he said quietly. 'I shall not go away. Every day has its evening. There's something else I want to ask you . . .'

'Then what can I do for you, rabbi?'

'Nicodemus, give me your cares.'

'My cares?'

'Yes, friend. That was what we agreed, that time. Now the moment has come. Give me your cares today. I need them, I've been waiting for them. I still lacked just them . . .'

'I don't understand,' I stammered. At this stage I find it quite impossible to understand what he is getting at. But even at the beginning, he didn't explain to me what he meant by being 'born again.' He rarely likes to explain his meaning. His teaching is not like that of the Greek philosophers. They explained the world, they told what it was like, in one talk. He likes a man to pass from discovery to discovery, to explain all the mysteries to himself. He doesn't equip you for life. He says incomprehensible things. At times he seems to contradict himself. I've heard him say many a time: 'Be as children; you must be like children.' And yet he says things incomprehensible, and almost seems to be saying: 'You must grow up to them.' But a grown-up is no longer a child, and a child must reconcile itself to not understanding the world.

But he made no explanation. He only pointed me to a stool

and gazed at me. There was a look of warmth, of love, of devotion in his eyes. He was like someone who is pleading, humbly pleading. He repeated: 'Give me your cares.'

'Give me your cares,' I pondered. It sounded like a sneer, if he had been capable of sneering. Of course, I'm ready to hand them over at once. I've no desire to keep them. That was why I had come here through the night, by pathless ways. I had brought them with me, but here they had increased even more. He hadn't taken them from me when we first made the agreement. Over a mug of warm milk which Martha brought me I gazed at him. I expected him to say something more. But he had his eyes again fixed on the fire, and the look of inner conflict and suffering returned to his face. 'He's only a weak man.' I have thought that again and again during the past three years. And yet I felt convinced of I don't know what.

It was late at night when I realized that it was time for me to return. Martha slipped out to bring my ass from the stable. I rose and went to Jesus. He seemed to be asleep, with his face in his hands. But when he heard my footsteps he raised his head, and I saw that his cheeks were wet with tears. He must have been weeping a long time, without a sound.

'May the Eternal be with you, rabbi,' I said.

'So you're going now?'

'Yes. The night is almost gone. The cocks will be crowing soon.'

'Yes,' he whispered, seemingly to himself. 'The night is almost gone . . . and the cocks . . .' He sighed. 'I could wish it to pass swiftly, and I could wish it to endure without end,' he made the incomprehensible confession. 'An unforgettable night . . .' It stuck in my memory that he said 'unforgettable.' 'Remember,' he said, turning back to me, 'that I wait for your cares. Peace be with you, child.' This man, younger than I, spoke like a patriarch. He stretched out his hand and passed it over my face. I have never known a more moving touch. Not even that of Ruth when she touched my face to comfort me in my despair over her.

Outside I found Martha waiting with the ass, and someone else. Heavy clouds were rolling across the sky, obscuring the light of the moon. But at that moment it swam clear, and I saw that the second form was Judas.

'Would you allow me to go with you to the city, rabbi?' he asked. 'I have to make certain purchases there.'

'Certainly,' I said. I was quite pleased at the proposal, for his companionship would distract me from my thoughts. I said 'the Lord be with you' to Martha, and we set off. Judas walked beside my ass. We passed into the shadow of the trees. Dogs barked occasionally. But when we drew away from human habitations we were engulfed in a silence that was disturbed only by the rustle of olive leaves in the wind.

'I think you were right,' I remarked after we had been travelling in silence for some time. 'The teacher is completely broken up. Where has his power gone?'

'He himself has got rid of it!' Judas whispered passionately. He added with a growing violence of tone: 'I've told you already, rabbi, he's thrown it away. He could have conquered. He could have sent packing all that band of wealthy scoundrels, thieves, exploiters, parasites. He could have destroyed them.'

'I'm afraid,' I answered, 'that if the leaders of the Sanhedrin learn of his weakness they will not stop to think twice. They'll keep him under surveillance and take action against him as soon as the people have gone home after the Holy Days.'

'They won't wait for the end of the Holy Days,' he broke in as violently as before. 'They'll kill him. It may be today, it may be tomorrow. He's finished!' He impulsively laid his hand on my ass's neck and plucked at its mane. 'He's finished already,' he repeated. 'And I've never had even as much as five coppers for myself!' His voice in the darkness sounded like the wail of a dying man. I felt his burning breath on my face as he leaned towards me. 'I've never even had five coppers of my own to buy wine, oil, and love . . . He says he loves people. He doesn't understand that nobody ever loves a beggar or anyone who's wretchedly poor. People gave him money. But he might just as well never have had it. I couldn't live like that,' his voice quivered. 'I just couldn't. Never having wine, never having friends, never having a decent robe to my back, never a woman who would give me herself . . . for herself . . . I just couldn't.'

He staggered for a moment like a drunken man, breathing heavily. Then I heard a jingling sound: evidently he had some coins in his hand.

The track led us down into the black depths of the ravine. The ass walked more slowly and cautiously. Above us rose the rocky sides of the gorge, dark, yet seeming to steam with the light that filtered down into it. The chill, or possibly my inner confusion of thought, set me trembling. What did he mean by: 'Give me your cares?' That must be yet another of his mysteries – terrible, painful, yet, like all his mysteries, concealing an unexpected peace at its heart. Or were they only the half-delirious words of a man plunged into despair? This last talk with him brought back to mind that other talk on the hill, when he had said: 'Take my cross and give me yours.' Then, too, I hadn't understood what he meant. I had half-consciously expected him to heal Ruth. Her illness had been my heaviest cross at that time. But he hadn't taken that on himself. And now – who knows? – perhaps a real cross awaits him. I have never been able to watch a crucifixion, it is such a horrible method of torturing a man. I cannot imagine what it would be like. I should think Judas, too, is afraid of a cross. Was it to drown his fears that he kept on jingling the coins? I felt like shouting to him to stop, but I refrained. So I rode on in silence between the patches of dazzling, twinkling moonlight. But Judas walked beside me continually jingling his shekels.

On reaching the city that morning I went to a workshop situated close to my house. I intended to order some work to be done, but it was so pleasant there that I sat on a baulk of timber and listened to the merry clatter of the hammers. The workmen sang as they worked, and their cheerfulness dispelled my anxieties: I began to forget the evil visions that had been

plaguing me during the night. But Ahir appeared at the doorway and beckoned to me. My heart sank. I knew that my care-
free moment had passed, that my servant was summoning me
back to the world of fears and troubles.

Outside, I found John and Simon waiting for me. Ahir had
fallen in with them close to Siloh, and they had come with him
to tell me the teacher had asked if he could have the upper
room of my house for the evening. He wished to eat a 'Galilean
passover' with his disciples. This request deepened my anxiety.
I didn't want to refuse, and in any case it is not permissible to
refuse one's house to pilgrims who wish to eat their passover
feast in it. But why had he asked me? Why did he propose to
come through the twilight to the city where danger is always
lying in wait for him? And, to make matters worse, he planned
to have the feast in a house a stone's throw away from the
palace of the high priest, in the house of one whom the Sanhedrin suspected of being his disciple. Was it just a terrible lack
of consideration on his part, or was he deliberately tempting
the Most High? I told Simon:

'Since the teacher has asked, of course I shan't refuse. But I
implore you not to do anything stupid! No more triumphal
processions into the city! Come quietly, in little groups, mingling with the crowds. Don't let anybody know that you intend
to spend the night in Jerusalem.'

John nodded his understanding. But Simon is impossible. He
was once more filled with an overweening self-confidence and
arrogance. He set his arms akimbo and said in his trumpeting
voice, sufficient in itself to attract everybody's notice:

'The teacher has no need to be afraid of anything. Let anyone try to attack him! I'll show him!' He struck his hand on a
parcel he was carrying under his arm. He unwrapped it and
triumphantly showed me two short, broad swords.

'They may come in handy,' he bragged as he wrapped them
up again. What a fool the fellow is! He actually thinks of fighting the Temple staff and the Grand Council guards! I again
began to imagine the worst.

They had their feast upstairs and sang hymns, while I anxiously paced up and down my room and listened to every sound that came from outside. Night had fallen when I heard them departing. I flung myself down on my bed and fell asleep at once. But I did not sleep for long. I was aroused by Ahir tugging my shoulders. He said someone wanted to see me. In a moment I was fully awake; I wrapped myself in my cloak and went out to the caller. It was James, John's brother. James has a habit of dressing neatly, his hair is always tidy, and in all his being he expresses cleanliness and care. But now his cloak was dishevelled, his hair wet and unkempt, his feet were muddy and bloodstained. As he stood there he was trembling from head to foot. For a moment or two he could not say why he had come. Then he choked up the words:

'They've caught him . . .'

Although I had been expecting some such news, I sank beneath it. My legs refused to support me. I sat down on a stool, my head went quite empty, black spots floated before my eyes. 'And so after all . . .' the words began to peal through my head, 'and so, after all.' All my thoughts, all my talks with him were focused down into those four words.

'And so after all,' I said aloud, 'he did not manage to escape, to hide . . .

I must have sat a long time with my head bowed, racked with a shivering fit. When I looked up James was still standing in front of me. As I gazed at him I realized that the most terrible thing for him was not simply that his master had been captured. His eyes expressed not only pain and terror. There was despair in them too. I felt drops of cold sweat on my forehead, and my teeth chattered as I whispered:

'How did it happen?'

'How did it happen?' he repeated, as though he needed to find an explanation for it himself. 'We ate the passover in your house, rabbi . . . He . . . He was sad. He spoke . . . I didn't understand everything he said. He said that before long he would be going away and would return again soon after, because he didn't want us to be left orphans . . . So perhaps they'll let him go. What do you think, rabbi?'

I shook my head dubiously.

'We said we would go with him wherever necessary and we weren't afraid even of death. He smiled mournfully, as though he didn't believe us. And he told us to love one another as nobody has ever loved before. We were to remember that he was always with us, and in our love for him we were to do our duty. He talked a long time: I can't repeat all he said. And after the meal he washed our feet. Peter didn't want him to, but he said it was necessary. And then, although we had finished the passover meal, he took bread and gave each of us a piece. Then he gave wine to each of us. And he said it was his body and his blood, and we were to eat and drink it. We didn't know what to make of all this.

'Judas went out immediately after. The teacher said something to him, reminding him: "Do it quickly." Then he told us again to love one another. And that whoever saw him saw the Father. That was because Philip had asked him: "What father?" and because we wanted him to show us the father. I can't remember clearly all he said. But John and I said we would be the first in the kingdom. Simon was indignant at that, and James cried out he would be the first because he was Jesus's "brother." But the teacher told us to be silent. He said that in this world kings are first, but in his kingdom he who is first must be as the most unimportant servant. And then he asked us if we had ever lacked anything when we went with him about Galilee, Pereia, Samaria, and Judaea. We said: "No." You see, we had always had food and drink, even though he had told us not to think of the morrow. But now, he said, it wouldn't be like that. Now we must think of providing ourselves with a wallet for the shekels and for food, and if any of us hadn't a wallet he was to sell his cloak and buy a sword. Simon cried out that he had already bought swords, and set two swords in front of him. But he didn't even look at them. He sat for a time with his head bowed in his hands, as though we had caused him great sorrow. Then he rose and said: "Enough! Let us go."

'The evening was getting late, the moon had risen above the Temple towers. We set out quietly in the direction of Ophel. Suddenly we saw someone in front of us. It was his mother Mary. She had been sitting under a fig tree, waiting for us to come out of the house. We halted. She and Jesus stood side by side in the moonlight. "Son," I heard her say, "I implore you not to go." He answered her very quietly, so that only she could hear. She cried out with pain, fell back and covered her face. He went to her, bent over her, and stroked her as if he were a mother trying to wipe the pain and tears from the face of her child. Then he gently but firmly pushed her away, and went down towards the Gate of the Source. He did not look back. She called after him: "I shall watch . . ." None of us knew what she meant. We walked past her and left her standing under the fig tree, her hands stretched out towards him.

'We went down towards the pool, leaving Ophel on our left, like a forest of bushes. Cedron was roaring in the night like a sea in a storm. We had hardly left the city when he began to talk again. He halted by a vine, and laid his hand on it. "We are like this vine," he said. "I am the trunk, and you are the branches. Love one another," he said again, "especially in the times of greatest difficulty." We didn't understand him, and he realized that we didn't. He said: "You'll understand everything when I send you the Comforter. He will teach you everything. I have to go away, for otherwise the Comforter would not come. But I am going away to my Father."

'Then John and I thought we knew what he was getting at. There was a time once when we and Simon were with him on a hill-top. We've never told anybody about this, for he told us not to. I don't know whether I ought to tell you, rabbi. But now we thought that he would be going to his father, just as he had that time on the hill-top. And that there would be another miracle like that one, only this time everybody would see it. All the world! So we now said we believed everything he said.

But instead of rejoicing he looked at us sorrowfully. "So you believe already, do you? The time has come when you will flee and leave me all alone. But I am not alone." Then he prayed.

'The moon rose higher and higher, and flooded the ravine with light. We were worn out, for we had had little sleep during the past few days. Our heads were bursting with all we had heard. He had decided to spend the night in the Garden of the Olive Press. When we passed under the trees we began to remove our cloaks and stretch them out on the ground. But he didn't sit down. "Sleep here," he said; "I shall be a little farther on." That didn't surprise us. He often prays at night, while we are sleeping worn out. But as he went he called to me, John, and Simon: "Come with me."

'We went to a spot below the cliff. He halted and said: "Watch and pray. I shall be praying too. I feel as sad as a man about to die." He said this in such a tone that we all stared at him. He had been sad ever since the day of the feast in Lazarus's house, but his sadness had never prevented his talking to us and giving us instructions. But now he seemed frightened, seized with despair. "Pray, and watch," he repeated several times. "The spirit is full of enthusiasm, but the body is so wretched!" He went on, but not far, only a stone's throw. We saw him fall to his knees and bow his face down to the ground. Simon said: "Let's pray, since he has asked us to." We didn't kneel, for we were very tired; we simply repeated "Hallelujah!" John fell asleep at once. My eyelids felt heavy and the prayer died away on my lips. I didn't even notice just when Simon began to snore. Then I came round again. I had no idea how long I had been watching, or even if I had been asleep. Then I rested my head against a trunk and went off at once.

'I was awakened by the teacher's voice. I started to my feet. He was standing over us and saying in a wail like that of a beggar at the Gate of Ephraim: "Why are you sleeping? Couldn't you watch just for this one hour?" He was standing in a patch of moonlight, and I saw his face. By the brow of Moses! It looked terrible! Have you ever seen the face of a man who has been stoned to death, rabbi? It was just like that: white, twisted with pain, as taut as a harp string. Or rather, it was like the face of a man who has been strangled, who has had to fight for every gasp of air. The night was cold, but his forehead was wet with sweat; the drops flowed almost like blood. If I'd been able to, I'd have jumped up and run away as though from a bad dream. But I seemed to be rooted to the ground. He stood over us, and repeated: "Why are you asleep? I warned you not to sleep. I need you. Pray! Watch! Only the first temptation comes alone. The tenth comes with the fifth, the twentieth with the ninth. The last with all the others."

'He raised his hand and passed it over his face. Then he returned to the spot where he had been praying. For a moment he was a hardly perceptible shadow in the darkness; then the moon shone and picked him out again. He slowly dropped to his knees. He repeated something, the same words over and over again. I don't know what he was saying, but sometimes he said it faster, feverishly; sometimes slowly, hesitantly. I grew more and more alarmed. He had told us to pray, but the words of the psalm froze on my lips. Simon muttered that we mustn't sleep, because the teacher needed us. But he had hardly said the words when . . . You see, rabbi, sleep seemed to me the only refuge from fear. When I heard Simon snoring I felt envious . . . He was no longer afraid, but I was still afraid.'

'So you went off to sleep again?' I asked.

He groaned like someone struck on an open wound.

'I was so afraid,' he said through his chattering teeth; 'so afraid.'

'And then they came and took him away?'

'No,' he answered; 'he came to us yet again. He was no longer groaning or weeping. He only said mournfully: "You can sleep now." We rubbed our eyes and gazed at him. We felt ashamed of having gone off to sleep. But why didn't he tell us that was the last moment? He said again and again: "Watch together with me." But how were we to know?

'Suddenly we heard shouts and we saw the crimson glow of

torches through the trees. Guards had surrounded the garden, and they approached from all sides. We started to our feet. I felt like running away. But Simon snatched his sword from his girdle and asked fervidly. "Am I to fight, master? Am I to fight?" I heard the others shouting as they were disturbed from sleep. The Temple guards closed around us in a ring. I saw swords, sticks, and spears, angry faces, I heard shouts. Simon leaped forward.'

But do you know, Justus, it appears Jesus rebuked his favourite disciple! Simon inflicted a wound on one of the high priest's servants, and he healed it. Surely he could have escaped even at that stage? He had slipped away from the crowd so often. It appears he had said: 'There will be no more miracles now; now you need to have a wallet and a sword.' But what sword did he mean, if he didn't allow Cephas to use his?

I had no hope of getting any further sleep. So I sat down to write all this to you, and had just finished when someone knocked at the house door. My heart stopped beating. I thought at once that they were intending to have done with all the teacher's friends too, this night. Instead of going to the door I ran up to the roof. But there was only one man standing below. 'Who's there?' I called.

'It's me, Chaim!'

I recognized one of the Temple staff. 'What do you want at this time of night?' I asked.

'The high priest has ordered me to tell you to come to his palace at once, rabbi. All the Sanhedrin is assembling there now. The rebel from Galilee is to be tried.'

'At night? A trial can't take place at night. The Law forbids it . . .'

'I don't know about the Law, rabbi; I'm not versed in the Scriptures. I've simply been told to tell you. And I have to go on to others.' He disappeared in the darkness.

I returned to my room on the ground floor. James was sitting by the wall, motionless, wretched. He could not forgive himself for falling asleep. But what is the good of regrets? I myself fell asleep many a time when watching at Ruth's bedside. In any case we wouldn't have been able to save him. Nor shall we, if he cannot save himself. Cannot, or doesn't want to? A Messiah who has come but doesn't wish to conquer: that puts an end to all faith in the Messiah. But if he is not able? That would mean that he is not the Messiah. Which is better: to know we have been mistaken, or to know that the faith itself is a delusion? I cannot solve that problem; I must go to the Sanhedrin. But perhaps it would be better to pretend I am sick? But what would I gain by that? They will condemn him in my absence. But supposing he has surrendered himself into their hands only in order to demonstrate all his power before their court? Then I would be like a swimmer who drowns in the very sight of land. No, I must go. I must show that I am a man. I must put up a fight for him. I don't wish to be like this fellow James, who sits weeping and doesn't dare to show his face in the street. True, I have come at the very end of the day, like the worker who came late to the vineyard in his parable. I thought it would be a moment of triumph. But it has proved to be a moment of bitter defeat. That can't be helped: that is always a possibility when one plays for high stakes. Maybe I shall regret all my vacillations; and maybe I shall reproach myself for not vacillating even more than I have. But enough! I must drink my wine down. I am going. I shall roll up this letter and take it with me. If I fall in with a departing caravan I shall send it to you by their hand. Oh, why aren't you here, Justus? You might be able to explain what he meant when he said: 'Give me your cares.' Why does he want to take my cares? And how can we arrange so that I can give them to him? Unfortunately, I have no one who can tell me that. He said: 'I wait; remember that I wait for them.' And he said it as a man speaks of water in the desert. But now he is a prisoner under threat of death. One can hardly put more burdens on a man who is a prisoner. And yet if he cannot take them, who can? He is the only one who has expressed such great desire for them.

'Give me all that fetters you . . .' So he once said. And when Ruth died I thought I understood that he didn't want to make her well. But why has he repeated 'Give me your cares' at this juncture? Why does he want to take them on his shoulders? And how does he propose to do it? Who can answer these questions?

For it is too late. Now he is a prisoner under threat of death. What can a prisoner do for a free man?

Accompanied by two servants (for I did not want to go through the streets alone), I went to the high priest's palace. Guards had been posted even outside the walls, each man leaning on his spear. In the courtyard fires were burning, and Temple guards, servants, Levites, and others whom I didn't recognize were around them.

As I entered the courtyard a Levite came up to me.

'Welcome, rabbi,' he said courteously. 'The Sanhedrin is still assembling. Meanwhile the prisoner has been taken to the revered Ananias. Perhaps you'd like to go and hear what he has to say?'

I said I would, and walked through the courtyard. The high priest's house is connected with his father-in-law's palace by two courts. Everywhere men were standing around fires. The Sadducees had turned out all Jerusalem. The Levite conducted me by a side entrance to a large hall built in the style of the Roman atrium, with a reservoir in the centre, which was open to the sky. Ananias was sitting on a low throne under the surrounding colonnade. With him were a number of priests and Sadducees, also Pharisees and doctors of the Law. I was amazed to see how swiftly the age-old hatred between the Pharisees and Sadducees had been transformed into friendship. Almost immediately after I entered, Jesus was brought in through another door opposite the throne. I halted as though transfixed.

Jesus was a wretched sight: his hands were bound behind him, and he was belted with a stout, wrought-iron belt, to which ropes were attached. These enabled him to be dragged along by the guards without their touching him. He must have been dragged in this manner all the way from the Garden of the Olive Press, and he must have stumbled and fallen again and again; his cloak and robe were filthy, mud-stained, wet and torn to ribbons; his hair was dishevelled. His feet were stained with blood. But even so he towered in height and in authority above the men around him. His face had a sorrowful expression, but he evidently was self-possessed. He gazed calmly straight at Ananias. If he felt any fear it was concealed in the depths of his being like a stone in a lake. As he stood there, erect and silent, I recalled that as he stood under the sombre trees he had said: 'Here I am. You are looking for me, so let these others go.' His bearing must have impressed his captors, for there was a silence, broken only by the crackling of torches. Unexpectedly I heard a grating sound, as Ananias laughed. The Sadducees and Pharisees around him echoed him. After a moment he said:

'Ah, so it's you, Jesus of Nazareth? What an honour it is for us to see you here. But what is this? Didn't you come of your own free will? And where are your disciples? Your servants? Where is your kingdom?' He suddenly changed his tone, as he struck his open palm against the arm of the throne. 'That's all finished now! You've sinned enough! We've had enough of your blasphemies! You have desecrated the Lord's Temple. Did you really think you'd always be able to go scot free?'

He spread himself more comfortably on his throne. Others took up the tune he had set. They rushed up to the prisoner and waved their fists in front of his face. They hurled invectives at him. The spell of that first impression he had made had been broken. When one of the guards struck him and he fell to the stone pavement the others also rushed to beat and maltreat him.

I looked on in horror. I had the feeling that a hitherto concealed malignant spite had been released in these men. I should have protested against such treatment of a prisoner; but my voice stuck in my throat. Even so I might have been moved to saying something, if Ananias himself had not restrained their ardour. The teacher rose to his feet.

'It's all finished now!' the former high priest repeated. 'And now tell us, what have you been teaching the people? Let us, too, listen to your fables. Well, speak!' he shouted in a threatening tone. 'What, have you lost your tongue?'

Jesus's voice sounded just the same as ever: calm, even and measured, and very sad:

'I have proclaimed my teaching openly. I have spoken in the Temple courtyard and in the synagogues. Every man could hear what I had to say. If you wish to know, ask those who listened to me.'

He did not finish the sentence, for someone struck him in the face with his fist. It must have been a powerful blow, for Jesus fell again. His assailant kicked him, roaring:

'You scum! How dare you talk to the most reverend rabbi like that?'

Jesus rose to his feet yet again. A stream of blood was flowing from his broken lips and nose. He said with difficulty, in a changed tone:

'If I spoke badly, then tell me. But if well, why did you strike me?'

Instead of answering, the servant spat into his face and burst into a raucous laugh. Taking a sidelong glance at Ananias, he snarled: 'To see you don't dare talk like that again!' I remembered I had seen that face somewhere, and after a moment I recalled it: it was Gadi, whom Jonathan had once sent with guards to take Jesus prisoner. Evidently, after being thrown out of the service of the Grand Council, he had taken employment with Ananias. The others were about to rush at Jesus again when Chaim entered, made an obeisance to Ananias, and announced that the Sanhedrin was now fully assembled and waiting for the prisoner.

The Sanhedrin holds its meetings in the house of Caiaphas. The council hall is always kept ready for use, with its benches arranged in a semi-circle. Despite the unusual hour, which in itself violated all the prescriptions, far more than the twenty-four members necessary for a quorum had arrived. The benches were crowded. Jonathas, as president, was sitting in the centre next to Caiaphas, as also was the vice-president, Ishmael, son of Fabia, husband of Ananias's daughter. Ananias's family had taken possession of all the administrative positions. Other sons of Ananias were sitting on the Sadducees' benches, including Eleazar, Ananias, Jehudah, and all the senior priests with Simon the Cainite, Jesus the son of Damayosh, and Saul at their head. To reach my usual seat I had to pass between our brethren: Simon son of Gamaliel, Jonathan bar Azziel, Eleazar bar Chetah, Jochanan bar Zakkai, Simon bar Poira, Joel bar Gerion, and others. I greeted them with a nod, but I noticed that when they saw me they began to whisper among themselves. Joseph of Arimathea was also present, and I sat down beside him. The president called on two scribes, the defence and the prosecution, to take their places at the ends of the semi-circles of benches. Then he rose to his feet:

'Most reverend fathers and teachers! We are assembled here in order to judge a man whose conduct and teaching have become a danger to the faith, to morality, and to the very existence of the Israelite nation. You all know whom I mean: the carpenter from Galilee.'

'But why have we been summoned to meet at night?' Joseph asked, rising from his seat. 'Isn't there another free day left for trials?'

Joseph has a rough voice which reminds me of the sound of a trumpet. I must admit he shows more audacity than I. But such as I am, I am. It was I who should have spoken up, not Joseph, for he doesn't know much about the teacher. Only what I have told him. He has never spoken to Jesus himself. Perhaps he intervened even now only out of friendship for me. Or, still more likely, simply in order to oppose Jonathas.

'Worthy Joseph!' Jonathas bowed his head in a gesture of reluctant respect. 'The matter is very urgent . . .'

'Not even in the most urgent matter are we allowed to make decisions at night.'

'Oh yes we are!' rabbi Jochanan exclaimed. This was a genuine surprise, for a Pharisee was coming to the aid of a Sadducee.

'No we're not!' Joseph stuck to his point.

'Of course, if a question of human life is involved we are not allowed,' several uncertain voices remarked from the benches.

'But there is a gloss which says . . .' Jochanan began.

'But it is not in the Scriptures,' Joseph sharply retorted.

'But if a doctor has pronounced . . .' someone remarked from the Pharisees' benches.

'The opinion of a learned doctor carries weight when it is accepted by the Sanhedrin.'

'No!' another of our brethren cried. 'The words of the teacher are as sacred as the words of the prophets were in the past . . .'

This caused some confusion among the Sadducees, and several called out:

'That's not true! That's an invention of the Pharisees!'

'Quiet! Quiet!' Jonathas hurriedly tried to restore order. 'We shall not decide that question now. We have an urgent issue to settle, and the dispute over the Torah teaching has been going on for many years. Let us agree for the time being. For if we all agree that a learned doctor's opinion can become the law – and we all do, don't we? – what could be simpler than to take this course in regard to the opinion which the reverend Jochanan bar Zakkai expressed?'

'But it's a question of principle,' a young Pharisee observed.

'We shall not discuss principles today,' the president suggested, and rabbi Jochanan agreed. Our senior Pharisees nodded their assent. Deserted by his elders, the young Pharisee sat down. But Joseph was not ready to yield.

'I don't agree,' he said. 'It is not permissible to try anyone at night.'

'But if the doctors have agreed with the priests . . .' Jonathas began.

'All the same I don't agree,' Joseph roared, banging his fist on the bench.

There was an embarrassed silence. The counsellors on the Pharisees' and Sadducees' benches put their heads together and whispered. But Caiaphas exploded:

'What does the opinion of one member matter? We're only wasting time! Let us judge this fraud at once!'

'But I propose that we yield to doctor Joseph,' rabbi Oncelas spoke up unexpectedly. That Greek always finds a way out of the most complicated situations. 'Without doubt the case will be a protracted one. We shall consider it: so much we are permitted to do. But we shall pass sentence after daybreak. Then we shall be in agreement with the Law.'

'Very true! Very sound!' Everybody spoke at once. Jonathas smiled with relief and whispered something to Caiaphas. The high priest nodded and gave Joseph a look of hate.

'Then let us begin the inquiry,' the president said. 'Bring in the prisoner and the witnesses.'

The teacher was brought in first. He was no longer bound, and there was no blood on his mouth. But his lips, nose and cheeks were swollen and turning blue. His hair was still dishevelled. He must have been very tired, for he shifted heavily from foot to foot every other moment. He had not lost his bearing. But he did not look at the assembly. He bowed his head and appeared to be counting the coloured tiles of the pavement.

A crowd of witnesses came in behind him. They were a desperate-looking lot, and the more honest faces among them seemed to be suffering from mortal terror. It was obvious that they had been persuaded to come here by threats or bribes. Jonathas read out the prescribed formula:

'Always remember that you are to speak the truth. For otherwise the blood of an innocent man will fall on you.'

A scribe took one of the witnesses by the arm and led him before the president. 'What is your name?' Jonathas asked.

'Chuz . . . son . . . son . . . of Simon,' the man stammered.

'What do you know about this man's crimes?'

'I . . . I . . . saw him . . . eating together with . . . sinners . . . with heathens . . .'

'The Sadducees often do that,' a young Pharisee said to his neighbour, but so loud that everybody heard it.

'What else?' Jonathas hurriedly asked.

'He said . . . that it is not permissible . . . to give a bill . . . of divorcement . . .'

'Did you, too, hear him say that?' Jonathas turned to the next witness.

'Yes, your reverence. He said that in former times there were no bills of divorcement.'

'And that it is not permissible to issue them?'

'No, your reverence. He only said they didn't exist in former times.'

'Take this fool away!' Caiaphas exclaimed impatiently.

'What do you know of this Galilean's crimes?' Jonathas asked a small, hunched fellow who looked like a beggar.

'Oh, I know a lot, your reverence. A lot! He made people well. I mean, everybody thought he made people well. But it wasn't really so. Many of them fell ill again.'

'So he worked magic?' rabbi Joel suggested to the witness.

'Without doubt he worked magic. Whenever he healed people he always called on Satan . . .'

'Don't say that word aloud, you fool!' the high priest said sternly.

'And did you, too, see people fall ill again after he had made them well?' Jonathas asked the next witness.

'No,' the man replied, staring at Jesus with terrified eyes.

'He told one man,' another witness started out of the group, 'that if he sinned again he would fall even more ill than before . . .'

'Shut your mouth!' the high priest struck his fist on the desk. 'Nobody's asking you!'

'Who else has heard that the illness returned?' Jonathas asked.

But no other witness was prepared to support that statement.

'Well, and what else do you know?' the president turned back to the beggar.

'He didn't offer sacrifices in the Temple . . .'

'You're not lying, are you?'

'May I drop down dead if I've told a lie. When the collector came to collect the dues from his disciples they told him their teacher had forbidden them to pay.'

'Bring the collector before me.'

A wretched, terrified little man was thrust violently out of the crowd.

'Listen closely to what I am about to say,' Jonathas told him. 'Is it true that the disciples of this . . .' he pointed to Jesus, 'didn't want to pay you the Temple dues?'

'Most reverend sir,' the man replied, swallowing violently, 'when I went and told them they had to pay . . . and this was, your reverence, in the month of Tishri, for he was not in the country during the month of Adar . . .'

'We're not interested in that! Tell me, did he pay or didn't he?' Caiaphas said fiercely.

'Why sir, I was just saying . . .' the man danced from foot to foot. 'His disciples went to him . . . to ask him, reverend sir . . .'

'And they didn't pay?'

'I'm just coming to that. They went and asked him. And he said . . .'

'That they were not to pay?'

'I'm just saying that they were to pay. For he said . . .'

'But they didn't pay, did they?'

'I'm just saying, your reverence, that they did pay . . .'

'Take him away! Next!'

The next witness was a gloomy, shrivelled man with phylac-

I

teries on his brow and arm and a beard falling to his chest; he looked like a Pharisee. He spoke slowly and smoothly, in a language more cultivated than that of the unclean individuals who had preceded him.

'This man,' he said, 'ordered his disciples to collect large sums of money. It was said to be intended as alms for poor widows and orphans. But the money went to him. He talked of repentance, but he himself went about with street-walkers. A whole band of loose women followed him. He gave great feasts for them . . .'

'How do you know all this?'

'Everybody saw him going about with women.'

'And did you see him too?' Jonathas turned to a tall man standing a little to one side.

'Oh yes,' this man replied. He was obviously a Galilean, for he used the dialect of the Tiberias district. 'I myself saw rabbi Nahum of Nain invite him to a feast, and some street woman came and washed his feet . . .'

'What is this unclean fellow dragging in somebody at Nain for?' rabbi Simon commented angrily.

'Can anyone else confirm that this man went about with loose women?' Jonathas hurriedly asked the other witnesses. 'Well, didn't any of you see him?'

'Has this court been called to meet at night,' Joseph's voice boomed out, 'in order to try a man for going about with street women?'

'Patience, Joseph! There are more serious charges to come,' Jonathas said. 'You'll hear something more interesting in a moment. Come here, you,' he called a Levite out from the witnesses. 'What have you to tell us?'

'This man ate the passover today,' the Levite said.

'Sacrilege!' the shouts broke suddenly from the benches. 'He's broken the Law!'

'Not at all!' Joseph outshouted them all.

'Wait a moment; let Joseph tell us!' Jonathas observed with a sneer. 'I understand this feast was held in the house of his friend, the reverend rabbi Nicodemus, a member of the Pharisees' Grand Council.'

'Of course I'll tell you!' Joseph retorted. 'He's a Galilean, isn't he? What do the prescriptions say concerning the right of the Galileans to eat the Passover feast on the eve of the Passover Sabbath?'

'You're digging a pit for yourself. The Sabbath begins this evening.'

'But the Passover Sabbath has already begun. Have you forgotten that you have consolidated two sabbaths into one? And we all know why: you wanted to have less bother . . .'

The hall was silent. Then someone muttered:

'That's true! The Galileans can take advantage of this right if they wish . . .'

'But we didn't know whether the Passover feast was held in accordance with the prescriptions . . .'

'Since when has "we don't know" been acceptable as proof of a man's guilt?' Joseph shouted.

'His own disciples,' Jonathas said through his teeth, 'assured us that after the feast he poured out wine and broke bread . . .'

'Where is this disciple? Let him speak for himself.'

But no disciple was found among the witnesses.

'We'll manage without him!' Joseph scoffed. 'I tell you the ancient prescriptions lay down that in token of friendship and brotherhood one can share wine and bread on the eve of the Passover, provided it is after the feast has been celebrated.

'That custom has fallen into desuetude,' Caiaphas intervened. His gaze was like a knife thrust into Joseph's breast.

'But it still exists,' Joseph commented.

'Next witness!' Jonathas put an end to the dispute. I heard him say quietly to Caiaphas: 'I have plenty more to come.'

'This man,' another Galilean testified, 'did not observe the fasts.'

'Did he say why he didn't?'

'He said he would fast later on . . .'

'But when?'

'I don't know, your reverence. He said the time would come for that . . .'

'And did you hear him say that?' the president asked another witness.

'I heard him say something rather different, your reverence. He said mercy was more important than fasting . . .'

'But you both saw that he didn't fast?'

The witnesses looked at each other questioningly.

'I didn't see that,' the Judaean muttered.

'But the people said he never fasted,' the Galilean swiftly added.

'Who else saw that this man doesn't observe the fasts?' Jonathas asked.

There was silence again. An unclean individual looking like a working mason broke it:

'But I did hear him say it wasn't necessary to observe the rite of ablution. He said the Pharisees washed themselves on the outside, but that it was sufficient if you were clean inside . . .'

'That's a serious charge,' rabbi Jochanan said. 'Allow us to ask this witness one or two questions,' he asked the president. Jonathas nodded his agreement, and Jochanan questioned the witness: 'Tell me, did you ever see this fellow dip his hands into water before eating?'

'No, never,' the man declared.

'And did you ever see him wash all his body after returning from the town, where a man who is clean is always in danger of coming into contact with a sinner?' rabbi Eleazar intervened.

'No.'

'And did you ever see him or his disciples wash the copper utensils used for preparing food?' rabbi Joel inquired.

'Or a mug from which a stranger might have drunk?'

'No.'

'Or the couch on which one reclines at a feast?'

'If you question this man on every matter in which you insist on purification we shall find the night too short for the inquiry,' Ananias son of Ananias interjected.

'How can you talk like that?' rabbi Jonathan retorted indignantly. 'These are very important questions.'

'But if these are the crimes with which this man is to be charged, let's go home to bed,' Joseph commented. 'Before long the Pharisees will be wanting to wash the stars and the moon.'

'Rabbi Nicodemus,' Jochanan turned to me; 'your friend and collaborator is sneering at the purification rites which you, I am sure, never neglect . . .'

'Of course I observe the rites,' I defended myself. 'But I don't like to see them exaggerated . . .'

'What do you call exaggeration, Nicodemus?' Joel demanded.

'It's an exaggeration, as the great Hillel taught, to insist that the whole pot shall be washed if only its handle has been touched by an unclean hand,' I reopened the age-old dispute.

'That's wrong, that's wrong!' rabbi Eleazar jumped to his feet. 'The handle forms one whole with the pot. If the handle . . .'

'But are we trying a blasphemer or quarrelling over a stupid pot?' Caiaphas snarled.

'We are establishing how profoundly unclean this Galilean is,' rabbi Oncelos observed in hypocritically honied tones.

'Joseph is quite right. Before long the sun itself will not be clean enough for you,' Simon the Cainite laughed.

'The man who doesn't care for the purity of his body will not care for the purity of his heart either,' rabbi Jochanan answered.

'Enough of this argument, reverend fathers!' Jonathas cried. 'We shall not try this man for his uncleanness. After all, he is only a common fellow. And they are all sinners, aren't they?'

'Jonathas is right,' rabbi Jonathan admitted on behalf of the Pharisee benches.

'Next witness!' the president called. 'What do you know about this Jesus?' he asked the man who stepped forward.

'He said his body was bread and every man should eat it; and his blood was wine . . .'

'Horrible!' Jehudah bar Ananias pulled a face.

'Only a sinner or a madman could talk like that!' several other Sadducees commented.

'That's not sinning, that's lunacy,' the young Pharisee at the end of the bench observed.

'What else can you tell us about him?' Jonathas asked.

The man raised his hands in indignation: 'He said the Temple would be destroyed.'

At this, horrified exclamations rose from the benches.

'Who will destroy it?' the president asked.

The man thought for a moment, then said: 'The Romans.'

'The hand of Edom will never destroy the Temple,' Ananias son of Ananias said sternly. 'The Temple is everlasting.'

'But surely you remember what the Lord said to the prophet Jeremiah: "It shall be with the Temple as with the house in Siloh,"' Joseph pointed out.

'You are wise, Joseph; and you know the Scriptures,' Ananias son of Ananias hissed. 'So you should remember that Jeremiah was speaking of the invasion led by Nebuchadnezzar (may Sheol have no mercy on him!). But afterwards he prophesied the return of the Israelites and the rebuilding of the Temple.'

'I know all that; you don't have to teach me the prophecies.' Joseph stood facing the Sadducees, but his gaze was fixed on space beyond them. 'Much of what Jeremiah said has come to pass. But not all. And much of what has come to pass can come to pass a second, a third, and even a tenth time. Which of us knows what new convenant the prophet was speaking of? What is meant by the sentence: "Every bird knows its time, but the people of Israel did not observe their time."? Don't you think that there is something stirring, that some great cause which can be won, or can be lost, is at stake?'

'Now Joseph is beginning to play the prophet!' Caiaphas remarked in his grating voice. 'We're quite ready to listen to his prophecies some other time. But we have other work to do today.'

Jonathas turned back to the witness:

'So he said the Temple would be destroyed?'

'Yes, your reverence.

'By the Romans?'

'No,' another witness cried. 'I heard him say he himself would destroy the Temple and then rebuild it.'

'What? All by himself?' the high priest started from his seat, and began to question the man feverishly. 'He himself intends to destroy the Sanctuary?'

'Yes, I remember now,' the first witness joined in. 'He even said he'd rebuild it in three days.'

'In three days!' the younger Ananias snorted. 'That certainly would be a miracle!'

'And he said he would rebuild it but not with hands,' the second witness added.

'No he didn't,' the other objected.

'But he did. Surely you heard him?' the second stuck to his point.

'The witnesses are not in agreement,' Joseph observed.

'Well, make up your minds!' Caiaphas said in a crafty tone. 'Did he say it or didn't he?'

'No!' cried the first.

'He did!' the second contradicted. 'He said the Son of God would rebuild the Temple.'

There was a hushed silence. This unclean fellow had allowed himself to mention the name of the Most High. By rights he should have been thrown out of the hall, proclaimed a sinner outside the Law, and deprived of the right to enter the court-yard of the faithful, and all synagogues. I saw Joel stuff his fingers into his ears and knock his head against the desk. I looked at Caiaphas, and was astonished to see that his face, which had been distorted with rage, had cleared as though at an unexpected revelation. He rose from his seat and extended both hands above his head. We realized that he proposed to speak invested with all the authority of his high office. There wasn't really any need for the high priest himself to declare this fool accursed. We all sat silent with expectation. But Caiaphas did not address himself to the witness, who was terrified at the effect his words had had. He turned his gaze on Jesus, who was standing with bowed head: a tree stripped of its leaves, but still exalted and unyielding.

'Listen, you!' Caiaphas shouted. Then he spoke in a profoundly solemn tone: 'In the Name of the Most High I command you to answer: are you the Messiah and the Son of Jehovah?'

We involuntarily bowed our heads and closed our eyes. Only the high priest is permitted to utter the terrible name of Him who Is, and then only when resorting to such an adjuration. My heart beat violently. I looked at the teacher. No matter what sort of man Caiaphas is, when he speaks in this manner he ceases to be an ordinary mortal. I knew that Jesus would have to reply. Would his words once more open an abyss beyond them? He slowly raised his head. At that moment his face, though swollen and bruised, had an expression of the same mighty force as when with one curt word he had cast out devils or had called down into the dark opening of Lazarus's tomb. In this beaten, maltreated prisoner a change was accomplished which exalted him to superhuman stature. Then perhaps he had been waiting for this moment? Perhaps now indeed he would overthrow all that he had come to overthrow? I breathed hurriedly. My life hung on his lips. I half expected a thunderbolt to fall and demolish Caiaphas's house. 'Perhaps this Samson has grown his hair again,' I thought. Everybody — the Sanhedrin, the servants, the guards, the witnesses, all Jerusalem — was gazing into the teacher's face. With his adjuration Caiaphas had challenged fate. When the reply comes, I thought, only one of these two will be left alive: Jesus, or the high priest.

'Atali kemartah,' I heard the words. But that voice did not sound like a thunderbolt. The incredible confession was spoken not with lightning, but with painful, swollen lips. 'You have said so yourself . . . And for this reason you will see the Son of Man only when he comes in the might of the Lord . . .'

Caiaphas's solemnly upraised hands fell to his neck. He thrust his fingers into his throat as though he were suffering from shortness of breath. I heard the sound of rending cloth. With the convulsive, violent action of a man for whom the ritual prescribed is quite inadequate, the high priest rent his garment down to the hem.

'Blasphemer!' His voice passed from a hysterical shout to a wail, and sank to a whisper: 'Blasphemer!' The high priest turned to the benches: 'Did you hear? Did you hear? Is it necessary to call any further witnesses? Are we not all of us witnesses?'

The members of the Supreme Council started to their feet. Above the shouts of 'Blasphemer! Blasphemer!' came the sound of rending garments. 'Remember to rend them from the bottom up!' Jonathas cried. Despite the general uproar, the president had retained his self-control, and reminded us that the ritual permits only the high priest to rend his robe from top to bottom.

I had a few words with Joseph, then I went out and wandered by myself about the courtyard. I thought; and my thoughts almost burst my head, as heavy melons burst a fragile basket. What did it all mean? He had answered the high priest's solemn adjuration by admitting that he was the Messiah and the Son of the All Highest. And yet, with these words he had not destroyed his enemies. Why is it that with him the most superhuman things are made to come in such an ordinary human manner? Is it for this that we have been awaiting the Messiah for centuries – for him, by his own admission, to ensure himself death? I had no doubt whatever that he had been condemned even before the trial began. The break which we are now observing in the proceedings has been arranged only to ensure that the sentence is passed in daylight. True, a death sentence has to be confirmed by Pilate; but I'm quite sure that brute won't hesitate for one moment. So death is waiting for Jesus. Who will vote against it? Myself,

Joseph, perhaps one or two more. Not even six votes altogether. Joseph says we must oppose the sentence, must shout that a nocturnal trial is not valid, that the teacher was not allowed any defence, that the term 'Son of God' is to be found in the Scriptures. But this issue is no longer one of nomenclature. For I remember that only a few hours ago James told me Jesus's words, in which he assured his disciples that he and the Father are one. He regards himself as literally the Son of God. But who is he, really? For three years I have been watching, both close at hand and from a distance. He has said and done tremendous things. There never was another man like him. I have written 'another man.' For even when doing such amazing things he has always remained a man. He has raised the dead, but he himself has shivered with cold in the chilly morning. I have seen these contradictions in him again and again. So perhaps Judas was right? Perhaps he did grow afraid? Perhaps he could have remained the Son of God, but failed to come up to that exalted level? Perhaps he could have ceased altogether to be a man, yet preferred to remain one?

My head ached with these thoughts. The people round the fires were quiet, half asleep. The only noise to be heard came from the farther side of the palace. When Jonathas ordered the guards to take Jesus from the hall it seemed likely that the teacher would be torn to pieces. The guards, the servants, even members of the Sanhedrin rushed at him with raised fists. They beat him and kicked him; and only when Jonathas cried: 'Don't kill him! Remember he hasn't been sentenced yet!' did they abate their zeal a little. Instead of beating him they spat in his face again and again. Joseph tried to defend him, but they dragged him away to the next hall. I slipped into the courtyard. There's nothing I can do for him. Why am I such a coward? James was in despair because the disciples had scattered and fled. But what help could these unclean individuals give him? Or I, either? If I could bribe anyone I should not spare the money. I'd give all my fortune. I am ready to carry out our agreement. 'Give me your cares and take my cross . . .' A cross? I felt a cold shiver run down my back. He has talked of a cross so often. Just as if he knew he had to die. For if he is condemned to death, it will be to death on a cross. We asked Pilate for an assurance that he would not crucify anyone. Now he will say: 'You yourselves want it.' How am I to take Jesus's cross on myself? Am I to allow myself to be crucified with him? But that would be suicide. Nobody wants my death. Why should I, a prudent, delicate, wise, respected man, go and myself ask for that most heinous of deaths? I cannot think of a more horrible death than to be extended, nailed up in the eyes of all, and then wait for hours until the physical spasms smother the movement of the heart. It is not death that is terrible, but dying; and crucifixion is a dying without end. Whenever I think of my own death I always pray for it to come swiftly, like dropping off to sleep. But how do I know when Ruth began to die? Or when her crucifixion began?

People say: 'He died an easy death.' But what man dies easily? No, there is no power that could compel me to take up his cross tonight. Why didn't his disciples do it? They fled; and am I to die? No, no! Better to close my eyes to all that has been and will be. Our agreement? What of it? What, after all, have I gained by it? Ruth died; and now I too will die, of terror. At the most he will perish for his teaching, for his talk of his kingdom, which obviously doesn't exist. If the Most High is so remarkably merciful, as he has said so often, He should know that every one of us human beings is a miserable wretch incapable of overcoming his fears. There may be men who never think of what is to come. But I am always thinking of it. I am absorbed in the terror of prevision. In what respect is Jesus's teaching any more pleasant than the ancient teaching which says that cold, dark, mournful Sheol awaits every man, whether good or sinful? How can one stake one's life on something which may be a miracle of happiness, but which is something unimaginable? Why did he come to tell us about some other world which a living man's eyes cannot see? Why did he come at all? He brought his frenzied dreams into a world in which we were making shift for ourselves somehow or other. When Ruth died, I thought: 'Nothing is left.' And yet life is stronger. I began to eat, to sleep, to arrange my future again. Evidently a man can survive the death of those closest to him. So why talk about that . . . kingdom?

I walked about shivering with cold. I stood by the fire, but I was unable to keep still, so I wandered off again. Somewhere beyond the city wall a cock crowed. The roar of the people on the farther side of the palace was like a noise which we have no means of silencing: a noise almost menacing.

Suddenly the uproar began to draw nearer to me. I ought to have fled. But my feet were rooted to the ground. I stood tense, my eyes screwed up, like someone expecting a blow on the head. A crowd of raging, furious men came towards me. Others rose from around the fires and hurried to meet that crowd. Suddenly a huge fellow with his face half covered ran past me in the direction of the gate. Something about him struck me as familiar. But I had no time to stare after him. A horde of servants, guards, young Levites and Pharisees went in a procession right past me. They were escorting the teacher, shouting and whistling as they went. I saw him for only one moment: a sort of fool's cap twisted from straw was on his head, his hands were tied behind him, his grievous gaze passed over the men surrounding him. For a moment that gaze rested on me. None of the might of the miracle-worker was left in it. Only an hour before, when Caiaphas had adjured him, he had been a personality uttering words capable of sending other men to their knees. Now he was only a man, thrust to the very bottom of human misery: a beggar, a leper, a sick man, a prisoner – all in one person. He went past me like a spectre, but his picture remained behind my eyelids. The crowd went on, pushing him, spitting at him, bowing to him ironically. I was utterly broken. If even a little of the teacher I had known had remained in him! Then it would have been easier for me to defend him! But how can you stand in defence of a man whose own weakness has made him — I don't quite know how to put it — has made him almost repulsive?'

Dawn came on suddenly with the grey of the moment before sunrise. The servants summoned us back to the hall. As though to hasten the coming of day, the lamps had been extinguished. Caiaphas rose to his feet impatiently. He himself gave the order:

'Bring in the prisoner.'

Jesus stood slumped, his head drawn down between his shoulders in a semi-conscious attitude of defence. There were blades of grass in his hair, and white patches of half-dried spittle on his cheeks.

Resting one hand on his hip, Caiaphas asked:

'Repeat to us a second time what you have already dared to maintain: that you are the Messiah.'

He replied without raising his head, in a voice quivering with weariness:

'What if I do repeat it? You will not believe me, nor will you release me. But this is your hour . . .'

Caiaphas laughed brutally.

'And so you are the Son of the Most High, are you?'

I had the impression that Jesus summoned up a great effort to overcome the weakness which possessed him. He drew himself erect, and raised his head. He said:

'You have said it yourself. I am He.'

Then his head dropped again and his body went limp. He did not appear to hear the shouts that broke around him. He stood indifferent to all that was occurring. He did not even tremble when Caiaphas asked the counsellors:

'What sentence do you pass?'

'Death!' Jonathas was the first to utter the word. It ran round the benches: 'Death! Death! Death!'

'No!' Joseph cried. 'I don't agree. This trial is invalid. The sentence is invalid. And this man is innocent.'

'Innocent?' Caiaphas shook with rage. 'Innocent? Since when,

Joseph, is it permissible for a sinner to say he is the Messiah and the Son of the Most High?'

'But supposing he really is?' my friend demanded.

'He?' the high priest interrupted indignantly. 'He? Take a good look at him, Joseph. Does he look other than what he is? That filthy, unclean clod the Messiah?'

'He worked miracles.' Joseph held his ground.

'With the aid of the unclean spirit,' bar Zakkai cried.

'But supposing that none the less . . . Listen!' Joseph turned to face the benches. 'I don't know . . . I'm only a merchant. I've never talked to him. I have never thought over these questions. But from the first moment I saw him, the moment I heard him speak, I felt troubled. What will happen if he proves to be the Messiah after all?'

A muttering from the benches rose into shouts:

'Don't talk nonsense, Joseph! He's not the Messiah, he's a liar. Has he cast a spell over you? The Messiah will not come from Galilee.'

Joseph's bearing gave me new heart. I started from my bench and cried:

'He doesn't come from Galilee. He was born in Bethlehem . . .'

But my feeble and ineffective cry was shouted down:

'Anyone can say that now the genealogical tables have been destroyed. You've done too much for him already, Nicodemus. You went around with him, you entertained him in your own house. You shouted in his honour when he rode into the city on an ass. Do you want us to bow down to any unclean individual? We all know what the signs of the Messiah's coming will be.'

'We won't waste any more time,' Caiaphas exclaimed. 'We shall pass sentence.'

'Wait a moment! This man . . .' I cannot remember Joseph ever speaking before like that. Some change in his sober and calculated way of thinking must have occurred. 'Listen! Does nothing disturb you whatever? Haven't you noticed that all your accusations fall off him like dry mud off leather? To tell the truth, I wasn't interested in this man. I defended him only because you were trying him fraudulently. But now I don't know . . .'

'If you don't know, go back to bed and sleep,' Ananias son of Ananias cried. 'There are enough of us here to pass sentence without you.'

'Let us pass judgement,' Caiaphas urged.

'Then what sentence do you pass?' Jonathas asked the assembly.

'Death! Death! Death!' The word came like blows of a hammer.

'Do you all vote in favour of death for this blasphemer?' he asked further.

'I don't!' Joseph said resolutely. 'I regard this judgement as illegal.'

'And so do I,' I added, attempting to master the shake in my voice.

'And so do I.' This third, unexpected voice came from the young Pharisee at the end of our benches. 'This man cannot be guilty. I admit that I don't know who he is. He only spoke to me once. But he is innocent.'

Caiaphas broke into a coarse, exultant laugh. 'Innocent! As innocent as a babe!' he ground his teeth. 'But your opposition counts for nothing. This is all your doing, Joseph! You think that because you're the wealthiest man in the country you can do as you like. But you'll live to be sorry for your pity. We shall settle accounts with you. And with you, Nicodemus! You're traitors!' he snarled.

My head swam as though I were standing on the edge of a precipice. Beside me I heard Jonathan's whisper:

'You've betrayed your loyalty to the brethren, Nicodemus. You're defending a man who sought to make us a shame and disgrace in the eyes of the people. We haven't finished with you yet.'

We left the hall in a dead silence. At the door I turned and

271

looked back at Jesus, I felt a last flicker of hope that he would do something that would change the situation completely. But he stood with drooping head, leaning forward as though about to fall to the ground.

We went out. From the Temple came the sound of silver trumpets; the tips of the towers of the Asmodeus Palace flamed with rosy light. The morning was chilly and fresh. We walked along slowly, without exchanging a word. But at last Joseph swore:

'By the beard of Moses! What scum! And they threaten us too! But I shall show them . . .'

'Where are you going?' I asked him.

'Home to bed. There's nothing more I can do for him.'

'I'm afraid I couldn't sleep. I shall go to the Temple and wait for Pilate's decision.'

We halted. He was about to say something more, but he only waved his hand angrily and walked away. The young Pharisee stood irresolute.

'Did you know him well, rabbi?' he abruptly asked.

I shook my head uncertainly. 'Yes, and no. I tried to get to know him. But . . .'

'He only spoke to me once,' the young man said. 'But then it was as though he had thrust his hand inside me and drawn out all my entrails. Who is he, rabbi Nicodemus?'

I slowly shrugged my shoulders: 'How should I know?'

'But you said he was born in Bethlehem.'

'So I have been told.'

'Why is it we know nothing of a certainty about him?' he burst out. 'He is a man concealed in mist. Can one fight for someone you don't know?'

I left him with this question on his lips. I walked slowly away. The sun was glittering more and more brightly on the golden plates of the Sanctuary. The first pilgrims were making their way up the road. Suddenly, at a break in the wall I saw a man lying with his head thrust between the stones. At first I thought he was some drunkard sleeping off his nocturnal revelry. But then, by the spasmodic heave of the shoulders I realized that this man was crying. Going closer I recognized him by his cloak. There is so much to come between us, those unclean fishermen have always failed to win my sympathy. But now I felt sorry for this great lout (or was it really only sorrow for myself?) I bent down and put my hand on his shoulder.

'Peter,' I said. Just why it came to me to use the name which the teacher had given him I really don't know. He flung himself round.

'Ah, so it's you, rabbi!' he sobbed. 'Don't call me by that name,' he exclaimed miserably. 'I'm no rock. I'm earth, ashes, roadside dust. Do you know what I have done?' He seized me by the edge of my robe, as though afraid I would go without listening to him. 'I . . . I've denied him. I said I didn't know him . . . I declared I'd never seen him before . . .'

'Where did you do that?' I asked.

'In the courtyard of the high priest's palace,' he groaned. Then I realized that it was he who had jostled me in the darkness. Even so, I was amazed to think that he had ventured to go there at all.

'Don't cry!' I squeezed his shoulder strongly in the attempt to comfort him. 'These things do happen. Man . . .'

But he was not to be comforted. He broke into even more violent sobbing:

'I betrayed him . . . I denied him . . . Him, who loved us so much.'

'These things do happen,' I repeated. 'There are times when fear is stronger than love. But possibly,' I replied to my own inner query, 'possibly he isn't the one he gave himself out to be . . .'

'I'm too stupid to know who he is,' Peter wailed. 'But he loved me, and I him . . . I thought I loved him . . . I was so sure of myself . . . I was furious with Judas for betraying him. And then I go and do even worse, even worse . . .'

That's true, I thought. Jesus did love so much. One always felt that if he had to bear for any one of us all that he has in fact borne during these past few hours he would do it without even stopping to think. Simon feels that. But as for me? I haven't denied him. But that may be only because nobody has asked me with threats, as Simon has been asked. They may expel me from the Sanhedrin, from the Grand Council. So much they could do to me. But they could get rid of Simon without even asking Pilate. Perhaps that's the only reason why I haven't gone so far as to deny him. But I have doubted. Simon has denied him, but he has no doubts. For me it is still a question of faith. For him it is a question of love.

Perhaps I, too, should weep, as he is weeping. But I have no tears. I wept my last tears over Ruth, the day I knew she would die. I have no more tears, and no confidence. Simon weeps, but he doubtless feels quite sure that despite his betrayal the teacher still loves him. As for me, I have ceased to believe that he is waiting for me. And so I cannot weep.

From the terrace above the porch I saw the colourful line of people making their way along the narrow and winding streets. It was not a very numerous crowd: guards went at the head of the procession, clearing the way with shouts and, when shouts were inadequate, with blows from sticks. Behind them, side by side with the elders of the Grand Council, walked the priests in all their panoply of head dresses, purple cloaks, ephods, and golden chains. Immediately after them Jesus followed under escort. He was surrounded with guards, and a double cordon of guards held back the mob pressing and shouting at the rear. They were the usual city rabble, ready to do anything for money, plus a few idle gapers.

But when the procession crossed the bridge and entered the Temple courtyard it was completely lost amid the solid mass of pilgrims who were coming so early to purchase sacrificial animals and to change money. The infamous market which he had dispersed had grown up again like a pruned bush. The procession attracted general attention. Thousands of people began to swarm around it. And the hostile shouts and whistles were drowned by the astonished roar of voices from men who, to their amazement, saw the prophet from Galilee bound and surrounded with guards. I thought I could discern the angry cries of Galilean peasants amid this hubbub. That sobered me. When I left Caiaphas's house an hour ago, I felt convinced that the teacher's fate was sealed. But now a new hope was born within me. What though the Sanhedrin had passed sentence? The Sanhedrin was not everything, and nor was Pilate. There were also the crowds who a few days previously had been hailing Jesus by the name of Son of David. The Galileans would not surrender their prophet. I ran down swiftly. My weakness had gone; I was ready once more to fight for the teacher's life. I forced my way ruthlessly through to the procession, which now was slowly circling the Temple. But I would never have caught up with it if it hadn't occurred to me to take a shorter route through the courtyard of the faithful. Then a surge of people carried me to the farther side of the Sanctuary, right under the walls of the sinister pyramid of Antonia. As I went I heard snatches of comment:

'They've caught the Galilean! Last night. But that won't come off! The damned priests! Where are they taking him? He worked miracles, he restored people to health . . . He's the Messiah . . . That's blasphemy . . . He's a great and good teacher . . . No, he's an accursed sinner. But supposing he really is the Messiah? Let's go and watch. What will the Romans say?'

The Romans must have been alarmed by this procession and the hubbub, for as we approached Antonia we heard the shrill sound of trumpets and drums inside the fortress. A triple rank of legionaries, their helmets drawn over their eyes and their shields held at the guard, welcomed us outside the gate. The garrison commander, Sarcus, leaned out of the window over the gateway and shouted:

'Halt! If you are not rebels, halt! What do you want?'

The procession and the accompanying throng poured into the narrow street leading to the fortress. At the Roman's command the Sanhedrin members stopped short several paces away from the ranks of soldiers. I noticed that there were many Pharisees moving around through the crowd, and paying particular attention to groups which had obviously come from Galilee. The tightly-packed street was roaring like some great fire. I saw rabbi Jochanan say something to one of our younger brethren; the young man climbed on to another Pharisee's shoulders and shouted at the crowd:

'Quiet! Silence! The high priest wishes to speak.'

So we Pharisees had come to the point of silencing the people in order to let the Sadducees speak! The hubbub died away. Caiaphas spoke in his hoarse, panting voice, addressing the Roman officer:

'We have come here to see the worthy Procurator on a very serious matter. We have brought him a conspirator who has been organizing disturbances. Go and ask the Procurator to come and hear us. We cannot enter the castle for, as you know, tomorrow is a great Holy Day, and at such a time we are not permitted to cross the threshold of a man who is not of our faith . . .'

Before Sarcus could reply Pilate appeared at the window. He stood with legs straddled, his arms folded across his chest. In all probability he had been drinking, for there were bags under his eyes. All his bearing expressed the fury of a man who has got out of bed the wrong side and is looking for someone to vent his spleen on. He stood silent, with screwed-up eyes, seemingly calculating the size of the crowd. Caiaphas nodded, and the guards pulled roughly on the chains and ropes, hauling their prisoner to the front. Pilate turned his eyes from the crowd to the members of the Sanhedrin, and then to the figure of Jesus. He asked mordantly:

'Is this the man you've come to proffer a charge against? I see you haven't waited for my judgement. That fellow is barely alive . . .'

He spoke the truth. During this past night the teacher had been reduced to a shadow of his former self. His face was bruised and battered, clotted with mud where the dust had mingled with his sweat. His right cheek was swollen, so that the line of the nose was obliterated. His hair was dishevelled and tangled, and filled with dust. The guards must have torn out his beard by the handful, for his chin was a brown clot of flesh, blood and hair. His parted lips were dry and black: blood had caked in the corners. Beneath the mud-caked brows the eyes seemed to find it an effort to see at all.

'He is a great criminal,' Jonathas replied. 'If he weren't we should not bring him to you.'

'If he has done so much evil you should have tried him yourselves,' Pilate sneered.

'We have tried him,' Ananias said. 'And we have judged him deserving of death. But we are not allowed to carry out such a sentence, worthy Procurator . . .'

'Of course you're not!' Pilate snapped. 'In all Judaea I alone have the right to decide on life or death. If it were in your hands . . . Your sentence doesn't mean much to me,' he added. 'I shall decide for myself what is to happen to him. Hand him over. Why, the man's hardly breathing!' he exclaimed angrily, for when the guards tugged at Jesus he fell to the ground. 'Are you asking me to try someone you have already tortured to death? What have you against this man?'

'Read the charge,' Caiaphas said to one of the Levites. The man raised a scroll, and began to read as though intoning a psalm:

'The high priest of the Most Holy One whose Name no man is worthy to pronounce, Joseph Caiaphas, son of Betus, after taking counsel with the most reverend and wise priests, teachers, doctors of the Law and the Torah in Israel, have decided to declare Jesus, son of Joseph, a carpenter of Nazareth, guilty of the crime of calling on the people to refuse to pay the tribute due to Caesar . . .'

'That's a lie!' Pilate interrupted. 'I know who pays the taxes and who doesn't want to pay!'

'Read on!' Caiaphas said with suppressed fury.

'And also guilty of the crime of stirring up the people and proclaiming himself king of Israel . . .'

'A king?' Pilate's choler turned to biting irony. 'Ah, so it's your king that you've brought to me! Well, in that case we'll try him. Bring this king here,' he ordered the centurion standing at his side.

The Roman soldiers took the ropes from the guards and dragged the teacher into the great courtyard. Servants brought out a ceremonial chair for Pilate and opened a baldachin of purple linen above it. Pilate sat down in the chair, with a lictor standing beside him, while a scribe knelt to take down the evidence. I could not hear what was said, but from Pilate's gestures I could surmise the nature of the conversation he had with the teacher. He was forced to ask his questions more than once, for Jesus appeared to be deaf to his words. The Procurator ordered the scribe to read out the Sanhedrin charge again. He asked a further question, pointing to the scroll, and the teacher answered. At that Pilate contemptuously shrugged his shoulders. He leaned forward and said something more; now the prisoner spoke for some time. Pilate listened, then leaned back in his chair and gazed at the teacher fixedly. He ran his eyes up from the feet to the tangled hair, and then back to the bloodstained feet of the man standing before him. When he spoke again, his attitude seemed to express not the bored reaction of a wearied judge, but a questioning doubt. Jesus replied, speaking for some time. But without waiting for him to finish Pilate shrugged his shoulders impatiently, got up from the chair, and went to the stairs. A moment or two later he appeared at the window above the gateway. He raised his hand for the crowd to be silent.

'I fail to see the crimes of which you are accusing him,' he said curtly.

There was a moment's silence. It was broken by Caiaphas:

'He's a criminal! A conspirator! A rebel!'

Other members of the Sanhedrin joined in: 'He's a dangerous man . . . He's committed many crimes . . .'

'I fail to see them,' Pilate broke in. The shouts of the Sanhedrin members increased in fury, but the crowd behind them was silent, not knowing what to think of these charges brought against the teacher. Pilate knew Judaea too well not to realize that the views of the priests and doctors were of no importance so long as the people did not support them. He clapped his hands. 'Don't bawl like that,' he said, almost as though trying to provoke them still more. 'In the last resort,' he rocked on his heels and licked his lips, 'since you're so anxious to get this man sentenced you can take him to the tetrarch. The man is a Galilean, so I pass him over to him.' He turned and left the window. The soldiers thrust Jesus outside the gate and handed him back to the guards, who pulled spitefully on the ropes.

The crowd slowly withdrew from the street. The priests and elders followed, with their escort of guards. As they passed me I observed that they were discussing something excitedly. Of a certainty none of them wished to go to Antipas. Pilate knew that that coward would not dare to raise his hand a second time against any man who enjoyed the people's esteem. And I began to feel convinced that if this Roman brute were on his side the teacher would escape alive. True, he himself had given warning of his fate. But that might have been only a test. Somewhere deep in my heart the thought lurked: 'He is able to save himself.'

Then I noticed that Joel, Oncelas, and Jonathan bar Azziel slipped through the ring of guards and called together the Pharisees mingling with the crowd. Evidently they were issuing fresh instructions. But when I approached they gave one another warning looks.

I followed some distance behind the Sanhedrin. The procession moved slowly through the porch, crossed the bridge, and went on to Khystos, where Antipas built a palace for himself when the Romans took over Herod's former palace. As the hours passed more and more people came flocking from all sides. Even the need to prepare the Passover did not hold the people back. And during this march from one end of the city to the other the mob succumbed to the childish pleasure of shouting, howling and whistling. This affair was gradually beginning to absorb and stimulate the people, as do the races in the hippodrome with which Herod defiled the slopes of Zion. The discussion over the teacher grew more and more excited. Then I heard a Pharisee say to the people around him: 'Don't forget that the Romans have always released one prisoner on the eve of the Passover. We must shout for one to be released.' 'Yes, they must release a prisoner, curse them!' the crowd responded. 'We'll shout all right!' 'Then shout for Barabbas to be released,' the Pharisee suggested. 'He fought against them.' Barabbas? I pricked up my ears in astonishment. What a suggestion! That bloodthirsty bandit had never attacked the Romans. His victims had always been defenceless people. The Sadducees had even asked Pilate to rid the city of him once. And now?

The head of the procession arrived at the palace. The leaders opened negotiations with Antipas's majordomo, for they were not willing to go inside, since they did not trust the tetrarch's house to be clean. He, for his part, being afraid of the people, refused to come out to them. Finally the prisoner was handed over to four of the tetrarch's guards and escorted inside. The priests, doctors, and the crowd remained in the street.

We did not have to wait long. The guard escorted the teacher out again. As before, his hands were bound and there was a rope around his waist, but a white sheet had been thrown over his torn and filthy clothing. Standing at the top of the steps leading to the palace, the majordomo announced:

'The most noble king of Galilea and Peraea, Herod son of Herod, requests you to tell the worthy Procurator that he thanks him for sending him this prisoner, and hands the prisoner back to you. The king will not judge him. This man is feeble-minded . . .'

The soldiers pushed the teacher down the marble steps. The ropes were once more handed over to the Temple guards. Caiaphas said something to them in a voice choking with fury.

They began to beat and tug at Jesus frenziedly. The procession turned back towards the temple; the guards tortured their prisoner at every step he took. I thought in horror that perhaps, since they had failed to obtain judgement against him, they intended to murder him summarily.

We came again to the gate of Antonia. Pilate came out, smiling sarcastically:

'Well? So the tetrarch also was unable to find this man guilty of any of the crimes you have laid at his door?'

The Sanhedrin made no answer, but they clenched their fists with fury. Caiaphas turned to rabbi Jonathan, who nodded in reply. The Pharisees mingling with the crowd muttered to the people: 'Shout for the prisoner now! Now!' Somewhere at the back of the crowd a voice was raised:

'A prisoner! Release us a prisoner!'

Others joined in, and gradually the voices merged into a single shout:

'A prisoner! We want a prisoner released!'

'What are they bawling about?' Pilate asked Jonathas.

'It has been the practice, worthy Procurator, for you to release a prisoner at the time of the Passover,' the son of Ananias replied, forcing himself to be polite. 'And that is what they are calling for.'

Pilate smiled venomously. He must have been getting a good deal of enjoyment out of this game he was playing against his former friends. He made a sign to indicate that he wished to speak, and waited until the shouts had died away:

'So you wish me to release a prisoner? I am quite willing.' He raised his voice, and gazed over the heads of the Sanhedrin members into the crowded street. 'I am holding two prisoners: Jesus, whom you call the Messiah, and Barabbas. Which of these do you wish me to release?'

There was a dead silence. A smile of triumph flickered over Pilate's clean-shaven face. He had made a clever move. So far the crowd had only been acting as spectators, but now its reply was bound to be sensible. For two years Barabbas had been the terror of merchants and pilgrims. But I had no illusions as to Pilate's motives. He was not interested in saving Jesus's life, he was only concerned to annoy the Sanhedrin.

Unexpectedly a single voice shouted from the crowd:

'Set Barabbas free!'

I had no doubt that it was one of our brethren shouting. The voice was not that of a common fellow. The cry was taken up by several others:

'Set Barabbas free!'

If Pilate had calmly replied: 'Those who are calling for Barabbas are not representative of your people,' I am convinced that nobody would have repeated the call. But he fell into the trap: he could not think of anything better to say than cry impatiently, and sarcastically:

'Well, hurry up! Have you chosen? So you want Jesus? But perhaps some of you prefer the bandit to the carpenter from Nazareth? No? Then I release Jesus . . .'

'No!' someone shouted back. 'We want Barabbas!'

This time more people took up the shout. A crowd is like a child, which allows itself to be guided so long as it is not conscious of the reins. 'We want Barabbas! Release Barabbas!'

'Barabbas?' Pilate said in an indignant tone. And, as one might have expected, the crowd in the street thought that Pilate was taking Jesus's side. They, too, were not interested in saving his life, they only wanted to score off the Roman. The struggle against the Sadducees and Pharisees was changing to a struggle against the Romans. The crowd instinctively felt that Pilate was caught in two minds. And a thousand voices shouted:

'Release Barabbas! Barabbas!'

The cry was taken up by everybody. Now 'Barabbas' was no longer the name of a bandit, it was a slogan: 'Barabbas! Set Barabbas free!'

Pilate's face revealed his fury. He must have been raging at the thought that he had handed his weapon to the crowd, only to find it turned against him. A Greek youngster came up and said something hurriedly to him. He replied curtly. Turning back to the window, he rested his hand on the balustrade and leaned out. He spoke over the heads of the men of the Temple, as though he still thought he could outbid them:

'So you want Barabbas and not Jesus? Then what am I to do with Jesus?'

For a moment or so there was a silence. My heart thumped like a hammer. Possibly if I had cried: 'Release him too,' the crowd would have taken it up. But I don't know the art of directing the masses. I'm afraid of them. My voice stuck in my throat. From the Pharisees scattered among the crowd came another shout: 'Crucify him!' My forehead was beaded with sweat. It seemed incredible that a crowd numbering several thousand people would follow this call. But Pilate again came to the aid of our brethren. In all eyes his face twitched with rage, his teeth grated, he beat his fist angrily on the wall. And at the sight the crowd roared exultantly:

'Crucify him!'

He turned to the priests and Pharisees. 'So you want me to start crucifying again?' he asked sarcastically. 'Are you yourselves asking for that now?'

'The people desire it,' Jonathas answered, folding his arms, while the shouts continued unabated:

'Crucify him!'

The Procurator bit his lips. But he was mastered by a savage determination to turn the crowd against the priests at all costs. And that was understandable: then he would have won the glory of a man who could govern Judaea. Nobody so far had done that. In this game Jesus's life was simply the stake.

Pilate summoned a centurion, and gave him orders. A moment or two later several soldiers came through the gateway and took Jesus over from the guards. Pilate went down and reseated himself on his chair. The prisoner was led off into the palace – I could not see where he was taken. But then a whisper ran through the crowd, some of whom could see right into the courtyard: 'They're scourging him!'

The punishment took some time. We heard the shouts and laughter of the soldiers in the depths of the courtyard, and the bleating of sacrificial lambs in the distant Temple. From time to time I thought I heard the crack of Roman whips. The people gathered around me breathed hurriedly, painfully. I began to think that if it went on much longer they would call for mercy instead of death. But I was wrong: the whipping inflamed their passions, and made them all the more impatient for the final act of execution.

A group of soldiers marched up to the Procurator. He rose to his feet and stared at them: no, not at them, but at someone among them. Then he went to the steps. The soldiers followed. He appeared at one window, and Jesus was pushed up to another, next to it.

I heard Pilate say:

'After all, this is a man.'

I closed my eyes, my throat was clasped as though in a vice; my stomach turned over, my heart beat like a bell. This was no man: the form standing at the window was a pitiful shell. A man flayed of his skin. The head, fixed on the rigid neck, was wearing a leafless crown, a garland of thorns. Beneath it the eyes were dark pits, with no sign of life in them. The cheeks were caked with blood, the beard was dripping blood. All the body was red with blood. The soldiers had thrown a scarlet cloak round him, and it made him look like a wine-presser just come from the press. Blood was dripping to the ground from his chest, his arms and thighs. His lower jaw had dropped as though he were dead. A cane had been thrust into his tightly-clenched hand.

From the leading members of the crowd came the cry:

'Crucify him!'

I almost felt like crying too: 'Crucify him! Put an end to all this!' This sight was not to be borne.

'Crucify him yourselves,' Pilate angrily answered.

'Does that mean, worthy Procurator' (it was rabbi Jonathan who spoke), 'that you wish to let him go free? For we ourselves may not crucify him. Yet he must perish, for he has declared that he is the son of the Most High.'

Pilate's face again twitched spasmodically. He looked round at his men as though anxious to assure himself that they were close at hand. Without a word he returned to the courtyard, and dropped into his chair. The soldiers led the prisoner before him. Then he rose to his feet. A white figure stood confronting the crimson one. They talked together. With his hands clasped behind his back, Pilate took several paces to and fro. Then he returned to the window.

'For the last time, I tell you,' he said with no conviction in his tone, 'I can find no crime that this man has committed. I have punished him and will now let him go.'

'Crucify him!' the mob howled.

'Crucify him!' shouted the priests, the Levites, and Sadducees.

'Crucify him!' The Pharisees and doctors took up the cry.

'But he is your king.' Now Pilate was behaving like a tethered dog furiously scattering its bed. 'Do you want me to crucify your king?'

'We have no king but Caesar,' Jonathan cried.

'Do you want us to make another visit to Capri to lay a charge against you?' Possibly this came from Ananias himself.

'The crowd will never agree. You'll have bloodshed before the day's out. And you know Rome won't like that!' rabbi Oncelos cried.

'Crucify him!' the shouts continued, more and more insistently.

'Do you want another rising like that in Caesarea?' Ananias asked again.

'Good!' Pilate said at last, grinding his teeth. He went back to his chair. Sitting erect, with his palms on his knees, he uttered a brief sentence. Probably it was the Roman formula: 'Ibis ad crucem.' When the words were passed to the lictor, I knew that it was as I had guessed. Soldiers marched out and drew up in rank. A horse was brought up. The scribe laid aside his tablets and set to work to write something on a large board.

Once more the Procurator appeared at the window. Beside him stood a lad with a ewer and a tray. With the air of a priest performing a religious rite Pilate ordered the boy to pour water over his hands. As he shook them dry, he said:

'I take no responsibility for this blood . . .'

'But we do,' Caiaphas shouted.

'We do!' Jonathan bar Azziel cried, and the Pharisees took up the cry.

'We do!' the crowd roared, drunk with victory, and ignorant of what it was shouting.

A procession came through the gate. At its head was a centurion on horseback, followed by some twenty soldiers. The teacher came behind them. Now he was wearing his own clothing; but it was filthy and torn, and he looked like a beggar in rags. His shoulders were borne down with the beam of a cross; the head in its ring of thorns projected from beneath the beam. He came with tottering step, wandering from side to side. If he had not been controlled by lads holding ropes fastened to his waist he might easily have turned off the road and stumbled blindly into the crowd. Two of Barabbas's band, also bowed down under crosses, came immediately behind him: they were to suffer the death their leader had escaped. The rear of the procession was brought up by further soldiers. At the sight of the bloodstained, stumbling form the crowd broke into a roar. Now they saw him only as someone the Roman had tried to save, and whom they had succeeded in wresting from his hands. Fists were shaken, stones and peel were thrown. The soldiers had to line the route in order to protect the prisoner. Pilate stood at the window, contemptuously watching the procession as it departed. Suddenly Caiaphas ran right into the gateway. Spitting with fury, foaming and brandishing his fists, he shouted:

'What have you done? Why did you have that inscription written? It can't be left like that!'

For a lad walking alongside the teacher was carrying a board under his arm. On it was written, in three languages: 'Jesus of Nazareth, king of the Jews.'

Pilate shrugged his shoulders. He was like a man who in defeat has ceased to reckon with his enemies. He turned his back on them and cried across his shoulder:

'What I have written, I have written.'

I did not see him conducted to the place of execution. The procession went down the hill, then, from the bottom of Tyropeon it climbed up to the city gate. The roaring and shouting of the accompanying mob did not cease for a moment. In order to get a good view many rushed ahead, or stood on tiptoe, trying to see him across the people's heads. From time to time there was a halt, and immediately a wild surge of people tried to force themselves closer to him.

I dragged along right at the end of the procession. I lacked the courage to walk at his side: I was afraid, afraid of seeing his face beneath that wreath of thorns. From time to time I heard shouts of savage glee: 'He's fallen! He's lying down! Get up! Hurry up! Get a move on!' And I hadn't the courage to witness this sight either. At one spot, as I stumbled along with my eyes fixed on the ground I saw the crimson trace of a foot on the stones. It must have been from his foot. I trembled at the very thought that I would see him again. Why is it that the human body, which can be so attractive, can also be the most horrible sight imaginable?

We passed through the gate. The procession turned below a small hill between the road and the walls, and halted. At the top of the hill there were several bare posts. The stony sides, overgrown with grey vegetation, but bare in places like the skin of a mangy ass, were the cemetery of the condemned. White signs painted on the rocks conveyed warnings to anyone afraid of defilement. The self-respecting faithful followed a path which could take only two or three persons abreast. But the impatient, heedless mob rushed straight across the stones and the graves.

When I struggled to the summit the act of nailing the bodies to the crossbeams was almost completed. The two bandits were already extended on posts standing one on either side. A central beam, rising higher than the others, had been allotted to the teacher. The blood of many criminals had flowed over its planed surface, soaking into the wood like resin returning to the trunk. The tablet with the insulting inscription was already nailed at the top. For one moment I saw Jesus's head across the mass of heads. But then it vanished: the executioners had ordered him to lie down. Through the hubbub I heard the heavy beat of a hammer. Then someone gave an order, and the men standing behind the post began to haul on the rope. The crossbeam slowly crept up the main post, bearing the teacher with his arms stretched out across it. His mouth was gaping, his head stiffly bent to one side; all his muscles were straining. The appearance of the crucified body was greeted with a roar. Slipping up the post, the crossbeam came at last to the mortise. As it dropped into position a shiver of pain passed over the racked body. The sound of a hammer rang out again. His feet were being nailed at the bottom.

Now Jesus hung between the greyish-azure sky and the top of the hill, which was covered with a swarming mass of people. His body strained as though trying to break away. When nailing him down the executioners had pulled with all their strength on his arms, so that the excessively distended chest could not relax. He was choking. His face turned blue, the veins in his neck swelled to bursting point, a whistle came from his open mouth. Except for a narrow girdle he was quite naked, and his body revealed all the marks of the tortures he had suffered. It was one open, suppurating wound. I could not but gaze at him, and I could not endure the sight. That torment expressed something more than pain: it conveyed a kind of grievous, helpless bashfulness which had been violated. I remembered Ruth's eyes when the doctors removed the coverlet from her deformed body. Now she was constantly in my thoughts. It was as though she were hanging at his side.

Through the panting breath of these crucified men I could almost hear her breath too.

The crowd grew silent. Here and there people talked quietly; a woman began to sob. But, as though some had not yet had enough, a voice cried:

'Hi, you! Maybe you'll come down from the cross?'

There was a sneer in the tone; but perhaps it was also a desperate challenge. Others took it up:

'Come down from the cross. Come on, why don't you? You could talk well, and you worked miracles . . . Why don't you talk now? Come down when we tell you!'

The shouts rose in intensity. And the more they increased, the more they seemed to have an insistent, feverish quality:

'Come down from the cross! You were going to destroy the Temple! You fraud! You cheat! Come down! You Messiah! You king! Son of the Eternal! Come on, come down!'

One voice seemed to come from overhead. I looked up: one of the crucified bandits was shouting too:

'Get down! D'you hear?'

I saw the teacher turn his head and look at the man. In that look was neither anger nor reproach. But the bandit appeared to take offence: he took a deep breath and spat at Jesus. 'You liar!' he coughed out.

The man hanging on the teacher's right hand broke in:

'You fool! You're blaspheming. We know what we are being crucified for. But he . . .' His voice trailed away: he was short of breath. 'Rabbi,' he turned to Jesus, 'if . . . you go to . . . your kingdom . . . perhaps you . . . will remember . . . me.'

The teacher's head turned slowly on its rigid neck. It seemed incredible, but over his swollen and bloodstained face passed the flicker of a smile. He said:

'Today . . . we shall be there . . . together.'

Then he again gasped for breath, his mouth gaping.

It suddenly struck me that the shouts of the mob had died away. Entirely absorbed in watching Jesus, I had failed to notice what was happening around me. The crowd had lost its interest in the crucifixion, and was looking about in alarm. For although it was now the sixth hour, the light of the sun was fading. In the middle of the day it grew darker and darker. Crimson mist like smoke crept over the surrounding hills, through the damp, rainy air. A wind blew up, raising little columns of dust. The sky turned a colour like the fallow sun-scorched wilderness of Judaea, and the clouded sun left only thin shafts of light. Someone shouted: 'The earth is quaking,' and though I didn't feel it myself I was seized with a blind, animal fear. Nor I alone. The mob scattered like a flock of sparrows startled by a stone. An anxious murmur arose as it fled down the hill, leaving at the summit only the representatives of the Sanhedrin, the soldiers, and a handful of the most intrepid onlookers. The wind whirled and whistled; the day grew gloomier and gloomier, as though a rain of ash were sprinkling from the sky. In this ruddy brown haze only the nearest objects were visible. The city wall and the road to Joppa had been obliterated. I went closer to the cross. There was hardly anyone left at the foot; some soldiers shifted about uneasily, a few figures with cloaks over their heads stood almost at the foot of the beam carrying the teacher; others remained a little way off like a flock of frightened sheep.

'Did you hear that?' someone asked. 'He called on Elias.'

'I'll give him a drink,' someone else replied. 'He asked for water.'

'Let Elias come and give it him himself,' a third voice commented, half sarcastically, half afraid.

I looked round; now the members of the Sanhedrin had gone, leaving one Pharisee, as though to act as guard.

I went closer still. The wind was blowing strongly. The heavy post gently swayed. Among the people standing beneath it were several women and one man. I recognized him: he was John, son of Zebedee. At his side was Jesus's mother. Her face was turned upward and was taut with pain, it looked as though carved in stone. Her hand was resting on the creaking timber. Thin streams of blood slowly flowed over her fingers. His blood, I thought, is mingled on this wood with the blood of the greatest of sinners. Through the gloom we could hear the rattle in his throat. His feet were level with my eyes, I noticed they were laid one over the other, and fastened with a long nail. The strain of the muscles was evident even down to the tensely outspread toes.

In the sunlight I hadn't dared to look at him. But in this gloom, standing right at the foot of the cross on which he was hanging I felt more at ease. Surely something will happen now, I could not help thinking. This gloom, this night at noonday, this fearful tension must come to an end at last. It must . . . Either he is really who he claims to be, or else . . .

Unexpectedly a voice, broken into single words, dropped on us from above. It began quietly, then passed into a prolonged cry like the scream of a nocturnal bird. I thought I heard:

'Abba . . . Father . . . into . . . Thy hands . . .'

I raised my head and listened. But now nothing was to be heard except the creaking of the post and the whistle of the wind. The others standing at the foot also listened intently. No further sound reached our ears. The gloom had veiled the form above us, but I thought I saw the knees twitch convulsively and remain bent.

'He's dead,' said John, and he covered his face with his hands. The women began to weep, and beat their heads against the ground. Only his mother remained standing as before, with dry eyes turned upward, her face fixed and grey. I was rooted to the spot, gazing at those two pierced feet. Behind me someone, probably one of the soldiers, said in Greek:

'This was no ordinary man . . .'

I stood helpless, as though I were yet another post driven into the ground. So he is dead, I thought. For those who believed him to be the Son of the Most High this must be the defeat of defeats. But even for me . . . I confess that right down to the last moment I had expected something to happen. That he should have died such a common death . . . he who had worked so many miracles. My former thought, that he would be able to save himself, stung me like the memory of a slap in the face. He hadn't been able to . . . But nor had we been able . . . I had defended him, I had exposed myself to conflict with all the Sanhedrin and the Grand Council. And yet I don't feel that I have done all I could. Yet what else could I have done?

As I had not noticed when it began to turn dark, so now I did not notice when the gloomy mists began to disperse. The day returned. The cliffs, the hills, the serrated city wall, the deserted road, all emerged again from the mist. I raised my head. His body was hanging heavily; it was no longer held up by the straining muscles. His head had fallen to his chest, his hands extended like limp lines. The violet hue of his face had gone, leaving it deathly white. Right above me I saw the staring eyes and half-open lips, revealing the teeth. In its last spasm the body had contorted in an ugly twist. By comparison with the distortion of his body the other two looked like Greek sculptures, they retained human proportions. In this body there was no symmetry, no harmony whatever. It was as though before he died on the cross he had been stricken with leprosy and paralysis. As though all the diseases in the world had entered his body.

In this death there was no aspect of dignity. It was one screaming horror, over which one wanted to throw a sheet as quickly as possible. The other two were still alive: I saw them gulping for air. In an hour or two they would be dead and like him. One of our consolations in the presence of death is belief in its majesty. But in reality death has no majesty whatever. One dies rebelling. The face hanging above me expressed only despair before superior might. I could not tear my eyes away from him. I expect you know the attraction of a mirror, and the incomprehensible, irresistible desire to make faces in it? That body seemed to be a mirror. One saw one's own face in it. I could not force myself away. It seemed that I would go on standing there without end. That which in the living man was horror, in the dead acquired the aspect of infamy. I have no complaint against him that he died. But I cannot overcome the affront that he died in such a manner!

On this post dozens of men had died. Like him they had panted, rattled, coughed, ground their teeth. And then they had remained hanging limply. He had gained nothing by my proximity. One dies alone. I had not heard Ruth's last sigh, as I had heard his cry. And yet their deaths were so similar, they might have been side by side. Far away from me – and very close . . . As though their death . . .

I turned to look at the man crucified on his right hand. He was rattling in his throat, and panting. I remembered what Jesus said to him. Those words were typical of him. His death, as well as his life, was always one blessing. And yet . . . he has died. Of a truth, Job's revolts were unwise. There is no answer for those who resist. But supposing it was by his own wish that he took all this infamy on himself? I have said it often: why has this fallen to me, just to me? But perhaps it needs to be put differently: perhaps these things come not to the man who has done wrong, but to him who loves? But I love so little . . . I love so poorly . . .

He is dead. The day returns to its ordinary cares and fears. Now I begin to realize what effect my words at the meeting of the Sanhedrin will have. He who dies does at least go to the realm of silence. Perhaps to his kingdom . . . If it only existed . . . despite this death! What would I have given if he had said to Ruth the words he said to this bandit – and if I had heard them!

The ruddy gloom dispersed at last, and the sun emerged from the mists, crimson of face as though angry or ashamed. The cloud which had brought the mist passed beyond the Mount of Olives, leaving behind it the scent that arises after a thunderstorm. I was torn with anxiety; I could not occupy myself with anything; I returned home in haste. I went to the upstairs room. Everything was left untouched, as it had been after their departure last night. A linen cloth was spread over the table; mugs, goblets and plates, pieces of bread, and bones, were scattered over it. The ritual cloaks and pilgrims' staffs lay thrown down in one corner, beside a pitcher of water and a large bowl for washing the feet. I sat down on the bench and was lost in thought. I gazed at the goblet from which the teacher had drunk, and which he had handed round for the others to drink. I felt so strongly that something was seething and bubbling in it that I had to get up and look. But there was nothing in it, really.

I was so deep in thought that I didn't hear steps on the stairs, and I raised my head only when I felt a touch on my shoulder. It was Joseph, with John the son of Zebedee. The young man's face was pale, swollen with weeping. His dishevelled hair fell over his forehead, his long lashes fluttered like the wings of a fleeing bird.

I felt that they had come to summon me to something. But all I wanted was quiet and oblivion. I asked peevishly:

'What do you want?'

Joseph sat down on the bench beside me and set his hands on his knees.

'I don't know whether you've already heard that he's dead. He died quickly. This lad says with truth that when the news reaches Caiaphas, the high priest will remind Pilate of the prescriptions of the Torah, which require the burial of a condemned man's body before sundown. And then they'll throw him into a common grave. Don't you agree that this man deserves honourable burial? If you do, we must go at once to the Procurator and ask him to hand the body over to us. There isn't much time. The Sabbath will begin within an hour.'

I raised a weary gaze to Joseph.

'You intend to ask for his body? Pilate will never agree to that,' I assured him, in my instinctive desire to have nothing to do with this scheme.

'But he may agree,' Joseph said. 'He'll be sure to demand money, but he should agree. In any case we can try. I think you felt respect for this man . . .'

'Yes, of course I did,' I stammered. But I still sought some way of evading this task. I was terrified at the prospect of going straight to the Procurator and chaffering with him over the body, and then undertaking all the trouble of the burial, so exposing myself further to the Sadducees and my brethren. That called for more strength than I possessed. 'Pilate won't want to talk to us today,' I said. 'He's furious. He's just as likely to vent his anger on us.'

Joseph looked at me closely.

'That's by no means excluded,' he admitted. 'I know him well. But this lad is so insistent. And his mother and some other women are still standing beneath the cross. We agreed that he had been condemned unjustly. But of course it would be better if I went to Pilate alone. I've had talks with him before. I've never asked him for anything . . .'

I started up from the bench.

'You can't go by yourself,' I exclaimed. 'If you insist . . . If you insist . . . ,' I repeated angrily, forgetting that if Joseph was anxious to try to ransom the teacher's body he probably did it chiefly for my sake. 'It will have a bad end, you'll see. But when you're in one of your obstinate moods you always . . .' I walked fuming about the room. But I stopped abruptly, for again the goblet from which the teacher had drunk appeared to be filled with seething liquid. Of course it was only an illusion. But it brought my thoughts back to the dead man. Suddenly my irritation seemed rather unpleasant: as though I were chaffering with a beggar over a penny. Maybe he wasn't what people thought he was, and what he himself thought he was. But, after all, he had died like a hero. Joseph was right.

'All right, I'll go alone,' Joseph said calmly. 'You're tired . . .'

'No, no!' I suppressed my fears. 'I'll go with you.'

The streets were so crowded that it was difficult to pass through them. The cloud had vanished completely, the sky was pleasant, the sun shone over the tower of Antonia, making it flame with light, as though it were a torch raised high above the city.

We gave in our names at the gate, and a Syrian page went to inform the Procurator of our arrival. I nudged Joseph and reminded him that we would be defiling ourselves by entering a heathen house. He replied:

'I'm sure your teacher would never stop to think about that, Nicodemus.'

He was right. For Jesus the act of mercy was above all law. But there was no time for meditation: the page returned and said the Procurator was waiting for us. We passed through the courtyard up the stairs to the atrium. A fountain was playing in the centre, reminding me of Pilate's robbery of the Temple treasury. He came to meet us with a smile on his face. When we bowed to him, he raised his hand in response.

'Welcome!' he said. 'What brings you to me on the eve of your greatest festival? This morning your elders would not cross the threshold of my house. Just as though I were a leper!' I felt that he was sneering at us, and the thought made me uneasy. But he genuinely tried to be amiable. He pointed us to chairs, and himself sat down. Joseph explained why we had come.

'What?' he exclaimed. 'Dead already? Impossible!' I had the impression that he was relieved, as though a great weight had fallen from his shoulders. 'I must send a soldier to check your statement.' He struck a gong and summoned a centurion. 'Listen, Longinus,' he said to the officer. 'Hurry and see whether it's true that that Galilean is dead already, as these visitors inform me.'

The centurion went out. Pilate got up and walked to the balustrade of the terrace, which gave a view of the city. Across the housetops he could see Golgotha, black against the sunlight, and the outlines of the crosses, with people standing at their foot.

'Hm!' he muttered to himself, rubbing his hands over his shaven cheeks. 'Already dead?' He sat down again and turned to us: 'It appears he called himself the son of Jove, or something of the sort, didn't he?' He wiped beads of sweat from his forehead. 'This day has wearied me,' he declared. 'Nothing but tumult, stink, and all the other things inseparable from your priests . . . And so you've come for his body, Joseph?'

'We want to bury him as is fitting. This man was a great prophet. I'm of the opinion that he was innocent of the charges brought against him.'

'Of course he was,' Pilate admitted. 'But what of it? Not all your people are as sensible as you. The priests and the Pharisees and the crowd were all shouting "Crucify him!" If I'd refused there would have been scenes, riots and possibly even a rising. I'd have had to send out soldiers to restore order. It was better to allow one . . . prophet, as you call him, to perish than to have to kill many later. I'm not cruel, though I understand the Jews think I am. I try to act in accordance with the philosophy of moderation in all things. But there's no place for philosophy when you're dealing with madmen. You can shut one madman away in a dungeon. But what can you do when a whole people goes out of its mind? Your kinsmen, Caiaphas and Jonathas, tried to threaten me this morning. But I gave them a nasty knock in return. I expect you heard how they whined: "Don't put it like that; say he ordered that he was to be called a king." But I wouldn't yield to them. I expect you read the inscription: "king of the Jews."' He laughed and rubbed his hands. 'Your Sanhedrin is beginning to think I'll dance for them like a monkey on a string when they start to play. They can get that idea right out of their heads. And you can tell them so!'

The centurion returned, halting at the threshold.

'Well?' Pilate asked him.

'It is, my lord, as the Jewish teachers have said. The Galilean is dead. To make quite sure I pierced his side. Blood and water flowed out . . .'

'So of course he's dead,' the Procurator said under his breath. He turned to me. 'I gather that when he was alive he worked miracles, healed sick people, and even raised the dead. Someone told my wife so. That's always the way: these magicians do their tricks, and then when something comes upon them they go to Dis like every one of us. This world is stupid and it always will be stupid. And the most stupid of all are those who try to find some sense in the stupidity.' He summoned a Syrian page. 'Bring me papyrus.' He wrote a few words on the papyrus, and the lad sealed it.

'Here you are!' Pilate said to us. 'On showing this you will be given the Galilean's body.'

We bowed our gratitude. But I felt sure that was not the end of the matter. I was surprised that he hadn't made any conditions. Both Joseph and I had gold in our wallets, and we planned to give him a debit note if we lacked sufficient cash.

'How much are we to pay for this, worthy Procurator?' I asked.

A sour look crossed his face. He was about to say something, but refrained. He walked meditatively across to the balustrade. The sun was sinking behind the hills.

'Well then, possibly . . . yes,' he began, turning back to us. 'But no! No!' He breathed heavily. 'No!' he said yet again. 'I give you his body. Take it and bury it. Bury it properly. As I have given it to you you needn't spare the perfumes and oils. After all, it's costing you nothing; bury it properly. I'm doing this to punish them.' The evil expression cleared from his face. As though enjoying to the full the surprise he had caused by his munificence, he added: 'I've given them one on the nose. They'll never forget this! A good joke! King of the Jews! Ha! Ha! Ha!'

Joseph went straight to Golgotha with Pilate's order, on the way collecting some men to help him. But I went to the market to buy myrrh and aloes. The stalls were already closed, but I knocked at one of them. I bought all the perfumes and oils I could, and hired two lads to carry them. The shadows were lying in the depth of the streets; only the roofs were still bathed in sunlight. I took the road to Lydda, which runs round the foot of Golgotha. When I had left the hill that afternoon the slopes were still crowded; now it was deserted: only a handful of people were moving about on its summit. I could hear the far-carrying sound of voices, and the knock of a hammer. I hurried to the spot.

When I reached the level area at the top, Jesus's body was already taken down from the cross. It lay stretched out stiffly on a piece of linen, reddish brown with dried blood and crimson in the light of the setting sun. The unnaturally elongated arms still retained the shape of a cross, and extended far beyond the shroud. The head had fallen back, to reveal the face. These were not the features I knew: the face with its pleasant smile. They had none of the rest and peace of the dead. The mouth was set in a cry of pain and despair, it still seemed to be suffering. The only resemblance left to the former Jesus was in his height. In his life he had always towered a good head above the crowd; now he seemed even taller: a giant spreading out his body over all the hillside.

He was surrounded by a little group of people. In the middle his mother was watching over her son. With her face uncovered, and still looking astonishingly youthful despite its expression of grief, she half knelt, half squatted on the ground. She was not weeping or sobbing, she was not talking to her dead son, as one talks to the dead. Her eyes were fixed on his swollen face. As I looked at her I felt sure that while her son's torture was at an end, her's had far from ended.

I called Joseph aside and showed him what I had bought.

'Why haven't you washed the body yet?' I asked. 'It's getting very late. And the soldiers are growing impatient,' I added, as the guard which had taken down the bodies beckoned to us to hurry.

'They don't want to wait, though I've offered them money,' Joseph agreed.

'Then what are we to do?'

'There's only one thing we can do. As it is we wouldn't manage to do all that needs to be done. I have a tomb in the side of that hill yonder. We'll pour oils over the body and lay it there for the time being. Then, early in the morning after the Sabbath it can be washed and anointed properly with what you have brought . . .'

'But how about the prescriptions, Joseph?' I exclaimed.

He waved his hand impatiently.

'You and your Pharisaic prescriptions! Look at the way she's gazing at him!' he pointed to Mary. 'I hadn't the heart to take the body from her just because of stupid prescriptions. Maybe I'm a sinner, but . . .'

The officer in charge came up to us:

'Hurry!' he said. 'Take these remains away. Dusk is falling, the Jews will quite likely attack us for disregarding their holy day . . .'

There was nothing else we could do. We called John and told him what Joseph proposed. He made no protest, and did not seem upset at the idea of putting the body unwashed into the tomb. He went to Mary and pointed to the setting sun. She made no objection, but yielded up her son, laying his head back on the sheet. John crossed the arms over the chest. As the body was moved, blood and water again flowed from the open wound in the side. At last a kerchief covered Jesus's face. But in concealing it from our eyes it did not conceal it from our memories. In me at least that look was carved as though burnt out with a red-hot iron. I thought I would feel better when I no longer saw that dread, bloodstained face. But it was not so; hardly had it been lost to my sight than I felt the lack of it. I felt that if I didn't see it again I should die, of hunger, of thirst, of revulsion against all that that face was not. Believe me, when the teacher's face was concealed I felt a terrible thirst to return to it again as soon as possible. Not that it should return to me, but I to it. It was like a call from Sheol. Whenever I talked to him I felt that I could read a call in his eyes. And I always felt guilty for not obeying that call. That face is calling me now! But in life it was beautiful, serene, and good. After death it seems to be crying out with pain and to be foretelling pain. I am always telling you that I'm afraid not so much of what is as of what I imagine will be . . . But that pain is itself a call. Do you understand that, Justus?

Of course, as the following day was a Holy Day I could not go to the tomb. But when the Passover ended at sunset I could hold back no longer. I ran out of the house. The moon was shining like a lamp, round, enormous. The city gates were closed, but I know wickets through which one can pass beyond the walls at night. I hurried as though someone were waiting for me. Only when I reached the plain beyond the city did I feel uncomfortable. I thought at once of the robbers who are always lurking close to the walls, especially at times of festival. I walked as though bewitched along the serrated line of light and dark cast by the wall. The night was cold, I trembled despite my thick cloak. Round the corner of the palace of Asmodeus I saw the hill of Golgotha. In the moonlight it really did look like an enormous skull: two hollows resembled eye sockets, and the dark bushes at the sides seemed like hair. I walked hurriedly, catching my cloak in the bushes, knocking my legs painfully against projecting stones. I made straight for a belt of shadow lying at the foot of the hill like a cloak thrown off a man's shoulders. But I had hardly passed into the darkness when I heard the unexpected shout:

'Halt!'

I stood rooted to the ground. My heart came into my mouth.

'What do you want?' the voice asked.

The speaker emerged from the shadow, and his armour gleamed in the moonlight. He was a Roman soldier, armed with spear and square shield. I was alone, so he approached me disdainfully. But he held his spear at the ready.

'What do you want?' he repeated.

'Oh . . . nothing . . . I was only coming . . . to the tomb,' I stammered.

'To the tomb?' he laughed. 'What for? The dead don't need

to be visited by night. Tell me at once what you're doing here, unless you want me to take you for interrogation . . .'

I felt sick, almost ready to faint. My mind was already imagining my body racked with torture. I was prepared to say anything, whether truth or falsehood, so long as it satisfied the soldier. But fortunately for me another Roman came out of the darkness. I heard a voice which I knew well:

'Drop it, Antonius. This man's an eminent teacher. I know him.' He came right up to me. 'Do you recognize me, rabbi?' he asked.

'Yes, of course I do!' I hastened to answer. I had given this decurion a few denarii once for some small service he had rendered me. He was an old, grey-haired soldier, and a rare joker. I was saved. 'Of course I recognize you, Lucian. What luck that you're here. I shan't forget this. But tell me, what are you doing here?'

He laughed. 'We're freezing and cursing! Don't you know, rabbi? We've been ordered to guard this Galilean prophet. The doctors and priests asked the Procurator to arrange for a guard. At dusk they set a great seal on the stone. I can show you. But you can't go into the tomb.'

'But the body hasn't been washed or anointed,' I exclaimed.

'I can't help that, rabbi,' he answered. 'We were ordered to guard the tomb until tomorrow at sunset and let nobody enter. The priests and doctors have promised us rewards too. But what an idea: guarding a dead body! Thank goodness there's only another night . . .'

'So the guard will be taken off tomorrow evening?'

'Yes. Apparently the Galilean prophesied that he would rise again within three days. And if he doesn't rise within three days he won't rise at all! Because people believe such yarns, we've got to freeze and lose our sleep. Come to the fire and have a warm, rabbi,' he added.

I went to their fire; several soldiers were lying round it.

'Why, there are quite a lot of you,' I remarked.

'All my troop,' Lucian replied. 'Enough to deal with anybody who tries to break into the tomb. And if he himself does rise again we'll put him back behind the stone. Shan't we, boys?' he cried cheerfully.

There was a roar of coarse laughter. 'He won't rise!' the men retorted. 'But if he does we'll kill him off a second time.'

That raised another brutal and savage laugh. One of them broke into a bawdy soldiers' song. The words played on my nerves: at that moment all I wanted was quiet and an opportunity to think. I went slowly to the cliff. Lucian followed me. Possibly he was afraid I would touch the seal. But I was constrained by his presence. I wished to be alone for a moment with this death.

'Lucian,' I said, 'I promise you not to touch the seal. But let me pray here, by the stone. Only for a moment or two. And get your comrades to be quiet, will you? I'll gladly give them a bottle of wine.' I hurriedly took some coins from my wallet and put them into his hand.

'We've been forbidden to drink a drop while we're guarding the tomb,' Lucian said craftily.

'Then buy it later. Here's some more. Just allow me to remain here for a little while . . .'

He stood rocking on his feet, astonished by my request. But the silver outweighed his scruples. He went slowly back to his comrades. I heard him say something to them. There was a roar of laughter, but then silence fell.

The rock was hard, cold, and damp, repellent to the touch. When I put my face close to it I almost had the feeling that I was close to the face of a corpse. I passed my hand over the smooth stone. Behind it, in a narrow stone bed, lay the man I had watched for three years. I had followed him from afar, never able to bring myself to take the final step. I had not experienced the joy, hope, and ecstasy which his disciples had known. I had turned to him at a time of misfortune and overwhelming suffering. And possibly for this very reason I had shared only one feeling with him: the feeling of fear. Half consciously I had been afraid of the moment when that strange doctrine of the kingdom, beginning seemingly with nothing and drawing into its orbit everything, would emerge from the swathing bands of infancy. I had felt that it would not always be only a melodious Galilean song. Its words would germinate like seed. Every one of us was to be the earth into which that seed fell: good earth or bad, rich or barren. What kind of earth had I been? I remembered so well what he had said about the soil which needed digging and dunging, and the seed which had to be protected from fire and flood. His words had not been like weeds, which spring up at once, and when you cut them down send up new shoots from the root. Yet at a certain stage they had begun to grow. One hadn't noticed just when it had begun, nor when they grew into a tree. A tree whose roots had undermined the house. I had been living a life seemingly peaceful and secure. But today I was like a land shaken with subterranean shocks.

I had followed him from afar. I had talked with him only once or twice. I had gone to him to ask him for something, but had never put my request into words. And Ruth had died. He hadn't healed her, though he worked such magnificent miracles. Instead, he had offered me incomprehensible words. What had he meant by 'being born again'? What had he meant by 'take my cross, and I'll take yours.' What had he meant by 'give me your cares'?

But, although they were incomprehensible, those words grew within me. At one time they had seemed like initiation into a great mystery. But they had revealed no magical powers. Their sounds had not made anyone superhuman. As for himself, at times it has seemed to me that nobody was more human in his nature than he. Greek philosophy created heroes – people who, for the sake of ideals of truth, beauty and goodness, raised themselves to the heights of superhuman renunciation and sacrificed their life with tranquillity and dignity. He, too, had given his life. He could have saved it, he could have fled, not even by resorting to a miracle, but simply by hiding when we warned him. He had given his life. But in what very different fashion from those Greeks. The death of the Greek heroes is always beautiful. His death was horrible. The beauty of their death is a picture executed by an artist. But who would wish to portray his death, which was devastating in its horror? Always, to the end of my life I shall see that body extended on the cross, as I shall always see Ruth in the arms of the women supporting her. Such a picture sows a grain of uneasiness, and it grows. The beauty of the death of a Greek hero is beauty consummated. This death was not beautiful, nor was it the consummation. Though he is dead, and though his church, consisting as it does of a few cowardly simpletons, will be scattered within the next few days, we who heard his words will never be able to forget a single one of them. He taught that everything is nothing, that mercy is everything. Whatever he said, this was always the essential meaning of his words. He died simply for that one truth. He did not flee before that most fearful of deaths, and this refusal itself seemed to say that the compassion he had always in mind was to be found even in an infamous death on a cross. But he proved nothing. Ruth's death was horrible. But his death was even more horrible. And when we took that body with its clinging blood and sweat down from the cross, there was not even time left in which to wash him, as one washes the faithful, even the poorest, before laying him in the tomb. He did not die with a smile on his lips, the death of a Greek sage. We laid his body, still filthy from that execution, in the tomb and hurriedly, almost as though ashamed, rolled the stone in front of it. And then the men of the Sanhedrin had come and sealed the stone. And so the testimony of compassion was refuted. He died for a truth which is no truth. Jairus's daughter rose again; Lazarus rose again. He died, and now lies crushed beneath the seal of the sacred sanctuary as though under Caiaphas's prophecy, and crushed beneath the boots of the Roman legionaries. Nobody will resurrect him, any more than he resurrected Ruth. One is almost inclined to think that he deliberately surrendered only himself and her to death. But then, what for? Simply that by their deaths they should prove that law is more than compassion, that the Most High can punish, but has no desire to forgive . . .

I turned away from the rock. While I meditated, the area of shadow had extended, and the moonlight had lost some of its glassiness. I returned to the fire. Several of the guards were playing dice, the others were walking about to keep awake.

'Thank you, Lucian,' I said to the decurion. I shook all the money I had left out of my wallet and gave it to him. 'I am very grateful. If you should ever have need of me . . .'

I left the spot. Behind me one of the soldiers started up his filthy song again. 'So you are not spared even that,' I thought. Tomorrow at dusk the soldiers will return to their barracks. They will sneer at the Jewish king who died like some wilderness bandit, and who then was guarded to make sure he didn't rise again. Their contempt had been turned into a sneer, and will remain only a sneer. No one jests at hemlock. But what could save a cross from scoffing?

So I came back home. But I cannot sleep. I am sitting writing to you. Oh, Justus, I am suffering terribly. It's as though everything that had already died within me once were dying again. I should be glad that I kept my distance from them, that I was not his disciple. The Sanhedrin and the Grand Council may forget that I spoke in his defence. I should be satisfied. Meanwhile, on the contrary this feeling fills me with despair. I cannot help thinking that those who always followed him, who believed in him, have preserved something none the less, despite this death and disappointment. I have saved nothing. For me he has died like Ruth, taking everything with him. It is as though I were again feeling the pain that the Most High did not wish to let me keep her. Yet at the same time . . . Oh, Justus! It is incomprehensible, but I feel as though at the very bottom of my despair some change has been accomplished. His saying that one must be born again is sounding in my ears once more. Why should I be thinking that perhaps this very night is to be the night of my second birth? What has his death in common with births? All my body is aching, like the body of a woman in travail, or possibly like the pain, unknown to a man, of a child entering into the world. But I know this night will pass – and all will end. For although it seems endlessly long, in truth it is passing swiftly. A pallid greyness is beginning to spread over the still black sky. All is quiet, but now in this ringing silence I think I can hear a footstep. My pain is still with me. It seems to be increasing. If it lasts much longer I shall be born again and then shall die at once. What is death? Why did I never ask Lazarus? A dying man apparently sees all his life pass before him in the twinkling of an eye. And I, too, am seeing all my past life. My homilies, Ruth – and his cross. The cross which I was to take on myself . . . But I did not. He died in order to show me that he is ready to do all things for me. I don't know why it is so, but he died for me. That was my cross to which they nailed him. My cross? But what of his cross? What have I taken on myself? Nothing, nothing! Simon snatched up his sword, Judas apparently ran to Caiaphas and flung the money down at his feet. But I? What have I done? I haven't done even that. I have done nothing. I wished only to look on. I kept my fears, my cares, to myself. Now I know who I am! I am barren soil . . . I shall not be born again. I shall not write homilies about him. I shall die before the dawn comes . . . I shall die from disgust with myself . . . I shall die . . .

Someone has just come running to the door of my house.

Justus, it was that decurion. He stood before me trembling, as I had stood before him last night. He was panting, the sweat was pouring down his cheeks, though the early morning is icy cold. He had money in his hand. Beating his fist on his chest, he shouted at me: 'But I tell you, rabbi, we didn't sleep. And we didn't drink! I swear to you that it was not a dream.'

For he says that Jesus came out from the tomb.

So he says . . .

Justus, what can I write now? I am choking, and shivering from head to foot. It's impossible! It is impossible! I have not taken up his cross. That would be too much . . . They simply must have imagined it. That would be too great a mercy . . . Why try to deceive ourselves? It only results in the wretched feeling as if one had awakened from a dream in which Ruth was still alive and no longer suffering.

DEAR JUSTUS,   TWENTY-THIRD LETTER.

How can I describe it all to you? It is something one should make a song of, and not simply talk about. Is it possible to speak of miraculous events in our miserable, ordinary human speech? That is the most terrible concomitant of his gospel, that a man feels as though cast far beyond the earth, in the sphere of the stars, and yet still possesses a heart and body just as human as before.

I shall try to tell you of all that has happened, but events are galloping past like runaway horses. The Roman soldier had hardly left me when I heard the oncoming tread of further occurrences. This time it was Joseph and John again. But now both of them in their eyes and their faces had an expression of consternation, of joy mingled with terror. For some time my friend said not a word, but sat down opposite me and stroked his beard and passed his hand over his hair with a gesture of embarrassment. John stood behind him; his black eyes seemed to be twinkling, his parted lips were quivering.

'Hm!' Joseph began. 'I don't suppose you've heard yet . . . But it's an amazing story. I just don't understand it. Listen: this lad says that very early this morning a whole flock of women ran to the tomb to wash and anoint the body. But you tell what happened yourself,' he turned to John.

'The women, rabbi,' the son of Zebedee began, 'say that the moment they got outside the gate opposite Golgotha there was a kind of earthquake . . .'

'I didn't feel anything of it,' Joseph interrupted.

'Nor I,' I admitted.

'Nor I,' said John. The lad seemed to be in a fever, but he tried to speak soberly and to the point. 'But they say it was so. And then something that looked like lightning struck the rock. They heard the roar, they saw the flash. Then they saw running soldiers . . . Just imagine, rabbi! The Romans fled, throwing down their shields, helmets and spears . . .'

'Yes, I've heard about that,' I nodded. I could still see Lucian's sweating, mortally terrified face.

'The women were frightened too. Some of them turned and ran; but others went up to the tomb despite their terror. We disciples had spent the night in the house of the tanner, Saphan, in Ophel. Not one of us could sleep. Suddenly Joanna, the wife of Chuz, ran in and cried that when she and the others went to the tomb they saw the stone was rolled away. And beside it stood a man in a cloak; he was flashing like sunlight. They declare it was an angel. He spoke to them, telling them the teacher was no longer there, for he had risen. Then they fled. We tried to calm her down. We said they must have imagined it all. But the other women all supported her; they were shouting and laughing, weeping and talking all in one. We were still talking to them when my mother hurried in and said that she and Mary had been to the tomb and heard the teacher's very voice. My mother didn't see anything, she only heard Jesus speaking to his mother. We didn't know what to make of it all; we shook with excitement. Thomas declared we'd lost our senses. But the women shouted, and we shouted too. To add to the excitement, Mary, Lazarus's sister, ran in, panting, with her hair falling about her shoulders: she looked just as she had when she was still possessed with Satan. She cried out that she had seen him. We were seized with terror. We felt convinced that something of terrible importance must have occurred. I laid him in the tomb myself, and you were with me. He was cold and stiff. But she says she has seen him alive. She didn't recognize him at first, but he spoke to her,

309

and that seemed to open her eyes. She fell at his feet; and she declares she saw the marks of the nail. He wouldn't let her touch him. He said it was too soon for that! Then he disappeared. And she ran to us as fast as she could. We couldn't remain in the house any longer. Simon and I ran out, and I reached the tomb first . . .'

'Well, and what did you see?' I exclaimed. 'Did you see anything?'

He took a deep breath, as though preparing for another run.

'The tomb was certainly open . . . I didn't have the courage to go in alone. I waited for Simon, and we went in together.'

'And then? What then?' I could not wait for him to finish.

'The body wasn't there. There's nothing whatever in the tomb. Except the linen in which we wrapped the body. The traces of the body have been left on the shroud. Even the rag with which we stopped his mouth has been rolled up. We brought everything away with us . . .'

He was silent. I, too, said nothing. Joseph asked in his stentorian voice:

'Nicodemus, what do you make of it all?'

I shrugged my shoulders helplessly. 'I don't know,' I said. 'I don't know. The women say the earth trembled, but nobody in the city felt it; lightning fell from a clear sky; men who are not men are seen, wearing gleaming robes; ten Roman soldiers flee in terror. Others say they heard and saw him; the tomb is empty. But taken all together it doesn't add up to sense. Let us ignore visions, I don't believe in them in any case. The one certain thing is that the body has disappeared from the tomb. One can have various explanations for that. First solution: Caiaphas wanted to defile the body, and ordered it to be taken from the tomb and thrown into a common grave. And he paid the soldiers to pretend they were afraid . . .'

'That doesn't make sense,' Joseph interrupted. 'Neither Caiaphas nor Ananias would dare to do that. Remember, Pilate allowed us to have the body and gave us permission to bury it. Let us assume that it was they, and they did it in such a way that nobody would know who had done it. But why didn't they wait till tomorrow? The guard was to be withdrawn this evening. And besides, the tomb was closed with the Sanhedrin's seal.'

'That's true,' I said. 'But in that case the disciples must have taken the body.'

'Nicodemus! You're talking pure rubbish! The disciples?' He nodded at John. 'Look how terrified they are. Think of the courage this lad had to summon up to stick his nose outside his hiding-place in broad daylight! Do you suggest that they had pluck enough to attack Roman soldiers? But if they didn't do it, who did? Did Jesus have any friend of sufficient standing to dare such a thing, apart from you and me?'

'No. But perhaps Pilate . . . I've been told his wife is interested in Jesus's fate . . .'

In his irritation he smacked his hand against his knee.

'You make me laugh!' he exclaimed. 'So now you're suggesting that the Roman Procurator stole from his own soldiers the body of a man whom he himself had sentenced to death two days before! I know Pilate! He'll never forgive those guards for fleeing like a lot of cattle in the sight of all Jerusalem. No, you can leave Pilate out of it.'

'But then who did do it?' I asked in my turn.

He sat looking from under his eyebrows, first at me, then at John.

'But supposing he really has risen?' he said slowly.

'Do you believe he has?' I asked.

'No,' he admitted. 'I accept only what I can weigh, measure, and touch with my hands. I had great difficulty in believing that Lazarus had risen from the dead. But I had to believe, because I saw him walking about the city. But that someone should have risen from the dead and then have vanished – that strains my credulity too much. Yet on the other hand I can't find any other explanation for it all. So I ask: supposing he really has risen?'

'He said he would rise from the dead,' John exclaimed. 'He said it again and again.'

'But what is your view?' Joseph asked me.

'As a Pharisee, of course, I believe in resurrection. But I think of it as going to happen some day, by which I mean at a time when changes will occur rendering it possible for us to believe it. I believe in resurrection, but not resurrection in the world as it exists at present.'

'In that case, fundamentally we are in agreement. But do you believe he has risen?' Joseph turned to John.

'Yes, sir,' he declared. 'He has risen . . .'

Joseph knitted his brows and shrugged his shoulders. He got up, took a couple of turns about the room, then sat down again. He was about to make some remark when my servant ran in to tell me Jonathas son of Ananias had called.

'Jonathas?' I exclaimed in amazement.

'Well, well!' Joseph nodded. 'I'm as surprised as you. John, you'd better clear off. He mustn't see you here. Go back to your people; but let me know at once if anything fresh occurs.'

I went out to welcome the unexpected guest. Jonathas had arrived in a magnificent litter. I escorted him into the hall.

'Oh, so Joseph is here too?' he remarked. He was effusive in his greeting to us; one would have thought there had been no quarrel between us the previous day. 'It's very convenient for me to see you both together.' He sat down with a rather challenging smile, and allowed water to be poured over his hands. 'I see you are as faithful as ever to the prescriptions,' he remarked. 'Well, Nicodemus,' he continued as he wiped his hands, 'you certainly have made fools of us all.'

'What do you mean, Jonathas?'

'Now, don't pretend you don't know. Strictly among ourselves, I'd never have suspected you of playing such a trick.'

'But what are you talking about?'

'Why, your hiding the body . . .'

'My hiding the body?'

'Well, it would hardly be me, would it? Listen, rabbi, don't take us to be such fools. We know you've stolen the body.'

'I haven't stolen the body.'

'Ha! Ha! Ha! Really, you're magnificent! Of course you haven't taken it yourself. As a true Pharisee you wouldn't touch a dead body. But you're wealthy enough to pay for the service. You can't deny that you went to the tomb last night . . .'

'I did . . .'

'Exactly! And you agreed with the soldiers that you would pay them well to flee at the sight of a "ghost." Don't deny it! I must admit you've taken a fine revenge. When Caiaphas heard of it I thought he'd choke on the spot, he was so mad. I don't know whether you paid Pilate too, but he issued wine to the soldiers instead of sentencing them to be whipped. In all my life I've never heard such a story! He gives you, the two wealthiest men in Jerusalem, the body for nothing, and then graciously allows his invincible soldiers to flee through the city, bawling like women with terror. You've certainly been clever!'

'But I did not take the body,' I repeated.

'Good! Good! Let's say you didn't. Obviously it evaporated into thin air. Only, you see, we just cannot have dead bodies walking around Jerusalem on their own feet. I admit that we treated you rather roughly at the Sanhedrin meeting. But in return you've made a fool of Caiaphas. An eye for an eye. But now let's call it a day. We'll come to an agreement, Nicodemus. None of us will take the body away. For that matter none of us had any intention of doing so. On the other hand, you tell us where it is now. All we want to know is that it is in a certain place, behind a certain stone . . .'

'But I tell you, Jonathas, that I did not take the body.'

'We're wasting time on empty talk . . .'

'For the last time, I tell you I haven't got the body.'

'Then who has? Joseph?'

'I haven't it either,' my friend said. 'But I know where it is.' He flung out his hand and pointed at Jonathas: 'You've concealed it.'

The president started up in his chair. He began to laugh, but the laugh was patently forced.

'You're a good actor, Joseph,' he said, 'but this time nobody will believe you. We took the body, indeed! It was you who took it. Listen: we've had enough of this pig-headedness. I've come to you as a friend. I know, I know, we've had disputes and arguments, we've given one another cause for offence. But I don't like squabbles, and insincerity angers me. Let's forget the past. Caiaphas is really furious. And when he decides on vengeance he sticks at nothing. Better a living dog than a dead lion, Solomon says. But I tell you there are times when a dead lion is better. Give the lion the funeral it deserves, and there will be peace. What do you say?'

I looked at Joseph. His face had a serious, concentrated look, as though some thought were troubling him to his depths. He shook his head seriously.

'I like sincerity too, Jonathas, and I'm not in the habit of concealing my actions,' he said. 'You want to tell us that it was we who stole the body? Then I assure you on the word of a merchant and an Israelite that neither I nor Nicodemus have had anything to do with it.'

Jonathas's courteous demeanour dropped away like a mask.

'You're the only ones who could have stolen it,' he exclaimed angrily. 'That Galilean rabble would never have dared to do such a thing.'

'All the same we did not take it.'

'I suppose you'll be suggesting next that Pilate did it for the sake of his wife, Claudia?'

'No.'

'Then what has happened to the body? It hasn't dissolved into the air.'

'Jonathas!' Joseph rose, went to the president, and leaned over him: 'Nicodemus and I have been asking ourselves that same question ever since sunrise. And we have not found any answer. Or rather, we can find only one answer . . .'

'Oh!' Jonathas laughed again: a grating laugh like a saw running against a knot. 'Joseph, you're not a doctor or a Pharisee. You're a sensible merchant. Let Nicodemus believe that yarn. You and I know it's rubbish! Stupid nonsense, and who's likely to profit by it? The one certain thing is that the cause of the Temple and the Torah would suffer by it. I tell you again: better a dead lion than a snapping dog. Enough of this game! That "ghost" has got to be put back behind the stone!'

'If he rolled the stone away himself,' Joseph said slowly, 'it won't be any good putting him back behind it a second time . . .'

'He didn't roll it away himself. I know it was you who buried him, but I also know a soldier pierced his heart first. And a man who has had a Roman spear between his ribs is dead beyond all possibility of doubt.'

'Yes, he was dead beyond all doubt,' Joseph nodded.

'And so he did not roll away the stone. You put him in the tomb, and you took him out again.'

'We did not!'

'Joseph! Nicodemus! I came here with good intentions. With words of reconciliation. But I warn you again: Caiaphas is prepared to go to any lengths. I know he's been to see rabbi Jonathan, and they won't let the matter rest. I don't want to frighten you, but if you're obstinate they'll find ways and means of forcing you to hand over the body.'

'You don't want to, but you're doing your best!' Joseph said sarcastically.

'I'm only warning you.' Jonathas rose to his feet, and changed to a more easy, friendly tone. 'In the last resort what does it matter what you've done with the body? We're only concerned with the tomb, and we only want you and Nicodemus to assure everybody that the Galilean is still lying in it . . .'

'But there won't be any body in it.'

'We can always find a body.'

'Of course; the Zealots will see to that!'

'Joseph! Remember that neither your relations with the Romans, nor your money . . .'

'I know: you needn't warn me. Goodbye, Jonathas. Give my regards to the high priest, and tell him I was sorry to hear about the curtain being rent . . .'

'That's only a stupid rumour! A Levite had a dream, and now he's talking nonsense. The crowd is repeating it because they're fond of "sensations".'

'But I heard the curtain was torn from top to bottom.'

'Well, it wasn't. In any case, you know we're always having earthquakes. And so the curtain . . .'

'Of course!'

'Well, perhaps you'll think it over? Why try to fight Caiaphas? I don't know whether you've heard, but he has demanded that both of you be expelled from the Sanhedrin.'

'If you didn't expel me, I'd resign . . . The Sanhedrin is no longer the Sanhedrin since it passed that sentence.'

'Is that your last word, Joseph?'

'My very last.'

'And how about you, Nicodemus?'

'Joseph has spoken for me.'

'In that case I have nothing more to say. I personally advise you to clear out of the city. Caiaphas will never forgive you for this . . .'

After seeing the president back to his litter I returned to the hall. Joseph was pacing to and fro, his head sunk on his chest, his arms folded behind him. I dropped into a chair. I felt myself inwardly shivering, feverish, in a mood of anxious expectancy. At last he halted in front of me, and said:

'That pleasant little talk has made two things perfectly clear to me. First, they haven't given up their fight against Jesus. They intend to go on fighting his "ghost", as Jonathas put it, and everybody who believes in that "ghost". And second: it has completely dispelled any suspicion I had that they have hidden the body. Jonathas was not exaggerating either, when he said that Caiaphas would stick at nothing. And that goes for Jonathan. That's quite understandable. The teacher is even more dangerous to them now than he was when alive. He has become a symbol, and often a symbol is more threatening than a living man. Listen, Nicodemus! Their fury will cool off in time. But at the moment they might well send Zealots to attack you. They know you were at the tomb last night. You didn't tell me that. What made you go?'

'That tomb seemed to call me,' I admitted.

'It certainly does,' Joseph said. 'Even now that it's empty. But to return to you. I think that since you've offended Jonathas it would be better if you left the city. You have a house between Emmaus and Lydda, haven't you? Take Cleophas with you: you know, that young Pharisee who voted against the sentence. They'll be taking vengeance on him too. Well, what do you think?'

I don't like having to make a sudden decision to go away, especially at present, when every moment brings fresh news. But Joseph is right. I wish he would come with me. He is so energetic, and all the courage and energy I ever had have seeped out of me. Not that I ever had much. Jesus should have had Joseph to turn to in his days of difficulty. Joseph mentioned more than once that he would like to meet him, but I never did anything to arrange it. I was always preoccupied with myself and my own affairs. Even though Joseph is my friend, I don't really know him at all well. I always thought his only interest was in trade.

'But how about you?' I objected. 'I'm not going to leave you behind.'

'You needn't worry about me. I'm on good terms with the Romans, nobody will dare to attack me. But you go. Go at once.'

'All right, I'll go,' I decided after a moment's thought. I still felt uncomfortable at the idea of leaving him to face danger alone. 'But you . . .'

'Nothing threatens me,' he repeated, calmly laying his hand on my shoulder.

I suddenly realized how much I owed to this man, who does so little to observe the prescriptions of the Law. For years he has been like a spreading oak, against which I have been able to rest the feeble bush of my life. He did a great deal for Ruth. He brought me gold when I had neither the time nor the inclination to trouble about financial matters. He lived quite near to me, but although I took so much from him I simply didn't see him, so to speak. But now my eyes were opened. I stretched out my hand in a feeling of gratitude.

'Joseph,' I said, my voice quivering. 'You are **my** true friend . . .'

He returned the squeeze of my hand, but shook his head.

'No,' he said, 'you're wrong. It seems to me that I am only on the track of what friendship should be like. Go, and return in safety. Each of us will ponder over the mystery of this body's disappearance, and exchange our conclusions later. Good?' He smiled, then stood thinking. 'There are mysteries,' he reflected, 'into which one must fling oneself in order to know them through and through, just as we fling ourselves into water, confident that it will yield before us. Farewell, Nicodemus. But don't you agree that there are some things which one must first accept before one can understand them?'

We walked along slowly, for the day had turned warm; one would not have thought it was the month of Nizan. At first we didn't talk much; we were both sunk in thought. The road to Emmaus drops down the side of the rocky plateau on which stand Jerusalem and Hebron. Emmaus is situated on the last rise. Beyond it, along the coast stretches the plain of Sharon, which at this season is covered with rich vegetation.

We arranged to spend the night at Emmaus, and to travel on to my village next morning. We had accomplished about half the journey when Cleophas, who had been dragging along moodily, with head drooping, snorted like a young horse and began to talk in a tone expressive of suppressed indignation:

'No, I just cannot understand it. Let us grant that he has risen from the dead. Though that is improbable. Men have been resurrected in the name of the Most High, but nobody has risen from the tomb of himself. But let us say that's what has happened. In that case, answer me, rabbi: what was the point of that trial, that torture, that death? A man capable of raising himself from the dead should not die the death of a slave. I shall never understand that. Unless you, rabbi, can explain it to me. You surely have a deeper understanding. You knew him . . .'

'I knew him,' I replied. 'But that doesn't in the least help me to understand what has happened. Truly, in his life-time there were occasions when he behaved as though he wanted to frighten his disciples, and was testing them . . . Then the dangers vanished; they proved to be illusory, or he overcame them. But much more frequently he allowed life to overcome him. He possessed a great power, but nobody knew when he would be prepared to use it. The miracle of resurrection is the greatest miracle of all. You're quite right, Cleophas; any man who can rise from the dead ought never to allow himself to be tortured with life. But in any case, what is the point of such a resurrection? He has risen, and he has vanished. Only his mother and a converted prostitute have seen him. If this resurrection were intended to be a sign that his doctrine is true others also would have to see him . . .'

'Everybody would have to see him!' the young Pharisee exclaimed.

'Of course . . . For the people who didn't see him wouldn't want to believe in him . . . The Messiah's triumph cannot be only in the heart . . .'

'Rabbi, do you think he was the Messiah?'

'How am I to know? But if he was, this Messiah was different from what the prophecies foretold. He brought something different from what we were expecting.'

'What do you mean?'

'He brought one thing: love.'

'And yet apparently he said that anyone who wished to be his disciple must hate his mother, his wife, even his children.'

'Yes, I've heard that too. But they were strange words, they seemed to be expressing only one side of the truth . . .'

'Do you think, rabbi, that he commanded us to hate?'

'Hatred, Cleophas, was a word foreign to him. I can assure you he didn't know what hatred is. He hated nobody. I even rather feel that he gave himself into their hands simply in order to show that hatred can be overcome . . .'

'But it was hatred that overcame. And they killed him . . .'

'True,' I admitted.

And each of us was again buried in his mournful thoughts.

Our two shadows went before us, slanting across the track. I didn't notice just when we were joined by a third traveller. When he caught up with and walked between us he looked like a wayfarer accustomed to long journeys, for he strode easily, hardly touching the earth with his feet. There was nothing about him to attract our attention: he was very tall, carried a stick, had his robe tucked back for the journey, and was not carrying any bundle. We didn't hear his footsteps as he came up, though he must have moved astonishingly fast, for I had seen no one a moment before, when, at a turn in the path, I had looked back to see whether we were being pursued.

'What are you discussing?' he asked. 'You seem to be filled with sorrow.'

Cleophas shrugged his shoulders. 'You've come from Jerusalem too, judging by the path you have travelled, so surely you know . . .?'

'Know what?' the man asked.

'You must have only passed through the city; you certainly couldn't have been staying there during the holy days. Things have happened . . .'

'What things?' Our new companion's questions sounded impatient, as though he were afraid he would not have time to talk with us. Cleophas was too agitated to speak calmly of the past two or three days' events, so I replied:

'You must have heard of the prophet from Galilee, who went about all over the country, teaching and working marvellous miracles? He even resurrected people from the dead. When he came to the city a few days ago our priests and doctors gave orders for him to be arrested; they tried him, condemned him to death, and handed him over to the Romans. And the Romans nailed him to a cross. This man had worked such wonderful miracles and his doctrine was so beautiful that many of us considered he had come from the Most High in order to free Israel. I thought so too. Unfortunately, he died. And to-day is the third day since he was laid in the tomb . . .'

'So he died and was buried . . .' the man who had attached himself to us did not seem satisfied with my story. 'And what happened then?'

Cleophas made a hopeless gesture.

'There are some,' he said almost angrily, 'who believe he has risen from the dead.'

The man looked at us. 'And you . . .' he asked. 'What do you think?'

I looked at him rather distrustfully. I didn't like his questions. I began to think he knew the whole story and was questioning us simply in order to discover what we thought. Perhaps he was a spy sent by the Sanhedrin? However, we were two to one. And besides, although he did not seem any different from an ordinary traveller, something about him encouraged one to talk.

'As a matter of fact,' I responded, 'several women went to his tomb before dawn this morning. They came back and said they hadn't found any body in it, but they had seen an angel, who apparently told them the dead man had risen. So his disciples ran to the tomb, and they, too, couldn't find the body.'

'And what do you make of that?' he asked when I stopped again.

He was no longer inquiring as to the further course of events, but was demanding to know what I thought. Doubt and suspicion crossed my mind again. He wasn't questioning like someone simply interested in the latest news, but as though he had every right to ask.

'I don't know,' I said hesitantly. 'I don't know . . . This Galilean was certainly out of the ordinary. At one stage I believed he was the Messiah. Nobody has ever worked miracles like his. And nobody has ever spoken as he spoke. But the Messiah must be someone higher than any ordinary man.'

'Do you, a scholar learned in the Scriptures, say that?' he interrupted me. 'Don't you remember what Isaiah said about "the root from the stem of Jesse"?'

'I do. But Ethan and Ezrahite said: "I have sworn unto David my servant that I shall establish his seed for ever."'

'And you think that will not be fulfilled?'

'How can it be? With the royal throne divided and in the hands of foreigners? But even if he were the descendant of David he died a cruel death. If you had seen it . . .'

'Man of the sluggish heart!' he said in a suddenly stern tone. 'Teacher who does not teach others, and who doesn't wish to recognize the truth himself!' (I cannot remember anybody ever speaking to me like this before. Yet I did not think it insulting.) 'Don't you see that all has been fulfilled that had to be fulfilled? Didn't our forefather, Jacob, say that the one Expected and Sent would come at the very time when Judah had lost the throne? Have you failed to read anything clearly in the sacred books, friend? Listen . . .' (The words of the prophet Isaiah came easily to his lips.) ' "The people that lived in darkness shall see a great light," and glory will flow over the land by the sea, in Galilee of the heathens. Have you not been in Galilee and seen it?'

'Yes, I saw it,' I whispered. I had so often heard men cry: 'The Messiah will not come from Galilee.' But this man brought out the prophetic prognostications from the sacred books like a cunning fisher fishing a small fish out of a river. The ignorant people of Galilee, the people of unclean people,

322

had seen the light. That was true. I raised my eyes to him. But he went on:

'Where was he born? Didn't you yourself go there, in order to be convinced that it was true? Haven't you read: "Bethlehem in the land of Judah . . . from thee will come a governor of the people"? Who gave him birth? Was it not foretold to you: "Behold, a virgin shall conceive and give birth to a son"? Haven't you heard that they had to flee with him as far as the land of the Pharaohs? Then what do you make of: "Out of Egypt I have called my son"? And who foretold him? Doesn't the prophet say: "I shall send an angel to prepare the way before you"? "A voice crying in the wilderness, make straight the way of the Most High." '

'That is true, every word of it,' I said. The sun was sinking lower and lower, growing steadily more crimson. I wiped my forehead, for it was streaming with sweat. The stranger's words filled me with amazement and simultaneously with dread. How was it that I hadn't noticed all this before? Every text he quoted hit me like a heavy block of wood. I had lived with the sacred prophecies under my hand, but I had not been able to interpret them. The teacher had reminded me with justice more than once: 'Are you a doctor and a teacher, and yet you don't know that?' I had been intoxicated with the sound of the scriptural passages and hadn't noticed their meaning. Like others, I had blindly and obstinately demanded the fulfilment of prophecies that suited me, that were in tune with my own conceptions, that raised the triumph of a shout and not the triumph of silence.

'Didn't he teach,' the traveller continued, 'just as it had been said he would, telling in parables things hidden from the beginning of the world? Didn't he send out his disciples like fishermen, so that they could catch people from every hill, from every cavern? Weren't even his miracles foretold? Didn't the Most High have to conclude a new covenant with him, a new Law, written and carried not on the body but in the heart?'

'You speak the truth,' young Cleophas said feverishly. 'Every word you say opens the books more clearly to us. But if this is all so, why did he die?'

'And why did he die such a death?' I cried. 'So wretchedly, so painfully, so horribly, infamously . . .'

We gazed at him with dilated eyes. We were conscious that this man was far wiser than we. He seemed to know all that we did not know, and in our ignorance we were filled with fear. He did not rebuke us. Gently, as though humming to the accompaniment of a cithara, he answered:

'Don't you recall that either? "I am a worm, not a man, made the contempt and laughing-stock of the mob." "The people cry and nod their heads: he put his trust in the Most High, let Him save him." "I have been encompassed with a band of evil men roaring like lions. I have been surrounded by ravening dogs. They have pierced my hands and feet, and have counted every bone." "From his feet to the tip of his head there is no health in him . . ." "One wound and bruise . . ." "Neither attraction nor beauty . . ." "We saw that he was as nothing, yet we desired him . . ." "A man regarded with contempt, the most wretched of men, a man of sorrows, who knew every weakness . . ." "Our diseases have been passed to him, our sufferings have touched him . . ." "We treated him as a leper, condemned by the Eternal Himself, to perish in infamy . . ." "He was destroyed for us, for our spite . . ." "But his bruises have made us whole. We have gone astray, but the Most High has laid our sins on him. And he himself desired that . . ." "He did not open his mouth to defend himself . . ." "He suffered with criminals and prayed for criminals . . ."'

'Oh, Adonai!' I whispered. My lips were as dry as though I were wandering through a waterless wilderness.

' "I gave my body to be scourged, and did not turn my face away from the smiters," ' he continued. ' "I was as a meek lamb, led to the slaughter . . ." '

For some time we had been too absorbed to notice the road along which we were travelling. Now, when he said these last words, he stopped as though about to take leave of us; and then we realized with surprise that we were already in Emmaus. He seemed to know that we intended to remain here, while apparently he was going on. Without stopping to consult each other Cleophas and I exclaimed as one:

'Rabbi, remain here with us. We would like you to tell us much more. Look, it is already evening . . . You can go on in the morning. Remain with us.'

At first he seemed to be thinking it over. But when we asked him again and again he nodded, and went with us to the inn. Fortunately, it was empty. The innkeeper brought a table and set it under a fig tree, and prepared refreshment for us. The heights of the hills from which we had descended were burning crimson, like logs in a dying fire.

'So he was the Messiah?' Cleophas asked with quivering lips.

Instead of answering the question, the stranger quoted again:

' "In those days the deaf will hear the words of the books, and the eyes of the blind will see in the darkness. Those who are quiet will make merry, the poor will rejoice in the Holy One of Israel . . ." "Those who did not seek me before will seek me, and I shall say: 'Here am I, to the nation that never called me . . .'" "The nations will come from the ends of the earth." '

His voice suddenly sounded through the grey evening like a call of triumph and gladness. After the mournful words depicting that sanguinary vision it was like a chorus of silver trumpets sounding a song of victory to heaven. Our hearts beat faster. But we looked at each other uneasily. The same thought was burning both our minds. If all this were true, and we had failed to see it even though we were looking for it, what fate awaited us and all the chosen who had been blind to the prophecies, and had rejected and crucified him? It was a terrible thing to wait for the Messiah for a thousand years. But what would be the end of this waiting, in view of our realization that the Messiah had come but we had not received Him?

As though guessing our thoughts, he said:

'All this had to be in order that the Scriptures might be fulfilled. And they have been fulfilled. The Son of Man died in order that you should not die, and he lives in order that you should live. He had to die in that fashion so that every one of you might be saved. For the prophet said: "Though your sins be as scarlet, I shall make them whiter than snow and wool." '

We sat in silence, and the wind stirred the leafless branches of the fig above us. He reached for the bread which our host had set before us, broke it, and gave each of us a piece. And then . . . O Justus! That movement of His . . . In a moment everything was clear. I saw at once what I had been unable to perceive before: the pierced hands, and the smile, like no other smile in the world, the smile of love which has no bound. And I burst into tears. For, having revealed Himself to us, He vanished. He was no longer sitting between us. But the bread remained . . . and the wine . . . and the words . . . and that overwhelming joy into which He had changed our despair. We started up from our seats. The sun sank into the sea. The night was spread open above us like a tent. But we were possessed with one overmastering, compelling thought: to go back, to go back at once, to tell the others that He had risen indeed. There was nothing more important in all the world than this news. We felt a need to tell everybody to cry it from the housetops.

We gulped down the bread and set off. We walked in a fever, sometimes we ran. Neither of us felt that we were running uphill, that we were short of breath. We did not exchange a word, we only turned to each other occasionally to ask a question:

'Do you remember when He said . . .'

'I do. My heart beat . . .'

The first star was lit in the sky. We walked, we ran, back to the city. Not for one moment did I recall the dangers from which I had fled only that morning.

Nor do I remember when I reached the house of Saphan the tanner. As I ran through the night along the twisting, narrow lanes of Ophel – I would never have ventured there in former days, least of all at night – I trembled with impatience. The low door was fastened. I beat on it with both hands. The news I was bringing was burning my lips like live coals.

The door was not opened at once. I heard a rustling noise, and I guessed that someone was peering through a chink to see who was knocking. In my impatience I cried out:

'It's I, Nicodemus! Open! It's Nicodemus! I bring important news.'

There was a quiet scrape as the door was drawn back.

'Come in, rabbi,' I heard Simon the Zealot's muffled voice. 'Come in, and don't shout. If you're heard you may put us in danger.'

Danger? I was not conscious of it. I was not afraid of it. I passed inside. Beyond a small passage was a spacious room, which was probably used for drying the skins, for it was filled with the pungent smell of tannic. The room was crowded with people. Nobody was asleep, though it was late at night. By the light of the fire I saw all His disciples except Thomas and Judas. His mother and sister, Martha and Mary, were there too, as well as other women and several men who looked like craftsmen. They seemed startled at my abrupt arrival.

'We've already heard about Joseph,' James son of Zebedee hurriedly said.

I interrupted him with an impatient gesture. I had no idea what he was referring to, but there could be no news more important than that which I brought. I cried:

'I've seen Him! I've seen Him!'

There was a momentary silence, then they all began to talk at once:

'There you are, he's seen Him too. Yes, and he's suffering from delusions too. But Mary saw him. Mothers often think they see their dead children. But I tell you He's risen from the dead. That's impossible. But I saw him!' Then I heard Mary's low, almost masculine voice: 'I fell at His feet.' 'You're distraught with grief, you imagined it!' 'Mary saw Him and I've seen Him,' Simon's voice boomed out. 'You imagined it, Simon!'

'But I really have seen Him,' I cried. 'He walked along with me for quite a distance. He spoke, He explained the Scriptures; He said He had to suffer as He did in order to save us . . .'

'Rabbi,' said James, the Teacher's brother, 'it's clear that you're overcome with sorrow too. Stop shouting!' he turned to the others. 'D'you want all Ophel to come running here? You'll have the Temple guards down on us. Listen, rabbi!' he turned back to me. 'Believe me, we're sincerely sorry . . . But don't give way to delusions like the others. He's dead, and the Temple people have stolen the body. And now they're saying we took it. If we start telling everybody he's risen from the dead they'll seize us and beat us. You may have seen his ghost . . . There are people who have seen the ghosts of the dead.'

'It wasn't a ghost,' Mary, Martha's sister shouted, shaking her head with its auburn hair violently. 'It wasn't a ghost. I could have touched Him if He'd let me . . .'

'It wasn't a ghost,' Simon repeated. But I did not sense in his voice the inflexible confidence that sounded in Mary's tones. 'I didn't touch Him either,' he added. 'But I heard Him speak. He spoke like this' (he lowered his voice still more): ' "Peter" . . . Could a ghost speak like that?' he asked me.

'It was not a ghost,' I spoke up. 'He sat down at the table with us, and broke bread and gave it to us. I'm the last man to believe incredible things. But I, too, was so close that I could have touched Him . . .'

'But none of you have touched him,' James retorted.

'If it were only possible to see Him even as a ghost,' John cried out unexpectedly, 'we should not be so filled with sorrow . . .'

'No, John,' Mary said. She speaks rather like her Son; though her tone is low, her words always carry weight. 'No, John, He has not risen simply as a ghost. His spirit never died. It departed from us for a time, and now it has returned. But He has risen again in the flesh so that our human eyes might see and our human lips might tell . . .'

'But if that is so . . .' James began.

'Did you hear what Mary said?' Simon exclaimed. 'I must

speak, I must.' He struck his great fist against his chest. 'I must shout it aloud . . .'

'We must not keep it to ourselves,' I confirmed his affirmation.

And at that very moment He was standing among us. The door did not open to let Him in, but nor did the gleam of the fire fade, nor did we hold our breath. We were still in our world, and He was standing in it too, just as in past days: tall, with arms outstretched in greeting, and an appealing smile on His lips.

'Shalom aleichem! Peace be with you,' He said.

Nobody answered, nobody stirred. We stood rooted to the ground. There was a deathly silence, faintly disturbed by a distant barking and the sound of the wind rustling the cypresses.

'What are you afraid of?' He asked. 'Why do you search your minds for answers which are more difficult than the one which is obvious? It is I. Look: examine My hands and feet. Touch Me. I am not a ghost without flesh and bones. Are you still afraid? Don't you believe Me even now, My children? Have you anything to eat? See: I shall share your fish and your honey. Do you still refuse to believe that I am with you?'

'O rabbi!' John cried out and, falling to his knees, pressed his lips to the hem of His robe.

'Rabboni!' Mary, Martha's sister, cried. She, too, dropped to her knees and went on her knees to Him, her hands outstretched and her face radiant with happiness.

'Teacher!' Peter sobbed.

'Lord,' James cried, 'forgive me my failures to believe . . .'

'Jesus, my Son,' His mother whispered.

They all pressed around Him, kissing His hands and His clothing, weeping with joy and ecstasy. And He gathered them to Himself, as though He, too, were glad He had returned and was among them again.

I was the last to go to Him.

'Master,' I said. 'We walked many miles together, and only at the end did I recognize You. And then You vanished. I do not deserve to have the grace of Your Presence close to me. I failed to recognize who You are, I did not leave everything to follow You. If You drive me away from You it will be punishment well deserved. For I . . .'

'Friend,' he interrupted in His kindly tone. 'My friend, to whom I gave my cross, welcome. Come closer, let me press you to My breast . . .'

The Greeks have a legend which tells of the sons of the earth goddess, who were invincible, for whenever they dropped to their mother earth they recovered their strength and went back to the battle with renewed vigour. That legend is a kind of vague adumbration of Him. For, the moment I touched that burning breast, all my weakness was turned to strength. He made me whole. O Adonai! He raised me from the dead.

We sat down in a circle on the floor. He stood in the midst of us, as He had so often before, and once more He explained that He had had to die in just that manner in order that the Scriptures might be fulfilled and that the grace of redemption from sin might be granted to all.

'But you will be My witnesses,' he ended. 'You are to go out into all the world, throughout its length and breadth, and carry the Father's promise to every man . . .'

In the early morning He departed as He had come: the man who had submitted Himself to the laws of the world, so that He might overcome those laws.

Just as I was about to leave the house next morning, John called me aside.

'Rabbi,' he said, 'don't go back to your home for the time being, lest you suffer the same fate as Joseph . . .'

'Joseph?' I cried out. I felt a pain in my heart. 'What has happened to him? Tell me! I know nothing.'

'It didn't occur to me that you didn't know,' he answered in amazement. 'Your friend is dead, rabbi. He went to the teacher's tomb, and there he was murdered by Zealots . . .'

Joseph dead! I could not reconcile myself to this news. My

friend, my one friend, who had given me so much, and whom I had come to know thoroughly only a moment or two before his death! I went into a corner of the room, sat down on a bench, and covered my face with my hands. But I did not weep. That morning I could not weep. One does not weep when one has been pressed to the breast of the Son of God. So I shall call Him so henceforth. Can it be blasphemy to mention the name of the All Highest, when one names Him with that Name? But Joseph is dead. Unfortunately, I am still human. The joy with which He infected me is like a puff of wind: it hardly brushed my cheek, and now is gone. It has not liberated me from pain, any more than it has liberated me from the world. But both the world and the pain are different now. I shall miss Joseph. The void which came into my life when Ruth died will be still deeper. But one thing I do know . . . Not that I really know it, but I feel it. The void will be only mine. Both Ruth and Joseph are with Him. His death has created a region of incomprehensible joy. And they are there. It is nothing that I shall go on missing them to the end, that nobody can take their place in my life. They are missing nothing. They are with Him in the Kingdom. What does it matter, Justus, that one is in danger, when the heart is at rest concerning those who are your nearest and dearest?

DEAR JUSTUS,   TWENTY-FOURTH LETTER.
    I had begun to think that we were waiting for nothing.
    We have been coming together every day for common prayers, and every day, kneeling in a semi-circle round the spot where we had seen Him, we have tensely pleaded for the coming of the promised comfort. But in vain. How well I know the feelings of a man who has pleaded for something right to his last strength, but it has not been granted him: then he feels not even bitterness, only emptiness. Day after day has passed since His departure. His glory is being erased from our

minds with every hour. Alas, there is no such thing as a miracle which lasts for ever. The pictures fade from our eyes, the fingers of our hands grow fresh skin. There is nothing which has the power to convince a man once for all. From even the greatest of joy one returns to despair. We have prayed. But how do I know what are the feelings of the others as they pray? Theirs may be different from mine. But my feelings have been of increasing sorrow. It is not that doubts are returning. It is something quite new: the consciousness that one is abandoned. The feeling that happiness has been with one, and has departed.

Lord, I have thought as I knelt, I no longer doubt now. I know You are the Son of God and God Himself. Only God could rise from the dead and ascend to heaven. But after revealing Your Divinity to us You have departed. You came among us unobserved, bringing us more than earthly happiness. Then for a moment You shone, You shone with radiance: only to vanish. And now You are no longer, as You were not during those two endless nights. What are memories? Life for us is still a journey ahead of us. Evil or good, its end still lies before us. But why did You have to reveal Your divine love, if everything is to return to what it was at the beginning? Jesus, I prayed, You have overcome death, but You have not vanquished death within us. We are still a continual dying. When You had departed, those who had always been with You kissed the stone which retained the imprint of Your feet. For those who loved You so much, who had been so faithful to You, that imprint is sufficient. But I, so it seems to me, did not love You. I admired You, I respected You, and now I believe in You. But I must not say that I love You. You shook me as a hurricane shakes a house. You tore me from my foundations and set me down on them again, but differently, so that I can no longer feel that I am what I once was. I need to feel You. In his loneliness man must touch someone. He seeks a friend, a woman, even a dog . . . Even though he knows it is all delusion; for even the best of friends will not understand everything; a woman will want him in turn to comfort her and to share her sorrows; a dog goes off at the barking of another dog. But I have no such delusions: Ruth is dead. Joseph is dead. But I cannot touch You.

The others are happier. You chose them and filled their little lives with Yourself. You did not choose me. I came to You of my own choice. Fearfully I knocked at Your door by night. And You spoke of the wind, that night. 'Do you hear that wind?' You asked. 'It blows wherever it likes . . .' I waited for the blowing of Your wind, as a loving woman waits to be mastered. I waited, but I was not able to give You anything. I agreed to take Your cross. But those were only words. I did not act like these others, who abandoned homes and all things. I received You with only half my heart. But if You had spoken to me! I am a man who expects a clear, definite word. A summons. A command. Right to the end I didn't know whether You really wanted me nor what You wanted of me. It seemed to me that You were demanding that I should write about You. But now it seems to me that even this was only my own desire. And again I realize that I do not love You.

Thus I spoke to Him, Justus; but He was silent. Now He was God in the height. When He was on earth He seemed to weep with every weeper. When He departed, the others stood with eyes turned to heaven, an expression of joy on their faces. For them He was their Master, who now had openly become God. They are too simple-minded to have foreseen that after a few days they would begin to sigh, to groan, to be afraid again. But I had that presentiment. So long as He was, so long as He made an appearance unexpectedly, half Spirit and half living man, everything seemed easy and beautiful. Too easy and too beautiful! It was like the period when a sick man is being cared for. But now the sick man has been declared well again. So He has departed. He left us with a promise which we did not really understand. As soon as we rose from our knees we began to discuss it: 'How will it happen? Perhaps He Himself

333

will come down to earth a second time? But this time in power and glory? What will the promised comfort look like?'

Simon cried:

'I tell you He will send angels and they will restore the kingdom of Israel. And a second David will be born.'

There was a murmur of assent from the others. Thomas remarked:

'Of course, if we are to be His witnesses right to the ends of the earth, He must first subject the earth to us . . .'

'But remember, He said the Kingdom is within us,' John commented thoughtfully.

'That's true,' Philip said. 'But if I want to impart to another what I feel within me I must speak. And you try going out and teaching! The Temple guards would seize you at once and run you before the high priest . . .'

As he said this they all involuntarily looked at the great beam fastening the door. They came secretly to meet in my house, secretly and fearfully. Their uneasiness, which had been lulled during the days of His return, awakened again.

I never speak. They knew Him well, they remember so many of His sayings. My memories are more modest. But I have often returned in thought to the time, a few days ago, when we were standing on the summit of the Mount of Olives. And He, shining with glory, like a cloud behind which the sun is concealed, rose into the heaven. I still seem to be hearing His words: 'You will receive power . . .' Power? When will it come? What will it be? A change in the world's destinies which will free us from all terror of the Grand Council, the Sanhedrin, the high priest, Pilate, the Roman Legate, the tetrarchs, the distant Caesar? Or possibly, I sometimes think fearfully, it is only a promise like the promise of the Messiah, which fills us with fear all through the ages, and then is fulfilled unexpectedly, against all the desires that have been read into the promise.

The disciples grew hot in dispute. Only His mother was silent. Does she know rather more of what is to happen than they do? Her last cry of pain was uttered on the Mount of Olives. 'Oh, my son,' she cried then, 'do You want to leave me again? Take me with You; don't leave me behind . . .' She threw herself at His knees; but He bent over her, whispered something to her, just as they were in the habit of talking together, face close to face. When He ended she slipped still lower, she fell with her face to His feet. He did not raise her up as a son would; He withdrew from her like God who commands and departs. She rose and stood quietly in the circle. And when He had departed she went with the others to kiss the stone which bore the imprint of His feet. The women ran up to lead her away. But she shook her head. She walked unaided down the hill, not as she had gone down from Golgotha, when they had had to drag her. Her face seemed set like stone. But that lasted only a brief while. Suddenly she halted. She waited for the disciples, and raised her hands, as though she wished to take them all into her protective embrace.

'Come, children,' she said. She took us all in with her gaze. 'Let us go together to pray, and together in prayer we shall wait.'

We followed her obediently. We went down towards the Garden of Olives. It was down here that it all began, I thought; and it is up there on the Mount that it has ended. All on the one hill. Opposite us, on the farther side of the valley, the Temple shone gold, white, and proud in the sunlight on the height of Moriah. She led us among the trees, into the green depths of Cedron, across the torrent to the gate, then through the empty and deserted city.

Now she said to us every day: 'Let us kneel and pray.' Kneeling in a ring, we sent our prayers up to heaven. The first day, we were sure our prayers would have immediate results. But on the ninth day we no longer knew what to think of His silence. Yet none of us was in a position to go on praying like that any longer. Life is life. One can live and pray, but one can not endlessly pray and not live. We prayed and we did not live!

The city began to stir again with movement and hubbub. The Feast of Weeks was approaching. Burnt with the sun, attired in sheaves and branches, the people came in from the fields. They went singing through the streets. We did not notice them. We prayed, and we prayed. But prayer was becoming increasingly difficult. Life beat its way through to us, through the walls. 'We have got to go on living somehow,' the thought persistently plagued us, as though all that had happened had never been. God had come down to earth, had laid bare His heart – but the earth remained earth. Before many years were past we would think it had all been imagination. His life, His death, and His rising again. A God in heaven is for every day. But a God Who has suffered and died must continually rise again, so that we may remember Him.

I often rested my eyes on His mother. That was the one comfort, the one hope. The others recalled their days in Galilee, all the events they had known. She never turned back to the past. She prayed for the future. She grew conscious of my gaze, and raised her eyes and smiled at me. I had the feeling that she understood my difficulties, and with that smile was encouraging me to further effort. I went back to my prayers. I repeated fervently: 'Lord, send that which You have promised to send. Send it swiftly. One can go on waiting for centuries for Your coming. But once You have allowed us to hear Your voice, further waiting is not to be borne. Nine days have passed, and nothing has come. For You a thousand years is as one day. But for us a day often lasts longer than a thousand years.'

Until . . .

Dusk fell; the festival began. All the city poured into the street. Processions bearing torches made their way to the Temple. There were shouting, laughter, singing everywhere, until it seemed as though even the walls were singing.

We ate supper, and returned yet again to our prayers. She summoned us; she demanded more of us that day than on any previous day. Sleep clung to our eyelids, but we exerted all our strength to overcome it. We recited psalms in chorus. Time and again we returned to the prayer which He had taught us: 'Thy Kingdom come . . .' Surely the Kingdom would be coming together with the comfort? The night passed over us, as heavy as on that night of the Passover. We are wrestling like Jacob with the angel, I thought; and as He had wrestled, when alone in the garden He had wrestled with His Father. But we were only human beings. Even she, the Mother of God, was a human being. With the last remnants of our strength we recited the psalms. Every few minutes one of us would doze off. Our knees burned. Every tiny speck of dust was like a sharp needle piercing them. That night seemed endless. My spirit revolted: shall we go on praying like this till morning? I raised my eyes to her impatiently, almost angrily. But she went on starting one psalm after another. Seeing our faces strained with effort she encouraged us with a smile: 'A little more, children . . . just a little more . . . Hold fast!'

We returned to our murmurs, we flung ourselves into prayer as though into a river with a distant farther bank. Extinguished by the snuffer of the day, the lamp light faded. Until at last the first rays of the sun fell across the wall. They were feeble, pale, rosy; but the light grew stronger and stronger, it grew in power, in clarity, in its golden hue. We prayed on and on. The wall before us seemed to be flaming. Our eyelids were dry. I was at the end of my strength. My knees felt like open wounds, as though my lower limbs had been cut off and I was standing on the bloody stumps.

Suddenly Mary stood up, raised her head, and threw her arms wide open. At that moment she was like a high priest who has made a sacrifice, and is waiting for the fire to fall from heaven to consume the gift. She said something quietly. We stopped praying. We gazed at her as though entranced. And then . . .

Something fell into the midst of us. Something dropped on us from on high, like an invisible mass of heat and power.

When a hurricane blows it is as though some invisible giant

has come into the midst: he stands impatient at first, then begins to rend, to strike blindly, to kick, to fight. Then it is an evil being making us conscious of his anger, a madman ready to tread us underfoot in order to satisfy his frenzy.

But the giant which we now felt among us did not come with anger. It fell on us like a burning wind, but it restrained its strength so that it should not burn us alive. It was someone merciful and remembering our weakness. It flew into the room like a great bird whose wings sweep across the face and make a menacing sound, but whose flight is tranquil and sure. It made invisible circles above us, sinking lower and lower, until at last it rested on our heads. It could have crushed us: we knew that very well; but it did not. It only lightly touched us with a touch full of love. Tongues of flame whirled in the air, rested on our foreheads, penetrated into the depths of our minds. That which was occurring outside us poured itself into us. We took great gasps of air, but it pierced to our hearts and brains, and burnt our lips as the coal burnt the lips of Isaiah. It destroyed us, but in such wise that we desired this destruction. We were like a woman ready to perish in her lover's embrace. We realized that we were all shouting. Despite its goodness, the Power that rested on us tore us to shreds. If it had remained longer we should have ceased to exist. Its kiss was enough to compel a man to leap free from the bonds of his own will. Another moment, and we would have become flames flying through the air, like flowers plucked from their stems. But that terrible breath had already vanished. It had touched us with a caress that could turn clay into flesh pulsing with life, and had departed. Of all that Power which had been poured through us something was left within us. When we rose with unceasing cries we had the same bodies as before, requiring food and sleep, and the same crushed knees. But our misery was like a cage for flame capable of scorching the earth. Our internal equilibrium was destroyed. We had to cry out, for within us there was more than the framework of our bodies could keep confined. We stood in a ring, impatient, ready to go off somewhere that very moment. Will burned within us, like a pyre flooded with oil. It took us a long moment to realize that that which had been manifested within us was our own being, only now, suddenly, astonishingly mature. I realized in very deed what it meant to be born again. To be born again means to be reborn in the fulness of all one's possibilities. We human beings bear infants which are only potential somethings. But God gives birth to giants, who tear down the gates of cities and shatter whole armies with an ass's jawbone. O Justus, so many things now suddenly became clear to me. I understood, too, what I was shouting. I was shouting the wisdom of the world, and those around me were crying the same wisdom. But don't imagine that I in a moment became a great scholar and that I have surpassed you, my teacher, in knowledge. I know only that which is necessary to me. The road before me is straight and clearly defined. I know where I have to go and what to do. I know all this, and I have the means to accomplish it. Woe upon me if I do not use those means! But I shall go. How could I remain? Not one of us could hold back.

We ran out of the house. Outside was a crowd of local merchants, pilgrims, visitors from distant parts. At the sight of us they broke into laughter. We must have looked ludicrous: a throng of people with feverish eyes, a shout on our lips, waving arms. They asked one another who we were and why we were behaving so oddly. I heard strange languages and dialects around us. Suddenly I realized that I understood certain of these tongues. Nor was I the only one. Each of us had been given knowledge of the language of the people entrusted to him. We could talk to them in their own tongue. We stood dumbfounded by the power which had been given us, and overcome by the command which was conveyed in this very capacity. How often we free ourselves from some obligation with the assurance: 'I cannot find words for that.' But now we could not escape the obligation. One experiences such a moment only once in a lifetime. I know already that the Power which has been given to us also has its limits. One can flee from it, again

339

and again. But an arrow flies swiftly, and once it has reached its target it remains embedded in it for ever.

We stood facing one another: the laughing crowd and we few, trembling but reinforced. I know I'm a coward. I have not stopped being afraid or foreseeing difficulties. But the command had come, and it was stronger than my fear. Now I understood: this is His cross. Formerly I could not have raised it. He knew when it would be possible to transfer it to me. The invisible Bird which He had sent us had left in our hearts some of His love, that love which changed the laws of the world. A man is bound to feel fear. But love casts out fear, as sunlight dispels the chill of the night.

'Hey you, drunkards!' someone shouted from the crowd. 'What are you making all this row for? What are you disturbing the peace of the Holy Day for?'

'They've been drinking new wine, and it's gone to their heads!'

I realized that it was I who should speak now. My Pharisee's garb would enforce respect. But I stopped to reflect. I understood, but I was still obstinate. Now I know that it was for me that He wrote in the dust: 'Why don't you go?' It was me He called 'hard and barren soil.' I saw Simon step forward. His broad face was crimson, as though he really had been drinking. I thought: 'What can that unclean clod find to say?' But he stood with his feet planted wide apart, and when he began to speak his stentorian voice immediately drowned the shouting. I had often heard him break into impulsive speech, and then stop short like a scolded boy. But now he began slowly, seriously, keeping a tight rein on his impetuosity.

'So you say we're drunk? That's a lie. Nobody drinks so early in the morning. But don't imagine that nothing has happened. On the contrary, the moment has come which the prophet Joel foretold, when he said the Most High would send His Spirit down on every man.'

How has it come about, I wondered, that this Galilean, this fisherman from Bethsaida, can speak like that? His words were simple, but they went to the very heart of the matter. And they impressed by their courage.

'I doubt whether you've forgotten Jesus of Nazareth,' he continued. 'He was still among us quite recently, working signs and wonders, healing the sick, raising the dead, listening to your requests. You had that same Jesus handed over to death, and the heathens nailed Him to a cross. But death could have no dominion over Him. King David died and was buried here, on Zion. But Jesus has died and risen again – and we are witnesses to this fact.'

He pointed to himself and to us. This was the man who only a few weeks before had writhed with fear in the courtyard of Caiaphas's house, and had cried: 'I don't know him'; this was the man who had not dared to go up to the foot of the cross and had not come to help us lay the body in the tomb. Now this same man was saying with inflexible resolution: 'We are witnesses.' I recognized that even with all the gifts I had been granted I would never be able to speak like that. In Simon confidence flames up swiftly, like lightning. I realized that I was seeing this man in a new light. If in the Kingdom of Heaven love is everything, then it is only just that He made Simon the first in His church. From what poor clay can the Lord's vessels be cast!

The people were no longer laughing. They stood silent, dumbfounded. Many of their faces expressed fear and regret. Suddenly someone cried:

'It wasn't us who killed him. It was the Romans.'

'It was the priests and the Pharisees,' cried another voice. 'We are poor people . . .'

'What are we to do?' This cry was taken up at once. 'What are we to do? He was good, He was kind. He always took our side, not that of those who strip us bare. We didn't want Him to be killed.'

Simon stepped closer to them. He opened his arms wide, with the same gesture that the teacher had so often used to draw the crowd to Him:

'Don't deny your guilt. But don't let it oppress you. He came to earth for your sakes, He suffered and died for you, for your children and for all who will come after. I am no better than you, for I, too, denied Him. But He forgave me. All He wants is that we should love Him. So give your love to Him, and let it change your lives. Repent! Love Him, and love one another. Spurn evil from your midst. Remember: you have been redeemed not with silver and gold but with the blood of the Messiah, the pure Lamb. Be baptized in His name. Let water flow over you and cleanse you, as it cleansed the earth in the days of the Flood. And then the Spirit Comforter will come to you also. It will come like the wind which blows through the generations, like rain on earth lying barren and thirsty, like a pursuer unwearying in the chase, like a judge always merciful, like a beggar waiting before the door of a house . . .'

They crowded round him, bringing him their wretchedness in their outstretched hands. They asked:

'Baptize me . . . and me . . . and me . . Baptize me in the name of Jesus of Nazareth.'

I took Simon by the arm.

'Look, Peter,' I began, feeling that I had to tell him something that I suddenly saw clearly. 'I'm so sorry . . . I have always thought I was better than any of you . . . In His Name . . .'

'Say no more, Nicodemus,' he interrupted me impatiently. 'Remember that I denied Him . . . But there's no time to go over that either, now. Surely you see that that Fire has set everything alight?' As though uncertain whether I understood him, he laid his enormous hand on my shoulder and bent over me: 'When He asked if I loved Him I told Him: "Lord, You know everything." He knows how much love there is scattered in human hearts. And He wishes to have it all. So we must gather it up for Him. Let us set to work quickly, Nicodemus, so that when He returns He does not find us idling . . .'

This letter will surprise you, I'm sure. It's so long since I last wrote. You may even have begun to think that I shall never write again, that I have forgotten you, or even that I am dead. But I am alive, and I still remember you, my master. I think of you these days even more than before. But truly it is not easy for me to write now, and I feel that it will grow more and more difficult.

You mustn't expect me to explain things which are born as a command within one. I have already told you: the task has been assigned, the means provided. I went on waiting for a sign. I don't want to undertake anything of my own volition. Now the sign has come. From this moment nothing can hold me back. I am going away. You many wonder where. As yet I don't know. I shall go where He sends me. To the people who have need of me.

And not I alone, but we all are departing. The Day of the Lord may come at any moment. So Peter declares. He called us together and said:

'Go wherever the Spirit of the Lord leads you. I shall remain here in the land of Israel, and with me James, the Lord's brother, and James the son of Zebedee. But the rest are to depart, and that quickly, for you may have less time than journey before you. And may Jesus, our Lord, be with you.'

When Peter commands, we listen obediently. We hitched up our robes for the journey, we took the pilgrim's staff in our hands, and those who had not been chosen by the teacher Himself knelt down to receive the blessing from Peter's hands. As we did so he commanded us to do the same to others, so that the gift of instruction should not come from each one individually, but, through our mediation, from those who were the Lord's first witnesses.

You, Justus, may be astonished to hear that I, a Pharisee,

knelt down before an unclean Galilean and accepted his blessing as a precious gift. But so much has changed! My last letter told of the coming of the Comforter and Peter's great speech. And so it has been ever since: he is always the first to speak now, and what he says we accept humbly. Though he has not changed. He still uses the speech of an unlearned, simple man, and at times he hesitates, he doesn't know how to begin. But he never hesitates in the face of danger. Before the Sanhedrin and the Grand Council he has shown a courage worthy of the Maccabeans. Sometimes he trembles when he is asked how one should pray, who may be baptized, or how the breaking of bread should be accomplished. And then he prays before he replies, and he is tortured like a woman bearing her first child. But in face of danger he never trembles. When the high priest summoned him before him, he gazed at Ananias (the son of old Ananias is the high priest now) and said: 'It is more important to listen to the All Highest than to men.' The high priest, doctors and priests stared at him hatefully. When they agreed on the sentence to be passed on the Galilean prophet they could never have expected that that sentence would not let them return to the old petty disputes, but would continually constrain them. But Simon raised his coarse voice, which roars like the waves of Lake Gennesareth when a storm bursts on the Great Sea: 'Jesus, whom you killed, He raised from the dead and made Him to be the Saviour of Israel. But we shall testify to this truth throughout the length and breadth of the world, whether you oppose us or go with us . . .'

The court sentenced him and John to be whipped, and they returned streaming with blood, but filled with joy. And they go on talking about Jesus in the Temple courtyard or in people's homes. And Cephas has become indeed a rock. Don't be surprised when I tell you I kneel before him and that my heart beats when his hand touches my brow, my lips and my chest. I am ashamed that I ever regarded him with contempt. He has changed, truly. But there are still times when I do not see eye to eye with him. And at times I even feel like saying, as of old: either him or me. But when he speaks, and I catch the heat of love in his words, a warmth such as none of the rest of us possesses, I am silent. And I remember what the Teacher said to him on the sea of Galilee: 'Feed my sheep.'

I have ceased to be a Pharisee. I have been proclaimed an outlaw, an accursed. The curse has been laid on me. I am no longer a member of the Sanhedrin. I am not allowed to enter the Courtyard of the Faithful, or any synagogue. That hurts me greatly. But I had to make some recompense for the incomprehensible joy I feel.

I no longer am wealthy. I have sold my home, my fields, shops, and flocks. I have given the money to the apostles, and they have ordered the people appointed for the purpose to share it among the needy. Now nobody wishes to keep anything for himself. For everything is the property of the Lord, and we are only the stewards, who have to account for every penny.

One thing I have not sold: the house in which He feasted on the night of His arrest, and in which the Comforter descended upon us. I gave it to Her, and She lived in it.

But now She, too, is no longer with us. The last earthly trace of His life was erased with Her departure. James, Judah, Joseph, Simon, the Teacher's 'sisters,' are all distant shadows of that life. She was something entirely different. Her face was His face, Her movements were His movements. He derived all His human qualities only from Her. Or perhaps She derived them from Him? Perhaps He, who had been for an eternity before He entered into Her as a child, impressed His thought, His goodness, His Smile on Her forehead, Her eyes and Her lips?

During all His lifetime She held Her peace. But after His departure She began to speak; and She spoke much, for the people wanted to hear about Him. They came long distances from Antioch, from Tarsus, from Alexandria, just for that purpose. And Her stories told always of only His words, His deeds. She Herself seemed not to exist in them. She was like a tree in the shade of which a legend is played out. Only twice did the branches of that tree bend low to intertwine in the story being told. The first occasion was when He was still a child and was lost in the Holy Place. She and Joseph returned to their home, not knowing what had happened; but then She ran back, Her hair flying, Her breasts heaving, Her lips quivering. There was much She did not understand, but Her heart said that the Child was the Treasure of the world, a Treasure that could not perish so long as it was in Her keeping. She ran up the slope of Moriah, jostling the people and forcing the Pharisees to step out of Her way in their fear of defilement. But when She found Him She did something which pained Her for years after: She reproached him for sitting calmly among the scribes while She was running about the city, out of Her mind with fear and despair. 'But He,' she said with a smile, only replied: '"What if you have been seeking Me?"' What hurt Her was not that He spoke like that, but the realization that He found it necessary to say it to Her, that He had to remind Her that in face of God's affairs fear and sorrow are nothing, and that God is not to be lost through lack of our care.

The second occasion came at the very beginning of His ministry. She told us: 'He was talking in Capernaum in the house of a devout man. A great crowd pushed their way in, in their desire to hear Him. Doctors, scholars, Pharisees came and angrily shouted that His teaching was from Satan. He answered them resolutely and sternly. I was not present, but some women and the sons of Alphaeus came running to tell me, crying that Jesus had gone beyond all bounds in His replies, and that if we didn't stop Him at once the doctors would accuse Him before Antipas and the tetrarch would put him in prison as he had John. I was seized with fear, and ran to the house. It was impossible to get inside: it was crowded and the people were besieging the doors and windows, even standing on the roof. I asked only that someone should tell him: "We are standing outside and we want you to refrain from saying any more. Come out to us." You see, I didn't understand, I still didn't understand. Over the heads of the crowd I caught His voice. He asked, just as He had in the Temple: "What if My mother and brothers have come for Me? You are My mother and My brothers. Every one who does the will of My Father is My brother and My mother." I was pierced with pain, the same pain that He must have felt when He said that. I always felt His suffering, even when I didn't understand it. But then He went on to answer the doctors' charges: "So according to you Satan has to cast out Satan?" He turned back to the people He had called His brothers and mother: "Did you hear what they called Me? The pupil is not superior to his teacher. If they have called Me Satan, what will they call you who are My family? But be not afraid, little flock." When I heard His words I wept. Not because He had called others His mother. But because, children, I remembered again that one must never be afraid for Him.'

One evening, four of us were sitting together with Her. There were Peter, John, Luke (the doctor from Antioch whom you sent to me to heal Ruth) and myself. It was a spring night outside. The heavy scent of flowers flooded the room. The table had been pushed back to the wall. She was sitting in the middle of the room, beneath a lamp, around which myriads of moths were fluttering. We sat opposite Her, on the floor.

That evening Her usual mild tranquillity had left Her. She had prayed alone all the morning, then had gone with the widows to distribute bread to the poor and to tend the sick. Although she could have spent all the rest of Her life surrounded with respect, and not needing to stir a finger, She was even more active than our other sisters. Perhaps She could not forget the words: 'My mother and brothers are those who do the will of My Father.' By Her own example She taught us how to give.

After a day of labour she was often weary. She would sit in silence and appear to be dozing. But that evening She was more animated than ever before. Her black eyes burned in Her swarthy face like two stars flung into a well. She was a mature woman, yet She showed no sign of the suffering and difficulties She had known. Those who have known Her for many years say She never changed from the day of Her Son's birth. And that evening She was just as one would wish to see someone who before long will be going away for many days.

Suddenly She said:

'My children, although I shall not be here, I shall not go away from you.'

We raised our heads. I felt my heart stop beating and die. There are words which only those departing can think of saying. Ruth, too, said something of the sort the night before she died: 'I am going away . . . you will remain.'

We did not understand those words, but all of us felt that She was saying something very important. We sat with our eyes fixed on Her. The roses of Sharon outside the window ceased to yield their scent. There was a profound silence, in which every sound was like a clap of thunder. We waited tensely, not knowing what we were waiting for. She went on in the same tone:

'I gave birth to the Hope which all men were awaiting; now I give birth again to compassion for you. I support the hand which is raised over you. You can expect everything from Me. You can ask everything. I am the steps which our forefather Jacob saw in his dream, with angels ascending and descending . . .'

Her voice, filled with goodness, was still vibrating in the air when something incomprehensible, as intangible as a dream, occurred. We shall never know how it happened. Suddenly She – Her face, Her form – seemed to be He. In a quivering glory of light and shade He appeared and overshadowed Her. We saw Him sitting on the bench, on that same bench from which He had risen, had broken the bread, and transformed it into His body. His hands, white and pierced, rested on His knees. Then again a curtain fell as if it were the dusk of the spring night, and when it passed neither He nor She was there. We started to our feet. She had vanished, though a moment before She had still been a living being. Her words still lived, but they were already dissolving in the silence. Her cloak lay on the bench, like Elias's cloak fallen from the fiery chariot. We bent over it in reverence. From it came the scent of roses. A bunch of white, hardly opened buds scattered over the floor.

'Where is She?' I asked in consternation, uncertain of my own voice. 'What has happened to Her?'

'Don't you know?' John answered. 'He has taken Her.'

Then I recalled what people said of John and the promise he had been given.

'Will He come for you, too, like that?' I asked.

'I have told you so many times,' he answered, shaking his head. 'He never said that I shall not die. But during that Passover I heard His heart. That is a great mystery. She was His heart. She was in Him. And so She could not die.'

So She has not died, Justus; She has departed, spirit and flesh. She will not fetter us to Jerusalem with Her presence. Now we can go off into the world, like grains of poppy seed which the wind has torn from the bursting pod. We shall be everlasting winged seed until we grow into a tree. As He promised . . .

I am going away. My road runs through Antioch, so for a time I shall be journeying with Luke. At first I could not bear the sight of him. He resurrected in me the memory of that struggle for Ruth's life. But now that is all past. Ruth is in Him — so how can I despair? Though I don't even see this, though I don't feel this, I believe it; and faith, though more painful than sight and feeling, is stronger, after all.

Luke has revealed to me a great secret: he would like to paint a picture of Mary's face. I was indignant when he told me, and explained that the Torah forbids the reproduction of the human form. I know Luke is a Greek, but from the day he joined us he was bound by all the sacred laws of the Old Covenant. Then he said he had another idea: he would collect all he has heard about the Teacher and write a story about Him, a kind of homily.

349

That was just what I had intended to do, do you remember? But perhaps Luke will do it better. In any case, I don't really know whether He would want me to write about Him. My homilies too long served for my own glory. Now I would wish that nothing should be done for myself, and everything for Him. Let it be as He wishes. Wherever He commands me to go, I shall go; when He commands me to die, I shall die. He lived, suffered, and died for me. Of what value would my writings be? To whom could I reveal Him as He was in very truth? We cannot find Him for others. Each man must meet with Him himself, just as I met Him that day on the road to Emmaus . . . And, perhaps, Judas also met with Him when he tore the silver from his heart and flung it on the Temple pavement? Would Judas have betrayed Him, if I had shared my wealth with him in good time? Every one of us will undoubtedly meet with Him some day. But it is also true that each of us may make that meeting more difficult for others . . .

Let Luke write! If He wishes to be written about, He has only to nod to the first man He meets. What joy it would be for me to write about Him! That would be a gift from Him. But even now I am His debtor. What can I give Him in exchange for all the love He has shown me? . . .

Printed in Great Britain by
Billing and Sons Limited, Guildford and London